MIDNIGHT SWIM

Hillary broke the surface of the pool with an accompanying splash, then drew in a breath of fresh air and smoothed the wet raven tresses from her face. It was not until she had paddled and waded to the water's edge that her eyes fell upon the other occupant of the pool.

Ryan stood poised waist-deep near the center, his handsome face betraying delighted amazement as his eyes raked over her exposed loveliness. Her chemise, the only undergarment she had worn that day, had been rendered virtually transparent by the water.

"What are you doing here?" she demanded, furiously treading water a short distance away in the deeper part of the pool.

"The same thing you are," he parried congenially. There was nothing lighthearted, however, about the look in his eyes.

"Get out of here at once!" she ordered, her voice rising on a note of increasing panic. "You've no right to intrude upon my privacy!"

"As I told you before," Ryan declared in a low but commanding tone, "I do what pleases me, no matter the cost, no matter the risk . . ."

Scoundrel's Bride

Catherine Creel

ZEBRA BOOKS
KENSINGTON PUBLISHING CORP.

ZEBRA BOOKS

are published by

Kensington Publishing Corp.
475 Park Avenue South
New York, NY 10016

First printing: May 1987

Printed in the United States of America

With love to Evelyn Gee and Phoebe Stell. These true friends have enriched my life.

And a special maururu roa *to all my readers.*

GLOSSARY

Note: There are only eight regular consonants and five vowels in the Tahitian language. All vowels are sounded.

Papeete (pah-pay-EH-tay)—the capital of Eastern Polynesia

Moorea (moh-oh-RAY-ah)—Tahiti's sister island

pareu (pah-RAY-oo)—traditional Polynesian garment

mauruuru roa (mah-oo-roo-OO-roo ROH-ah)—thank you very much

Tevaite (tay-vah-EE-teh)—a woman's name

upaupa (OO-pah-OO-pah)—a Tahitian dance

I

Tahiti . . . 1858

The early morning air was heavy with the usual fragrances of exotic flowers and fruits, with the aroma of food drifting on the warm, ceaseless tradewind, and with the unmistakable scent of horses. The waterfront market in Papeete, the oldest town in the South Pacific, was alive with the babble of voices—an intriguing blend of Tahitian, French, and English. Natives moved about easily, slipping over the dust in their bare feet as they made their selections and bargained amiably with the women who had come to sell their wares. Purveyors for the ships anchored in the harbor wandered amongst the makeshift tables and stalls, anxious to secure the choicest produce for their appreciative captains and crews.

The town itself, a conglomeration of brightly painted wooden buildings and thatch-roofed huts stretched along a dazzling beach under tall, sheltering trees, lay on a busy, crescent-shaped harbor on the northwest coast of the island of Tahiti. Its simple village streets, laid out as boulevards, formed pleasant, shady avenues that ended where lush green foothills rose toward jagged mountain peaks half-hidden in the clouds.

Several tall-masted ships were anchored in the deep aquamarine waters of the harbor, so close that their yards ran into the boughs of the gently swaying coconut palms and feathery casuarina trees that lined the shore. The wreck of an American whaler, its bow pointing up toward the sky, lay near the reef a few hundred yards from the waterfront. Beautiful, golden-skinned children scampered playfully about along the stone-edged quay. Small groups of Tahitian men, either bare-chested or clothed in loose cotton shirts above the customary flower-patterned *pareu* wrapped about their waists, sat talking together near the water's edge. The women of the island, most of them clad in a longer version of the same, toga-like robe that was wound about their breasts to fall in soft folds past their knees, laughed and sang merrily as they walked about with graceful, undulating movements that gave evidence to the fact that here, in this languorous, South Sea haven, "hurry" was a word unknown to them.

Hillary Reynolds was an exception.

She marched along at a brisk pace that was undeniably conspicuous, her purposeful steps leading her past the market's display of neatly strung fish, pyramids of papayas, mangoes, and watermelons, baskets of onions, tomatoes, and cucumbers, buckets of oysters and clams, and rows of woven hats, baskets, mats, and traditional shell jewelry. Several of the natives called a greeting to her as she headed toward the British consul's house a short distance farther along the shore.

"*Ia orana*, Missy!"

"*Maita'i oe*, Missy?"

10

"*Ia orana*," Hillary responded to the people with a preoccupied air, using the familiar Tahitian greeting. To the young woman who had inquired after her health with such warm sincerity, she smiled briefly and answered, "*Maita'i vau*, Titi."

The aromatic breeze tugged softly at Hillary's unbound hair, its lustrous, flowing raven tresses reaching to just above the unmistakably feminine swell of her hips. Since she had long since wisely discarded the near torturous restrictions of corset and crinoline, the slender yet shapely curves beneath her simple gown were well molded by the clinging folds of creamy white muslin. Her attire—considered highly improper by the usual standards of civilized society—easily set her apart from the other women gathered along the waterfront.

Her mode of fashion, however, was not the only immediately noticeable dissimilarity. Although her flawless English complexion was tanned to a light golden hue, the satiny smoothness of her skin was still several shades lighter than the deep amber tones of the Tahitians' scantily clad bodies. And, whereas the majority of those crowding Papeete's main street possessed guileless, almond-shaped brown eyes, Hillary's were large and luminous and of a splendid violet color that had prompted more than one admirer to compare them to two sparkling amethysts. Their owner had remained characteristically unmoved by such blandishment.

Having spent the past five years in Tahiti, the present Hillary Reynolds was a far different one from the Hillary Reynolds who had arrived from England to live with her aunt and uncle on their vanilla plantation. She had been no more than sixteen at the time, and accustomed only to the stifling, well-ordered confines of the London aristocracy. To

11

suddenly find herself transplanted into a tropical, delightfully lackadaisical world of such enchantment and freedom had been quite a shock, but one from which she had quickly recovered. She had embraced her new life with all the enthusiasm and vitality of her youth, and had suffered only occasional, increasingly fewer, twinges of homesickness as the years had worn on.

The British consul's spacious, whitewashed abode, with its glazed windows, wide verandahs, and an impeccably manicured lawn, was readily distinguishable by the familiar Union Jack flying overhead. Flanked by the quarters of the American consul on one side and the French on the other, it housed the two representatives of Queen Victoria's country, as well as their entourage of family and servants. The consul himself was a married man with three children, while the vice-consul was a bachelor by the name of Anthony Warren. The young, flaxen-haired Anthony was to be the recipient of Hillary's unexpected visit.

"New tariff indeed!" she murmured in obvious annoyance as she brushed a wayward strand of midnight black hair from her silken brow. Sweeping the hemline of her full skirts away from the thick layer of dust coating the stone walkway, Hillary approached the white picket fence lining the neat row of government houses. She was in the process of lifting a hand to the gate when she glanced up to take note of a man exiting the same building that was to be her destination.

As he turned to move down the front steps of the house, he donned his broad-brimmed Panama hat and negligently slung his dark blue coat over one shoulder, maintaining his hold upon the expertly tailored garment with one large, sun-bronzed hand.

He had traveled no farther than the bottom step when his eyes fell upon the beautiful young woman who stood but a few yards away.

Hillary felt a powerful, involuntary tremor running the length of her spine as her wide violet gaze encountered the startling, blue-green intensity of the suddenly immobile stranger's. He was without a doubt the most incredibly striking man she had ever seen. The hair beneath his seaman's hat was dark brown, yet streaked with gold as a result of many hours spent beneath the sun's fiery radiance, and his tanned, ruggedly handsome countenance also gave evidence of the fact that here was a man more accustomed to the vagaries of the weather on a ship's deck than the fine and fancy trappings of a shore-goer's parlor. He was quite tall, and the fitted lines of his spotless, white linen shirt accentuated the admirably hard-muscled breadth of his chest and shoulders, as well as a narrow waist that tapered down into lean hips. His trousers, fashioned of dark blue duck, molded a pair of taut, sinewy thighs and long legs that sported gleaming black leather boots. There was an aura of powerful, undeniable masculinity about the man, whose eyes, Hillary suddenly realized, were making an embarrassingly bold assessment of her feminine charms. His smoldering gaze raked over her with such thoroughness that she felt positively naked!

Inhaling sharply as she watched the stranger's chiseled lips curve into a slow, sensuous smile of obvious approval, Hillary drew herself up proudly and opened the gate. She was nonplussed by the erratic pounding of her heart, but she sought to ignore her inner disquietude as she swept down the stone walk and directly toward the spot where the man stood regarding her with what she could have sworn was amusement—and something else she dared not name.

Indeed, even though she endeavored to prevent her gaze from straying to his face again, she caught a glimpse of the disturbing gleam in his eyes—eyes that remained fastened unwaveringly upon her while she squared her shoulders and lifted her chin in an unconscious gesture of defiance. Gallantly removing his hat at her approach, the handsome stranger stepped aside and nodded wordlessly down at her as she marched rigidly past him and up the steps. Hillary offered him no response, though she was keenly aware of his close proximity. She was almost certain he had turned to stare at her, but she did not allow herself a backward glance before raising her fist to deliver a brisk rap to the door, which was answered in a mercifully short amount of time.

"Hillary! What a pleasant surprise!" Anthony Warren's fair, patrician face was wreathed in smiles as he swung open the door and placed a properly solicitous hand upon her arm. His pale blue eyes displayed a warmth for her that had steadily increased throughout their several months' acquaintance. "I was just on my way out. Queen Pomare granted me an audience for ten o'clock this morning," he announced, hastily shrugging into his frock coat while ushering her inside the brightly lit foyer.

Returning Anthony's smile with a brief, somewhat absent one of her own, Hillary lifted her skirts and moved through the doorway, unable to prevent tossing a look over her shoulder as she did so. A slight frown of puzzlement creased her brow when she saw that the bold stranger had disappeared.

"What brings you here so early?" queried Anthony, obviously torn between the desire to remain and talk with her and the duties calling him away. Only a trifle taller than Hillary, whose height was considered above average for a woman, he possessed an athletic build and was quite attractive in a typically Anglo-Saxon way. He had been groomed for diplomatic service from an early age, though neither he nor his family had ever expected his social polish and politic skills to be put to use in a place such as Tahiti.

"I wanted to discuss the new tariff, but it will wait," she declared with an audible sigh, her violet gaze clouding. No matter how hard she tried, she could not clear her thoughts of the devilishly handsome man who had stared at her with those laughing, vibrantly blue-green eyes. What on earth was the matter with her? She was accustomed to being stared at by newcomers—mainly whalers or merchant sailors—for the simple reason that there were only a small number of fair-skinned women on the entire island, much less in Papeete itself. Why then had she been so affected by the tall seaman's attention?

"Are you certain?" There was an unmistakable note of relief in Anthony's pleasant, mellow voice.

"You can't risk offending Queen Pomare now, can you?" Hillary reluctantly conceded with another sigh. "Oh well, perhaps we can discuss it over tea this afternoon. I'm sure Uncle Denholm will want to talk to you—if he's feeling up to it, that is." She had already crossed the threshold again, and she paused in the sunshine outside as Anthony caught up his hat and closed the door behind them.

"His health has not improved then?" he asked, his flaxen brows knitting together into a frown of concern.

Hillary shook her head, her glistening ebony curls clinging to the silken curve of her shoulders, left partially exposed by the deep, rounded neckline of her gown. "No. To tell the truth, I grow more worried with each passing day. I've mentioned the possibility of taking him back to England for treatment, but he stubbornly refuses even to consider going." Anthony drew her arm through his as they descended the steps and strolled down the walk together. In spite of her preoccupation with financial matters and her uncle's failing health, Hillary found herself looking about for any sign of the man who had virtually undressed her with his eyes. The tone of her voice was deceptively casual as she murmured, "Anthony, there . . . there was a man leaving the house just as I arrived—"

"Don't tell me the fellow dared to speak to you?" he demanded sharply, a scowl temporarily marring the aristocratic perfection of his features as he cast Hillary a searching look.

"No, of course not," she hastened to assure him. Dismayed to feel a telltale blush staining her cheeks, she quickly averted her face. How on earth could she explain her lingering curiosity about the man? She certainly couldn't calmly proclaim: I want to know who he is because he looked at me in such a way that I felt naked. She could envision dear Anthony's reaction to such a shameless admission.

"Whalers!" muttered Anthony, leaving no doubt as to his adverse opinion of the men who were notorious for being drunken and unruly when ashore. He was a firm believer in the old saying that whalemen hung their consciences on Cape Horn before sailing into the South Pacific. While some of them were decent and God-fearing, too many had earned the unfavorable estimation in which they were held. "The Americans are the worst of the lot. Even when one of them appears to be a cut above the others, it's wise never to believe so."

"So the man was an American whaler?" Hillary innocently probed. Suffering a sharp, inexplicable pang of disappointment at the thought, she released an inward sigh and firmly resolved to forget about the stranger. After all, she knew as well as anyone what whalemen were like. She had witnessed their public transgressions often enough these past five years. And the stories she had heard about them were enough to shock even the least shy and retiring young maiden.

"A captain, actually. He said he felt it his duty to inform me of the death of one of his crew, a British subject. While I must approve of the fellow's sense of moral responsibility, I cannot in good conscience condone either his manner or his vocation." They had reached the end of the stone walk by this time. Anthony relinquished Hillary's arm and opened the gate, then followed after her as she stepped into the tree-shaded boulevard. Smiling at her again, he said, "I would be delighted to join you for tea this afternoon. Please give your uncle my respects. And please inform Tevaite of my desire for some of those crumb cakes she presented on the occasion of my last visit!" He laughed softly and took Hillary's hand between both of his in an affectionate gesture of farewell before setting off in the opposite direction.

"Good luck with the queen!" she remembered to call after him. She stood and watched him for a moment, silently musing to herself that it was really quite remarkable, the way he always appeared so impeccably groomed in spite of the heat and dust and wind. Anthony was the epitome of an English gentleman—he did not allow himself to wilt or perspire, at least not while in the company of others.

Feeling unaccountably restless, Hillary spun about and swept back down the gentle slope of the unpaved street toward the bustling yet leisurely activity of the market. The morning breeze caressed her face as she reflected that Tevaite, the Tahitian women who was more her friend than her servant, would no doubt be finished with her shopping soon. By the time the two of them returned to Starcross, the day would be half gone, but it was highly probable that Uncle Denholm would not even have noticed their absence. If only his health would show some sign of improving—

Her silent reverie was interrupted by the sudden, nagging sensation that she was being followed. Reacting with characteristic directness, she came to an abrupt halt and turned her head to ascertain if her suspicions were true. Her breath caught in her throat and her violet eyes grew round as saucers within the delicate oval of her face.

Merciful heavens, the whaler! He stood poised only a short distance behind her, and his handsome, sun-kissed face was wearing a strangely disturbing expression that sent another sharp, involuntary tingle coursing down her spine. He must have been waiting for her to leave the consulate. But for what purpose? she wondered, her pulses racing alarmingly.

Whipping her head back around, Hillary sought to regain her composure. Why should I feel in the least bit threatened by the man? she sternly reasoned with herself. This certainly was not the first time she had been pursued by a lonely seaman anxious to strike up an acquaintance with a young woman who reminded him of hearth and home. There had been only two unfortunate occasions whereupon a sailor had taken it into his head that she was one of the *vahines* who considered it something of an honor to bestow their favors upon such men. However, she had been in no real danger. Since she knew practically everyone on the island, there was never

18

any lack of champions in times of distress.

Employing tactics that had proven quite effective in circumstances similar to the one at hand, Hillary turned to the tall American and favored him with a withering, coldly disdainful glare. The whaling captain's response was not at all what she had expected. Instead of appearing either duly chastised or discouraged, he looked more dangerously intrigued and determined than ever. A mocking smile tugged at the corners of his mouth as his narrowing eyes glowed with a fierce yet unfathomable light. Maintaining a negligent hold upon the double-breasted coat slung over his shoulder, he began moving slowly toward Hillary, his unsettling gaze lingering in turn upon the enchanting curve of her full young breasts and the delectable roundness of her hips beneath the clinging white muslin.

Hillary could feel her cheeks crimsoning. Indignantly deciding that she had had enough of the man's impertinence—and battling the sudden urge to catch up her skirts and run as fast as her legs could carry her—she whirled back around and marched resolutely onward, her steps brisk and measured. She could literally feel the man's eyes upon her, and she sensed that he had resumed his mysterious pursuit of her, but she refused to offer him any further demonstration of her annoyance. She would ignore him forthwith; she'd not let him see how very much his actions, his audacious scrutiny, had affected her.

Forcing herself to behave as normally as possible, she strolled amongst the wonderfully disorganized rows of the market. She responded politely to inquiries about her uncle's health and smiled at the children who came bounding up to greet "Missy," as she had come to be known among the islanders. Her eyes frequently scanned the waterfront for any sign of

Tevaite, and she was none too pleased by the fact that the woman was nowhere to be found. A surreptitious glance backward every few moments revealed the whaler's persistence. Although he pretended great interest in the fruits and baskets whenever he saw her flashing amethyst gaze straying in his direction, she was not so easily deceived.

Hillary grew even more indignant when it occurred to her that the man was enjoying himself at her expense. He was apparently playing some sort of contemptible little game with her, and she did not take kindly to the realization that she had been singled out as a source of amusement for the procacious American captain. She was sorely tempted to summon one of the French *gendarmes* posted at various points along the waterfront and issue a complaint against the insolent whaler, but she had to admit that such action would seem a bit drastic for so minor an offense as ogling. After all, the man had not directly approached her yet, had offered her no spoken insult. Why then did she feel so . . . so *touched* by him?

"Miss Hillary! Miss Hillary!"

She experienced no small amount of relief upon hearing the familiar voice calling her. It was Tevaite. The older Tahitian woman, who spoke almost flawless English as a result of missionary schooling, stood waiting in the shade beside the horse and wagon across the street. It was obvious from the many baskets lining the bed of the rather ramshackle conveyance that she had completed her weekly purchase of supplies for the plantation.

Hillary's beautiful, stormy features relaxed into a smile. After gracefully lifting a hand to indicate that she had heard, she emerged from the familiar disorder of the market and set off to join her friend, anxious to return home and forget all about the tall stranger who had caused her such a peculiar combination of outrage, trepidation . . . and breathless excitement.

Tevaite's dark liquid eyes were alight with their usual sparkle as she watched her young mistress hastening across the street. The Tahitian woman's silky, blue-black hair hung almost to her waist, and her noble features were smooth and unlined, making it difficult to determine her age. A member of the race whose people were on average the tallest in the world, she was considered somewhat petite, despite the fact that she and Hillary were much the same size. A mischievous smile spread across her face as she gathered up the folds of her crimson *pareu* and agilely climbed up into the wagon.

When a noticeably tense Hillary lifted her full skirts and settled herself beside Tevaite on the wagon seat a moment later, the older woman chuckled softly and remarked with irrepressible good humor, "You have won the heart of another."

"What on earth are you talking about?" Hillary demanded sharply, then flushed guiltily as her eyes met the knowing look in Tevaite's.

"I saw how the tall man followed you. He is watching you still," she cheerfully supplied, gazing past Hillary to where the handsome whaling captain stood surveying them on the outskirts of the market directly opposite. "There is no shame to have a man such as he—"

"The man is a whaler, Tevaite!" Hillary brusquely cut her off. She frowned darkly and gathered up the reins, refusing to give the insolent rogue the satisfaction of any further notice. "You know as well as I do that they're a rude, unprincipled lot who have brought us nothing but trouble!"

21

"There are good and bad among all men," the other woman pointed out with a philosophical shrug. While it was true that many whalers had taken advantage of the Tahitians' innate kindness and unselfish hospitality, others had proven to be compassionate and generous. A number of schools and churches in the South Pacific owed their existence in part to contributions from men whose hard, dangerous, and often boring way of life prompted in them a need to feel that they had counted for something more than their thankless domination of the sea. "He does not have the look of a devil," opined Tevaite, leaning forward to subject the faintly smiling American to a wide, speculative look.

Hillary's only response was to snap the reins together abruptly above the horse's back and maneuver the wagon toward the crowded wharf. Several men, mostly Tahitians, were straining their backs to load barrels of sugar, flour, and other supplies aboard a French merchant ship that had finally been granted its turn to dock at the quay. The full barrels were large and unwieldy, and it was no easy task for the men to roll them across the splintered wooden planks to the ship's lowered gangway. The vessel's chief mate stood on deck, bellowing orders in a garbled mixture of Tahitian and French. His voice momentarily ceased its strident roar as his eyes fell on Hillary, who was now driving the wagon past the quay. A surge of mingled homesickness and lust welled up deep within the Frenchman, and he mentally cursed himself before tearing his gaze away and resuming his duties.

Suddenly, a shout from one of the Tahitians alerted the others to the fact that he and his fellow worker had lost control of a barrel. There was a great commotion on the wharf as everyone frantically scurried out of the way of the barrel, which was heavy enough to crush a man, as it went careening wildly out into the street.

"Missy! Missy!"

"*Attendez*, mademoiselle! *Attendez!*"

A loud gasp broke from Hillary's lips when she glanced up to see the barrel thundering directly into her wagon's path. She jerked back on the reins, trying desperately to control the horse as the shrilly protesting, panic-stricken animal reared up on his hind legs, then lurched backward, sending the contents of the wagon spilling into the dust beneath the wheels. The runaway barrel rolled perilously close to the horse's front hooves, continuing onward until it smashed into the market displays across the street. Tevaite clutched at the side of the wagon seat for support, watching in helpless fear while her young mistress sought to regain control of the violently twisting horse.

Before Hillary knew what was happening, the very man from whose bothersome presence she had been intent upon fleeing was there before her, grasping hold of the frightened animal's bridle with an awe-inspiring mastery that caused the crowd of onlookers to marvel at both his courage and his abilities. He placed his other large hand on the horse's sleek neck and commanded in a low, resonant tone, "Steady, boy, steady." His deep-timbered voice, combining with the soothing pressure of his strong fingers, achieved the desired effect of calming the animal. Within seconds, the chestnut gelding had quieted and stood complacently while his subduer rewarded him with several gentle strokes along his flowing mane. "Ease up on the reins," the tall stranger instructed Hillary, his unique turquoise gaze flickering only briefly over her stunned, wide-eyed countenance before returning to the horse's placid face.

Hillary Reynolds suddenly found herself at an uncharacteristic loss for words. While her pulses raced wildly and a tiny voice at the back of her mind observed that the bold captain appeared even more breathtakingly handsome at such close proximity, her wounded pride pointed out that not only had the man subjected her to an embarrassingly bold appraisal for the past several minutes, but he was now issuing orders to her with a wholly masculine air of superiority that made her feel like an incompetent schoolgirl!

"I'm perfectly capable of controlling my own horse!" she snapped, then colored furiously as the captain favored her with a quizzical half smile. His eyes, virtually dancing with amusement, issued her a silent challenge.

"Are you indeed?" he softly quipped. There was a pleasant lilting quality to his speech that bespoke his Yankee origins, but Hillary was in no mood to appreciate it. Her bright gaze kindled umbrageously as her fingers clenched the reins even more tightly. Painfully aware of the crowd gathering about the wagon, she felt her annoyance with the man increasing tenfold when she took note of the smiles and looks of avid curiosity being directed at them. Tevaite, having alighted by this time to retrieve the provisions scattered on the ground, added her merry glances to the others as she hurriedly lifted the baskets and returned them to the wagon bed with the assistance of several friends.

The blush staining Hillary's cheeks deepened. Quite anxious to put an end to the discomfiting scene, she faced the captain squarely and forced herself to declare with icy politeness, "While I

24

undoubtedly owe you a debt of gratitude for your assistance, Captain, I—"

"Gallagher. Captain Ryan Gallagher," he determinedly supplied, reaching up to sweep the hat from his head in a gesture that should have been gallant but instead seemed every bit as mocking as the faint smile still playing about his lips. "Master of the whaling bark—"

"Would you be so good as to stand aside?" she cut him off. Her eyes flashed and narrowed before sending him a chilling glare that had discouraged lesser men. Captain Ryan Gallagher, however, held fast to the gelding's bridle, prompting Hillary to demand imperiously, "Let go of my horse!"

"Not until you promise to go easier with the poor fellow. As with women, there are times when a strong hand is needed . . . and times when a gentler touch will do," drawled Ryan, his gleaming, blue-green gaze full of meaning as he raised his eyes to Hillary's face.

She inhaled upon a gasp, shocked at both the implication of his words and the effect of them upon her innermost, feminine emotions. Considerably dismayed to feel an unfamiliar warmth spreading throughout her entire body, she was relieved when Tevaite climbed back up to the wagon seat a scant moment later.

"All is ready again, Miss Hillary," the Tahitian woman announced with a sly glance in the handsome young captain's direction. Hillary did not hesitate before briskly snapping the reins above the horse's back, thereby forcing Ryan to make a swift choice between maintaining his grip on the bridle—which would necessitate a battle for control over the hapless animal's allegiance—or releasing it and removing himself from the wagon's path. He chose the latter, for the simple reason that he was fully confident he and the young woman known only to him as "Miss Hillary" would meet again. And soon—very soon, Ryan Gallagher silently vowed.

Hillary, her color still high and her eyes still ablaze, refused to look at him again as he stepped aside. She drove away at an unusually abrupt pace, bringing a worried caution from Tevaite to avoid running down any of the people who were wisely scurrying to get out of the way.

Ryan stood and watched until the wagon had disappeared, then sauntered back across the street to retrieve his coat from where he had dropped it in his haste to aid Hillary. There was a meditative glow in his eyes and a distinctly purposeful set to his sun-bronzed features as he negligently shook the dust from the coat and slung it over his shoulder once more.

Traveling homeward along the northwest coast of the island, Hillary and Tevaite spoke little. Tevaite, sensing her young mistress's inner turmoil—and secretly attributing it to the American captain—gazed tranquilly about her as the wagon bounced and jostled over the road that completely encircled the larger part of the island, called Tahiti Nui by the natives. The route continued onward for halfway around the smaller part, known as Tahiti Iti. There was only the one road, and it owed its origins to the queen's late father and the members of the London Missionary Society, who had caused it to be built some thirty years earlier as a means of punishment for sinners who crimes had ranged from petty thievery to murder.

Hillary, normally quite appreciative of the island's

tropical beauty whenever she made the trip to Papeete and back—even after five years—was now too engrossed with disturbing memories of her recent encounter with a certain devilishly attractive seaman to take much notice of the peaceful, sunlit scenery. Plagued by the persistent image of Captain Ryan Gallagher's face swimming before her eyes, she was scarcely able to concentrate on guiding the horse along the path winding through an endlessly diversified landscape.

Tahiti was dominated by the twin, towering peaks of Mount Orohena and Mount Aorai, two long-dormant volcanoes the slopes of which were covered with dense rain forests of incredible verdancy. The island was a natural paradise where there was fresh water in abundance; where there was enough food and warmth and beauty so that the majority of its inhabitants had no ambition to struggle for anything more. It was a place where clear turquoise lagoons lapped gently at white sand shores; where aromatic, flamboyant trees displayed gigantic blooms in various shades of red, orange, pink, and yellow; where cascading waterfalls plunged into deep, sparkling pools fringed by nodding palm trees.

The coastal plains boasted coconut trees, mangoes, banana trees, taros, breadfruit trees, and others. The interior was a wild region of deep, narrow valleys, fragrant lime trees, swift rivers, wild coffee bushes, and steep, jagged mountains, which cut sharply into the skyline and were concealed beneath an almost perpetual mantle of clouds and rain. Surrounding the island was a protective barrier of coral, where the eternal surf of the Pacific thundered upon the reef.

Once away from the main city, there were charming little villages where the thatch-roofed huts—open on all sides to the breeze—were scattered haphazardly among the coconut and breadfruit trees. Fishermen paddled in outrigger canoes, *pareu*-wrapped women strolled along the road and washed clothes in the innumerable streams that flowed into the beckoning waters of the lagoon, and naked brown children ran carefree amongst the lush vegetation. Goats, pigs, dogs, cows, and horses added to the population of each small, close-knit rural community.

The wagon was soon rolling past Matavai Bay and Point Venus. Matavai Bay was where the early visitors to the island had dropped anchor—men such as Wallis, who had claimed the island for England in 1767, Bougainville, who had proclaimed French sovereignty over the island in 1768, and the great English explorer, James Cook, who had followed a year later. Here, there was a lovely, crescent-shaped harbor and a black sand beach, very tall palm trees that curved far out over the beach and lagoon, and a steep hill at the western end of the bay, which blocked Papeete from view.

Point Venus, situated at the northeast tip of Matavai Bay, had been named by Cook. He and his men had made their camp at this exact location during a visit to the island in June of 1769, having been sent to view and record the transit of the planet Venus. Although they failed in their original commission, their observations regarding Tahiti and the islanders served to bring the South Pacific into prominence as an area of the world to be explored and utilized. Cook's visit had been the fateful turning point—life for the Tahitians had been irrevocably altered, and it was still a point of great dissension within the "civilized world" as to whether or not the change had been for the better.

Not long after leaving the bay behind, Hillary was

slowing the horse and wagon to a halt near the main building at Starcross. Her uncle and his late wife had started the plantation some eleven years earlier, shortly after the introduction of vanilla to the island. Denholm Reynolds, in a rare moment of sentimentality, had seen fit to bestow upon his new home the name of his mother's birthplace in England, a quaint little Devon village where he had spent many happy boyhood hours.

"Tehura will help me with the baskets. Your uncle will want to see you," proclaimed Tevaite with a gentle smile at a somber-faced Hillary. Climbing down, the native woman was greeted by her daughter, a plump little beauty of fourteen with eyes shaped like almonds and shimmering, blue-black hair reaching almost to her knees. Tehura flashed her mother and Hillary an impish smile.

"The *ari'i* is better today," the girl announced, using the Tahitian word for chief. The designation in this particular case was part playful, part respectful. "He asks for much food!"

Hillary's features momentarily relaxed into a smile at the news. She secured the reins, then gathered up her skirts to alight, recalling that her uncle had displayed little appetite throughout the past several weeks. Indeed, she mused with an inward sigh as her feet met the ground, Denholm Reynolds's once-portly frame had been so ravaged by illness that his clothing now hung in loose folds upon his gaunt body.

"Has he been awake long?" she asked Tehura. She was already moving toward the open doorway of the two-storied villa, a large, airy structure in the colonial style with a traditional thatch roof, louvered windows, railings with worked posts, and wide verandahs on all sides. The main house, or *fare*

29

vanira as it was called by the natives who lived and worked on the estate, was well off the road and nestled among the thick tropical foliage beneath an emerald canopy of palm trees. Several outbuildings, with walls of bamboo and raised roofs of thatched pandanus leaves, were scattered about the premises. The fields containing neat rows of fragile vanilla plants lay only a short distance away from the small hut where Hillary taught school to the workers' children in the afternoons.

"Not long," Tehura responded with a slight shake of her head. Having scampered up into the wagon bed, she was nonchalantly leaning back against one of the larger baskets in the wagon. "He asks for you, then asks for food."

"He will not get his wish for food unless you help me!" Tevaite admonished her, though there was no accompanying sharpness in the older woman's tone. Tehura's melodious laughter rang out before she offered her mother a saucy retort. Hillary seemed not to hear their good-natured bantering as she climbed the front steps of the house and disappeared inside.

The furnishings assembled by Denholm and Louisa Reynolds for their island home were an intriguing blend of Tahitian and European—the floors were covered by both woven palm mats and Oriental rugs; the walls were adorned with paintings of pastoral English scenes and with brightly colored native art; and the furniture consisted of wooden tables and chairs carved by local craftsmen as well as chintz-upholstered sofas and chaises brought from the Reynolds's homeland. Although there was an undeniable sense of prosperity about the place, there was also a noticeably well-worn look that increased with each passing year. Denholm Reynolds had never been the same since the death of his wife more than three years earlier—he had lost most of his enthusiasm for life, and Starcross had naturally suffered. It had fallen to Hillary to maintain the plantation's twice-yearly production of vanilla pods.

However, neither the vanilla crop nor the newly imposed tariff on it took precedence in Hillary's mind as she crossed to the staircase and hastened up to her uncle's room. She was inordinately pleased to find him dressed and seated in a chair out on the upper verandah. It was the first time he had left his bed in nearly a week's time.

"Good morning, Uncle! Tevaite and I just this moment returned from Papeete. Tehura tells me you're quite impatient for your breakfast," Hillary remarked with a soft laugh as she bent to brush his cheek with her lips.

"It seems the memory of past delights has made itself known to my long-neglected stomach," the pale, gray-haired man confessed a bit ruefully.

"An improved appetite is a very significant sign of improvement," asserted his niece. She sank down into a white wicker chair beside his and turned her violet gaze upon the gently swaying crowns of the trees, which were level with the verandah. Absently scrutinizing a lone blackbird who sailed downward on the breeze to perch atop a coconut, she inhaled deeply of the warm, sweetly scented morning air. In the next instant, her brows drew together in a gesture of renewed disquiet that seemed at variance with the serenely beautiful surroundings.

"Did you speak to Anthony about the tariff?" queried Denholm, noting her frown. He readjusted his wire-rimmed spectacles and smoothed a faintly trembling hand across the top of his balding head. Though in reality he was not yet sixty, his appearance was that of a man at least ten years older.

"No," Hillary answered with a sigh. "Queen Pomare had summoned him to the palace. But he'll be coming for tea this afternoon. I hope to discuss it with him then." She idly reached up to gather her thick, luxuriant mass of hair and lift it from her neck. As she allowed the raven tresses to fall back into place a moment later, the unbidden recollection of a pair of vibrant, blue-green eyes studying her with wicked boldness suddenly insinuated itself in her mind once more.

Captain Ryan Gallagher. Her face flamed anew at the embarrassing memory of her traitorous body's reaction to his appraisal . . . to the sound of his resonant, deep-timbred voice . . . to his undeniable masculinity . . .

"Hillary, my dear, is something wrong?"

"What?" she blurted out, starting guiltily as she was drawn out of her disturbing reverie.

"Is something wrong?" her uncle repeated patiently. "You took a bit flushed. Perhaps you should rest a while. I think sometimes you try to do too much." He released a heavy sigh and shook his head sadly. "I know I'm only more of a burden to you. If only—"

"Nonsense!" Hillary discounted his words with a determined brightness. Rising from the chair, she hurried to his side and knelt to place an arm about his frail shoulders. "You will get better soon, Uncle. Until then you're not to worry, understand? Tevaite and I will take care of everything." She prayed her assurances held more conviction than she truly felt.

After pressing another kiss to Denholm's cheek and promising to send up Tehura with his breakfast soon, Hillary left the room and closed the door behind her. She stood leaning back against it for several long moments. Her thoughts centered briefly on the slight improvement in her uncle's condition, and she felt a small glimmer of hope that he would return at least to some semblance of his former self. When the morning's incident in Papeete then pushed into the forefront of her introspection, she murmured an exclamation of self-reproach and took herself off to help Tevaite put away the provisions.

II

The following morning was radiantly calm, but the early afternoon brought with it the distant rumble of thunder and the heavy, unmistakable scent of approaching rain. Hillary, musing that she would be glad of a respite from the heat, swept through the doorway of the thatch-roofed building that served as a school and set an armload of books atop her carved wooden desk. She turned to smile at the nearly dozen children who sat cross-legged on their woven coco-frond mats with such angelic innocence.

They were miniature versions of their parents—the girls each wore an overlapping length of bright *tapa* cloth about their slim little bodies, while the boys wore only waistcloths fashioned of the same felted material that was made from the inner bark of breadfruit or mulberry trees. Hillary had both witnessed and participated in the process of making *tapa* many times. The peeled bark was first scraped and soaked in water, then beaten with a club until soft and pliable. Afterward, the fabric was stenciled or painted in bright colors, or the design printed by using blocks of carved bamboo. She had always preferred the latter method herself, but realized it was because she had never been terribly adept at painting. Her Aunt Louisa had despaired of teaching her the "finer arts" of sketching and embroidery the first year she had come to live at Starcross.

Hillary's smile faded as her gaze scanned the room and she became aware of Tehura's conspicuous absence. Tevaite's daughter was the oldest of her pupils and a very willing helper. It wasn't at all like her to be late.

"Has anyone seen Tehura?" she asked of the class. Before her question could be answered, she looked up to see the missing girl framed in the doorway. It was immediately apparent that something was wrong, for Tehura's usual vivaciousness had been replaced by an air of abnormal sobriety. She ducked her head before entering the hut, her bare feet padding noiselessly across the dirt floor as she hastily took her place near the front. "Tehura? Tehura, what is it?" demanded Hillary quietly. A worried frown creased her brow, and she bent down to place a solicitous hand on the girl's arm. "What—" she started to question again, only to break off with a startled gasp when Tehura reluctantly lifted her head. A dark, purplish bruise marred the amber-hued smoothness of one cheek, there were several scratches and bruises on her arms, and a telltale redness and puffiness was visible about the younger woman's eyes.

"I . . . I am sorry, Missy, but my mother, she says I am to come to school," Tehura declared in a voice scarcely above a whisper.

"Oh Tehura!" breathed Hillary. She did not wait for the explanation Tehura was about to offer, but instead drew the girl up beside her and swiftly ushered her back outside, away from the wide, curious stares of the other pupils. After leading her a short distance away, Hillary urged, "Tell me what happened to you."

"*Aiti e peapea,*" murmured Tehura, suddenly turning evasive. She lowered her eyes and clasped her hands together behind her, in the same manner as a child who knows he will be reprimanded if he admits the truth.

"It *is* important!" Hillary dissented. Seizing the girl's arms in a firm but gentle grip, she commanded, "Tell me, Tehura. Tell me who hurt you!"

"The man from the ship," Tehura finally revealed. Her almond-shaped brown eyes glistened with sudden tears, and her lower lip trembled as she confessed, "I go with him last night when he says I am to be his *vahine*. He—"

"You *what?*" interrupted Hillary, her expression one of shocked disbelief.

"I go with him," Tehura reiterated.

"How . . . how could you do such a thing? Why, you're only a child!" Hillary's arms dropped to her sides as Tehura gave her a look of mingled amusement and confusion.

"I am no child, Missy."

Her beautiful face flooding with color, Hillary was unable to think of a suitable response. She was well aware of the fact that Tahitian girls matured much earlier than their European counterparts, but she had always believed Tevaite's daughter to be different when it came to such things. With the islanders, there was no false modesty about the celebration of physical love—young girls from the age of ten or so would readily grant their favors and suffer no condemnation for it, at least not among their own people. Still, Hillary reflected as she met Tehura's dark liquid gaze, she had never before contemplated the thought of her young friend giving herself to a man, and particularly not to some degenerate sailor

37

who would so cruelly mistreat her.

"He says he is the *tapena,* but I do not believe him. How can he be the *tapena* when other men from the ship say he is not?"

"It makes no difference if the blackguard is a captain or not—what matters is what he did to you!" Hillary feelingly asserted. Her eyes flashed in rapidly growing indignation, and she raised her hands to grip Tehura's arms once more. "How did this happen? What were you doing in Papeete last night?"

"My mother's brother, Mahi, he tells me I can ride on his horse when he goes to Papeete yesterday. It was dark soon. I go with the man from the ship. At first he is happy, but then he becomes like a *demoni* and hurts me. I scream and run away. Mahi finds me. We ride home this morning," she recounted with childlike simplicity.

"What did your mother say when you returned?"

"She says to come to school. I tell her you will not like what happened, that you will say I have done wrong, but she says to come."

Realizing that Tevaite and Mahi had apparently reacted with typical insouciance, for it was nothing out of the ordinary for a young Tahitian woman to spend the night with one of the seamen in port and to receive rough treatment occasionally, Hillary was nonetheless infuriated that the attack on Tehura would go unpunished. She was thoroughly disgusted with the way the islanders were time and again taken advantage of. It was useless to report the incident to the authorities in Papeete, she silently reasoned. They would merely dismiss it with an indifferent shrug and a callous remark that the girl had only gotten what she deserved. Hillary had witnessed that reaction before. There had to be something she could do, some way she could ensure that Tehura's assailant would be taught a lesson.

"We go back to school now, Missy?" the girl suggested with a tentative smile, hoping that her teacher's anger had passed.

"Do you happen to know what ship the man was from? Do you know the name of it?" Hillary surprised her by asking.

Tehura's eyes grew very wide, and she hesitated a moment before nodding and reluctantly answering, "Yes, Missy. It is called the *Falcon*. It is a ship for catching whales."

A whaler, Hillary's mind repeated. I might have known! Captain Ryan Gallagher's handsome face swam before her eyes once more. Mentally consigning him and all his kind to the devil, she sought to control her perilously rising temper. There was only a slight, telltale quaver in her voice as she calmly instructed her oldest pupil, "You will teach the class today, Tehura. Please concentrate on the reading lesson I assigned last week." She gathered up her skirts and whirled about to begin marching purposefully toward the house.

"But where do you go?" a very puzzled Tehura called after her.

"To see that justice is done!"

The journey from Starcross to Papeete was accomplished in record time. Hillary's righteous indignation grew with each bump and jolt of the wagon— and with each drop of rain that pelted her as the heavens opened up and released a life-sustaining deluge upon the countryside. When she pulled the weary horse to a halt before the quay, her eyes were ablaze with a magnificent amethyst fire and her thick ebony curls were plastered in a damp curtain across her back and shoulders. She had drawn a slicker over her as protection against the rain, but the loose canvas garment had been unable to prevent a partial soaking of her hair and clothing during the brief, tropical thunderstorm. The storm had passed now, leaving heavily scented perfumes to emanate from the wet earth as the sun's rays broke through the clouds.

"Ia orana, Missy!" several of the workers on the busy wharf sang out when they caught sight of Hillary. She responded with a brisk nod and wave in their direction, then hurriedly alighted from the wagon and approached one of the Tahitian men who stood upon the shore. Asking him which of the ships in the harbor bore the name *Falcon,* she was satisfied when he pointed at one of the vessels anchored alongside the quay. He told her that it was an American whaleship, and that it had finally been given permission to dock the previous evening.

"Mauruuru roa," she hastily thanked the man before setting off toward the three-masted ship he had indicated. The *Falcon* had a bulky, tub-shaped hull and bluntly curved bow, for she had been built for endurance instead of speed. Painted black with white ports, she carried three whaleboats on the port side and two on the starboard, and her rigging, Hillary vaguely noted as she drew closer, was that of a bark, with fore-and-aft sails on her mizzenmast. During the five years she had lived on the island, Hillary had learned a great deal about the various types of ships that put in at Papeete—and the various types of men.

Without pausing to contemplate the wisdom of her actions, she started up the lowered gangplank of the *Falcon.* She staunchly ignored the comments—

both harmlessly appreciative and otherwise—from the seamen gathering on the wharf to watch her as she boarded the whaleship. It had long been a custom in the South Pacific for island girls to swim out and greet any ship arriving in port and to extend their particular brand of hospitality to the woman-hungry crew, but Hillary was clearly an exception to that illustrious tradition. Not that a "decent" woman's presence was an unheard-of sight aboard a whaler; quite the contrary was true. Many a captain's wife had insisted upon accompanying her husband on his voyages, voyages that were apt to last three years or even longer. All the same, it certainly was not a common, everyday occurrence to see a beautiful young woman of obvious quality marching proud-as-you-please onto a whaleship.

Upon reaching the top of the gangplank, Hillary suddenly found her path barred by a very tall, very burly man in drab sailor's attire whose coarse, weathered features were screwed into a darkly menacing scowl. He stood with his arms folded across his huge chest and his booted feet planted squarely apart on the ship's deck.

"What would you be wanting aboard the *Falcon?*" he growled, squinting down at her with cold gray eyes. A ragged, unruly thatch of black hair hung from beneath his cap, and an equally unkempt beard hid the lower half of his face. Hillary could not help wrinkling her nose in distaste as she was assailed by the foul odor given off by the hostile giant's clothing.

"I wish to speak to the captain of this vessel at once!" she imperiously proclaimed, evidently not in the least bit discouraged by his intimidating stance.

"The captain don't allow women aboard." His eyes narrowed even further as they raked over her in an openly rancorous manner that left little doubt as to his opinion of the female sex in general.

"Then the captain will have to make an exception, for I *am* coming aboard and I *shall* see him!" declared Hillary, her own eyes virtually shooting sparks as they refused to fall before his. "Now stand aside, please!" Her whole demeanor was one of such proud, angry defiance that the man was clearly given pause. He stood glaring down at her for several moments longer before apparently conceding defeat. Although he muttered a blistering oath under his breath, he took a step backward nonetheless and finally allowed her to board.

"Wait here," he commanded with a surly air. "I'll fetch the captain."

"That won't be necessary!" retorted Hillary, already sailing past him and making straightaway for the quarterdeck.

"Where do you think you're going? The captain don't like to be disturbed when he's in closed quarters!" the man ground out, moving with surprising speed to intercept her before she could reach the companionway leading to the officers' cabins below. Effectively blocking her path with his bulk again, he snarled in disgust. "This ain't no 'hen frigate'! You can't go below decks. Them's private—"

"Private or not, I'm going down!" decreed Hillary. Armed with an obstinancy borne of womanly outrage and a fierce desire to see Tehura's abuser punished, she merely detoured around the bearded giant and continued on her way. She had a clear notion of where the captain's quarters were located. Gathering up her skirts and disregarding the startled looks sent her way by the few members of the crew on duty that afternoon, she quickly descended the narrow steps of the companionway.

Pausing before the cabin that lay directly below the

skylight, Hillary raised her hand to knock at the closed door. Her lovely countenance was quite flushed, her heart was pounding, and her breasts rose and fell rapidly beneath the fitted bodice of her pale lavender gown, but it was all due to still-smoldering fury, not apprehension.

The captain will be made to listen! she silently vowed, her chin tilting upward in a gesture of unwavering determination. I will convince him to punish the cowardly fiend responsible for Tehura's injuries! She rapped firmly upon the door, then waited impatiently for the forthcoming response.

It was not quite what she had expected.

The muffled curse she heard coming from within the cabin was savagely unrighteous enough to provoke a rush of hot color to her cheeks. In the next instant, the door was flung open to the accompaniment of a deep, familiar voice thundering, "Blast it, Josiah, I distinctly recall leaving orders—"

Hillary's eyes grew very wide, and she suffered a sharp, highly audible intake of breath at the same time the handsome young captain of the *Falcon* broke off to stare down at her incredulously. Their startled gazes met and locked, and neither of them spoke for what seemed to Hillary an eternity. Following the initial flash of recognition in the captain's well-remembered eyes, the impression in their smoldering, blue-green depths swiftly changed from astonishment to delight, then to something that bespoke much more than mere pleasure.

Dismayed to find herself seized by a sudden lightheadedness, Hillary blushed fierily and battled the temptation to beat a hasty retreat. She finally recovered voice enough to break the silence, but the uncharacteristic nervousness she was experiencing caused her words to tumble over one another in a most embarrassing manner.

"*You* are the captain of this vessel?" she breathlessly queried.

"Captain Ryan Gallagher, master of the whaling bark *Falcon,* of New Bedford, Massachusetts," he confirmed, a disconcerting twinkle in his eyes as he nodded down at her. "At your service, Miss Hillary." His mouth curved into a smile of appreciative irony.

"My name happens to be Reynolds—*Miss Reynolds,*" she informed him, visibly bristling beneath his amused gaze. "And I have something of the utmost importance to discuss with you!" Why in heaven's name did it have to be *him?* Hillary silently lamented. She was acutely conscious of the way he was towering above her, of the way his tall, muscular frame filled the doorway as they faced each other in the dim light of the companionway. He was every bit as dangerously attractive as she remembered—she had been woefully unsuccessful in driving all memory of him from her mind the past day and a half. The insolent rogue had even invaded her dreams!

"Indeed?" Ryan parried softly, the look in his eyes growing even more alarming. "Then may I suggest you do so in the privacy of my cabin?" He gallantly stepped aside to allow her entry, swinging the door wider.

His words struck a dissonant chord with Hillary's better judgment, and she felt a rapidly intensifying uneasiness deep within. However, she stubbornly refused to let the captain see any evidence of her reluctance—downright fear, if she were honest with herself—at being alone with him in such intimate quarters. Lifting her head proudly, she bravely responded, "Of course, Captain Gallagher." She did not glimpse the unholy light of amusement in his eyes as she moved rather cautiously past him and through the narrow doorway, taking care to ensure that her full muslin skirts did not come into contact with his polished leather boots.

Once inside, Hillary's troubled gaze made a quick, encompassing sweep of the cabin. The captain's quarters actually consisted of two small rooms—a main cabin that served as both an office and a sitting room, and an adjoining stateroom where he slept and washed. The room in which Hillary stood contained very little in the way of furnishings—there was a table where the captain made entries in the ship's log and kept an eye on the compass overhead, and a horsehair sofa placed across-ship at the stern with cuddies or recesses taking advantage of the overhang of the stern itself—but it nevertheless had a cramped feeling about it, for every single space was occupied with books, charts, instruments, and other para- phernalia attesting to a life at sea. The cabin's only outlooks were an overhead skylight with panes of glass set in a barred frame, and a small stern window. If a man were tall, as in Ryan's case, it would be difficult for him to stand erect anywhere save between the overhead timbers.

"What exactly is it you've come to discuss?" Ryan questioned with deceptive nonchalance as he closed the door and turned back to her. He was wearing much the same attire as the previous day, and Hillary could not help noticing how very suited the white linen shirt and dark, fitted trousers were to both his coloring and his physique.

She mentally shook herself before declaring a trifle unsteadily, "It . . . it's a very grave matter concerning one of my students, a girl by the name of Tehura." She caught her breath on an inward gasp when he suddenly began advancing upon her. Taking an instinctive step backward, she released a faint sigh of relief when he merely sauntered past her to resume his place at the table.

"Please be seated, Miss Reynolds," Ryan politely directed without betraying any of his secret amusement at her obvious skittishness.

"I would prefer to stand!"

"Very well. Then we will stand."

Hillary eyed him dubiously, then apparently changed her mind. He watched as she sank down onto the edge of the sofa, still holding herself stiffly erect and still doing her best to maintain an air of businesslike composure. Ryan bent his tall frame into an oversized wooden chair, only the suggestion of a smile on his sun-bronzed face as he gazed across at his unexpected but eminently desirable guest. Musing to himself that the somewhat bedraggled but undeniably beautiful young woman before him was even more captivating than he had remembered, he gave silent thanks for whatever, or whoever, had brought them together once more.

"I have reason to believe one of your men is guilty of mistreating Tehura, Captain Gallagher, and I demand that you take action!" Hillary bluntly asserted, her eyes flashing their brilliant amethyst fire as her indignation returned to hit her full force.

"When did this alleged mistreatment take place? And what makes you believe one of my men is responsible?" he asked evenly. Ryan found himself unable to concentrate fully on what she was saying. He was instead wondering if she had ever lost her heart to a man, if she had ever known love. The surge of jealousy such a possibility provoked in him was inexplicable but very authentic. It was a bit unnerving, the way she set his blood afire. He was unaccustomed to feeling so strongly about a woman—

at least the sort of woman Hillary Reynolds was—from the first moment he set eyes upon her.

"Last night. I was unaware of the . . . the crime until Tehura came to school today. The poor girl bears visible marks of the brutal, unwarranted attack upon her! When I questioned her about their cause, she admitted that she had . . . had 'kept company' with a man claiming to be the captain of a whaler, and that he was off this very ship!"

"Are you accusing me of the crime, Miss Reynolds?"

"The thought had occurred to me, Captain, but Tehura expressed doubts as to the validity of the man's claim."

"It's a relief to know I'm no longer a suspect," he wryly assured her.

"I'd venture to say your own conscience is not entirely clear when it comes to the women of this island!" she remarked with biting sarcasm.

"Haven't you heard, Miss Reynolds?" countered Ryan, a sardonic grin playing about his lips. He leisurely folded his arms against his broad chest. "Whalers, particularly American whalers, have no consciences."

"Are you going to treat this matter with the seriousness it deserves?" challenged an increasingly annoyed Hillary as she came abruptly to her feet. Things weren't going at all as she had planned.

"By all means," he solemnly declared, standing as well. "If you'll simply tell me which of my men—"

"I've no idea which of your men is responsible. I was expecting *you* to supply his identity. As the captain, you naturally have the authority to question the crew."

"That may prove more difficult than you think. You see, Miss Reynolds, the men serving aboard this ship, aboard any whaleship, tend to balk at any sort of interrogation involving—"

"I'm well aware of the types of men serving aboard this ship, Captain Gallagher! I've been in Tahiti long enough to know that they are a despicable lot indeed. It is said that whalers are a nuisance to the authorities, the despair of the missionaries, and quite often the ruination of the natives. I quite agree!" She stepped forward and gripped the rounded edge of the table, her violet eyes aglow with unquenchable spirit, her color becomingly high. "In the early days of the white man's exploration here, the women of this island traded their favors for nothing more than a handful of nails. But things are changing. There are those who are doing their utmost to put an end to the exploitation of these innocent, generous people. You yourself, Captain Gallagher, if you have any sense of decency at all, can help to ensure a better way of life for the Tahitians. You can make certain the man who abused Tehura is found and punished!"

"First you offer up an indictment of all whalers in general, and with the next breath you tell me there's a possibility I have a sense of decency," Ryan noted idly, his aquamarine eyes full of ironic humor as he braced his hands on the opposite side of the table and leaned toward her. A shaft of sunlight, turned to a soft rainbow of colors by the prism effect of the glass above, fell upon his head and set his dark hair aglow. "It may surprise you to learn, Miss Reynolds, that I'm very familiar with these islands and the problems of the natives. While you may not believe it, I've done all I can to keep my men in line. But in no way is it possible for me to prevent every unfortunate incident such as the one involving your pupil."

"Are you saying you will do nothing?" she indignantly demanded, dismayed to find herself noticing the tiny flecks of gold in his eyes.

"Not at all. I give you my word I'll question the crew at the first opportunity. If the guilty man is found, then I will see that an appropriate punishment is meted out," he promised with quiet authority.

Hillary did not know exactly what to say at this point. She was still angry, and she was plagued by a certain vague dissatisfaction. Telling herself there was no longer any reason to remain, and feeling decidedly bothered by the fact that the captain was staring across at her so intently, she drew herself proudly erect and finally spoke with icy politeness. "Thank you, Captain Gallagher."

She had already gathered up her skirts and turned to leave when she heard him utter in a low, vibrant tone, "I knew we'd meet again, Miss Reynolds. I'm a firm believer in destiny, you see."

Hillary, not at all certain she had heard him correctly, whirled back around with a look of startled confusion on her face. "What was that, Captain?"

"Destiny," he repeated. A slow, disturbingly meaningful smile spread across his rakishly handsome countenance. The gleam in his eyes grew even more intense as he began moving unhurriedly from behind the table.

"Destiny?" Hillary echoed a trifle breathlessly. Her eyes grew enormous as he drew closer, and she was once again assailed by a wildly erratic heartbeat. "I . . . I don't know what you mean!" Ryan paused mere inches away from her, and she suddenly felt quite small—and frightened, though she would not admit it, even to herself.

"I would have lent the fates a helping hand if you had not returned to Papeete today," he readily confessed, his gaze boring deep into hers as he towered ominously above her. "After yesterday—"

"I do *not* wish to discuss what happened yesterday," she angrily proclaimed, "except to tell you that your behavior was unpardonably rude!"

"Yes, it was, wasn't it?" admitted Ryan with a disarmingly unrepentant grin. His expression sobered somewhat as he explained, "For reasons unknown even to me, I felt compelled to follow you. It wasn't as if I hadn't seen many a comely face and figure in my time—although your face and figure, Miss Reynolds, are without a doubt among the most comely—"

"Why, how . . . how dare you!" she sputtered indignantly, her cheeks crimsoning and her eyes flashing.

"I dare because there's so little time." His deep voice was tinged with a slight huskiness, and Hillary was alarmed once more by the strange light in his eyes, by the purposeful set to his swarthy features. She fought the cowardly impulse to take flight.

"I've always found there to be ample time for the things that truly matter, Captain Gallagher, but the satisfaction of your . . . your masculine curiosity about a woman is not one of them!" she scathingly asserted, her bosom heaving beneath her fitted, lace-edged bodice. "Perhaps from this moment on, you will confine your attentions to those who would welcome them. Since you claim to be so familiar with this island, you should be aware that there are certain areas of Papeete where men of your 'inclinations' can find willing partners in . . . in . . ."

"Fleshly pursuits?" Ryan obliged by finishing for her. The mockery in his tone was unmistakable, the smile now tugging at the corners of his mouth decidedly roguish. He folded his strong, linen-clad arms across his chest again before challenging in a lazy drawl, "Tell me, Miss Reynolds, why is it you seem so distressed by the fact that you are a beautiful young woman? Could it be that you have no real understanding of what occurs between the members of my sex and yours, no real understanding of what it means to love?"

"I have a perfect understanding!" Hillary retorted with spirit. Then, as if suddenly realizing that the conversation had taken a highly improper, not to mention exceedingly dangerous, turn, she hastily put what she believed to be a safer distance between herself and the bold seaman and reached for the doorknob. "Good day, Captain. Our paths shall not cross again!" she firmly ordained. She had no sooner grasped the knob with trembling fingers when he was there behind her, his large hand closing upon her arm to forcefully detain her.

"If there's one quality I'm certain you possess, my dear Miss Reynolds, it's backbone," murmured Ryan, the pleasant Yankee lilt to his voice more pronounced than ever. "Why then are you so anxious to turn tail and run?"

"Let go of me!" Hillary cried, her temper flaring to a perilously high level. She tried to jerk her arm free, but he held fast. "I'm warning you, Captain Gallagher! Either you release me at once, or I'll . . . I'll scream!"

"Scream all you like. This is a whale ship, remember? Surely you don't believe the men aboard this vessel will find anything unusual in the sound of a woman's scream coming from the captain's quarters?" he smoothly taunted.

Hillary, deciding that she had endured quite enough embarrassment and discomfort at the hands of Captain Ryan Gallagher, finally lost control of her carefully guarded emotions. She, who had never

51

before struck another fellow human being in the entirety of her life, now raised her hand and delivered a resounding blow to the sun-bronzed ruggedness of Ryan's cheek

The long silence that followed was heavily charged. Aghast at what she had done, Hillary stood mutely staring up at her handsome captor with wide, sparkling eyes that reflected her inner turmoil. The expression on Ryan's face was at first impassive, then forebodingly grim. An almost imperceptible narrowing of his fiercely glinting eyes signaled the coming response as his fingers tightened upon the tender flesh of Hillary's arm.

A sharp gasp broke from her lips when he seized her other arm and yanked her up hard against him. Her damp raven locks tumbled riotously about her shoulders, and her muslin skirts swirled around the captain's booted, lean-muscled legs. Unable to make her body obey her brain's frantic commands to struggle, Hillary stared up at Ryan in breathless anticipation, her luminous violet gaze betraying her mingled fear and excitement.

"There's a fire burning inside of that cool, prim-and-proper exterior of yours, Hillary Reynolds, a fire waiting to be unleashed by the right man. And *I* am that man!" Ryan avowed in a low, resonant tone that sent an involuntary tremor coursing down Hillary's spine.

"No!" she denied, her own voice little more than a frightened whisper. She dazedly shook her head as she choked out again, "N . . . no!"

But he paid her no heed. Before Hillary could do anything more than raise her hands to push weakly against the unrelenting hardness of his broad chest, Ryan's warm mouth crashed down upon her parted lips with a demanding fierceness that both alarmed

52

and thrilled her. His strong arms masterfully encircled her trembling softness to pull her even closer, to mold her womanly curves to the length of his virile, masculine form while his velvety tongue plundered the moist sweetness of her mouth.

Hillary had never been kissed before—or rather, she had never been so *thoroughly* kissed before. There had been a handful of chaste, almost brotherly kisses from Anthony, but certainly nothing to compare with what was being done to her now. Although barely capable of coherent thought at the present moment, she told herself she should fight the captain, should prevent this wildly enchanting embrace he was forcing upon her.

Forcing? a tiny voice at the back of her mind derisively challenged.

She was given no time to argue with her own conscience, for Ryan's kiss deepened at that moment, his lips growing even more insistent, his hands sweeping boldly downward across the slender curve of her back to the beguiling swell of her hips. Hillary gasped inwardly when she felt his hands cupping her buttocks, when she felt his fingers intimately caressing her rounded flesh through the scant protection of her thin muslin skirts and single petticoat. As was her custom during the warm and rainy season, she wore little in the way of undergarments.

Just as she was made shockingly aware of Ryan's hard masculinity, his lips finally relinquished hers and began searing a fiery path downward to the silken column of her neck . . . to the inviting hollow in her throat where her pulse beat so rapidly . . . to the scooped neckline of her bodice where a modest but provocative portion of her full young breasts swelled above the lace . . .

Hillary's eyes flew wide at the first touch of his warm, persuasive lips upon her breasts. She inhaled sharply and bit at her lower lip to stifle a cry as a wave of growing panic washed over her. No man had ever dared to treat her like this! What was worse, *she* had never dared to forget herself like this!

"No! Dear God, no!" she feverishly gasped out, now pushing in earnest against Ryan. When he would not desist, she entangled her fingers in his thick hair and administered a none-too-gentle yank.

"What the devil—" Ryan ground out, scowling down into her flushed, visibly alarmed countenance. His heart twisted when he glimpsed the look of sheer desperation in her glistening eyes, and he hesitated only a brief second longer before reluctantly loosening his hold upon her.

Hillary, fighting back hot tears of shame and embarrassment, spun about and groped blindly for the doorknob. Ryan's gaze darkened as he watched her wrench open the door and disappear through the doorway in a flash of muslin and lace. Stumbling back up the steps of the companionway, she emerged into the bright sunshine once more and flew back across the deck of the *Falcon*. She passed Josiah on her way to the gangplank, but she was too distraught to notice the look of smug triumph on his craggy features. Choking back a sob, she hastily made her way through the crowd on the quay, back toward the cluster of palms along the shore where she had left the horse and wagon.

"Hillary?" a familiar, masculine voice hailed her in obvious surprise.

She inwardly cursed her luck at having been seen by Anthony Warren, of all people, at such an inopportune moment. Sorely tempted to behave as if she had not heard him at all, she heaved a sigh and mused to herself in annoyance that the young British vice-consul was most assuredly the sort who would persist. She halted beside the wagon, dashed impatiently at her tears, then turned to face her would-be suitor with a tight, forced smile on her face.

"Hello, Anthony," she managed to say calmly enough.

"What are you doing here?" he immediately questioned, his attractive face wearing an expression of deep concern—and what she could have sworn was disapproval. He swept the hat from his fair head and raised a hand to grip Hillary's arm lightly. "Why, you've been crying!" he observed, noting the telltale moistness clinging to her sooty eyelashes.

"It . . . please, Anthony, it's nothing at all," she lied, still feeling so mortified and upset that it was all she could do to be polite to him.

Abruptly whirling about to climb up into the wagon, she had done no more than place a foot on the step when he startled her by demanding accusingly, "It's true, isn't it?"

Hillary turned back to face him with a look of irritated bewilderment. "What are you talking about?"

"One of the natives came to the house a short while ago to inform me you'd actually ventured on board a whale ship! I didn't believe him, of course. You see, I was certain I was well enough acquainted with you to know you'd never be so lost to propriety that—"

"Oh, but I *am* so lost to propriety, dear Anthony!" she interjected with a bitter little laugh, battling the fresh tears that sprang to her eyes. She knew it wasn't fair to vent her anger on him, but she couldn't seem to help it. Her beautiful face was quite stormy as she flung herself into the wagon seat and snatched up the reins. "Not that I owe you an explanation, but it was on Tehura's behalf that I jeopardized both my reputation *and* your estimation of me!" she added caustically.

"Tehura?" he echoed, his aristocratic brows drawing together in a puzzled frown. "How is Tehura involved? Why would—"

"Perhaps you should ask Captain Gallagher!" Hillary angrily blurted out. Then, as if realizing she had already revealed too much—she couldn't say exactly why, but she hadn't wanted to enlist Anthony's assistance in the matter—she bid him a hasty farewell and drove away.

Although she rigorously chided herself for such weakness, Hillary was unable to prevent her gaze from straying to the *Falcon* as she traveled past the quay. Her eyes widened and her face flamed anew when she spied Ryan Gallagher standing on the quarterdeck, looking for all the world like a man who is seldom thwarted in any of his pursuits.

III

"I love this part of it, Uncle. It may be hard work, but there's a certain degree of excitement to it all." Hillary smiled down warmly at him, her violet eyes aglow as she swept the single braid of hair from her bare shoulder and readjusted the ties of her crimson, ankle-length *pareu*. "Besides, you know as well as I do that the harvest would be a disaster without my supervision."

"Supervision—not participation," Denholm Reynolds gently admonished. Leisurely appraising her attire, he returned her smile with an indulgent one of his own. "You look like one of them yourself this morning."

"It would be difficult to do this sort of thing wearing skirts," she retorted with a soft laugh, allowing herself the luxury of taking a seat beside him at the table. A quiet sigh escaped her lips as she leaned back against the white wicker and raised her face to the sweetly scented morning breeze. Having been at work in the fields since before dawn, she was grateful for the respite.

Tevaite stepped out lightly onto the lower verandah a moment later, her hands bearing a tray laden with plates of fresh coconut and *fei*, a red mountain banana that grew wild in the island's practically uninhabited interior, and steaming mugs of coffee flavored with vanilla bean and coconut cream. The Tahitian woman set the tray on the table and grinned approvingly at her young mistress.

"You will soon grow wise and wear little clothing all the time," she predicted.

Hillary shook her head as she amiably dissented, "No, Tevaite. It seems I'm destined to cling to my old ways—just as you are."

"Ah, but I have adopted new ways, too, Miss Hillary." She transferred the contents of the tray to the rounded surface of the table, then soundlessly padded back inside the house.

Denholm, chuckling after she had gone, lifted one of the mugs and sipped carefully at the hot brew. His spirits were much improved of late, due in part to his niece's insistence that he spend at least half an hour a day partaking of the fresh, sun-warmed air.

"Perhaps Tevaite is right," he philosophized aloud, his pale face wearing a faint, thoughtful frown. "Perhaps we shouldn't cling to certain reminders of our former way of life. When your aunt and I first came here, we were so rigidly determined to make Starcross a bit of England in the tropics—a bastion of British culture and morality in the midst of what we perceived to be a heathenish world." His thin lips curved into a sad, ironic smile of remembrance. "We soon discovered how very misguided our determination had been. Instead of Starcross becoming a symbol of what we had left behind, it became instead a symbol of what we had found."

"And yet you didn't embrace the Tahitian way of life to the exclusion of all you had known in England," Hillary pointed out. "The same has been true for me. My life has become what I believe to be a satisfactory blend of both cultures." She drank only a little of her own coffee before reluctantly drawing herself upright again. "Though I wish I could remain and talk, I must get back to the harvesting. Mahi and the others will find the temptation to leave the work and go fishing entirely too irresistible if I am not there to 'encourage' them." Indeed, she mused with an inward sigh, because there was no greed among the natives, it was at times next to impossible to induce them to work the plantation. They would use their skills for no reward, but rather for the pleasure of using them and knowing others would be grateful for them.

"You'll share tea with me later, won't you?" her uncle queried hopefully. Still too weak to do anything more than sit, he was beginning to feel increasingly bored and restless.

"Of course. Providing Tevaite actually serves tea!" she laughingly assured him, bending down to drop a light kiss on his forehead. "I must confess, I've still not acquired a true appreciation of her coffee." She stepped down from the verandah and set off toward the fields where the ripened vanilla pods were being picked from the vines by Tevaite's brother and several other men, women, and children who had been persuaded to help.

Hillary had not gone far when her ears suddenly detected the sound of hoofbeats approaching. She turned about just in time to see a lone rider slowing his mount to a halt in front of the main house. It wasn't until he swung down lithely from the saddle, however, that she was afforded a clear view of his face—a face that was all too familiar.

Ryan Gallagher! her mind cried in stunned amazement. Merciful heavens, the infuriating captain was here at Starcross! But how? How had he known where to find her? More importantly, what was he *doing* there?

"Good day to you, Miss Reynolds," he casually proclaimed, crossing the distance between them with long, unhurried strides. He swept the hat from his head as he approached, and his eyes twinkled irrepressibly down at her in spite of the solemn expression on his handsome countenance.

"How dare you come here!" she seethed, her own eyes lit with a virulent fire. She was fairly quaking with the force of her anger . . . and with that alarming, inexplicable weakness that held her in its grip whenever she was near him. Ever since her humiliation at his hands the previous day, she had been tormented by painfully vivid memories of his warm lips branding hers, of his powerful arms pulling her close, of his sensually persuasive fingers offering their bold caresses to her trembling, pliant body, and these memories returned with a merciless vengeance now that he stood before her again.

"The fates needed a helping hand," Ryan declared with a meaningful half smile. He paused so close to Hillary that they were almost touching. She was made acutely conscious of his superior height, and of the faint, masculine aroma of soap and leather hanging about him. "You see, I didn't think you'd be returning to the *Falcon* any time soon."

Hillary took an instinctive step backward before demanding, "How did you know where I lived?"

"It wasn't difficult to find out. Your friend was more helpful than he intended," he explained, his smile broadening into a wry grin.

"My friend?"

"Anthony Warren. He, too, paid a call on me yesterday. But his visit didn't hold my interest the way yours did." His penetrating, blue-green gaze moved over her with bold unhaste, taking in the highly intriguing details of her attire—or rather, the lack of it. His eyes lingered upon the creamy smoothness of her bare shoulders and the spot where her *pareu* was knotted across the fullness of her breasts.

Noting the direction of his gaze, Hillary flushed in renewed embarrassment. She did her best to ignore the disquieting flutter in the pit of her stomach as she loftily decreed, "You may very well get back on your horse, Captain Gallagher, and—"

"Hillary? Hillary, my dear, please introduce me to our visitor!" Denholm called out from the verandah. Hillary started guiltily at his voice, for she had forgotten all about him. She hastily glanced past Ryan's broad shoulder to see that her uncle was watching them from his seat on the lower verandah.

"Do as he says, *Miss Hillary*," Ryan instructed in a low, mocking tone. He did not appear in the least bit scathed by the venomous glare she directed up at him. In fact, there was a perplexingly complacent air about him as he turned to follow the young woman flouncing haughtily past him.

Hillary performed the introductions once she and Ryan stood upon the shaded coolness of the verandah. "Uncle Denholm, may I present Captain Ryan Gallagher. Captain Gallagher, this is my uncle, Denholm Reynolds." Her tone was one of noticeably wooden civility, earning her a sharp glance from Denholm before he extended a hand of welcome to their guest.

Ryan smiled as he took the proffered hand and shook it. "How do you do, Mr. Reynolds."

"Captain Gallagher," the older man responded with an answering smile. "Forgive me for not rising.

I'm afraid these spindly old legs of mine would cause me great embarrassment if I were to tax them in your presence." He motioned to the chair opposite his. "Please, Captain, be seated. Would you care for coffee?"

"I could do with some coffee," Ryan accepted with a nod. His gaze returned to Hillary, his hands taking an easy grip on the chair beside her uncle's and holding it in what was obviously a signal for her to seat herself in it. Hillary, in an unusually childish gesture of defiance, ignored him and instead elected to sit on the other side of the table. A grin of pure amusement tugged at Ryan's lips as he bent his tall, muscular frame into the white wicker chair. None of this was lost on Denholm Reynolds.

As if on cue, Tevaite appeared with another mug of coffee and a fresh plate of fruit. She tried, unsuccessfully, to hide a mischievous, knowing smile as her dancing brown eyes shifted back and forth between her young mistress and the handsome whaling captain she had immediately recognized as the man who could work magic with horses—and probably with Miss Hillary, too, she mused to herself with an inward giggle.

"What brings you to Starcross, Captain Gallagher?" Hillary's uncle questioned amiably as Tevaite returned inside.

"There is a small matter of business to be resolved between myself and Miss Reynolds," he replied, his penetrating, aquamarine gaze traveling back to Hillary once more. Her eyes grew very round in the delicate oval of her face, and she was dismayed to feel her cheeks burning anew.

This is a nightmare! she dazedly told herself. Ryan Gallagher couldn't really be here. She had believed she would never see him again. Why, oh why did he have to show up on her very doorstep?

"Business?" echoed Denholm. A puzzled frown creased his brow as he glanced across at his niece inquisitively.

Shaking herself out of her near panic-stricken reverie, she hastened to assure him, "It . . . it's nothing of great importance, Uncle." In the next instant it appeared as if she had developed a sudden and quite profound interest in the circular pattern of the spotless white tablecloth, for her troubled amethyst gaze fastened unwaveringly upon the linen where it clung to the rounded edge of the table before her.

"I see." The balding, gray-haired man turned back to Ryan, his still-perceptive gaze missing little. "Tell me, Captain, how is it you and my niece came to have business with each other?" he queried, smiling softly as his eyes met the younger man's. "Unless I am much mistaken, you hold the position of command aboard a whaler—*not* a merchant ship."

"You are entirely correct, Mr. Reynolds," confirmed Ryan, smiling as well. A look of silent understanding passed between them. "As to the business between myself and your niece, you'll pardon me if I reply that Miss Reynolds should be the one to explain it to you."

Hillary groaned inwardly at that, and she unconsciously bit at her lower lip in growing trepidation. Bristling when she finally raised her eyes to Ryan's again and glimpsed the unmistakable light of challenge in his, she abruptly rose to her feet and announced, "I'm sorry, Uncle, but any explanation will have to wait. I *must* get back to the fields."

"But Hillary, my dear," Denholm quietly objected, "we have a guest." Hillary visibly hesitated, torn between the desire to appease her uncle's sense of propriety and the desire to flee the impudent captain's presence as quickly as possible. She finally forced herself to face Ryan squarely as he, having stood as well, stared down at her in a disturbingly expectant manner.

"If you'll excuse me, Captain Gallagher, I'm afraid I have work to do. It's harvest time here at Starcross, and the vanilla pods must be gathered at their precise moment of maturity." Satisfied that she had done her duty, however unwillingly, she wished her uncle a pleasant day and spun about on her slippered heel to leave.

"Alas, we always seem to be shorthanded," she heard Denholm remarking as she stepped down from the verandah. "My niece insists upon toiling just as long and hard as anyone."

"Then perhaps I can be of some help," Ryan offered decisively. "If you'll excuse me as well, Mr. Reynolds." He nodded down at the startled older man, then strode after Hillary. She had not gone far when he caught up with her, his hand closing with firm gentleness upon her bare arm.

"What do you think you're doing *now?*" she demanded in a furious undertone as she rounded on him. Initially prompted to try and jerk free, she decided against such action when she glanced back to see that her uncle was still watching them. There was a frown of bemusement on his lined, pallid countenance. "Let go of me!" she whispered harshly. She was surprised when Ryan acquiesced, and she gazed up at him in mingled anger and confusion.

"I'm going with you," he calmly asserted, the rugged perfection of his sun-bronzed features wearing only the ghost of a smile.

"Going with—why, you most certainly are *not!*"

"I know for a fact you need the help. Why not

accept it with good grace and forget, at least temporarily, about what happened between us yesterday?''

"What happened between us yesterday has absolutely no bearing on this whatsoever! I don't want your help, Captain Gallagher, and I'll thank you to depart these premises at once!''

"There's no sense in being bullheaded when you—''

"I'm not being bullheaded!'' she hotly denied, her eyes blazing up at him murderously.

"Yes you are,'' he argued with maddening aplomb. "Your uncle told me you're short on field hands. Well, my dear Miss Reynolds, I'm strong and ablebodied and can do a full day's work with only a minimal amount of rest and nourishment.''

"But you're a whaler! You don't know the first thing about harvesting vanilla!''

"Did I fail to mention that I'm also a quick learner?'' A thoroughly disarming smile spread across Ryan's face as, evidently considering the matter settled, he executed a slight, mocking bow in her direction and bade, "Lead the way, Miss Reynolds.''

Heaving a sigh of complete exasperation, Hillary was forced to admit defeat. She reluctantly conceded to herself that there was no possible way she could prevent him from tagging along. However, it occurred to her in the next instant that in all probability he would be unable to withstand either the physical strain of the work or the heat of the broiling sun. Yes, she silently mused with a spark of vengeful confidence in her eyes, to a man who had no doubt done nothing more strenuous in recent years than maintain his balance on the rolling deck of a ship, the type of activity required of him in the fields would soon send him running back where he belonged!

With a secretive little smile playing about her lips, Hillary obeyed Ryan's self-assured command and led the way along a well-worn path through the trees. She knew his eyes were raking familiarly over her as she walked ahead of him, for she could literally feel his burning gaze upon the partially revealed curve of her back and gently swaying, *pareu*-covered hips. Although she held herself regally erect and did her best to ignore his unsettling perusal, she could not prevent a sudden tingle from dancing lightly down her spine.

Within seconds, they had reached the fields where the vines had been trained over small trees planted about nine feet apart. The fully developed pods, which had formed only after the virgin vanilla blossoms had been pollinated by hand at the exact moment they bloomed, were slightly yellow in color now that they were ripe. Ryan spotted several Tahitians, young and old, bending down to extract the pods from the vines and place them in large baskets.

"It's not as simple as it appears," Hillary coolly remarked, stealing a glance at him as they surveyed the sunlit greenery. "Great care must be taken to ensure that the pods are neither split nor cracked."

"I think I can manage that," Ryan drawled lazily. He favored her with another sardonic, faintly challenging smile before peeling off his coat and dropping it to the ground. His hat followed to land atop the coat. Then, purposefully rolling up the long sleeves of his white shirt, he turned back to Hillary and said, "Let's get on with it."

"I don't know exactly *why* you're doing this, Captain Gallagher," she murmured in a low tone of intense annoyance, "but if you're so set on making an utter fool of yourself, then so be it!" With that, she wheeled about and plunged into the midst of the neat rows of trees, resuming her place among the other workers.

Ryan, disregarding her ungenerous remarks, closely scrutinized the actions of the natives for a short time before moving forward to begin work. One of the men handed him a basket, and it wasn't long before he was congratulating himself on mastering the technique of separating the vanilla pods from the vines. His gaze frequently strayed to where Hillary bent and stretched to her task, her beautiful face wearing an endearing look of concentration. His eyes darkened in wholly masculine appreciation of her supple curves, so well revealed in the simple, unrestricting garment wound about her body.

The late morning hours crept by. The tropical sun, a brilliant golden fireball hanging in the cloudless blue sky, blazed down relentlessly upon the harvesters. Ryan, the only one clad in shirt and trousers, had long ago begun to feel the unpleasant effects of the heat. His dark, sun-streaked hair clung damply to his forehead, and the exposed areas of his hard body gleamed with sweat. As if in answer to his wishes, Tehura suddenly appeared at his side with a brightly colored waistcloth sent as a gift from her mother.

"You want me to wear *this?*" he asked with a crooked grin as he took the waistcloth from the impishly smiling fourteen-year-old and held it up for inspection. His eyes had not missed the bruise on her face, and he surmised that she must be the same young woman who had been mistreated by one of his crew.

"My mother, she say you will faint like woman if

you are stubborn!''

"Please tell your mother I accept her gift, and relay my gratitude for her thoughtfulness," he told her with great formality, prompting the plump and pretty girl to giggle delightedly as she turned away. Ryan, clutching the waistcloth in one hand and sauntering toward a nearby hut in order to change, smiled to himself when he caught Hillary hastily averting her gaze after watching him leave the field. When he emerged from the hut a few minutes later, his appearance had undergone a startling transformation indeed.

He had wrapped the length of *tapa* cloth about his waist as he had seen the Tahitian men do, leaving him covered only from his waist to just above his knees. His sleek, muscular arms and torso were tanned to a dark golden hue as a result of many hours spent shirtless on the deck of the *Falcon*. The taut skin of his long, splendidly athletic legs, however, had rarely seen the light of day, so that it was several shades lighter than the skin on the upper portion of his virile body. His bare feet were also ludicrously pale, as they were usually encased in a pair of black leather boots.

A pleasant trill of laughter suddenly went up from the field, followed by another, and soon another. The Tahitians were expressing their amusement at what they deemed to be a particularly humorous sight, but their laughter held no animosity or unkindness. His gaze sweeping leisurely over them as he headed back to the field, Ryan accepted their gesture of camaraderie and joined in with a self-deprecating chuckle of his own.

Hillary's violet eyes grew very wide as she looked up to see a half-naked Ryan Gallagher advancing upon her. She swallowed a sudden lump in her throat and quickly straightened. Her own silken, light golden skin was covered with a thin sheen of perspiration, and several damp, escaping tendrils of ebony-colored hair curled beguilingly about her face. She could feel a telltale blush rising to her face as she took note of Ryan's undeniably masculine physique. While it was true she had seen scores of island men thus attired every day for the past five years, there was a troublesome difference in her mind between them and the man who now paused to tower above her with such alarming equanimity.

"It's quite obvious I'm a man of the sea and not of the land, wouldn't you say?" he put to her, his gaze brimming with good-natured mockery.

"Haven't you carried this . . . this ridiculous charade far enough?" she indignantly charged.

"Why is it either ridiculous or a charade?" Ryan countered with a roguish grin. "I'm merely clad in the traditional Tahitian garb, just as you are, and I've caught on damned well at this harvesting, even if I do say so myself."

"Why?" demanded Hillary, striving to maintain her composure. "Why are you doing this? Is it merely to torment me further? Is that why you're here—to cause me even more unhappiness and embarrassment?"

"No." His expression grew quite solemn. "No, Miss Reynolds, that was not my purpose in coming here. Nor was it the reason I offered you my assistance." He stared intently down at her for several seconds longer before turning away without another word. Hillary was greatly perturbed by his evasiveness, and she released another disparate sigh as she reminded herself there was no time to waste on worrying about the motives of a man who was little more than a stranger.

A stranger? that inner voice of hers dare to impugn. Aren't the two of you already so much more than strangers to each other?

"Hillary Reynolds, you're an idiot!" she muttered aloud. After anxiously glancing about to make certain no one had heard her, particularly not the handsome, half-naked whaling captain, she took up an empty basket and began filling it with vanilla pods.

Anthony Warren dismounted and looped the reins over the post in front of the main house at Starcross. He frowned thoughtfully at the other horse already tethered there and munching on a generous pile of hay, then tugged the hat from his fair head and swiftly climbed the steps. Tevaite answered his knock.

"*Ia orana*, Mister Warren," she murmured, her smile lacking its usual warmth.

"Good day, Tevaite. I'd like to speak with Miss Hillary." His manner was one of noticeable impatience as he strode inside.

"I am sorry, Mister Warren, but Miss Hillary is not in the house."

"Oh. Then would you please tell me where I may find her?"

"She and the *tapena* are in the fields today," the Tahitian woman informed him with deceptive innocence. Though she was not in the habit of mixing her native Tahitian with her missionary-taught English very often, she did so readily when in the presence of those she considered non-islanders.

"The *tapena?*" he echoed with a deepening frown. A captain? In the fields with Hillary?

"Gallagher," supplied Tevaite, carefully scrutinizing his reaction from beneath her eyelashes. She was satisfied to glimpse the look of startled displeasure crossing his patrician features. While she believed the young Englishman to be a basically good man, she did not believe him to be the man for Miss Hillary.

"Captain Ryan Gallagher is in the fields with your mistress?" Anthony demanded a confirmation. When the woman nodded wordlessly, he grew quite red in the face and questioned in tight, clipped tones, "Where is Mr. Reynolds?"

"He is upstairs in his bed. He is not to come down again until the teatime."

"I see," Anthony ground out in barely controlled anger. "Very well. Thank you, Tevaite!" Wheeling stiffly about, he marched back outside and immediately turned his steps toward the green-canopied vanilla fields.

What he found there provoked a wealth of emotion—not at all pleasurable—within him. He was shocked enough to see Hillary so scandalously clad and working beside the natives as if she were one of them, but he was absolutely flabbergasted to discover Captain Ryan Gallagher toiling alongside her while wearing nothing more than a waistcloth.

"What the bloody—" Anthony started to swear, breaking off when Hillary caught sight of him and waved a friendly greeting.

Still feeling a trifle guilty for the way she had treated him the day before, she left her work to speak with him. She could have sworn she heard a low chuckle escaping Ryan's lips as she hurried past.

"Anthony! How nice to see you again. I'm afraid you'll have to pardon my appearance, but I wasn't expecting you to call today!" Hillary proclaimed with a breathless little laugh. She gracefully lifted the back of her hand to her forehead to smooth away a few damp curls. "We expect to be finished well before nightfall."

"What, may I ask, is *he* doing here?" Anthony nodded curtly toward Ryan, who was watching them out of the corner of his eyes. "Why is the captain of a whaling vessel working in your fields? And why is he in such an indecent state of undress?" he demanded with what he deemed to be totally righteous anger. A dull flush crept upward from the high collar of his shirt as his pale blue eyes narrowed.

"Please, Anthony, keep your voice down! Do you want everyone to hear you?" She cast an anxious look over her shoulder at Ryan and the Tahitians before her gaze returned to the outraged young man before her. "It so happens that Captain Gallagher was . . . was kind enough to remain and help when he came to call this morning," she explained in a low voice, hoping her words held more conviction than she felt.

"I'd no idea you were so desperate!" Anthony disobligingly retorted. Hillary's eyes flashed, and her own countenance grew increasingly stormy.

"Desperation had nothing to do with it, and you have no right to take me to task for either the way I run this plantation or the people I choose to allow upon the premises! The truth of the matter is, we *were* a bit shorthanded and Captain Gallagher *is* providing valuable assistance!" No sooner had the words left her mouth than the man in question suddenly materialized at her side, causing her to color furiously.

"Roll up your sleeves and join us, Warren. I'm sure Miss Reynolds could use your 'valuable assistance' as well," Ryan offhandedly suggested. His mouth curved into a lazily challenging smile as he folded his arms across the bronzed, softly matted expanse of his bare chest and met Anthony's wrathful glare.

"I thought I made it *quite* clear to you yesterday, Captain Gallagher, that you were to keep away from Hil—from Miss Reynolds!"

"You *what?*" gasped Hillary, rounding on Anthony with a look of wide-eyed disbelief.

"I went aboard the *Falcon* after you left town and confronted Captain Gallagher about your visit," Anthony confessed as if he were proud of what he had done. "Although he would tell me nothing of what had prompted you to such rash measures, he—"

"If I had wanted to make my business known to you, Anthony Warren, I would have done so myself!" she snapped indignantly. Glancing up at Ryan, she was vexed to glimpse the irrepressible amusement in his interested gaze. She sent him a speaking glare before endeavoring to regain her composure. "Please, Anthony, there's no sense in quarreling about it now," she told the younger and more slight of the two men with a conciliatory smile. "I'll be more than happy to explain everything to you, but it will have to wait until after the harvest is completed."

"Then perhaps I *will* lend my assistance!" he announced, shooting Ryan a look of stubborn defiance. He began shrugging out of his impeccably tailored frock coat.

"Anthony, don't be absurd! You're not at all accustomed to this sort of thing!" Hillary adamantly protested.

"Neither is the captain, I'll wager. If he can manage, then so can I!" he insisted with a wholly British arrogance.

"Take my advice and exchange those fancy trappings of yours for one of these things," Ryan was only too happy to recommend, negligently looping a thumb in the folds of his borrowed waistcloth.

"Otherwise, my friend, you'll soon find yourself—"

"I choose my friends very carefully, Captain Gallagher, and I have no intention of shaming myself before Miss Reynolds or the natives!" Anthony pompously declared, eyeing the other man's attire in open disgust. With necktie and cuffs still intact, he took a visibly apprehensive Hillary by the arm and escorted her into the field. A slow, smugly triumphant smile spread across Ryan's handsome face as he sauntered away to resume his own work.

"Really, Anthony, I *do* appreciate the gesture, but it isn't necessary for you to try to prove anything to me—or to Captain Gallagher!" Hillary pleaded with him.

"If you'll be so good as to demonstrate precisely how the harvesting is done, I shall apply myself with diligence," he solemnly promised.

Hillary sighed heavily, realizing she had little choice but to agree. If Anthony was so determined to engage in this perfectly nonsensical competition involving masculine pride, she reflected in exasperation, then there was certainly nothing she could do to stop him. She knew Ryan Gallagher had purposely baited him, and it was toward the captain that most of her anger was directed. From the first moment the infuriating man had forced his way into her life, her usual easygoing temperament had given way to an almost perpetual state of discontentment!

Hillary was the first person to reach Anthony's side when he succumbed to the heat and crumpled to the ground. Ryan was close on her heels, and it was he who lifted the slender, fair-haired man in his strong arms and swiftly carried him to the deeper shade at the edge of the field. One of the natives ran to the

74

house to fetch Tevaite while Hillary cradled Anthony's head in her lap and gently slapped at his cheeks in an effort to revive him. He had been laboring for little more than an hour, but his face had been burned to a bright scarlet by the sun's rays.

"Anthony? Anthony, can you hear me?" Hillary urgently appealed. Ryan dropped to his knees beside her and began loosening the young Englishman's necktie and collar.

"The blasted fool," he muttered, though he was genuinely concerned about the unconscious man's welfare. "I suppose I gave him too much credit for knowing when to call it quits."

"This is *your* fault! *You*, Captain Gallagher, are the one responsible for his condition!" she lashed out. Her eyes were glistening with unshed tears. "If you hadn't taunted him, if you hadn't dared him to prove himself—"

"I'm honest enough to admit there was a good-natured challenge in my attitude toward him, Miss Reynolds, but I'll be damned if I'll take the blame for his folly in carrying things too far!" Ryan dissented with a tight frown, his own eyes glittering coldly.

"Good-natured? Is that what you call it when you very nearly get a man killed?" Hillary charged irrationally. Ryan was about to offer her a suitable response, but thought better of it and clamped his mouth shut.

Tevaite arrived on the scene soon thereafter. The Tahitian woman immediately took charge of the situation, kneeling beside Anthony and pressing a cool, damp cloth to his forehead. She then brought forth a small vial and uncorked it, releasing the most ungodly stench and waving the concoction directly underneath the unconscious man's nose. Anthony came to with a start.

"What . . . where am I?" he demanded groggily, jerking himself into a sitting position. He groaned and clutched at his head.

"It's all right, Anthony. You're going to be fine. The heat was simply too much for you," Hillary explained soothingly. She refused to meet Ryan's gaze again.

"I'm afraid I've made rather an ass of myself," Anthony remarked with a sheepish little smile. His clouded gaze flickered briefly over Ryan, but he said nothing to the other man. With the aid of Hillary's arm about him, he climbed unsteadily to his feet and stood motionless for several seconds as he waited for the dizziness to subside. Tevaite, meanwhile, had summoned one of the male harvesters, who now moved forward at a signal from her.

"Mister Warren, it is best for you to come to the house," she proclaimed. "You need rest and drink. Mahi will take you back to Papeete."

"Yes, Anthony, you must go to the house and rest," Hillary quickly supported Tevaite's advice. Expecting an argument from him, she was pleasantly surprised when he allowed himself to be led away by Mahi. Tevaite followed after them, leaving Hillary alone with Ryan.

"I . . . I think it would be best if you left now, Captain Gallagher," she decreed uneasily, still finding it difficult to meet his gaze as she forced herself to face him. "While I cannot deny your assistance has been both timely and considerable, and I . . . I thank you for it, I do not know what it is you want from me." She finally raised her eyes to his, and what she saw reflected within those glowing, blue-green orbs caused a sudden, disturbing tremor to course through her body like wildfire.

"I never leave anything unfinished, Miss Reynolds," was all he said, his voice sounding particularly deep-toned and vibrant. His handsome face was inscrutable as he left her and walked back into the field.

Hillary stared after him. The strange, inexplicable restlessness crept over her again. Only this time, it was accompanied by a foreboding sense of a significant—and irreversible—change in her life.

The actual harvesting of the vanilla was completed even sooner than Hillary had expected. Feeling a great satisfaction, as well as profound relief that the routine would not have to be repeated for another six months, she thought of all that was left to be done. Now that the pods had been gathered, they would be put in heaps and lightly covered with flour sacks. For nearly a month, the vanilla would be exposed to the sun's rays for increasing periods of time each day, then confined to a sheltered hut and covered with blankets to keep them warm in the evenings. Once the fermentation process had been completed, the well-cured pods would be spread out in shallow layers and carefully sorted into different grades; the first to ripen would appear nicely wrinkled and supple. The flavorful vanilla would finally be packed with great care for shipping. It was Hillary's custom to leave the entire process in Tevaite's hands, for the older woman was quite a perfectionist in the matter and had always insisted upon overseeing it herself.

It was late in the afternoon when the Tahitians lifted the last of their baskets and carried them from the fields. Ryan, having already placed the fruits of his own labors beneath the swaying palms, went to retrieve his boots and clothing from the hut and was puzzled to find them missing. Shaking his head in mild bemusement, he strolled toward the main house. He had watched Hillary disappearing along the same path mere seconds earlier. But it was Tevaite who stood waiting for him on the front steps of the house.

"Mister Reynolds asks you to join him for tea, Captain Gallagher," she announced, her dark eyes brimming with merry humor. A secretive little smile played about her lips. As if possessed of the ability to read his thoughts, she added, "Miss Hillary will join him, too." A disarming, boyish grin lit Ryan's handsome countenance as his own eyes twinkled with amusement.

"Please tell Mister Reynolds—*and* Miss Hillary— that I accept the invitation." His gaze dropped briefly to his less than immaculate appearance. Again, Tevaite anticipated his question and was quick to provide a solution.

"A bathing pool will be found if you follow the path behind the house. Your clothes will also be found." Without any further explanation, but with a suspiciously complacent smile, she set off toward the spot where preparations were already underway for the first step in curing the vanilla pods.

"My thanks to you, madame. You are truly a *maiahi* in disguise!" Ryan called after her. *Maiahi*, he silently repeated, chuckling to himself as he strode away to find the path. The woman was indeed an angel of sorts—to him, anyway—for he had almost immediately recognized in her a valuable ally. He was soon to discover just how much of an ally . . .

The sunlight filtered softly downward through the thick cluster of trees, its illuminating radiance touching only a portion of the lush greenery surrounding the small, freshwater pool. The gentle roar of a cascading waterfall, pouring forth its sparkling contents from a rocky, moss-coated ledge above, echoed pleasantly within the intimacy of the clearing. The cool, moist air was filled with an intoxicating aroma of flowers—delicate, multi-hued orchids, colorful carpets of bougainvillea, towering hibiscus and pink cassia, jasmine and frangipani, and the white, heavy-scented gardenia called *tiare Tahiti* by the islanders.

To Ryan, who had paused at the terminus of the path to stare in appreciation at the secluded enchantment before him, the clear, turquoise waters of the pool looked too inviting to resist any longer. He wasted no further time before unwinding the waistcloth from his body and wading, naked, into the pool.

Hillary, blissfully unaware of the fact that her privacy was being invaded by the very man she would least prefer to do so, closed her eyes and lifted her face to the soothing spray just beyond the concealing curtain of the waterfall. She was reluctant to leave her favorite bathing spot, but she knew her uncle was awaiting her return.

And what of Ryan Gallagher? Is he awaiting your return as well? Or is he on his way back to Papeete— and out of your life for good? she mused silently.

Admitting to herself that it had been unpardonably rude of her to disappear without first offering the captain a formal declaration of gratitude and at the very least a polite farewell, she nonetheless refused to suffer any real degree of remorse. It was true that he had played a very significant part in the harvest, but it was also true that he had done so against her wishes. She had been forced to spend the entire day in his maddening presence. Why should she feel obligated to treat him with anything other than indifference? After all, wasn't he the same man who had . . . had *accosted* her the day before?

Idly slipping the beribboned strap of her chemise back into place upon the glistening creaminess of her shoulder, Hillary sighed. Reflecting that she would in all likelihood never see Captain Ryan Gallagher again, she wondered why the thought gave her no pleasure. She frowned darkly and plunged back into the water, emerging on the opposite side of the waterfall. She broke the surface of the pool with an accompanying splash, then drew in a breath of fresh air and smoothed the wet raven tresses from her face. It wasn't until she had paddled and waded to the water's edge that her eyes fell upon the other occupant of the pool.

He stood poised, waist-deep, near the center, his handsome face betraying delighted amazement as his eyes raked over Hillary's exposed loveliness. Her chemise, the only undergarment she had worn that day and the straps of which she had tucked into the ties of her *pareu*, reached only to just above her knees. Rendered virtually transparent by the water, it provided absurdly inadequate protection from Ryan's piercing gaze. He was afforded a brief, tantalizing vision of silken curves and rose-tipped breasts beneath the clinging white cotton, as well as an alluring hint of the triangle of velvety black curls that concealed the secrets of her womanhood.

A tiny, breathless shriek escaped Hillary's lips before she instinctively whirled about and dove back into the pool. When she finally came sputtering to the surface for air once more, her beautiful features were blushing scarlet in mingled outrage and embarrassment.

"What are *you* doing here?" she demanded, furiously treading water a short distance away in the deeper part of the pool.

"The same thing you are," he parried congenially. There was nothing lighthearted, however, about the look in his eyes. Their smoldering, blue-green depths were full of an impassioned intensity that Hillary did not fail to notice—nor to take alarm at. She trembled uncontrollably as her own fascinated gaze traveled with a will of its own over Ryan's naked, unabashedly masculine form. The bronzed smoothness of his powerful, lithely muscled arms and chest were slick and gleaming with moisture. Revealed in the clear water, below the indentation of his trim waist, was a shocking glimpse of lean hips and the forbidden darkness between a pair of hard thighs . . .

Hillary's wide violet eyes flew back up to Ryan's face. What she saw there was enough to make her inhale sharply and propel herself farther away in the water.

"Get out of here at once!" she ordered, her voice rising on a note of swiftly increasing panic. "I don't know how you came to find this place, but you've absolutely no right to intrude upon my privacy!"

"It so happens I'm innocent of the misconduct you're presently attributing to me," he told her, then smiled roguishly and confided, "but in truth, even if I *had* known you were here, I'd have been compelled to remain and watch you bathe."

Hillary gasped loudly at that, and her countenance grew even more stormy as she seethed, "How dare you! How dare you think you can—"

"As I told you before," Ryan broke in to declare in a low but commanding tone, "I dare because there isn't enough time to do things in the conventional manner. Once repairs on the *Falcon* are completed, I'll be sailing back to New Bedford. It will be many months, perhaps even a year or two, before I can

81

return to Tahiti.''

"Why should the particulars of your departure—
or your possible return—matter to me?'' retorted
Hillary, her pulses racing and her gaze clouding with
noticeable apprehension. Without allowing him the
opportunity to reply, she hastened to reiterate, "You
will either get out of this pool at once, or I shall call
for assistance and have you removed by force! We are
not aboard your ship now, Captain Gallagher, and I
can assure you that my screams *would* be heeded here
at Starcross!''

"By all means, my dear Miss Reynolds,'' he responded with one mockingly raised eyebrow, "do
as you see fit.'' He still did not display even the
slightest inclination to leave.

Hillary glared back at him in helpless fury. Her
arms and legs were beginning to tire, but she dared
not move toward the more shallow water near the
center of the pool. Dear Lord, she prayed as she eyed
Ryan warily, please make him go away! The last
thing she wanted was to have the natives witness such
a humiliating scene between herself and the captain.

Who is it you truly fear, Hillary—Ryan Gallagher
or yourself? an inner voice derisively challenged. And
what will you do if he decides to call your bluff?

It became apparent in the next instant that Ryan
had done just that. Without a word, he began advancing on her, his steps slow and measured as his
feet sank into the soft sand on the bottom of the
freshwater lagoon. Although his face was inscrutable,
his gaze was literally smoldering with a dangerous
steadfastness of purpose.

Hillary's eyes grew round as saucers before she
abruptly kicked about and started swimming in
retreat toward the waterfall. Any thought of scream-
ing for help fled her mind as she concentrated all her

efforts on escaping from the man whose very touch had set her afire the previous day. She was desperate to avoid a repetition of what had occurred aboard the *Falcon*, and her alarm increased tenfold when she recalled the fact that she was very nearly naked and the captain completely so.

She had no idea what she would do once she reached the other side of the waterfall, but she nonetheless hurried to dive underneath the cascading curtain of water. A sharp cry broke from her lips when, splashing upward in preparation for her descent, she suddenly felt two strong hands closing about her slender waist and dragging her relentlessly backward.

"No!" cried Hillary, struggling frantically to escape. She kicked and twisted and squirmed, sending showers of water everywhere as she fought Ryan like a tigress. His bronzed, sinewy arm clamped about her waist like a band of iron, and in spite of her highly physical efforts to prevent the inevitable, he easily hauled her to the center of the pool. When he stood waist-deep in the water once more, he stopped and brought his other arm forward across her shoulders and collarbone, just above the indignantly heaving swell of her breasts. Although she continued to resist with all her might, her back was pressed intimately against the granite-hard breadth of his naked chest.

Hillary's struggles came to an abrupt halt in the next instant. Her violet eyes widened in startlement, and she suffered a sharp intake of breath when her firmly rounded bottom, left only partially covered as the chemise's hemline floated upward, suddenly fanned across the hardness of Ryan's masculinity.

He groaned softly close to her ear as his arms tightened almost painfully about her. When he spoke, his voice was deep and edged with a strange huskiness that sent a tremor of mingled fear and excitement racing the length of Hillary's spine.

"Be still, Miss Reynolds," he commanded. "Be still, or I swear, things will progress a great deal faster than either of us planned." Hillary swallowed a sudden lump in her throat. Though she was battling a wave of light-headedness and confusion, she stiffened within Ryan's grasp and forced a note of haughty defiance into her own voice.

"I don't care *what* you may have planned, Captain Gallagher! You know as well as I do that your behavior at this moment is utterly contemptible! Now take your hands off me, you . . . you degenerate whaler!" She was startled to hear a deep rumble of laughter escaping his lips.

"Isn't that particular insult a trifle redundant?" he sardonically challenged. "Is it not true, my love, that all whalers are degenerate?"

"Why, you . . . how dare you call me that! I am most assuredly *not* your love and I—"

"But you shall be. And soon," vowed Ryan, his low, vibrant tone scarcely above a whisper as he gently rested his chin against her damp head. Hillary gasped inwardly. This can't be happening! she mused in alarmed bewilderment. I can't truly be standing here in nothing more than my chemise with a naked man's arms about me! Dear Lord, who *is* Ryan Gallagher and why is he saying and doing such wicked things to me?

"Never!" she finally decreed. Renewing her struggles with a vengeance, she bent her head and sank her teeth into the unsuspecting flesh of Ryan's forearm. He ground out a blistering oath and relaxed his hold, but only long enough to spin Hillary about and lock her into another embrace. Her arms were pinned at her sides this time, and her flailing feet, hampered by the natural resistance of the water, were unable to inflict enough bodily harm to do any good.

"Let me go!" she cried in frustrated anger, her eyes blazing up murderously into Ryan's. She endeavored to prevent her scantily clad body from making such bold contact with his, but to no avail. Her full breasts were partially flattened against his chest, and she was all too conscious of the fact that a mere fraction of an inch away from the most private sector of her womanly form was the corresponding maleness of Ryan's. Her cheeks flamed even more hotly than before. "I've had quite enough of your manhandling! Now let me go!"

"Not this time," murmured Ryan. His handsome face appeared disturbingly solemn, and there was a certain unfathomable glow emanating from his blue-green gaze, but Hillary had no time to ponder either its meaning or its significance as he began lowering his head with the obvious intention of kissing her.

Beyond caring about the embarrassment such action would undoubtedly bring, Hillary opened her mouth to scream. Her belated cry for help was effectively silenced by the forceful pressure of Ryan's lips upon hers.

She moaned in protest and squirmed against him, but only succeeded in bringing the lower half of her body into an even more intimate alignment with his. She trembled as the bare flesh of her thighs met his beneath the surface of the pool, and she hastily arched her back in a futile attempt to deny the shocking contact as his arms once again reflexively tensed about her softness. His kiss deepened, his warm tongue demanding and gaining entry to the sweet nectar of her mouth.

Hillary's senses reeled as another moan—one of awakening passion instead of maidenly protest—welled up deep in her throat. Aghast to feel herself surrendering to the enticing madness Ryan was so adroitly creating within her, she nonetheless returned his kiss with an enchanting fervency that sent his own raging desire careening very nearly out of control. She rose up on her toes, her arms entwining about the corded muscles of his neck, when his hands suddenly delved into the water to grip the delightfully feminine roundness of her derriere.

The hemline of her undergarment, the wet, translucent cotton of which was plastered like a second skin to her body above the water, had once again floated upward in the back, so that she was left essentially naked from about the middle of her buttocks downward. Ryan's long fingers curled about her bare bottom, splaying possessively across the shapely mounds that seemed to beg for his touch. Hillary shivered at his caress, and her eyelids fluttered open when she perceived the unmistakable evidence of his arousal against her supple, sparsely covered thighs.

Then, his fingers were tightening upon her buttocks as he lifted her higher in his embrace. His lips relinquished hers at last, and almost immediately afterward Hillary felt his mouth capturing the rosy peak of her breast. She stifled a soft cry when his tongue flicked gently back and forth across the nipple, and the highly erotic sensation of his lips suckling at her breast through the thin cotton of her chemise prompted her hands to clutch weakly at his broad shoulders.

Hillary knew that she was being swept away by a floodtide of emotion and longing, but she seemed powerless to resist. She had never felt this way before, had never been so aware of herself as a woman, nor of her body's appeal and purpose to men. It was something she had never allowed herself to think about—until Ryan Gallagher had come into her life.

"Hillary. My beautiful little love," he whispered hoarsely as his lips trailed back up to roam hungrily across her flushed face. She closed her eyes and gave herself over to his passionate, oh-so-persuasive attentions. Before she quite knew what was happening, he was bending down to lift her in his powerful arms. He began wading purposefully across the pool, transporting his precious cargo toward the shaded coolness of the sand along the bank.

Ryan's eyes, smoldering with intensity, probed the passion-clouded depths of Hillary's as he cradled her against his tall, muscular frame. In the deepest recesses of her mind, she dazedly realized that, unless she did something to prevent it, she was in very grave danger of losing herself completely in the wildly rapturous abandon beckoning her onward . . .

"Put me down!" she managed to choke out. Ryan's handsome, sun-kissed brow creased into a dark frown, but he did not waver in his progress across the lagoon. "Put me down!" Hillary repeated, her voice stronger and holding more conviction this time. The sudden awareness of her imminent, disastrous surrender was emphasized when she raised her hands to push against Ryan's chest. "Let me go, damn you!" she demanded, her swiftly rising panic causing the utterance of the first malediction she had ever spoken aloud. Her struggles intensified when her captor, his expression forebodingly grim, held fast and continued toward shore.

Hillary's mind desperately searched for a way to escape before it was too late. She didn't truly believe Ryan Gallagher was the sort of man who would resort to rape—but, heaven help her, she could no longer deny the fact that he had the power to render her entirely defenseless!

"No!" she defiantly proclaimed, for her own benefit as well as his. In one violent motion, she twisted upward within his grasp and flung her arms about his head, successfully upsetting his balance as his feet connected with a particularly soft patch of sand on the bottom of the pool. Ryan swore as both he and Hillary went toppling sideways into the lagoon.

She jerked away from him just as they hit the shallow water. In her efforts to scramble upright and flee, her foot made accidental, but highly effective, contact with Ryan's unguarded masculinity. He ground out another curse and doubled over in pain while Hillary splashed hurriedly to the shore. Without a backward glance, she snatched her *pareu* from where she had left it spread across a fragrant hibiscus shrub and flew back along the path.

Hillary, having quickly dressed and composed herself for her uncle's benefit, was greatly relieved to learn upon returning downstairs that their guest had tendered his regrets and taken his leave. Denholm Reynolds chose not to share his personal observation regarding Ryan Gallagher's hasty departure, nor his opinion as to what had prompted it. Unbeknownst to his beloved niece, he had seen the handsome young captain following the same path Hillary had traveled on her way to the bathing pool. And he had seen both of them, in turn, making their way back to the house a short time later.

As Hillary took herself off to prepare their tea, her thoughts were drawn to Ryan again. Though she was loath to admit it, she felt more than a twinge of disappointment that he had left without facing her again.

Ryan's troubled thoughts were following a similar course at that same moment. Telling himself that perhaps he had made a mistake in leaving before Hillary's reappearance, his fingers tightened upon the reins and his mouth curved into a faint, self-derisive smile. He had wanted to spare her further pain.

He hadn't meant to lose his head at the lagoon, but the glorious sight of her near-nakedness had prompted him to forget all about his admirable resolutions to woo her gently. There had been nothing gentle in the way she had made him feel!

Cursing himself again for losing control of the situation, he suddenly realized that he had neglected to tell Hillary about his questioning of the crew. None of them would admit to any knowledge of Tehura, or her mistreatment, but Ryan still suspected one man in particular. Sooner or later, he would have the truth.

And sooner or later, Ryan vowed as he breathed deeply of the fresh, salt-tinged air on his way back to Papeete, Hillary Reynolds would acknowledge what he had known from the very beginning—*she belonged to him.*

IV

Moorea's jagged peaks were silhouetted against a brilliant, red-orange morning sky. Traditionally called *Aimeo* by the natives, the incredibly lovely, triangular-shaped island was far less civilized than its larger neighbor. It beckoned across twelve miles of frequently uncertain seas, so that most visitors to Tahiti contented themselves with surveying its tranquil beauty from a distance.

In the event that someone did decide to brave the capricious waters, the crossing from Papeete was best attempted in the early hours of the day, just as Hillary and Anthony were preparing to do on this particular Saturday in April. They had secured passage on the only boat that regularly made the two-hour trip, and they were in the process of boarding when Hillary glanced up to see Ryan Gallagher, his tall frame easily recognizable in the crowd, striding leisurely down the quay toward them.

"Good heavens!" she breathed.

"What's that?" Anthony queried, a smile lighting his still reddened features as he reached up to assist Hillary into the boat. He wore a very broad-brimmed hat to protect his skin from further exposure to the sun, and he had even discarded his black frock coat, at least for the duration of the crossing, to ensure less chance of suffering the heat exhaustion to which he was so susceptible.

"Ry . . . Captain Gallagher is coming this way!" she revealed with a telltale blush. She was totally nonplussed at the way her heart suddenly took to pounding. It had been two days since she had seen him last. He had not come to Starcross again, and she had purposely avoided going into town. She had begun to wonder if she would truly never be bothered by him again, if he had perhaps finally conceded the futility of what she could only suppose to be his dishonorable intentions. Since that disgraceful incident at the bathing pool, he had invaded her thoughts and dreams with more disturbing frequency than ever. She had burned with shame—and something else she dared not put a name to—whenever the memory of their tempestuous embrace insinuated itself into her mind.

"Gallagher?" Hillary's fair-haired escort echoed with a sharp frown as he turned his head to follow the direction of her wide, anxious gaze. It was obvious when his eyes fell on the other man, for his entire body stiffened with annoyance. "I don't suppose it would do any good to ignore him," Anthony remarked a bit sourly.

"I'm *quite* sure it would not," murmured Hillary. She was still struggling to regain control over her absurdly erratic breathing when Ryan ended his approach at her side. His striking, blue-green eyes glowed with noticeable pleasure as they traveled briefly but thoroughly over her. She could read the approval in his gaze, and she was suddenly quite glad she had worn the pale lavender, sprigged muslin gown that fitted her slender curves to perfection and emphasized the violet radiance of her eyes.

"Good day to you, Miss Reynolds," proclaimed Ryan, negligently doffing his hat. Although he favored her with a slight, entirely proper inclination of his head, Hillary did not fail to glimpse the irreverent humor lurking in his gaze. "Mr. Warren," he said, nodding to Anthony in turn. "It seems we're of the same mind this morning, doesn't it?"

"What do you mean?" the younger man demanded with yet another frown marring his sunburned brow.

"Moorea. I've been of a mind to pay a visit to the island again myself. What a pleasant coincidence the three of us decided to go on the same day."

"Is it truly a coincidence, Captain?" challenged Hillary, eyeing him suspiciously. Why did *he* have to show up today, of all days? She had enough on her mind already without having to worry about Ryan Gallagher's shenanigans!

"Why should you believe otherwise?" he parried with a deceptively innocent smile. His eyes, boldly caressing the upturned loveliness of her face, offered a roguish tribute that sent her pulses racing.

Anthony, swallowing the bitter pill of the captain's presence on the upcoming trip, took Hillary's arm and tugged her insistently down to the boat's weathered deck. Still preoccupied with Ryan's bold perusal, she was unprepared for Anthony's action, and she very nearly lost her footing as the flounced hem of her skirts and petticoat were caught beneath the heel of her laced, white leather boot. Ryan was there to lend support in an instant, his strong arm slipping about Hillary's waist as he stepped agilely down into the boat. She gasped and jerked away from him as if the contact had burned her, while Anthony cast her gallant rescuer a sharp look of rebuke.

93

"Come, Hillary," said the young Englishman, "we should take our seats without further delay." He frowned severely at Ryan once more before leading Hillary to the far side of the deck.

The small sailing vessel, *Paradaiso*, was employed chiefly in the transport of mail and supplies to Moorea and accommodated no more than half a dozen passengers. At present, only Hillary and her two greatly contrastive swains had come aboard. She fervently hoped there would be other passengers as well, but in this she was soon disappointed, for the French captain of the boat ordered the crew of three Tahitians to weigh anchor and set sail a scant five minutes after Hillary and Anthony had settled themselves upon a splintered bench on the starboard side.

Ryan had chosen to stand. As the *Paradaiso* gathered speed on its way out of the harbor, he lifted a booted foot to the bench on the opposite side of the boat, rested his forearm atop his bent knee, and tilted his hat back upon his dark head at a rakish, devil-may-care angle. He appeared the very epitome of a dashing sea captain—a fact that was not lost either on Hillary or the increasingly jealous young man beside her. Although mentally chastising herself for it, she could not prevent her eyes from straying to the hard-muscled smoothness of Ryan's hip and thigh beneath the tightly stretched fabric of his trousers, nor to the rugged perfection of his handsome face, presented in profile and wearing only the hint of a smile.

"Does Pastor Witherspoon know you're coming?"

Hillary started guiltily at the sound of Anthony's voice. She hastily tore her gaze from Ryan and transferred it to her escort's reddened countenance.

"No," she replied, her own face a trifle flushed.

"But I told him I'd return within the month. I know he'll be pleased to see us."

"And to see the supplies you're bringing, no doubt," Anthony pointedly added. There was an unmistakable note of disapproval in his voice. "Really, Hillary, I'm afraid you're being much too generous—"

"Nonsense!" she cut him off with a soft laugh, forgetting about Ryan for the moment. "Even if I myself were not inclined to support the Academy, Tevaite would see to it that the supplies found their way to Pastor Witherspoon—without my knowledge, of course!" Indeed, she mused to herself, the London Missionary Society's South Sea Academy would always hold a special place in Tevaite's heart. The Tahitian woman had been educated there, and several members of her family still lived near the school on Moorea.

"Not that I mind in the least accompanying you, but was it truly necessary to deliver them yourself?" Anthony then asked. He had hoped the two of them would be able to spend his day off engaged in more leisurely pursuits, such as a picnic at Starcross or even—dare he think it?—a jaunt to one of the secluded lagoons south of Papeete where they could be alone. He had never been completely alone with Hillary, and it was only recently that he had begun to consider the possibility of accelerating his courtship of her.

"I wanted to speak with the pastor about the books and lessons he so generously lent me for my own pupils. And, to be honest, there *is* another matter of business awaiting me on the island," she reluctantly confessed. The wind whipped her full skirts about her ankles, and she was forced to raise a hand to her beribboned straw bonnet to keep it from being torn from her head. She stole a quick look at Ryan, but he still faced straight ahead and appeared to be totally absorbed in his observation of the boat's course through the deepening, brilliant turquoise waters of the harbor.

"Another matter of business?"

"Yes, Anthony." Hillary sighed and decided that it was time to reveal the truth. She hadn't wanted to deceive him, but she had concluded there was no other way to get him to Moorea and the meeting planned there later that day. "You see, it fell to me to bring you. Since the other members live on Moorea, I was the only one who—"

"Other members of *what?*" he demanded sternly, keeping a vigilant hand on his own hat.

"The newly formed Vanilla Association of Tahiti. We're going to conduct our first real meeting this afternoon."

"You know my feelings regarding such organizations, Hillary," Anthony reminded her with yet another frown. "And possessed of that knowledge, what in heaven's name prompted you to believe I'd ever consent to attending? I most certainly cannot offer an endorsement of this . . . this—"

"Vanilla Association of Tahiti," she calmly re-iterated. Fully prepared for his resistance, she was also quite confident that, with the correct methods of persuasion, she would be able to enlist his much-needed support. Following another surreptitious glance in Ryan's direction, she smiled winningly at Anthony and said, "Since you *are* the British vice-consul, dear Anthony, we thought it only fair that you be afforded the opportunity to attend the meeting and hear our grievances firsthand."

"What grievances?" he asked, studying her closely.

"The new tariff, for one. Surely you're aware of

how difficult it's going to be for any of us to make a decent profit when we must needs pay even greater taxes on our product?"

"My dear Hillary," he replied with exaggerated patience, as if speaking to a child instead of a young woman nearing her twenty-second birthday, "we've already discussed this matter at great length. As I told you, there's really nothing I can do."

"You could make a formal protest on our behalf!"

Anthony was obviously thrown into a quandary at that point. He was exceedingly fond of Hillary and would do almost anything within his power to please her; on the other hand, there was his position to consider, *and* his future in the diplomatic corps. How could he possibly risk jeopardizing his entire career—a career that the British consul himself had termed "promising"—for the sake of making a protest that in all probability would prove futile?

"I'm sorry, Hillary," he told her quietly, his pale blue eyes making a silent plea for understanding, "but I simply must not get involved. And neither should you. There's nothing to be gained by stirring up trouble, don't you see?"

"The only thing I see, *Mr. Warren*, is that your reputation is far more important to you than either our friendship or the welfare of the islanders!" Hillary reproachfully decreed. She failed to note the sharp glance Ryan cast her way. "Their way of life has changed drastically since the French took control of these islands eleven years ago. It is imperative that they learn more about the rest of the world, in order that they may know how to guard against further demoralization. The few of us who struggle to run the plantations here are committed not only to the education of the children, but also to restoring Tahiti to at least some of its former glory. After all, need I

97

point out that *we*, the British, bear the same degree of responsibility as the other 'civilized' people who have set foot here throughout the past ninety years?"

"I know how very attached you have become to this place. Your attachment cannot help but color your judgment," the young Englishman responded with a faintly condescending air. "I most humbly beg your pardon, Hillary, but I cannot in all good conscience agree with your estimation of the circumstances. In my opinion, the blame for any dishonor lies squarely on the shoulders of the whalers and other such mercenary, rapacious scoundrels who have been allowed to prey at will upon these shores." This last he spoke with a meaningful glower at Ryan Gallagher.

Hillary, her eyes following the direction of Anthony's decidedly unamiable gaze, felt herself flushing anew when she encountered the expression of tolerant amusement on Ryan's face. Apparently having taken no offense at the other man's words—though offense was clearly intended—he fixed Hillary with a keen look from those smoldering, blue-green eyes of his that served to make her feel positively unstrung. She dropped her eyes and twisted her head about in a moment of panic, then in the next instant furiously castigated herself for her display of weakness.

Why should she be afraid of Ryan Gallagher? He's only a man, she mused with a defensive set to her lovely features, only a man with all the same human faults and frailties as other men. What was there to fear? He was not going to harm her. He could not force her to do anything she did not wish to do—or could he?

"In light of my regard for you, dearest Hillary, I really must insist that you disassociate yourself from this unfortunate and ill-begotten organization. You must have nothing more to do with it. As soon as we have completed our visit to Pastor Witherspoon, we shall return to Papeete and—"

"Ill-begotten?" she indignantly challenged, her thoughts effectively diverted from the disturbing American. Her eyes flashed·at Anthony as she hastened to offer a heartfelt defense of her cause. "I'll have you know that each and every member of this 'ill-begotten' organization is a decent, hardworking individual whose foremost concern is for the effect of his endeavors upon the local economy! We seek nothing more than what is fair! And if neither you nor your esteemed colleague will agree to hear us out, then we will simply have to take it upon ourselves to petition the higher authorities for justice in this matter!"

"But—"

"And furthermore, you have no right whatsoever to dictate to me what I may or may not do! While it is true that I greatly value your friendship, Anthony Warren, it is also true that I possess brains enough to make my own decisions regarding either business or personal relationships!" She pivoted about angrily on the bench so that she was no longer facing the hapless young vice-consul, whose bewilderment at her outburst was evident in the way he stared open-mouthed at the rigid curve of her back.

Ryan Gallagher smiled to himself. Trouble in paradise, he thought in satisfaction. Judging from the disharmonious scene he had just witnessed, there was little to fear in *that* particular quarter.

Although the fair-haired Englishman attempted conversation with Hillary several more times, the remainder of the crossing passed in almost total silence. The boat encountered only a minimal amount of opposition from the sea as it sailed across the deep channel and through the pass where the ocean penetrated the reef-sheltered lagoon surrounding Moorea. The vessel dropped anchor in the fjordlike Opunohu Bay on the north coast of the island. As always, there was a small crowd gathered on the shore awaiting the arrival of the *Paradaiso*. Tahitians and Europeans alike were eager for the packets of mail and crates of supplies delivered on a fairly regular basis.

Hillary's destination was Papeto'ai, a picturesque village that boasted not only the South Sea Academy and a unique octagonal church built by the missionaries in 1829, but the first Polynesian printing works as well. It was also in the Opunohu basin, where Papeto'ai lay, that the first cultivation of sugar cane, coffee, and cotton had taken place. Now however, the fertile, emerald-cloaked valley was the site of a number of vanilla plantations, mostly run by British subjects who, like Hillary's aunt and uncle, had nurtured the dream of carving out their own empire of sorts in this land upon which nature had poured out its bounty. But, also like Hillary's aunt and uncle, they had soon discovered that reality and romantic visions of success do not always go hand in hand.

"Hillary! Oh, Hillary, I'm *so* glad you've come!" enthused a pretty young woman standing with her equally attractive young husband at the end of the narrow quay. She moved forward to embrace her friend as Hillary stepped hastily from the boat without so much as a backward glance at either Ryan or Anthony. "Where is Mr. Warren? Donald and I were only a moment ago arguing about whether or not you'd be able to convince—" The green-eyed strawberry blonde broke off and flushed guiltily when her gaze lit upon Anthony, who had finally disembarked and was striding toward them. It was apparent from the unusually grim set to his aristocratic jaw that something was amiss.

"I'm afraid, dear Constance, that Mr. Warren will not be present at our meeting after all!" Hillary disclosed in tight, clipped tones. She was aware of the fact that Anthony had paused just behind her, but she refused to turn about and acknowledge his presence.

"Good day, Mrs. Bainbridge. Mr. Bainbridge," Anthony declared with stiff cordiality, his blue eyes glinting dully. He shook the other man's hand as Constance's husband of two years joined them.

"Are you truly declining our invitation, Warren?" the sandy-haired Donald questioned with a frown. He leisurely drew his wife's arm through his, while Hillary, moving to Constance's other side, caught a glimpse of Ryan Gallagher from the corner of her eye. He reached up to tug the brim of his hat lower upon his head as he sauntered past the two couples. He cast not a single glance in their direction, but Hillary was certain he was listening to every word. Still more than a trifle nonplussed by the fact that he had not spoken to her since they had boarded the *Paradaiso* in Papeete, she could not prevent her troubled gaze from straying to his broad back as he stopped a short distance away and began negotiating with one of the natives for the use of a horse.

"I have already made my decision known to Miss Reynolds," Anthony proclaimed a bit haughtily, making no secret of his true feelings in the matter.

Donald gently cleared his throat and replied, "Yes, well, then there's nothing more to be said, is there?"

"Nothing at all!" seconded Hillary. Favoring Anthony with one last reproachful glare, she told him, "Your escort is no longer required, Mr. Warren.

101

I shall not be returning to Papeete until tomorrow."
With that, she whirled about and marched regally to
the shore. The Bainbridges, noticeably discomfited
by the situation at hand, were given little choice but
to follow after her. Murmuring a hasty "Good day!"
to Anthony, they left him standing alone—his pride
and principles intact but his heart aching—on the
quay.

Hillary sailed resolutely past Ryan, who, employing his limited command of the Tahitian language,
had by this time secured a rather sway-backed but
sturdy looking animal as a means of transportation
about the sparsely populated island. Involved with
making some necessary adjustments to the stirrups of
the ancient leather saddle, Ryan was nevertheless
aware of Hillary's every move as she settled herself in
the Bainbridges' carriage nearby. His eyes, following
the open conveyance from England until it was out
of sight a few moments later, glowed with satisfaction once more when he saw the look of curiosity
Hillary tossed back at him over her shoulder.

Anthony Warren noticed the look, too. A surge of
jealousy welled up deep within him. He jammed his
hat atop his head and began marching in Ryan's
direction, intent upon demanding to know the
purpose of the other man's visit to Moorea. Before he
had reached the end of the quay, however, the tall
American had already mounted up and set off down
the same dusty road taken by Hillary and the
Bainbridges.

Hillary's anger had thankfully cooled somewhat
by the time Donald pulled the horses to a halt before
the main building of the South Sea Academy. Pastor
Witherspoon, a bespectacled, middle-aged man with
a kindly face and disposition to match, came bustling
out of the forty-year-old stone structure nestled

beneath the palm trees to greet the unexpected but welcome visitors. Children, most of them Tahitian, but a few English cherubs as well, swarmed gaily from the building in his wake and surrounded the carriage.

"Miss Reynolds! And Mr. and Mrs. Bainbridge as well! What a pleasant surprise!" The gray-haired vicar was forced to raise his voice to be heard above the din, but he seemed quite accustomed to it. "Please, do come inside!" A matronly woman appeared on the scene to round up the children and usher them away, allowing Hillary and her friends to alight and follow their gracious host as he led the way to his study.

Sensitive to the fact that Donald and Constance were no doubt impatient to be about their business at home, Hillary kept her visit to the mission school brief. She returned the teaching materials Pastor Witherspoon had lent her, answered his questions about the children at Starcross, inquired after the progress of the Academy's pupils, and informed him of the supplies she had arranged to be delivered later that day. His thanks were sincere and profuse, and it was with a much lightened heart that she climbed back up into the carriage and waved good-bye.

"Now, my dearest Hillary, perhaps you'll be so good as to tell me why you and Anthony Warren are at such odds with each other!" said Constance once they were on their way again. Her lovely, heart-shaped face looked especially youthful, framed as it was by a becoming cascade of strawberry blond curls. She was several inches shorter than Hillary, her figure more rounded, and her attire a trifle more in keeping with the typical English custom of dressing to the hilt even in the tropics. Constance Bainbridge might never have given serious thought to dispensing with

some of her undergarments, but she was not a conformist in all ways. Dress like a proper Englishwoman she might, but behave like a proper Englishwoman—not always. It was due to her warm, impulsive, and at times eccentric, nature that she and Hillary had formed such a close attachment. They considered themselves kindred souls.

"I would have thought the reason was obvious," Hillary responded with an ironic little smile. "The friction between us stems from his refusal to aid our cause, of course."

"Then it has nothing to do with that other man?"

"What other man?" countered Hillary, feigning ignorance but painfully aware of the sudden rush of color staining her cheeks. She quickly averted her face, turning her clouded gaze upon the sunlit glory of the passing landscape.

"The one who sailed with you and Anthony from Papeete. He's very handsome, isn't he? I couldn't help but notice the way you looked at him. Do you know him well?"

"No!" Hillary denied with startling vehemence. The young Mrs. Bainbridge favored her friend with an expression of wide-eyed bemusement before exchanging a knowing look with her husband. Hillary, quickly recovering her poise, took a deep breath and sought to explain. "That is to say, I . . . I have indeed been introduced to the man, but our acquaintance does not extend far beyond that." Pleading silently to be forgiven the lie, she was once again plagued by vivid memories of her brief but turbulent encounters with Ryan Gallagher. Oh Lord, why had he come to Moorea? Why had he behaved so strangely on the boat? More importantly, where was he now?

"I thought perhaps you had finally hit upon a way to bring our reluctant young diplomat to heel," remarked Constance. She smiled impishly, and there was an accompanying sparkle of wholly feminine mischief in her eye. "You know, my dear, make the poor fellow insanely jealous and then—"

"Constance Bainbridge!" her devoted spouse felt it his duty to admonish. He turned to frown quellingly down into her upturned countenance, but managed to bring only the glimmer of a husbandly crease to his lightly tanned brow.

"Oh, Donald! I do so adore it whenever you attempt to look stern!" giggled his unrepentant mate. She hugged his arm before turning back to Hillary. "By the way, what is the other man's name?"

"He isn't the 'other man'! He is Captain Ryan Gallagher, a typically arrogant and insufferable whaler." Why did the very mention of his name upon her lips leave behind such a queer sensation?

"Really? Oh, how very exciting! You must tell me absolutely everything just as soon as we're alone together!"

"There is nothing to tell," Hillary stubbornly insisted. Grateful when she spied the familiar carved posts marking the boundaries of the Bainbridges' vanilla plantation, she made a silent vow to try to forget all about her personal troubles and concentrate solely on her preparations for the meeting scheduled to take place only a few hours hence. Her violet gaze traveled appreciatively over the whitewashed *fare vanira* situated at the end of a well-cleared path through the gently swaying trees. The house was much like the one at Starcross, as were the other buildings dotting the surrounding grounds.

Idly recalling the fact that Donald Bainbridge had brought his new bride to the tropical estate—purchased sight unseen while he was still in England—nearly two years ago, Hillary was pleased to note once more the evidence of his and Constance's hard work and unflagging perseverance. Jade Point, as it had been dubbed by the young couple who had known each other since childhood, was now perhaps the finest example of all the plantations, most of which were also located on Moorea. Donald possessed not only an innate talent for the business of producing vanilla, but also for communicating with the people he employed. Jade Point owed its success to the kindness and generosity of its owners. Some of the Vanilla Association's more pompous members, reflected Hillary, would do well to exhibit a little more of those same attributes.

As soon as he had assisted the two young women from the carriage, Donald kissed his wife and took himself off to inspect the progress of the curing vanilla pods spread out beneath the sun's benevolent radiance. Constance led Hillary up the steps and inside the house.

"We've some time yet before any of the others arrive. Let's get you settled, then have that talk!" the petite blonde determinedly suggested. In the next instant, she took her friend by the hand and revealed in a conspiratorial whisper, "I'm so glad you decided to stay until tomorrow, dearest Hillary, for I've heard there's to be a positively wicked, *forbidden* performance of dancing by the natives not far from here tonight!" Hillary's widening eyes sparkled with interest.

"A forbidden dance? Do you mean they're actually going to perform the *upaupa?*" she questioned in disbelief, knowing full well that any public exhibition of the dance was prohibited by law. Queen Pomare, yielding to pressure by the scandalized and outraged missionaries some years earlier, had authorized stiff penalties for any transgressors.

"And the *timorodee* as well, if my sources prove correct!" Constance confirmed with a nod and a dimpled smile. "You and I will be able to witness what few have ever seen!" Her smile was quickly replaced by a frown when she viewed the shadow of uncertainty crossing her friend's beautiful visage. "Oh Hillary, don't tell me you're not going to come with me? Why, without you, Donald will most assuredly withdraw his permission for me to attend!"

"Donald *knows* of your plans?"

"Of course he does, you silly goose."

"But . . . but what about the meeting?"

"We won't be going until after the meeting. As a matter of fact, I intend to invite the other wives to come as well. The men will be busy with their cigars and brandy by then, so they won't even have to know. Think of how much fun it will be!"

Hillary, while admitting that she had always possessed a certain curiosity about the infamous dances, told herself that she couldn't possibly agree to be a party to her friend's madness. Both the *upaupa* and *timorodee* were reputed to be lascivious and shocking and thoroughly unfit for the eyes of decent folk. And yet, she then mused, the dances were a part of Tahiti's culture, part of its past. They couldn't be all *that* scandalous. What harm could there be in merely watching them? It wasn't as though she were going to be a participant.

"Well, I don't suppose—" she reluctantly began to acquiesce, still feeling uneasy about the whole thing.

"I knew you'd agree!" Constance happily declared. Taking Hillary's hand again, she gathered up her skirts and started up the bamboo-railed staircase. "To tell the truth, I hope the dances *are* as wicked as I've heard. Some of the ladies—and I'm afraid you yourself will have to be included in this, dear

Hillary—are entirely too proper and could use a bit of influence from the islanders' glorification of love."

"Constance Bainbridge, you . . . you are absolutely incorrigible!"

"I know, my dear, I know." She laughed delightedly and pulled her friend into one of the sunlit bedrooms at the top of the stairs.

Wondering what Constance would say if she knew the truth about Ryan Gallagher and his shocking attempts to influence the proper Miss Reynolds with his own "glorification of love," Hillary ducked her head to hide a fiery blush and folded her arms tightly across her bosom to conceal a sudden, involuntary tremor.

The first meeting of the new Vanilla Association of Tahiti was pronounced by everyone in attendance to be a huge success. Nearly a dozen married couples had traveled to Jade Point, and all but four of those would be enjoying the hospitality of the Bainbridges for the night. The drafting of several important bylaws had been achieved by the conclusion of the assembly, an assembly at which Hillary and Constance had been the only females bold enough to voice their opinions, but no real resolution to the tariff problem had been found. Another meeting was planned for the end of the month, for the sole purpose of drawing up and voting upon a formal protest to be sent to England. Hillary was secretly doubtful that the protest would do any good.

Following a time-honored tradition, the husbands and wives separated and sought the company of their own sex for the remainder of the evening. The men wandered into the library for their customary cigars

108

and brandy, while the women gathered in the parlor for conversation and tea.

The cosy, lamplit room was soon filled with the pleasant drone of feminine chatter. The windows had been thrown open to the night, and the sounds of rustling leaves and gently breaking waves drifted on the sweet-scented breeze as it whispered softly through the house. Perched on one of the cushioned windowseats, Hillary glanced at the massive grandfather clock in the opposite corner, then at Constance. The mistress of Jade Point, noting the direction of her friend's visibly apprehensive gaze, smiled as their eyes met. She wasted no more time before rising to her feet and spreading her well-manicured fingertips in a graceful request for silence.

"Ladies, may I have your attention please?" The room swiftly quieted as nine pairs of eyes fastened curiously upon Constance. "I know I promised you tea, and you shall have it if you are still of a mind to remain closeted here in the parlor, but I should like to invite you all to accompany me to a special performance of native dancing. My own dear husband has generously agreed to keep *your* lords and masters occupied, and I give you my solemn word that we shall return within the hour."

"Native dancing?" echoed Theodora Abbey, a rather sour-faced dowager who never dressed in anything but pale mauve. She had lived on the island for three years and was the self-appointed social leader of the group. "Why on earth would we be interested in such a thing, my dear Mrs. Bainbridge?"

"I . . . I don't think my husband would approve of my attending without him," pretty young Juliet Danbury murmured with properly Victorian meekness

There were other such dutiful protestations heard

wafting about the room, but an undaunted Constance raised her hands once more and announced, "Naturally, I leave the decision to each of you. I should simply like to remind you that this is indeed a very special exhibition, and one that *I* do not intend to miss. Hillary and I will be leaving at once, so those of you who wish to accompany us should let it be known at this time."

"Are you actually suggesting that we *steal away* to watch this exhibition?" Theodora's voice rang out in dire tones of disapproval. Her ample, mauve silk-covered bosom rose and fell while her gray eyes narrowed coldly. "Why, I cannot believe you are so lost to all sense of propriety, dear Mrs. Bainbridge!"

Hillary suppressed a laugh as Constance sighed dramatically and said, "I fear I am hopeless, Mrs. Abbey, for I cannot see anything so terribly wrong in wanting to learn more about the Polynesian culture. As for our 'stealing away'—what harm can there be in it? Our husbands are following their usual custom of neglecting us, are they not? I daresay the majority of them would not be in the least bit interested in how we choose to spend our evening."

Another buzz of lowered voices filled the parlor. Some of the women were strongly tempted to accept Constance's invitation, while others, among them Theodora Abbey, preferred only to comment disparagingly upon what they deemed to be young Mrs. Bainbridge's lack of experience and expertise in her duties as hostess. Finally, when it appeared no one was willing to be the first to speak up, Juliet Danbury amazed the others by standing and crossing tentatively to Hillary's side. Hillary smiled at her and silently applauded the young brunette's rare display of temerity. Another woman joined them, then another. Even some of those who had initially scoffed at Constance's idea now hastened to join in the adventure. Within seconds, only Martha Kitteridge, Jane Holmsby, Theodora Abbey, and Theodora's daughter-in-law, a timid creature who was loath to incur the formidable dowager's wrath, remained seated. It was obvious that no amount of persuasion would make them change their minds about the folly of the outing.

The eldest son of Jade Point's housekeeper, a handsome young Tahitian by the name of Arii, was waiting outside with several of his friends to provide an escort for Constance and her guests. Holding torches aloft to light the way beneath a star-filled tropical sky, the Tahitians led the excitedly whispering and giggling Englishwomen along a path through the tall trees and fragrant shrubbery. The trek was not at all a difficult one, and it took less than a quarter of an hour for them to reach their destination.

Hillary gazed curiously about her as she and the other, equally wide-eyed women emerged within a spacious clearing that was already beginning to grow crowded. A single, thatch-roofed hut stood guard at one end of the torchlit area, while the yellow-orange flames of a fire crackled and blazed heavenward in the center of the clearing. Giant chestnut, or *mape,* trees cast ghostly shadows on the ground as the cool night breeze sent their limbs into motion.

"I'd no idea there would be so many other spectators," Constance leaned close to whisper, nodding to indicate the men and women seating themselves in a large semi-circle about the fire. Though most of those who had come to witness the forbidden dances were islanders, there were quite a number of Europeans in the crowd.

Musing that word of the upcoming festivities had

apparently spread quickly, Hillary wondered why there had been no attempt by the authorities to prevent the exhibition. "Perhaps we should go back," she suggested to Constance, her uneasiness increasing with each passing second.

"Nonsense! Come, let's move nearer to the fire," the petite blonde eagerly directed. Hillary tried to hold back, but Constance merely tugged her forward. The rest of the group from Jade Point followed close behind, pausing to stand a little apart from the other spectators.

Seconds later, two Tahitian men, each clad only in a knee-length *pareu*, appeared on the other side of the fire and knelt upon the ground with drums fashioned of wood and sharkskin. They began beating out a loud, forceful cadence that echoed through the clearing and brought the fascinated crowd to an expectant silence. There was nothing but the hypnotic rhythm of the drums for several long moments. Then, a dozen young women, all wearing short skirts of *tapa* cloth tied low upon their shapely hips and sporting fresh blossoms of jasmine and hibiscus in their long black hair, emerged from behind the hut to form a ring about the fire. Their breasts were covered by nothing more than two large, mother-of-pearl shells fastened together with narrow lengths of handmade twine.

Following a signal from the lead dancer, the ring began to circle slowly. The tempo of the drumbeats increased ever so slightly as the lithe, golden bodies of the dancers swayed sideways in movements so natural and graceful that none who witnessed them could find their innocent sensuality offensive. Participation in the *timorodee* was limited to unmarried women—the dance had traditionally been performed as a means of attracting a mate. Now, however, its purpose was only to entertain.

And entertain it did. Much like everyone else's, Hillary's gaze was riveted upon the firelit activity before her. She was fascinated by the dance, and not the least bit scandalized by the dancers' scanty costumes.

The tempo quickened. The beautiful young natives began to sway and turn with even more enthusiasm, their increasingly abandoned movements in perfect unison with the pounding of the drums. Several of the Englishwomen with Constance and Hillary snapped open their fans and began waving them briskly back and forth in front of their flushed, visibly shocked faces. It soon became clear why the missionaries had been so outraged by the *timorodee*. By the end of the dance, the participants were flying round and round, their shell-covered bosoms heaving, their silken hair streaming wildly about them, their dark eyes sparkling as though they were lost in some sort of prurient trance.

A loud murmur rose from the crowd when the drummers finally stilled their efforts and the dancers disappeared behind the hut once more. Hillary was surprised to find her breathing so erratic. She lifted a faintly trembling hand to her throat and stole a quick glance at Constance. Taking note of the two bright spots of color on her friend's cheeks, she wondered if her own face displayed her consternation at what she had just witnessed.

"Good heavens!" breathed Constance at last. Her green eyes were shining as she turned to Hillary and pronounced, "That was without a doubt the most *provoking* thing I have ever seen!"

"I should say 'provoking' is an appropriate term with which to describe it!" Hillary retorted with a rather shaky laugh. Inhaling deeply of the night air, she swept a stray curl from her forehead and smoothed a hand along her sprigged muslin skirts. One of the women in the Jade Point group, a plump redhead by the name of Clarissa Dexter, suddenly rounded on Hillary's friend with righteous indignation.

"Constance Bainbridge, how dare you bring us to this . . . this disgraceful, immoral—"

"Have you no shame, Constance?" another woman sternly chimed in.

"You knew all about this, didn't you?" still another demanded with an accusing glare. "I daresay you were well aware of how very *special* this exhibition was to be!"

"Oh dear!" Juliet Danbury murmured, wringing her hands in distress. The last member of the group merely stared reproachfully at Constance and continued to flap her delicate lace fan.

"We will endure no more of this disgrace!" decreed Clarissa. "Ladies, let us return to the house at once!" Subjecting a strangely silent Constance to a withering look, she whirled about and flounced away. The others followed suit, all except Juliet, who stood glancing helplessly back and forth between her hostess and her departing companions. Constance released a heavy sigh and turned back to Hillary.

"I'm afraid I've little choice but to see them safely back," the pretty blonde reluctantly admitted. "But there's no reason for both of us to miss the *upaupa*, dear Hillary. You wait here."

"No," Hillary dissented, shaking her head. "I'll go with you. You'll need an ally when you face Theodora Abbey!" She didn't add that she had seen quite enough of forbidden dances for one night. She had never dreamt they would be so overpowering. *Provoking*, Constance had said. Yes, they were indeed that, mused Hillary.

"That old battle-ax? She doesn't frighten me a bit. No my dear, I insist that you stay and watch the dance. I'll leave Arii here with you. Hopefully, I shan't be long in rejoining you!" Without allowing Hillary the chance to protest further, Constance motioned to the young Tahitian man to remain, grabbed Juliet by the hand, and hurried after her fleeing, ungrateful guests.

Hillary sighed. She was torn between obeying her better instincts, which cautioned her to return to Jade Point at once, and the desire to remain—in spite of having been made uncomfortable by what she had seen—to witness the dance that was reputedly even more scandalous than the first one.

The decision was made for her by the drums. Their echoing rhythm began reverberating about the clearing again before she could force herself to leave. Voices died away as the spectators resumed their places upon the ground. Only Hillary and one man remained standing in the soft golden glow of the firelight.

Her eyes flickered absently in his direction. She gasped, her entire body stiffening and her beautiful face wearing a look of dawning incredulity and dismay.

Dear God, no! Not *him!* Not *now!*

V

Ryan Gallagher's lips curled into a slow, roguish smile as his gaze captured Hillary's. He had been startled to discover her there, for he had believed her to be safely ensconced in the Bainbridges' house for the night. Indeed, he had followed the carriage to Jade Point before riding off to secure accommodations for himself at a nearby hostelry that catered to seamen. The proprietor had taken great pleasure in informing his guests of the planned, "secret" defiance of the law. Since Ryan had experienced a mild curiosity to see the dances performed once more—he had first done so nearly ten years earlier while serving as first mate aboard his uncle's ship— he had followed the proprietor's directions and arrived upon the scene just as the *timorodee* was beginning.

He was both intrigued and delighted by Hillary's presence at the forbidden presentation. Having observed the hasty departure of her companions, he gave silent thanks for the fact that she was, at least for the moment, alone. The expression of mocking amusement on his handsome face was quickly replaced by an intense yet unfathomable look, and he hesitated no longer before advancing upon the beautiful young woman he had sworn to make his own.

Hillary's eyes grew wide with alarm as she witnessed Ryan's approach. Frantically wondering what to do, she was about to surrender to the impulse to take flight, when the swelling crescendo of the drumbeats signaled the momentarily delayed start of the dance. She glanced anxiously at Arii, only to see that he had wandered to the opposite side of the clearing to join another group of friends.

Then, Ryan was at her side, towering ominously above her, making her feel trapped. He spoke not a word; neither did he touch her. He merely stood close beside her, throwing her into further confusion by turning his attention back to the drummers on the other side of the fire. Hillary tried to make herself move away, but she could not. It was as if she were being compelled by some mystical force to remain. She was acutely conscious of Ryan's nearness, of the warmth of his hard, masculine body, of the astonishing fact that the two of them were there together beneath the stars, preparing to watch the dance that had upon more than one occasion been described as "the most indecent ever seen." She stole a glance up at his face, but he gave no indication that he was aware of anything but the dance.

Five half-naked young men had appeared in front of the hut by now. Their dark amber, smoothly muscular bodies gleamed in the firelight as, planting their feet firmly apart on the ground, they slowly began swaying and rotating the upper portion of their sleek torsos. Arms, hands, and fingers waved dexterously about; it appeared that each joint moved separately. Each motion was executed with a fluid, manly grace that held the audience spellbound.

Hillary swallowed a lump in her throat and battled to regain control of her breathing. Her luminous gaze moved surreptitiously upward to Ryan's handsome countenance with more and more frequency. Still, he did not look at her. She caught a glimpse of the fire's reflection within his magnificent, blue-green eyes, and she found herself staring at the patch of bronzed skin where the open collar of his white linen shirt fell back to form a deep V.

Her attention was drawn back to the performance when the drums suddenly pounded to an abrupt halt. There was a pause of several long seconds before the drummers took up their task again, with more fervor than ever before. Without warning, the dancers gave out loud, discordant cries and began miming scenes of violence, throwing themselves about as if possessed. The scene continued like that for a mercifully short time, after which the participants calmed their movements somewhat and settled into a rapid but sinuous rotation of their lower bodies.

The crowd roared with approval when five young women suddenly leapt up from within the ranks of the spectators to join in the dance. Hillary's eyes grew enormous within the delicate oval of her face as she watched the Tahitian women pair off with the dancers, positioning themselves face-to-face with their male counterparts. The women began a highly suggestive gyration of their shapely, *pareu*-covered hips while the men, their own movements increasing in frenzy as the inciting tempo of the drums drove them to even greater abandon, uttered wild cries of encouragement.

To Hillary, it seemed that the drums pounded in her brain. She bit at her lower lip and refused to look at Ryan again. Her cheeks burned, her breasts rose and fell rapidly beneath the thin muslin of her bodice, and her eyes sparkled brightly. She caught her breath and felt a warm flush stealing over her entire body when she saw the vibrantly attractive young men and women engaged in what was an undeniable simulation of the act of love—their lithe bodies, glistening with perspiration as a result of their exertions, were all but entwined, their pelvises were thrusting provocatively forward in unison, their arms were flung outward to allow greater freedom of movement, and the impassioned expressions on their faces gave evidence to the fact that they were celebrating their natural, most gloriously human impulses.

Before a dazed and breathless Hillary quite knew what was happening, Ryan's strong arm slipped about her waist. She had little time to protest before she found herself being spirited away from the dance. He bore her relentlessly backward into the concealing darkness of the lush green foliage, and when she would have screamed, he silenced her with the masterful pressure of his warm lips.

It was as if he had touched off a veritable powder keg of emotion. When his mouth crashed down upon hers, she immediately lost both the strength and the inclination to resist. Atremble with the astonishing force of her passion, she found her supple curves pressed boldly against his hardness as he enveloped her within his powerful embrace. She strained almost feverishly upward, entwining her arms about his neck, her lips parting beneath the rapturous onslaught of his while her luxuriant mane of midnight black hair loosened from the pins to tumble in wild disarray about her face and shoulders.

A short distance away in the clearing, the performers were caught in the throes of the dance's unrestrained climax. Without ever actually touching, the men and women completed the symbolic exhibition of love and collapsed, exhausted and joyous, beside one another on the ground. The drums stilled for a brief interval, but neither Hillary nor Ryan seemed to take any notice of the silence.

She moaned softly as his embrace swiftly grew more inflaming. His hands roamed across her back and down to her hips with such evocative urgency that her pulses raced out of control. She returned his fiercely demanding kisses with an answering fire of her own, and she did not offer even a token resistance when his fingers, displaying what she dazedly mused must be an ability borne of much practice, liberated the back fastenings of her dress and smoothed her bodice downward. The beribboned neckline of her chemise was soon untied and tugged out of the way as well, so that her breasts, full and firm and rose-tipped, were rendered totally vulnerable to the moist caress of his mouth.

Inhaling upon a gasp when his warm lips branded the satiny perfection of one naked breast, Hillary was only dimly aware of the resumed pounding of the drums. She did not know what Ryan did, that the *upaupa* would last for most of the night as other dancers came to take their turn before the fire. The sight of men and women expressing their sexuality so openly had aroused her own awakening desire, and Ryan had taken advantage of her momentary weakness to convince her, in the best way he knew how, that she was every bit as passionate a creature as those she had just watched. His ultimate goal was more than physical possession of her body—he wanted her heart and soul as well.

At the moment, at least a partial victory seemed assured. Hillary clung to him as if she were drowning, her soft gasps and moans urging him

121

onward as his tongue swirled with tantalizing unhaste about the sensitive peak of her breast. Her trembling fingers threaded within the pleasantly soap-scented thickness of his hair. She felt reality slipping away. There was only Ryan, only the inexplicable but overwhelming need to have him touch and kiss her the way he was doing now, to somehow ease the almost painful yearning that had flared to a fever pitch inside of her. She didn't know exactly what it was she wanted of him, or what she wanted of herself. All capability for rational thought vanished. She was being swept away on a rising tide of passion, engulfed by the most exquisitely tormenting sensations she had ever known . . . and she was powerless to prevent it.

His lips returned to claim hers as he lifted her in his arms, then lowered her gently to the ground. Hillary shivered when the bare skin of her shoulders met the coolness of the thick, cushioning blanket of fern. The hypnotic sound of the drumbeats echoed through the sheltering palms and wonderfully fragrant shrubbery as Ryan, stretching out on the soft earth beside his willing captive so that her head was cradled upon his arm, kissed her with such captivating ardency that she grew faint. The velvety warmth of his tongue ravished her sweet mouth, while his sensuously persuasive fingers stroked and caressed the delectable bounty of her breasts.

Somewhere in the benumbed recesses of her mind, Hillary became aware of Ryan's hand drawing her skirts and petticoat upward. With surprising swiftness, he pulled the folds of sprigged muslin and lace-trimmed cotton up about her slender white thighs, thereby baring her silken limbs and allowing him access to even more of her loveliness. She moaned against his mouth and trembled anew when his hand trailed purposefully upward along the quivering softness of her inner thighs. The convenient, open-leg design of her drawers provided no barrier against his questing fingers.

His lips seared a fiery path back down to her breasts as his hand reached the secret place between her thighs. She inhaled upon a sharp gasp when his fingers tenderly delved within the triangle of downy black curls to stroke the soft pink flesh hidden therein. Her head tossed restlessly side to side upon the carpet of fern, her thighs parting of their own accord as she felt herself soaring heavenward. His tongue flicked erotically across the nipple of her breast, prompting her back to arch instinctively, and her fingers to curl almost convulsively about the corded muscles of his neck.

Hillary was scarcely able to breathe, and she couldn't seem to prevent a series of soft, broken cries from escaping her lips as the longing deep inside of her intensified. Her womanly passions were being truly awakened for the first time by Ryan's gentle mastery of her body. She was willing to surrender herself completely to him in that moment, willing to yield her femininity to his masculine possession, though she would never have admitted it aloud. The fire in her blood, initially kindled by both the blatant sensuality of the dances and Ryan's bewitching kisses, was now stoked by her own long-repressed desires.

Ryan, however, made no move to take her. He concentrated fully on giving her pleasure, on initiating her into the delights of the flesh. But still he did not attempt to make her his own. Unversed as she was in the ways of love, Hillary was nonetheless quite certain there was more to lovemaking than what had taken place so far. *Why did he hold back?*

The sounds of revelry were carried on the night wind as the second performance of the *upaupa* drew closer to its inevitable climax. Ryan took Hillary's mouth with his own again, his fingers matching the tempo of the drumbeats as they caressed the very center of her womanhood and brought her emotions to their own vibrant, searing conclusion. He swallowed her breathless cry of release seconds later, then rolled to his back and held her lovingly within the warm circle of his arms when she collapsed, languid and more than slightly bewildered, against him.

"Hillary. My wild, sweet love," he murmured close to her ear. His deep voice was full of tenderness.

Reason quickly returned. And when it did, Hillary was assailed by several unpleasant emotions—a keen sense of disappointment, shame and disbelief at what she had done, a lingering ache deep inside, and a smoldering, irrational anger directed at Ryan Gallagher.

Fighting back the hot tears suddenly stinging against her eyelids, she yanked her chemise and bodice upward at the same time she rolled abruptly away from Ryan. A sharp frown creased his handsome brow as he lifted a hand toward her, but she jerked away from him and stumbled to her feet, hampered by her full skirts as well as the tropical greenery that closed about her and tangled within her disheveled locks. Rising to his feet in one quick motion, Ryan seized her arm in a firm grip and forced her about to face him.

"Let me go!" cried Hillary, clutching her gown to her heaving breasts as she twisted futilely within his grasp. Her hair swirled wildly about her stormy, crimson-cheeked face.

"What is it, my love? What's wrong?" demanded Ryan in a low, resonant undertone. The drums had

124

momentarily stilled again, leaving the starlit darkness filled only with the peaceful sounds of the sea and the gentle breeze.

Hillary opened her mouth to lash out at him, to tell him that she despised him and would never forgive him for what he had done, but no words would come. Her eyes flashed their brilliant amethyst fire as she gazed mutely up at him. His own eyes were glowing with such tenderness and warmth and desire that she felt her anger melting away. She was confused by the sudden urge to throw herself upon his broad chest and weep.

"Hillary—" he murmured huskily, slowly pulling her toward him again.

"Hillary! Hillary, where are you?" a feminine voice rang out from the direction of the nearby clearing.

Constance! Hillary's mind confirmed. Dear Lord, she had forgotten all about Constance!

She cast Ryan a look of helpless desperation. Without a word, he spun her about and quickly began refastening the buttons of her gown. Surprised and undeniably touched by his assistance, she felt herself growing light-headed once more, felt her skin burning where his fingers brushed against her back.

Then, he was giving her a gentle push forward. Not trusting herself to look at him again, she gathered up her skirts to return to the dance. She was certain she heard him vow "Until later, my love" behind her, but she did not pause in her hurried flight back through the thick, sweetly scented foliage.

Constance breathed an audible sigh of relief when she spied Hillary emerging from the darkness into the torchlit clearing once more. The petite blonde hastened to her friend's side, saying with a soft laugh,

"I was beginning to think I would have to send Arii and his friends to search for you! Where on earth did you disappear to?"

"I . . . I went for a walk," murmured Hillary. She hastily averted her face as she offered the lame excuse, knowing that the fresh tears starting to fill her eyes would give her away.

"For a walk?" Constance echoed with a slight frown of bemusement. She reached up to liberate a crushed hibiscus petal from Hillary's flowing ebony tresses. Her brow swiftly cleared as she negligently tossed the petal aside. "Well, no matter. I'm so glad there are more performances yet to come! Is the dance truly more wicked than the *timorodee?* It took a good deal longer than I expected to see the ladies back to the house, and Theodora launched into a sancti-monious tirade the very moment we set foot inside the parlor. I'm afraid I shall never be forgiven my misdeeds of this night!" Apparently taking no notice of the disquietude Hillary was doing her best to conceal, Constance laughed again and drew her along toward the fire.

Hillary's eyes swept closed when the pounding of the drums resumed and the next group of young men took their places before the hut. She inhaled sharply as the sudden, unbidden image of Ryan and herself, swaying their bodies close together in the seductive movements of the dance, forced itself into the midst of her troubled mind. When she quickly opened her eyes again, it was only to discover that Ryan had returned to the clearing as well.

He stood just beyond the semicircle of spectators. His devastatingly handsome countenance was in-scrutable, but there was no escaping the penetrating, blue-green intensity of his gaze as it fastened upon her.

Dismayed to feel the telltale flaming of her cheeks, Hillary folded her arms against her breasts in an unconscious gesture of defensiveness. She looked away and tried, unsuccessfully, to forget about her wild, shameful behavior and the way Ryan had so easily conquered her flesh. Although her nerves were strained almost beyond endurance, she somehow managed to suffer through the remainder of the performance without shattering into a thousand pieces.

Constance, her blue eyes shining and her lovely face flushed as the dance ended, declared with satisfaction that it was indeed more provoking than the first. Distractedly murmuring her agreement, Hillary was profoundly grateful when Arii came to escort them back to Jade Point. She could feel Ryan's eyes upon her as she escaped into the welcoming darkness.

Ryan was already there when the Bainbridges delivered their guest to the quay the following morning. The *Paradaiso* was just preparing to drop anchor as Hillary took Donald's hand and stepped down from the carriage. Though she could see Ryan from the corner of her eye, she did nothing to acknowledge his presence. She had known he would be there, but she was nonetheless unprepared for the way her heart suddenly raced within her breast.

How in heaven's name was she going to endure the next two hours? wondered Hillary, a knot tightening in the pit of her stomach. Would he dare to remind her of her shame?

She had tossed restlessly upon her bed all night as her troubled mind refused to grant her slumber. Since she had shared a room with two other ladies—

not, thank heaven, either Theodora Abbey or Clarissa Dexter—there had been little privacy and therefore no opportunity to release all her pent-up emotions. Feeling as if on tenterhooks, she dreaded the upcoming voyage back to Papeete.

The solution to her dilemma came from a completely unexpected source—Anthony Warren. As soon as the boat was secured against the narrow wharf, he disembarked and hastened forward to greet Hillary.

"Why, Anthony!" she breathed in surprise. Constance and her husband, exchanging knowing looks again, considerately remained beside the carriage.

"I had to come," said Anthony, his eyes full of contrition as he swept the hat from his head. "I slept little last night. Our quarrel weighed heavily upon my heart." Guiltily reflecting that her own wakefulness had stemmed from an entirely different reason, Hillary stole a quick glance at Ryan. She stiffened when she glimpsed the light of devilment in his eyes and the faint smile that touched his lips.

"I'm very glad you came," she told Anthony, managing a brief smile. She turned to bid a fond farewell to Donald and Constance, who reminded her again of the next meeting of the Vanilla Association. Constance, embracing her friend one last time, added in a mischievous whisper that perhaps they could arrange another exhibition of forbidden dances. Sudden color flooded Hillary's face, but she comforted herself with the thought that Constance would probably attribute it to nothing more than maidenly embarrassment over what they had witnessed.

Boarding the *Paradaiso* with Anthony, Hillary sat down upon the bench and turned so that her back was to Ryan, who politely tipped his hat at the Bainbridges as he sauntered down the quay. He took his place in the boat, choosing to stand as he had done the previous day, and blithely ignored the suspicious, calculating looks Anthony shot him while the vessel's crew followed the captain's orders to cast off.

The journey back to Papeete was even more nerve-wracking than Hillary had expected. Just as before, Ryan did not once speak to her or Anthony—a fact that kept her wavering confusedly between relief and disappointment. She found it exceedingly difficult to pay attention to Anthony as he apologized for his behavior of the previous day and begged her forgiveness. He went on to suggest, quite earnestly, that although his opinion of her involvement in the Vanilla Association had not changed, the two of them should declare a truce and do their utmost to avoid the subject entirely.

Hillary absently granted her forgiveness and requested his own. Gazing toward the beckoning island of Tahiti as the ship's sleek bow sliced through the whitecapped seas of the channel, she could think only of Moorea.

She was profoundly relieved when they finally reached Papeete. Painfully aware of Ryan's eyes upon her, she declined Anthony's invitation to remain and share a meal with him at the consulate. She murmured her thanks when he assisted her from the boat, then hurried down the wharf, grateful to find Tevaite waiting for her. Distractedly waving aside the older woman's questions, she climbed up into the wagon and snapped the reins above the horse's head. Her lips curved into a bitter, humorless little smile when she reflected that she was always leaving Papeete in a hurry of late—and always because of Ryan Gallagher.

* * *

129

Denholm Reynolds was awaiting his niece's return on the lower verandah of the house at Starcross. Watching the two women alight from the wagon, he flashed a welcoming smile at their approach and rose to his feet beside the wicker table. His smile quickly changed to a worried frown, however, when he glimpsed the visible redness about Hillary's eyes.

"Has something happened, my dear?" He reached out to place a paternal arm about her shoulders and draw her close. She managed a tremulous smile as she kissed him.

"No, Uncle," she lied, forcing a note of brightness into her voice. "I'm just tired, that's all. The night's . . . activities lasted longer than I'd anticipated, and the trip home this morning was a bit difficult." She was discomfited by the long, meditative look Tevaite bestowed upon her before disappearing into the house, but she gave no outward indication of her unease as she took a seat beside her uncle and tugged the straw hat from her head. Gracefully smoothing her full, white lawn skirts into place beneath the table, she smiled again and said, "It's good to see you outside. At the rate you're improving, it won't be long at all until you're well enough to drive into Papeete with me." How much longer would *he* be in port? she suddenly wondered, unable to suppress yet another thought of Ryan.

"I must admit to a certain eagerness to see the old town again after so much time," her uncle remarked with a quiet chuckle. His hand shook only a little as he raised a glass to his lips. He sipped at the fresh coconut milk, then coughed gently before instructing, "Tell me about the meeting, my dear. Was it a success?"

Hillary released a sigh and raised a hand to brush a stray wisp of hair from her forehead. Her violet gaze appeared troubled as she replied, "Yes and no. While we all agreed upon certain measures of conservation and employment, we have yet to make a clear decision about the tariff."

"Was Anthony able to provide any helpful suggestions?"

"Anthony refused to attend the meeting," she recalled with a frown, her eyes flashing anew. "He disapproves of the organization. He is afraid any involvement with us will do irreparable damage to his precious career!" She sighed again before admitting, "I suppose I shouldn't blame him for that. He *is* a man of principle, and he has been a good friend."

"Only a friend?" Denholm probed with a soft smile.

"Do you still cherish hopes he will become more?" she countered teasingly. Quickly sobering, she looked away and declared with a touch of sadness, "I *do* love him, but not in the right way."

"Is there someone else?"

Hillary's head abruptly snapped about once more. Her eyes grew very wide, and a dull flush rose to her face.

"Why . . . why do you ask that?" Though she sought to keep her tone steady and nonchalant, there was a noticeable quaver in her voice. Her gaze fell hastily beneath her uncle's close scrutiny.

"Because you've never before mentioned the word 'love' in connection with such a relationship. I was therefore curious to know if perhaps you had formed an attachment for—"

"No!" she denied with startling vehemence, then blushed in guilty embarrassment when she observed the way he was staring at her so intently. Hurriedly regaining her composure, she gently cleared her throat and clarified, "What I mean to say is, how I

131

feel about Anthony Warren has nothing whatsoever to do with anyone else." That said, she looked away again, pretending a great and sudden interest in the surrounding greenery.

"Not even Captain Gallagher?" he then challenged. The introduction of Ryan's name into the conversation took Hillary completely off guard. Her eyes flew guiltily back to her uncle's face. He was smiling at her with such fond indulgence and wisdom that she was certain he had guessed the truth about her stormy association with the whaler.

Her beautiful countenance displayed telltale anxiety as she blurted out, "Oh, Uncle, I am so confused!" She fought back a fresh surge of tears, miserably reflecting that she had never before been given to such deplorable exhibitions of weepiness. But then, her emotions had never before been in such utter chaos. *Why?* she asked herself, rising to her feet. She began to wander aimlessly about the verandah, while her uncle sat watching her in thoughtful silence. "To be honest, I don't know what I feel for him. He's arrogant and maddening and impossibly bold—" she enunciated quite feelingly, only to break off and spin about, her skirts twirling up about her shapely ankles. "But it doesn't really matter, I suppose, since he'll be leaving as soon as the repairs on his ship are completed. And then, thank heavens, my life will return to normal!"

"Is that what you truly want, my dear?" asked Denholm, still playing devil's advocate. He had, indeed, already surmised what she would not yet acknowledge—she was falling in love with the handsome American.

"Of course!" Hillary answered with unconvincing aplomb. "My life was both orderly and rewarding before I ever heard of Captain Ryan Gallagher. It will be again once he's gone." Then, apparently deciding she had revealed too much already, she hastily bent to kiss her uncle again and took herself off with the announced intention of changing into clothes more suitable for housekeeping chores.

Denholm Reynolds absently fingered the half-empty glass of coconut milk as he stared after his beautiful young niece. His gray eyes clouded with worriment. Time is running out, an inner voice cautioned him. Hillary would be left alone when he died. Something had to be done . . . and soon.

Wasting not a single moment on self-pity—he had accepted his plight and was in truth looking forward to the day when he and his beloved wife would be reunited—he thought briefly of Anthony Warren. He had always believed the young vice-consul would be the man Hillary would choose to wed when she finally gave up her independence. In fact, mused Denholm, he and Anthony had both counted on it, though there had never been any formal declaration of such. It had been understood between them.

But no, the fates had evidently decreed otherwise. Ryan Gallagher. An American. A whaler. Would the young captain treat her well? Would he know how to rule her headstrong nature? Would he know when to use a strong hand, and when to allow her spirit free rein? Would he be content to remain in Tahiti, or would he insist that Hillary leave Starcross and her adopted homeland forever?

"There is only one way to find out," Denholm concluded aloud. He smiled faintly to himself before raising his eyes to find Tevaite standing in the doorway. The Tahitian woman nodded across at him solemnly in silent understanding.

*   *   *

The master of the whaling bark *Falcon* stood alone in his quarters aboard ship. The late afternoon sunlight streamed unrestrainedly through the barred panes of glass above, casting a warm glow upon Ryan's dark head and the charts strewn across the top of the desk before him. An intense light gleaming within the depths of his magnificent blue-green eyes gave evidence to his troubled thoughts as he stared down, unseeing, at the vast array of nautical lines and symbols. He negligently raked a hand through his thick hair, then breathed an oath and wheeled to gaze outward through the small stern window.

Hillary. Memories of what had happened between them last night still burned within his mind. The recollection of her innocent yet impassioned response served to fire his blood anew, but the most vivid—and disturbing—memory was of the pain and confusion in her eyes afterward.

If there had been any doubt at all about the true extent of his feelings for her before then, it had been forever vanquished by the stirring of his heart when he had glimpsed the helpless desperation in her sparkling amethyst gaze. He loved her, loved her more than he had ever believed it possible to love anyone. His pursuit of her may have been prompted by less noble motives in the beginning, but no longer. While the desire to make love to her had certainly increased, so had the desire to cherish and protect her.

Ryan's mouth curved into a faint, self-mocking smile as he pondered the irony of it all. He had seen a great deal of the world throughout the past seventeen years at sea. From the tender age of fourteen, when he had followed family tradition and signed on as cabin boy aboard his own uncle's ship, he had wholeheartedly embraced the adventurous life of a whaler.

He had grown to manhood at sea, had tested that manhood in many a waterfront brawl during those younger, hell-raising days. In short, he had been much like his fellow whalemen who worked, fought, and loved hard.

But he was no longer the same. His dreams, principles, and temperament had undergone a gradual but inevitable transformation as he was matured by both time and experience. The transformation had eventually left him as he was now—a man who had begun to experience a certain dissatisfaction with his chosen way of life, a man who for the first time in years entertained thoughts of abandoning the sea and settling down in one place.

Hillary. He knew he'd never want to leave her once she belonged to him . . .

"Captain?" a familiar masculine voice interrupted his silent reverie. The man on the other side of the door knocked again, more loudly this time. Ryan frowned and rose to his feet.

"Come in, Connor." He watched as his first mate, a lean-bodied man who stood nearly as tall as himself, swung open the door and ducked his head to enter the cabin.

"Sorry to bother you, Captain, but I thought you'd want a report on the ship's repairs." Connor Reid tugged the hat from atop his curly black hair as he closed the door behind him. He smiled, his attractive features sporting a healthy tan above the collar of his white shirt. His golden eyes twinkled companionably across at the other man, and when he spoke again, it was with the easy informality he and Ryan shared whenever alone. "That bastard did a right good job on her when he ran her onto the reef!"

"I suppose we ought to give thanks for the fact she isn't rotting at the bottom of the harbor with the others," Ryan commented wryly, referring to the numerous wrecks that owed their origins to the ineptitude of certain government pilots. The captain of every vessel seeking anchorage at the port of Papeete was required to allow a government-appointed pilot to board and steer the ship through the dangerous entrance into the harbor. The pilots, however, were notoriously bad about running the ships onto the point of the reef, or even onto an outer buoy. Whaling ships and merchant ships alike had fallen prey to the infamous helmsmen; much cargo had been discharged from the wrecked vessels and stored ashore, and a vast amount of oil had been sent home on other ships—in each case, expenses had been paid by the French government to the owners. And, thought Ryan, there was always the added compensation of being forced to remain in Tahiti for extra weeks, or even months.

"Well, at least the damage was limited to that one section of the bow," said Connor, obeying Ryan's nod to take a seat on the horsehair sofa. "And if she hadn't been listing as she was, there'd now be the devil of a hole *below* the water instead of above it. Stokely claims she'll be right and tight within the week."

"I sense an inordinate amount of pleasure at the news." For the first time since he had returned from Moorea, Ryan's handsome features relaxed into a smile. His gaze was full of noticeable raillery as he sat back down behind the cluttered desk. "Tell me, Connor, is there any *particular* reason you're so anxious to sail homeward?"

The other man chuckled softly, knowing full well the hidden meaning of the captain's words. He and Ryan Gallagher had been friends since childhood. Connor's first voyage had taken place only a year after Ryan's, and on a ship commanded by one of Ryan's uncles. The association between the Reids and the Gallaghers extended far back into New Bedford's colorful history.

"We've been away nearly three years. I've probably no reason to hope she's waited for me—or that her father will have changed his mind about me—but yes, damn it, I'm anxious to get back and find out!"

"She'll be waiting," Ryan confidently asserted.

"I wish I could be as certain as you."

They both lapsed into thoughtful silence for a moment, during which time Ryan's gaze was drawn irrevocably back to the window.

Connor, taking note of the sudden shadow crossing his friend's countenance, remarked with a bantering note in his own voice, "It seems you've taken quite an interest in Tahiti of late. I don't remember your being so enchanted with the place when we were here last."

"Then perhaps your memory isn't quite as good as you think," parried Ryan. He folded his arms across his broad chest, and there was only the hint of a smile playing about his lips when he confessed, "Though I am indeed more than ever enchanted with Tahiti itself, I find my interest held primarily by one of the island's inhabitants."

"The most captivating inhabitant I've ever seen," Connor pronounced with a broad grin. "I'd have had to have been blind not to notice what's going on—so would nearly everyone else aboard this ship. By the way, who is she?"

Ryan experienced a sharp twinge of jealousy at the thought of the other men admiring Hillary's beauty, then laughed inwardly at himself for behaving like a lovesick fool. "An Englishwoman by the name of Hillary Reynolds. She lives with her uncle on a vanilla plantation not far from Papeete." A slow, engimatic smile touched his lips as he added, "And if all goes as planned, Miss Reynolds will soon become my wife."

"Your wife?" echoed Connor. His darkly attractive features displayed both surprise and disbelief. "Are you serious, Ryan?"

"Never more so."

"But what about—"

"Alison Bromfield and I were never formally engaged," Ryan pointedly reminded him. He frowned, his blue-green eyes glistening coldly now. "There may have been an understanding between our families, but our personal relationship did not quite meet Alison's expectations."

"Yes," the first mate now somberly recalled, "she did make quite a scene in front of everyone there to see us off that day, didn't she?" Connor well remembered how the spoiled and pampered only child of Ebenezer Bromfield had clung so possessively to Ryan on the wharf three years ago, demanding that he marry her before sailing away. When he had refused, with as much tact and kindness as possible under the circumstances, the beautiful but shrewish Miss Bromfield had vengefully announced to the startled crowd of family and friends gathered about them that she and Ryan had agreed to wed just as soon as "this last voyage" was completed.

"There was little I could do to smooth things over before leaving," Ryan grimly reiterated. "But it no longer matters."

"Then you're really planning to marry this English-woman?"

"I am. And I'm giving strong consideration to the notion of returning here to Tahiti and settling down. You know me as well as anyone, Connor—you're aware of the fact that Alison wasn't completely off the mark that day. This *will* more than likely be my last voyage."

"What about your family?"

"They'll have no choice but to abide by my decision."

"I see," murmured the other man. Since he did know Ryan as well as anyone, he knew it would be useless to try to dissuade him from either course of action. Once Ryan Gallagher made up his mind, there was no changing it. That's why he's been such a damned good whaling master, Connor mused to himself.

"Blast it, man, you needn't sound so down in the mouth about it!" Ryan growled in mock severity. A disarming grin lit his handsome face as he revealed, "After all, I'm going to recommend that you be given command of the *Falcon* once I've become a land-lubber." He stood and wordlessly extended his hand. Connor, rising to his feet as well, moved forward to grip it with his own.

"I can't say I haven't dreamt of being her master," the first mate confided with an answering grin. Growing serious in the next instant, he couldn't resist asking, "Are you sure about all this, Ryan?"

"About Hillary—yes. About abandoning the sea— not entirely, at least not yet. To tell the truth, I've been toying with the idea of starting up a small shipping line of my own for the past couple of years. David's well able to run the family business. He was groomed for it, whereas I was destined from birth to feel a quarterdeck beneath my feet." He shook Connor's hand once more before releasing it, then came from behind the desk as his friend and chief officer turned to take his leave.

"If you truly intend to marry the young woman,

then you'd best step up your courtship," advised Connor, the irrepressible twinkle returning to his golden eyes. "Stokely's proven his worth as ship's carpenter many times, and he'll more than likely have the job done within the week, just as he said."

"A week ought to be time enough," Ryan drawled lazily. He clapped the other man on the back amiably before sending him on his way with instructions to go to the galley and tell Josiah, the cook and therefore the most feared man aboard ship save for the captain, to come to his quarters before commencing preparations for the evening meal.

Alone again while awaiting the arrival of the burly, perennially scowling Josiah, Ryan wandered back to the desk and sank down into the sun-warmed chair. His pensive gaze scanned the cabin, his brain making a mental note of its contents. The entire room was a tribute to three generations of one whaling family, for both his father and grandfather had commanded the *Falcon* before him. If he carried through on his plans to retire from the sea, he'd be breaking an age-old Gallagher tradition.

It's time, his mind's inner voice supported what his heart already knew. It was time to accustom himself to another kind of existence, to discover once again what it was like to live with his fellow human beings—men *and* women—on the land.

He wanted no other woman but Hillary by his side when he set about relearning life's simple pleasures . . . and, God willing, he would have her.

VI

"I will come with you." Tevaite grasped the side of the wagon and lifted a foot to the step board.

"No. Please, I . . . I want to go alone," Hillary insisted. She gave the older woman a brief smile of apology as she settled her skirts about her on the seat and took up the reins. "Besides, you said yourself the pods need attention this morning. Please tell my uncle I'll be back well before noon."

"But why must you—" Tevaite started to question again, only to break off when her young mistress flicked the long straps of leather above the horse's head. The worn springs creaked in protest as the wagon wheels rolled down the tree-shaded drive to the main road.

The day promised to be one of those gloriously warm and lazy ones for which Tahiti was famous. The morning air was fresh and scented with the wondrous aroma of flowers, the endlessly diversified landscape aglow with sunlight, but Hillary could not shake the heaviness of her heart.

Hillary Reynolds, what are you doing? an inner voice indignantly demanded. She had vowed not to return to Papeete until receiving news of Ryan's departure, and yet she was on her way to town now. You could not stay away, could you?

Lifting her chin in a gesture of self-defiance, she told herself once more that it would be cowardly and absurd to let Ryan Gallagher prevent her from going about her business. Starcross was in need of supplies —while that was true, she was using it as an excuse to rationalize her decision. She had a nagging feeling that neither Tevaite nor her uncle had been fooled. The two of them had looked at her, and each other, so strangely when she had told them she was going. They had seemed unaccountably perturbed at the news. Uncle Denholm had said little, but Tevaite had raised a number of thoroughly unconvincing objections.

Hillary sighed disconsolately and gave a flutter of the reins. She reached up to reposition the unadorned straw hat atop her head. Her lustrous raven tresses were pinned into a rather severe chignon upon the nape of her neck, while her beguiling curves were encased in a plain, serviceable gown of dove gray cotton. The lace-collared neckline was buttoned all the way to her throat, the long fitted sleeves fastened at her wrists, so that the whole effect was one of unapproachable primness. It was as if her guilty conscience had demanded she arm herself with an outward show of rigidness and decorum—not only as a penance for her body's traitorous response to a certain sea captain the night before last, but also in order that she would appear less desirable to that same captain should she perchance encounter him while in town.

Perchance? the voice derisively challenged. Isn't it true that you—

"Stop it!" Hillary blurted out, totally exasperated with herself *and* her conscience. The chestnut gelding slowed and cocked back an ear at her in confusion. "Not you, boy." She smiled as she gently flicked the reins again. The smile faded once the horse resumed its unhurried pace, and Hillary's silken brow creased into a frown of growing apprehension.

The waterfront in Papeete was alive with its usual flurry of activity. Since it was a Monday, the market was even more crowded than usual. Hillary returned the waves and greetings of several acquaintances as she guided the horse and wagon to her customary stopping place beneath the trees. She tried to concentrate on what she was planning to buy, but she could not. With a will of its own, her gaze traveled ahead to where the three masts of the *Falcon* towered above the wharf.

Was he there on the ship now? she wondered breathlessly, her violet eyes wide and sparkling with uncontrollable interest. Was he below in his quarters at that particular moment, in the small, cluttered cabin that had been so effectively dominated by his presence?

"I wasn't expecting an escort."

A loud gasp broke from Hillary's lips as she jumped in alarm. Twisting about abruptly on the wagon seat, she found herself staring down into the piercing, aquamarine depths of Ryan Gallagher's eyes. He met her startled gaze squarely, a roguish smile lighting the sun-bronzed planes of his face.

"Wha . . . what did you say?" she choked out, groaning inwardly when she felt the hot color rising to her face. Dear Lord, where had he come from? She had been taken unawares by his sudden appearance, and she felt herself growing more unnerved by his close proximity with each passing second. While it was true that she had been fully prepared to catch a glimpse of him while in Papeete, she had *not* expected to have him standing mere inches away and negligently bracing a hand on the wagon as he was doing now. She felt all her firm resolve to treat him with coolness and detachment melting away. Painfully vivid memories of what she had allowed him to do to her that night on Moorea came flooding back into the forefront of her mind. Why, oh why did I come here today? she wondered desperately.

"I said I wasn't expecting an escort. And certainly had no idea you'd be the one to come." His smile broadened, making him look more devilishly irresistible than ever.

Hillary averted her gaze and swallowed hard. She was about to bid him a curt farewell and drive on when the meaning of his words finally sank in. "What are you talking about?" she demanded in mingled puzzlement and annoyance. "I'm not here as any sort of escort, and most assuredly not for *you!*"

Ryan's handsome countenance sobered a bit. "Then you don't know about your uncle's invitation?" he asked, even though he had already guessed the truth.

"My uncle's invitation?" echoed Hillary, still baffled. Realization dawned on her in the next instant, prompting her eyes to grow very round. Good heavens, she thought in growing dismay, surely Uncle Denholm hadn't actually—

"Mahi conveyed the message to me last night. Your uncle was kind enough to invite me to lunch at Starcross today." His eyes twinkled across at her affectionately as he gave a low chuckle. "I should have known you had no part in it."

"Of course I had no part in it!"

"Nevertheless, I fully intend to keep my word to your uncle. And whatever the reason you've come to town, you might as well take me along when you return home.''

"I'll do no such thing!" she retorted indignantly. She bristled beneath his amused gaze, her emotions in an upheaval once more. "I'm terribly sorry, Captain Gallagher, but since my uncle neglected to inform me of his invitation—an invitation that never should have been issued *or* accepted—I do not feel compelled to honor it!" She turned away and snatched up the reins again, her obvious intent to drive away.

Without warning, Ryan's large hand shot out to close upon both of hers. "It's time we settled things between us, my love," he decreed in a deep, vibrant tone that sent a shiver dancing up Hillary's spine.

She caught her breath when her gaze encountered the disturbing intensity of his. Her thoughts were in utter turmoil, and she was greatly distressed by a sudden recurrence of the urge to cast herself into his strong arms and dissolve into tears. Taking refuge in anger, she wrenched her hands away and feelingly proclaimed, "There is nothing to settle! Don't you understand? I never want to see you again!"

Before he could offer a response, she pivoted back around on the seat and snapped the reins together. The wagon lurched forward as the startled horse took off, but Ryan held fast. In one swift motion, he swung up agilely into the wagon and snatched the reins from Hillary's hands. Forced to move over when he sat down beside her, she was at first too shocked to utter a protest. It wasn't until they had traveled well past the market that she came to life again and gave voice to her outrage.

"Why, how . . . how dare you!" she sputtered furiously, her eyes ablaze. "Get out of my wagon!"

When he neither spoke nor complied, she made a desperate attempt to regain control of the reins. Ryan, however, easily maintained his grip. Hillary then gathered up her skirts and whirled about to seek escape by jumping, but Ryan quickly intervened. Transferring the reins to one hand, he caught her about the waist and roughly hauled her back against him. She gasped when her backside made jolting contact with the hard wooden seat, and she struggled futilely against the bronzed, sinewy arm clamped like a band of iron about her midriff. They had reached the outskirts of Papeete now and were headed southward.

"Relax, my love," Ryan commanded with quiet authority. "I only want to talk to you. I give you my word I'll not—"

"The word of a whaler?" she parried with biting sarcasm, refusing to surrender. She inhaled sharply when his arm tightened about her.

"I'm not ashamed of what I am, Hillary. Even so, no man should be judged by the actions of others."

"My judgment of you, Ryan Gallagher, would be ill enough if it were based solely on what you have said and . . . and *done* to me!" Her beautiful face grew even more stormy when she heard him laugh. She was held so closely against him that she could feel the mirth rumbling upward from deep in his chest. Stung by what she perceived to be his scornful amusement at her shame, she fought back hot, bitter tears and made an unexpected lunge for the reins.

"What the devil—" Ryan ground out as she threw herself forward and grasped the leather straps. She tugged on them with all her might, then flung about and delivered a surprisingly forceful blow to the clean-shaven ruggedness of Ryan's chin. He swore, his eyes glinting dangerously as he tried to force her

146

back down to the seat, but she managed to break free. Trying to control the nervously stamping horse with one hand, he caught at her skirts with the other, his action followed by a loud, ripping noise as the fabric gave way. Heedless of the damage to her gown, Hillary scrambled down from the wagon and went crashing into the thick foliage on the downhill side of the road.

"Hillary!" Ryan hurriedly looped off the reins and jumped down to give chase. "Blast it, Hillary, come back here!"

She heard him calling her, but she did not stop. Glancing anxiously over her shoulder, she darted headlong through the clinging, fragrant shrubbery, only to emerge moments later onto a wide, deserted beach. She gathered up her skirts and flew across the sun-washed sand, almost blinded by her tears and driven by an overwhelming need to escape from Ryan and the turbulent confusion of her feelings for him.

Though she was well-accustomed to the heat and humidity, and her body conditioned by a daily regimen of physical activity, Hillary was nevertheless soon outdistanced by her pursuer's long, hard-muscled strides. She cried out when she felt his fingers closing about her arm. Her hat had been torn off by the wind, and her thick raven curls defied the restraint of pins to tumble down wildly about her shoulders as she battled Ryan's efforts to subdue her. He forced her roughly about, his other hand swooping up to the back of her head to entangle within her hair.

"Hillary, listen to me!" he commanded, his voice whipcord sharp.

"No!" She squirmed and struck out at him, but to no avail. A loud gasp broke from her lips when his arm clamped about her waist and yanked her up hard against him.

"Whether it pleases you or not, my love, you *will* hear me out," Ryan asserted in a low, resonant tone that warned her to obey. Hillary's luminous gaze shot upward to meet his, only to decipher therein a gleam of unmistakably menacing intent. A small tremor of fear shook her, and her eyes fell hastily before his. Though she despised herself for her cowardice, she ceased her struggles. She stood quiet and still, locked against him in breathless anticipation, refusing to look at him yet acutely conscious of his eyes upon her. Several long seconds passed.

Suddenly, he loosed his hold upon her. Hillary was astonished at her abrupt release, and even more surprised when Ryan muttered a savage curse beneath his breath and flung away from her. He took only a few steps toward the water's edge before rounding on her again.

"Damn it, woman, I don't know whether to kiss you or thrash you!" At that moment, he looked entirely capable of acting upon *both* urges.

Hillary's temper flared anew, and her anger made her brave enough to counter, "If you attempt to do either, Ryan Gallagher, I'll . . . I'll—"

"You'll scream?" he obligingly supplied, his mouth curving into a sardonic half smile. He slowly shook his head. "No, my love, you had the opportunity to do just that before we left Papeete. As a matter of fact, you've chosen to ignore that particular option every time we've been together. Admit it, my dear Miss Reynolds—you're not as averse to my presence as you'd like to make both of us believe."

"Why, I . . . I'll admit no such thing!" she indignantly retorted. Her eyes widened in renewed

148

apprehension when he took a step toward her, but she proudly stood her ground. Forced to tilt her head back in order to meet his gaze, she felt a strange fluttering of her heart.

"Can you honestly still deny what's between us?" he challenged, his deep voice scarcely above a whisper and his eyes aglow with a disarming mixture of tenderness and desire. "After what happened on Moorea—"

"Nothing happened on Moorea!" snapped Hillary, then blushed fierily at the implication of her words. Her gaze dropped again as she hastened to amend, "What I meant to say was that the . . . the incident should never have occurred!" She swallowed hard before raising her tear-filled eyes to his once more and bitterly proclaiming, "But rest assured, Captain Gallagher, I intend to put it completely from my mind, since indeed *nothing* truly happened!"

Ryan subjected her to a long, scrutinizing look. His handsome brow creased into a frown as his eyes traveled intimately over her flushed, stormy countenance. Finally, he smiled softly and asked, "Is that why you're so angry with me? Because I didn't—"

"No!" She glared up at him murderously, her irateness growing when his own eyes twinkled back at her in fond amusement.

"Believe me when I say nothing would have given me greater pleasure. But I want more than that from you, Hillary Reynolds. Much more."

She found herself unable to offer him the scathing reply that rose to her lips. The sweet-scented breeze played havoc with her long raven locks, just as Ryan Gallagher's nearness—and words—played havoc with her senses. She stared up at him in furious bewilderment, her mind racing to find the elusive answer to her dilemma.

"The *Falcon* will be seaworthy again in a week's time," Ryan quietly announced. "I would postpone her departure if I could, but the men are anxious to get home, and I must make all haste to deliver the oil to New Bedford." He took hold of her shoulders and gazed deeply into her wide, sparkling eyes. "We will be husband and wife before my ship sails."

Hillary's mouth fell open, and she blinked up at him in stupefaction. Good heavens, had he really said what she thought she'd heard? No, it . . . it wasn't possible!

"As you know, an inadequate amount of time prevented my courtship of you from following the usual, more conventional dictates." His fingers lightly caressed the soft flesh of her shoulders beneath the unbecoming gray cotton, and another warm, beguiling smile touched his lips. "But since it was all going to come to this anyway, I fail to see—"

"What are you talking about?" she breathlessly demanded, feeling as if in a daze.

"Three days. I'll allow you three days in which to plan the wedding—no more. I don't want to waste a single moment of the time we have left to us," he told her, the utterly masculine resonance of his voice making Hillary tingle all over. His blue-green eyes smoldered with barely controlled passion as he slowly drew her closer. Although she was perilously light-headed, the significance of his words finally sank in and brought her crashing back to reality.

Dear Lord, thought Hillary in growing fury, he was actually *commanding* her to marry him! She had never expected to hear him mention marriage at all, much less in this despicably high-handed manner!

"Take your hands off me!" She was too enraged to wait for his compliance. Her hands flew up to push at his chest, and she forcefully propelled herself from beneath his grasp. Ryan made no move to stop her as she clutched at her skirts and began scurrying back across the sand toward the road. A gleam of satisfaction lit his eyes when she came to an abrupt halt, then spun about to confront him again. "How dare you *order* me to marry you, Ryan Gallagher! Even if I were the least bit inclined in that direction—which I most assuredly am *not*—I would never, for one moment, even consider accepting such a . . . a loathsome, offensive, cold-blooded propos—"

"Cold-blooded? Hardly that, my love," he dissented in a low tone brimming with laughter. "My blood was set afire the first moment I saw you. And as was proven on Moorea, yours is every bit as hot as mine."

A fresh wave of embarrassment washed over Hillary. She trembled with the force of her indignation while her blazing eyes hurled invisible daggers at Ryan's head. Undaunted, he sauntered forward to tower above her again. She took an instinctive step backward, battling the temptation to flee—*and* the temptation to discover whether or not he would employ any physical methods of persuasion . . .

"It avails you nothing to try to conceal your true self beneath such puritanical trappings, sweet Hillary," he observed, his eyes making a swift, critical appraisal of her attire before returning to her face. "You are a beautiful, spirited, and passionate woman. Once we are wed, I will delight in teaching you all the pleasures of love."

She gasped at the bold possessiveness of his gaze. Hastily regaining her composure, she asserted quite vehemently, "There will be no wedding! When I marry, Captain Gallagher, it will be because I wish to do so and not simply because an arrogant scoundrel such as you—a *whaler*—has the insolence and audacity to decree it!" She whirled about, her furious steps taking her only a short distance away before she turned to face him again. Her beauty was heightened by her anger, and Ryan found it difficult to restrain himself from catching her up in his arms and kissing her until she begged for mercy.

"And furthermore," continued Hillary, obviously striving to convince herself as well as him, "I would never consider marrying a man of the sea! I would never be content to sit at home and wait while my husband went . . . went traipsing about the world, doing God-only-knows-what and . . . and easing his loneliness with other women while I worried if he were perhaps lying dead or injured somewhere—"

"That is not a valid argument in this case, my love. You see, I've decided to abandon my wild and adventurous ways and settle down."

"You . . . you have?"

"I want a different kind of life now. One that includes a traditional home and family. One that includes *you.*"

"Be that as it may, I don't wish to live anywhere but here. Tahiti is my home now!"

"And it shall continue to be so. Once I have fulfilled my obligations by completing this last voyage, I intend to make it *my* home as well." He smiled at her look of incredulity.

"You . . . you do?" she breathed, her eyes very round and luminous. Ryan nodded in silent confirmation, then unhurriedly closed the distance between them once more. He lifted a hand to tenderly smooth a wayward curl from her forehead. She did not protest. Her pulses leapt at his touch, and she found herself mesmerized by the vibrant glow in his eyes, by the way the sun's rays lit the golden streaks in his dark hair and cast intriguing shadows across his handsome, softly smiling face.

"We are well matched, Hillary Reynolds. Well matched in both temperament and passion," he murmured, his deep voice tinged with huskiness. He finally took her in his arms and claimed her unresisting lips in a warm, splendidly rapturous kiss that did little to help the chaotic state of her mind. When he released her nearly a full minute later, she was left feeling anything but defiant. She was only dimly aware of him saying, "Since you may require a little time to become accustomed to the thought of our marriage, I will wait until tomorrow to speak to your uncle. You can break the news to him yourself first if you like, but he *will* be told by tomorrow at the latest."

Hillary could do nothing more than stare dazedly up at Ryan. She was expecting him to kiss her again, but he did not. Unaware of the great effort it was costing him to hold back, she swallowed her disappointment and offered no objection when he silently led her back up to the road.

Still stunned and preoccupied, she failed to acknowledge Anthony Warren's greeting as she and Ryan drove through Papeete a few minutes later. Anthony was startled, and most unpleasantly so, to see that it was none other than the bold American captain who was driving Hillary's wagon while she sat—with what to his jealous mind's eye appeared to be complacence—beside him.

It was then that Anthony came to a decision, a decision he had been postponing until he felt the time was right. *Hang it all,* he told himself with uncharacteristic vehemence as he stood and watched the wagon ramble past the quay, *the time is now!*

*　　　*　　　*

153

"Thank you, Tehura. That should do for now. You may go and help your mother upstairs." Hillary drew the last loaf of bread from the oven, then straightened and released a sigh as she set the pan atop the flour-coated table. Casting a quick glance toward the open doorway, she idly noted that the afternoon light was already fading into dusk. She sighed again, recalling how Tevaite had protested such late work in the kitchen. The baking of bread was always done of a morning, the older woman had reminded her. But, thought Hillary as her eyes clouded anew, Tevaite had not known of the desperate need to divert her troubled thoughts elsewhere, *anywhere* but on Ryan Gallagher. Unfortunately, her efforts had met with little success.

"She is not there, Missy," said Tehura, her melodious young voice bringing her mistress back to the present. "She is with the *vanira.*"

"Oh. Of course," Hillary murmured, remembering the chore of transferring the vanilla pods to the special warming hut each evening. "Well then, perhaps you should occupy yourself with some of those books Pastor Witherspoon sent."

"We have no school now," the girl pointed out. She leaned upon the broomstick and smiled impishly, her almond-shaped brown eyes twinkling. "You teach school to the *tapena* now!" Hillary was dismayed to feel herself blushing. Feigning indifference, she turned back to extract the already cooled loaves from the pans.

"Don't be ridiculous. You know as well as I that school will resume as soon as the vanilla has been shipped. Captain Gallagher has nothing whatsoever to do with it."

"That is not what my mother says. My mother, she says—"

"Tehura!" Hillary admonished, her voice sharper than she intended. "I'm sorry, but I . . . I do not wish to discuss Captain Gallagher any further. Now please run along."

Tehura, giving an eloquent shrug of her deep golden shoulders, obediently set aside the broom and padded across to the doorway. Before disappearing outside, however, she braved one last, highly impertinent question.

"Do you become his *vahine* soon, Missy?"

Her mistress whirled about and shot her such a quelling look that she wisely took flight.

Hillary sank down into a chair and frowned at the smudges of flour on her dress. She had not bothered to tie on an apron. In spite of its soiled condition, the gown of pale rose dimity, which she had donned upon arriving back at Starcross, was still a good deal more becoming than the gray one she had worn earlier. Although, she mused, her prim garb hadn't discouraged Ryan in the least.

Lunch had been a disaster, or so it had seemed to *her*. It had lasted a mercifully short time. She had been forced to pretend nothing was amiss as Ryan and her uncle exchanged views upon a wide range of topics, from the weather in Tahiti and the production of vanilla, to how difficult it would no doubt be for a man who had been at sea the greater part of his life to suddenly embrace life on the shore. Almost certain her uncle had introduced *that* particular subject as a means of ferreting out the truth, Hillary had breathed an inward sigh of relief when Ryan, true to his word, had refrained from mentioning their "betrothal." Still, she had been on pins and needles throughout the whole affair, so much so that she could not recall exactly what Tevaite had served for the meal out on the verandah.

"Marriage," she whispered, her thoughts returning to Ryan's startling proposal—no, *command*—as she sat alone in the kitchen. What was she going to do?

The prospect of becoming Ryan Gallagher's wife did not alarm her as much as she might have expected. Quite the opposite, she realized, her face flaming at the wicked turn of her thoughts. She trembled anew at the memory of his kisses.

"No!" she defied aloud, jumping up from the chair to pace distractedly about the room. It was impossible! She couldn't marry a man she scarcely knew, even if he did possess the shameful ability to make her forget all else but his touch. How could she even be tempted to go through with it?

She had always vowed never to marry unless for love. Ever since she was naught but a girl, she had dreamt of what it would be like to fall in love, to experience the wild, sought-after madness of which she had heard so much. A wild, sought-after madness, her mind numbly repeated. It seemed to describe what she felt for Ryan.

What she felt for Ryan? Her violet eyes grew very wide and her heart pounded within her breast. Dear Lord, could it be . . . was it possible that she had fallen in love with Ryan Gallagher?

The fateful question remained unanswered, at least for the moment, as Anthony Warren suddenly materialized in the doorway. Hillary gaped at him in astonishment for a moment before gathering her wits about her and moving forward to greet him.

"Why, Anthony!" Hastily rolling down her sleeves and smoothing her skirts as she went, she managed a faint smile of welcome. "I . . . I did not know—"

"I came as soon as I could," he proclaimed with a

156

deep frown, his fingers tightening about the hat in his hand. Hillary, thinking that he was behaving quite unlike himself, stared at him in bemusement.

"Came as soon as you could?"

"Yes." His blue eyes glistened strangely, and there was a dull, angry flush to his aristocratic features that gave evidence of his intense displeasure. "I came to ask you something." Wasting no further time, he demanded, "What the deuce were you doing with Captain Gallagher today?"

"What?" she breathed in disbelief.

"I saw the two of you in town this morning. He was driving *your* wagon! Imagine my shock upon discovering that you were actually riding beside that . . . that blackguard!" The young Englishman fought against the jealousy-induced flaring of his temper, a temper that was rarely put to the test. "I've been unable to get it out of my mind the entire day. You told me there was nothing between you and Gallagher, and yet I saw the two of you together! Dash it, Hillary, the man always seems to turn up wherever you happen to be!"

Hillary was too stunned to offer an immediate reply. She was only dimly aware of Anthony striding past her to fling down his hat upon the table. When he turned back to her, his manner became more pleading than angry.

"Although there is no formal understanding between us, my dearest Miss Reynolds, I feel that my regard for you gives me the right to concern myself with your welfare. Therefore, I insist upon the truth—is he or is he not attempting to engage your affections?"

Hillary swallowed a sudden lump in her throat before replying in a voice that was not quite steady,

"While I am most grateful for your concern, Anthony, I fail to see why I should answer you at all."

"Because if there's even the slightest chance you're forming an attachment—" Breaking off, he crossed the room to stand directly before her. He drew himself rigidly erect, his pale features looking more Anglo-Saxon and patrician than ever above his stiff white collar as he declared a bit pompously, "If you're going to marry any man, that man will have to be me!"

His startling pronouncement was followed by a long, tension-filled silence. Hillary found herself musing that Anthony appeared every bit as surprised as herself. Anthony found himself musing that Hillary didn't appear to be overcome with joy. The two of them stared at each other, both knowing the truth but neither desirous of being the first to put it into words.

Finally, Anthony cleared his throat, smiled ruefully, and spoke with a note of self-mockery in his voice. "I should have expected as much. It was highly unrealistic of me to think you'd remain immune to the charm of any other man as long as I was around."

"Oh, Anthony, it . . . it has nothing to do with another man!" she told him earnestly, her eyes shining. "I'm sorry, but it's just that I don't care for you in that way. And, I think if you're truly honest with yourself, you'll find that your own feelings are far from what they should be. Dear Anthony, don't you see? It would be wrong of us to settle for anything less."

"And what about Gallagher?" his aching heart prompted him to retort. "Are your feelings what they should be for him?" He studied her beautiful face closely as her eyes fell and her cheeks grew rosy.

"I am not certain what my feelings for Captain Gallagher are."

"I see," murmured Anthony, though he didn't see at all. He slowly turned away from her to retrieve his hat from the table. Absently dusting the flour from the underside of the hat's brim as he headed for the doorway again, he could not refrain from pausing on his way out. "Promise me something, Hillary," he quietly directed, his gaze softening as she raised her eyes to his. "Promise you'll come to me if you should need help, that is . . . well, if things don't work out the way you want them to."

"Oh, Anthony." Fighting back tears, she threw her arms about his neck and hugged him close. "I wish I *could* love you the way you deserve to be loved," she feelingly declared. "And I do promise to come to you if I ever need help." She bestowed an affectionate but sisterly kiss upon his cheek before drawing away. It took him a moment to regain his composure.

"Well then, I suppose I should . . . be going. There seems to be a storm brewing, and I certainly don't want to get caught in a cloudburst after sundown." Settling his hat upon his fair head, he was about to make his reluctant exit when the sound of his name on Hillary's lips detained him.

"Anthony?"

"Yes, Hillary?" There was a faint glimmer of hope in his blue eyes as he gazed down at her.

Her own eyes were sparkling brightly, and she smiled up at him tremulously before appealing in a soft voice, "Please come again soon, dear friend."

Anthony, valiantly striving to conceal the pain and disappointment her words caused, nodded wordlessly and left. Hillary stared after him, watching until he disappeared around the corner of the

159

house. Her spirits were heavier than ever as she mentally shook herself and dashed impatiently at the tears that had finally begun coursing down her cheeks.

A short time later, when she was upstairs in her room dressing for supper, she wandered aimlessly over to the window and peered out at the darkening landscape. A thick mantle of clouds had begun rolling in from the sea to spread across the sky, blotting out the setting sun's last, yellow-orange fingers of light on the horizon. The wind, usually nothing more than a mere wisp of breeze in the evening hours, was quickly gathering velocity. Hillary watched as the palm trees bent and swayed in submission to nature's force, as the coco fronds were sent whipping about in the charged, rain-scented air. Anthony was right, she mused. There would indeed be a storm that night.

"A storm," she echoed aloud, her mouth twisting into a smile of appreciative irony. There was a storm of another kind already taking place in both her heart and her mind. She thought of Ryan . . . of Anthony . . . of all the unbelievable events of the day. Her emotions felt raw and strained to the limit, but she'd had enough of crying. She was a grown woman, not a child. Usually forthright and decisive, she detested the perpetual confusion that had plagued her ever since the maddening, overbearing, devastatingly handsome sea captain had come into her life.

But no more, she silently vowed, her eyes aglow with their brilliant amethyst fire. She would not allow herself to be manipulated by him or anyone else! If she did marry Ryan Gallagher, it would be because she wanted to, not because he had decreed it!

160

Spinning angrily about, she drew up short when a knock sounded at the door.

Tevaite sailed into the room, her perceptive gaze missing little as she smiled at her young mistress and announced, "Your uncle wishes you to join him. He is feeling well tonight. He wishes to eat downstairs."

"Thank you, Tevaite," murmured Hillary. "I'll only be a moment." The skirts of her white embroidered gown rustled softly as she moved across to the dressing table and took up her hairbrush. Acutely conscious of the other woman's eyes upon her, she could not prevent a slight, nervous trembling of her fingers. She hurriedly dragged the brush through her silken tresses, then expertly coiled them into a chignon and jammed the hairpins into place. Tevaite watched her all the while, finally breaking the silence when Hillary flung a lightweight shawl about her shoulders.

"The night grows cool," the Tahitian woman casually observed. "There will be rain soon. It is good Mr. Warren did not stay."

"How did you know Anthony had been here?" demanded Hillary, eyeing her suspiciously.

"Tehura saw him," Tevaite answered, her face inscrutable. Tehura had done more than just see him, she recalled with an inward smile. And like the dutiful daughter Tehura was, she had confided the results of her eavesdropping to her mother.

"Tehura sees entirely too much!" Hillary briskly asserted. Clutching the shawl tightly to her bosom, she went on to declare, "I would appreciate it very much if you would speak to her—or rather, *not* speak to her about something!" Tevaite merely responded with a look of questioning, wide-eyed innocence. Hillary sighed heavily before explaining, "I don't want you filling her head with ideas about . . . about

161

Captain Gallagher and me. As a matter of fact, I don't want you or anyone else here at Starcross to mention his name again!''

A slow, enigmatic smile spread across Tevaite's noble features. Her brown eyes shone with both affection and an understanding borne of life's seasoning.

"Truth not spoken is still truth, Miss Hillary." With that, she pivoted about gracefully on her heel and disappeared.

Hillary stared after her in perplexity. What *is* the truth? she asked herself. A sudden clap of thunder seemed to mock her. Muttering a decidedly unlady-like oath, she blew out the lamp and swept from the room.

VII

The crew of the *Falcon* hastened about on the pitching, rolling deck to secure the vessel against the gathering storm. The churning waters of Papeete's harbor swelled into whitecapped waves before the wind and slapped forcibly against the ship's hull. Ryan stood in the master's position on the quarter-deck, his deep voice ringing out above the din as he gave orders for the rigging to be checked and all hatches to be battened down.

"It's a good thing we're not still tied up at the quay!" remarked Connor beside him, forced to shout in order to be heard. "That temporary patch we put on her would likely be dashed to pieces by now!" He cast a wary eye on the roiling heavens. "Damn, but will you look at that sky? Black as midnight and not yet six o'clock!" The wind tore the words from his lips and threatened to send him crashing back against the railing.

"Looks like we're in for the devil of it, all right!" Ryan thundered back, his rugged features looking quite grim. He'd seen storms like this before, and he knew that the signs boded ill for the ships in the harbor as well as for the folk on shore. From April through June, there were long periods of calm, occasionally broken by exceptional tropical cyclones that tossed the smaller ships about like mere playthings and callously ripped apart the thatch-roofed huts of the natives.

Hillary. Her image suddenly floated across his mind. Would Starcross be spared the storm's savage fury? he wondered, his heart twisting at the thought of his beloved in the midst of such danger. But then, he reasoned with himself, she had lived in Tahiti for years and was of a certainty more familiar than he with the need to take precautionary measures. Nonetheless, he could not shake a strange uneasiness as his vigilant gaze drifted northward.

"The ship's secured, Captain!" yelled Connor. Ryan, acknowledging his first mate's report with a curt nod, gave the order for the crew to get below. He shot one last look in the direction where he knew Starcross lay, then battled the strengthening gale as he made his way across deck to the companionway. There was nothing to do now but wait.

The storm lashed mercilessly at the earth for what seemed like hours. The winds howled with dreadful ferocity, lightning flashed repeatedly across the sky and thunder roared its earsplitting response, the dark clouds whirled in a frenzied, circular motion as warm air collided with cool, but, strangely, there was no rain.

The men aboard the *Falcon* waited in the dimly lit closeness below, listening intently while the ship careened violently to and fro in the raging swells. Ryan and Connor sat together in the captain's quarters, their gazes drifting frequently upward to the skylight as they alternately talked and lapsed into long periods of silence. Great sheets of water, swept upward by the relentless whirlwind, crashed forcefully against the barred panes of glass. There was nothing else to be seen, save for an occasional glimpse of the black, boiling heavens.

Finally, when it seemed the worst had passed, Ryan, Connor, and the crew returned above deck to survey the destruction. The winds had calmed somewhat but continued to buffet and rock the ship. The atmosphere was still charged.

Glancing up at the sky speculatively, Ryan scowled at what his eyes beheld. "Witch's cauldron," he murmured, half to himself. The storm was defying any familiar pattern. There should have been a deluge by now, instead of this peculiar heaviness in the air.

"It looks as though she weathered it all right, Captain," pronounced Connor, his own gaze making a broad sweep of the deck as the men hurriedly checked the rigging. "I'll have the patch inspected right away." He bellowed the order, then gripped the railing for support and peered across the churning waters of the harbor toward Papeete. "The town didn't fare so well."

Ryan turned, his eyes following the direction of the other man's gaze. The land was bathed in a bleak gray light, so that the devastation wrought by the storm was clearly visible. The stalls and tables of the market were now nothing but splintered bits of wood littering the street. The roofs of several buildings had been torn asunder, and a number of uprooted trees lay sprawled along the shore. The windows of both the French and British consulates had been shattered, though the houses themselves had sustained no significant damage.

The town's inhabitants, some of them injured by the flying debris, slowly began emerging from whatever shelter they had sought, their faces appear-

165

ing dazed with a conflicting mixture of dismay and gratitude. Miraculously, the quay was still intact, as were all of the larger ships in the harbor and most of the smaller ones. The destruction was not as widespread as in past storms—this time, there had been no loss of human life.

Suddenly, the church bells began ringing. Ryan, wondering at first if their tolling was perhaps a signal that the danger had passed, found his gaze drawn instinctively northward once more. His blue-green eyes filled with stunned disbelief as they noted the huge cloud of smoke billowing upward from the base of the twin, towering peaks of Mount Aorai and Mount Orohena.

Sudden alarm gripped him. Recalling in the back of his mind that Starcross was nestled in the coastal valley just north of the mountains, he watched as the swirling gusts of wind fanned the rapidly thickening smoke in that direction. *Hillary! Dear God, what if the fire—*

"What the bloody hell is that?" Connor blurted out as he, too, caught sight of the smoke. "Why, it . . . it's a fire!"

"Launch the boats, Mr. Reid!" Ryan commanded sharply.

"The boats?" the first mate echoed in bewilderment.

"Aye, the boats! We're going ashore!" His eyes gleamed with an almost savage light, and his mouth tightened into a thin line. If there was even the remotest possibility that Hillary was in danger, he had to be there to help her.

"Going ashore, Captain? For what purpose?" Connor asked, still puzzled. It wasn't like him to question Ryan's judgment, but he was concerned about leaving the ship when the weather remained

166

so unsettled.

"To fight a fire, Mr. Reid! Now give the order, damn it! There's no time to lose!"

The coconut rats were the first to signal the oncoming blaze. Even before the telltale smoke began choking the air at Starcross, a veritable horde of the small, seldom-seen rodents appeared. Screeching in terror as they scurried across the wind-lashed grounds, they instinctively sought escape from the encroaching heat by heading toward the sea.

Hillary stood just within the doorway and watched in horrified fascination as the panic-stricken creatures raced past. Shuddering involuntarily at the rather ghoulish sight, she was grateful when her uncle moved to her side and placed a comforting arm about her shoulders.

"Why are they running like that?" she wondered aloud in perplexity. "What could be driving them from the forest?"

"The storm, perhaps," suggested Denholm in a deceptively off-handed manner. "The winds may have been a good deal worse up in the mountains." Secretly, he was more than a little concerned. In all the years he had lived in Tahiti, he had never seen anything like it. Something was very wrong.

"Then we ought to be doubly thankful for the fact that we were spared," murmured Hillary. Although the gale had ripped apart two of the outbuildings, the main house had sustained only minor damage. Tevaite had already begun organizing the natives, many of whom had fled their huts to seek shelter at the house, into groups to clean up the debris.

What about Ryan? she suddenly wondered. Had his ship come through it all right?

"We'd best get back inside, my dear," Denholm pronounced, tossing up a worried glance at the sky again. "Judging from the look of things, the storm's far from over."

"Yes, but it's a bit unusual, isn't it?" she remarked, her own eyes full of inexplicable disquiet as she, too, perused the dark, ominous clouds. "It should have started to rain before now." She slipped from beneath her uncle's arm and pressed a quick kiss upon his pale cheek. "You go on. I'll be inside shortly. I must speak to Tevaite about the children. I don't want them outside in the midst of all this thunder and lightning."

"Perhaps you'd better tell Tevaite to have everyone come into the house. There's no need to take any risks." Sparing one last narrow look overhead, he leaned heavily on his cane and returned inside.

The frantic exodus of the rats had ended by now. Hillary gathered up her skirts and set off across the verandah to where the older woman was directing the cleanup efforts. Several of the Tahitians continued to glance up warily at the sky as they hurried to do Tevaite's bidding. The still turbulent winds sent up such a fierce rustling of the leaves that it was difficult for her to be heard.

Hillary's long white skirts billowed and flapped about her legs. Her hair had come unbound, and the wind tugged almost painfully at the thick raven tresses as she bent her head against the force of the gusts. Reaching Tevaite's side, she raised her voice to declare, "We must get the children inside again!"

Tevaite nodded in agreement, then prophesied, "There will be rain soon! Much rain!"

"Tell everyone to leave the work until tomorrow," instructed Hillary. "If there's to be more of this, we—" She broke off when her nose was suddenly assailed by a faint, acrid smell. Before she had time to ponder its origin, a wispy fog of smoke blanketed the treetops and descended upon the clearing. "Why, something's burning!" she breathlessly proclaimed, her eyes becoming very round. "Something is . . . is on fire!" No sooner had the words left her mouth than the smoke thickened, and along with it the pungent odor of scorched vegetation carried on the wind.

The natives all ceased their efforts and stared in surprised bewilderment at one another and up at the sky. Within seconds, a mysterious amber glow appeared in the south. They were further baffled to hear a volley of strange, staccato noises, the sound of which was much like distant gunfire.

"Merciful heavens, Tevaite, wha . . . what could it be?" Hillary stammered in growing alarm as she gazed southward.

The older woman frowned thoughtfully and said, "I will send Mahi to see!" She hurriedly summoned her brother, who wasted no time in flinging himself onto a horse's back and riding away to find the source of the blaze. When he returned minutes later, he was out of breath and his face wore a look of undisguised terror.

"The *auahi*, the fire, it burns the land! It comes this way, Missy!" he gasped out. "It comes this way!"

"Dear Lord!" whispered Hillary, sudden fear gripping her heart as she raised a hand to her throat and gazed wide-eyed at the intensifying light in the sky. She whirled back to face the men, women, and children standing in front of the house. More than twenty pairs of eyes were fixed upon her—the Tahitians were obviously looking to her for guidance. What was she to tell them? What was she to do?

She repeated a silent, desperate prayer for wisdom.

The answer came in the form of her uncle, who had become worried upon detecting the unmistakable scent of smoke that suddenly wafted through the house.

"Hillary, what is it? What is burning?" Denholm called out from the doorway.

Hastening up the front steps, Hillary quickly told him what Mahi had said, then cried above the wind's ceaseless roar, "What shall we do, Uncle? How are we going to save Starcross if the fire—"

"Tell them to get all the buckets they can find!" he tersely directed, his voice gaining strength from alarm so that he sounded more like the man he had once been. "The roofs must be wet down right away! And tell Mahi to take some of the men to the fields— they're to dig a trench to the south and fill it with water!" Denholm Reynolds had never been forced to battle a fire in Tahiti before, but he had once done so back in England. Drawing on this long-ago knowledge, he gave further instructions to his niece, then took himself back inside to gather up several important papers and a few treasured mementos, along with some food, blankets, and medicines. He could only pray they wouldn't need the latter.

Hillary took charge of the bucket brigade, which was comprised mostly of women and children. She drew water from the well again and again, while the others hurriedly emptied the wooden pails onto the woven thatch roofs of the house and outbuildings. It was extremely tiring work that yielded scarcely enough results to be noticeable. Their labors were greatly impeded by the wind, for it whipped across the thatch and took with it much of the hard-won moisture.

The air grew heavier with smoke, and the popping sounds became more distinct as the fire swept closer.

The fresh scent of rain mingled with the smell of burning wood, but still the swirling black clouds did not release their needed bounty.

Dear God, please let it rain! Hillary beseeched in growing dread. She blinked back tears of helpless frustration, knowing that they would all soon have to abandon their efforts and take refuge nearer the sea. As much as she loved Starcross, she could not risk the lives of any of the Tahitians, nor her uncle's. But she would remain and fight against the consuming flames until the last possible moment.

The flames owed their origin to a single, well-placed flash of lightning, which had touched off a blaze in the dense undergrowth of the interior forest. The brush there was drier than the rest of the foliage and so ignited more readily. As it burned, the intense heat generated by the blaze caused the surrounding and taller vegetation to be kindled as well, and also caused the coconuts to explode, setting up the rapid, gunshot-like noises. There were in actuality two fronts to the fire—one close to the ground, the other following seconds later in the trees. As was all too evident, the blustery winds played a crucial role in the path of destruction, for they provoked the flames ever onward.

"Hillary, come! We cannot delay any longer!" Denholm seized her arm and began tugging her insistently along with him. The Tahitians had already fled, leaving only Tevaite behind with Hillary and her uncle. "We've done all we can!" he reiterated. His hand fell away when a spasm of coughing shook him, and Tevaite moved to place a supportive arm about his frail shoulders.

"We must go!" she sternly proclaimed, grabbing the younger woman's hand. "What will be will be, Miss Hillary! We must go!"

Hillary's anguished gaze shifted from them to the house, now silhouetted with stark clarity against the sky's fiery, yellow-orange glow. The smoke, wave after billowing wave of it, was becoming so thick and oppressive that it was difficult to breathe.

"There has to be something, some way—" She broke off, choking back a sob as she turned away in defeat. She knew there was little hope that Starcross would make it through the fire unscathed, in spite of all they had done. It seemed traitorous, somehow, to abandon it and flee.

Please, God! Please—

"Why, someone . . . someone's coming!" Denholm suddenly exclaimed in surprise. Hillary spun about to see two wagonloads of men, along with another half-dozen men on horseback, barreling down the front drive through the curtain of smoke. She gasped in stunned disbelief when her glistening eyes fell upon the lead rider.

"Ryan!" she whispered hoarsely, her hand tightening almost painfully about Tevaite's. Her blood pounded in her ears, and she experienced an inexplicable yet powerful sense of relief. It struck her in that moment that she had never been so glad to see anyone. His coming prompted a new surge of hope to spring to life within her—and caused her heart to stir as never before.

Reining to an abrupt halt before Hillary, Ryan leapt from his mount and immediately began thundering orders to his men. They jumped down from the wagons and hurried to obey, some of them heading for the house while others straightaway made for the fields. Within seconds, the grounds were alive with activity and shouts as the whalers took up buckets and wielded shovels.

Ryan turned to Denholm and declared above the

172

commotion, "We'll make a firebreak around the house! As soon as the flames move closer, we'll set a backfire!" His gaze finally fastened upon Hillary, and his features softened for only an instant before he scowled darkly and roared, "What the devil do you think you're doing, you little fool? Take the horses and get out of here!"

Stung by what she perceived to be his unwarranted harshness, Hillary glared back at him and defiantly retorted, "This is *my* home, Captain Gallagher! I have a perfect right to be here!"

"Not if you're endangering your life, and theirs as well!" he shot back, nodding curtly toward Denholm and Tevaite. "Now do as I say, damn it, and—"

"No! If you and your men are here, then there's no reason why I shouldn't stay as well!" She turned to her uncle and said, "You and Tevaite go on. I'll join you when—"

She got no further, for Ryan suddenly scooped her up in his arms and carried her to one of the wagons. Though she protested loudly and struggled within his grasp, she could not sway him. He deposited her none too gently on the seat, then quickly helped her uncle up beside her. Without waiting to be told, Tevaite climbed up into the second wagon.

"If we're successful, and there's every reason to think we will be, the fire will be diverted around the house and fields!" Ryan assured them. Before Hillary could do anything more than cast him a look of mingled fury and concern, he raised a hand and brought it slapping vigorously down upon the horse's rump. Hillary was forced to handle the reins when the startled animal took off. Tevaite followed close behind in the other wagon—the remaining horses had been tied to the back, and they snorted in growing panic at the smell of the fire as they raced

173

down the drive.

Satisfied that Hillary was on her way to safety, Ryan wasted no more time before wheeling about to take his place in the midst of the preparations. He placed Connor in charge of clearing a wide circle of land to act as a firebreak, then bounded up the steps of the back stairway to the second-story verandah. He climbed higher still, hoisting himself up to the roof. It was damp, but not nearly enough to keep it from burning. Concluding that the only way to save the house would be to remove the thatch, he balanced his weight on a supporting beam and called down for several of the men to help him in ripping loose the dried, woven coco fronds.

Minutes later, Hillary came riding back down the smoke-fogged drive. She had dutifully guided the wagon to the nearby sheltered cove where Tehura and the other natives waited. Once there, however, she had scrambled onto one of the whalers' horses and, heedless of her uncle's fervent objections, had urged the reluctant animal back along the road to Starcross.

She could not explain, even to herself, why she felt compelled to return. There was simply this overwhelming urge to be there, to take part in defending her beloved home against the force that threatened to destroy it. And there was also the undeniable need to be at Ryan's side—for whatever the reason, she couldn't sit idly by while he risked his life on her behalf.

Ryan's handsome face became a mask of rage when he caught sight of the lone rider pulling up before the house. He ground out a curse and climbed down from the roof with astonishing swiftness and agility, his eyes ablaze with a savage light. Rounding the corner of the house just as Hillary slid from the saddle, he stalked forward to seize her arms in a punishing grip.

"What the hell are you doing back here?" he roared, his smoldering gaze boring into her wide, startled one.

She had never seen him so angry, and though she inwardly blanched at the menacing gleam in his eyes, she lifted her head proudly and replied, "Following my conscience, that's what! Now let go of me! We've got work to do!" Her own eyes flashed up spiritedly at him. In spite of the fact that her face was smudged, her hair streaming wildly about her, and her dress torn and bedraggled, Ryan found himself musing that she was still the most beautiful woman he had ever seen. But, he reflected as his thoughts returned to the issue at hand, she had to learn to bow to his judgment, especially when it came to something as serious as the present situation.

"Damn it, Hillary!" For a fleeting moment, it appeared that he would strike her. If the look in his gleaming, narrowed eyes was any indication, he was certainly tempted to do so. His fingers tightened painfully about her arms. "We've no time to play these childish little games of yours! There's a fire bearing down on us, and I'll be damned if I'll let you stay!" He released her, but only to bend and lift her in his arms again. In spite of her struggles, he easily tossed her back into the saddle. "If you dare to defy me again, I swear I'll—"

"Captain! Captain, the roof! The roof's caught fire!" the voice of one of his men suddenly rang out.

Hillary stifled a cry at the news. Her gaze met Ryan's one last time before he sent her mount lurching forward. She sawed on the reins in a frantic attempt to stop and turn the horse, but the smell of fire, more intense now that there were flames so close,

175

prompted the frightened animal to balk at going back.

Shifting in the saddle to glance back anxiously over her shoulder, Hillary observed the damage done when a shower of red-hot sparks had been whisked up by the wind and conveyed over the swaying treetops to fall upon the roof. A flash of lightning split the sky as Ryan and several others hastened to battle the rapidly spreading flames that shot up from the thatch still in place above the kitchen.

"Get more water up here!" Ryan beat at the flames with a blanket while two of his men did their best to tear the surrounding thatch free before it caught fire as well.

Hillary jerked on the reins with all her might. The horse emitted a shrill protest, rearing up on its hind legs and spilling her from its back. She landed in a tangle of skirts, her fall cushioned by the damp earth and thick ground cover along the drive. Staggering breathlessly to her feet, she began hurrying back toward the house. Her eyes burned from the smoke, and she fought against rising nausea as she watched the flames on the roof dancing ever higher.

Her gaze moved to Ryan. She caught her breath when she saw the way he stood balanced on the roof, almost in the midst of the blaze. Apparently heedless of the danger stalking him, he strove valiantly to save the house—*her* house. She felt more than a twinge of alarm at the thought of what could happen to him, and she quickened her steps as she reached the clearing once more.

Suddenly, her worst fears came true. The beam supporting Ryan's weight gave way. There was no warning before the wood split and cracked, no warning before Ryan and one of the other men went crashing down through the burning roof.

"Dear God, no!" gasped Hillary, drawing up short in front of the house. She raised a hand to her tightly constricted throat, her eyes wide with horror as she stared up numbly at the spot where Ryan had been only seconds earlier. There was a sudden, sharp pain in her heart, as though a knife twisted within its abruptly stilled depths. "No!" she cried out brokenly. "No!" She clutched at her skirts and raced frantically around the corner, oblivous to the flames that now shot across the verandah.

"Josiah! Ewan! Give me a hand!" yelled Connor as he sped to rescue the two men sprawled amid the burning debris inside the kitchen. He went tearing through the doorway, moving first to drop down on his knees beside the man who was both his captain and his friend. "Ryan! Ryan, can you hear me?" He released a long, pent-up breath when Ryan stirred and opened his eyes.

Josiah was there an instant later, quickly helping Connor get their captain to his feet and outside. Ewan, the ship's cooper and a man almost as large and burly as the cook, took charge of the other man, hoisting him to his brawny shoulder and conveying him outside as well.

Several crew members were already working to extinguish the fire on the verandah, while others hastened inside the kitchen to prevent the flames from spreading to the rest of the house. The beam's collapse had achieved an unexpected benefit—the portion of the roof that had been burning was no longer in place.

With a desperate single-mindedness, Hillary shouldered her way past the whalers. Before she had reached the kitchen doorway, however, she caught sight of Ryan. Two men, one of whom was the same black-bearded giant who had barred her way aboard the *Falcon*, each supported one of his arms with a shoulder as they quickly moved away from the house. Though he was obviously shaken from the fall, he was conscious and did not appear to be seriously injured—in fact, he impatiently shrugged off the assistance of Connor and Josiah just as soon as they stepped down from the verandah.

Weak with the most profound relief she had ever known, Hillary gathered up her skirts and flew impulsively to Ryan's side. Her eyes were bright with tears as she reached out to grasp his arm.

"Oh Ryan! Are you all—" she began, only to break off with a sharp gasp when he rounded on her with frightening savagery. He glared down at her murderously, his emotions warring with one another as his searing gaze bored into her wide, startled one. Though he made no move to touch her in those few tension-charged seconds, Hillary felt certain that he was thrashing her in his mind.

The awful silence was broken when Connor, who had taken himself off to inspect the progress of the men's work, returned and declared, "The fire's closing in fast now, Captain! The break's about done here, and Ewan's gone to check on the fields."

"Tell the men to have their shovels ready," commanded Ryan. "We'll set the backfire now." He turned back to Hillary with another fierce scowl and ground out, "No matter what happens, you're to do exactly as I say! We may very well end up running for our lives!"

"Wha . . . what do you mean?" she asked, a noticeable quaver of fear in her voice. Ryan finally seized hold of her. His gaze hardened and his features grew quite grim.

"The blaze we set may very well stop the main

178

fire—or at least divert it around the house and fields—but it could instead send a wall of flames bearing down on us." Hillary winced as his fingers curled with bruising force about the soft flesh of her arms. "Listen to me!" he growled. "Stay close beside me, and when I give the order, run as fast as you can to the fields, understand? Even if the backfire succeeds for the most part, the flames could split. You'll be safer there."

"And what about you?" challenged Hillary, her heart pounding as she met his gaze squarely. He never answered, for Connor interrupted at that point to report that all was ready.

"Then let's get to it," Ryan quietly decreed. He looked at Hillary again, his blue-green eyes glowing with a strange combination of fury, concern, and love. "Remember what I said. And know that, whatever happens, your life is the dearest thing in all the world to me." With those astonishing words, he turned and led the way toward the trees.

The next few minutes were fraught with almost unbearable suspense for Hillary. She willingly obeyed Ryan's order to remain close to him, waiting and watching as he stationed more than a dozen men along the firebreak just to the south of the house and grounds. The rest of the men were already at their assigned posts in the fields; if the fire broke through into the clearing, then a second line of defense would be mounted at the fields. If the house could not be saved, they would at least try to save the vanilla plants. The plants would be a heavy loss indeed, for without them, Starcross could never be rebuilt.

"Stand fast now!" commanded Ryan, lighting the makeshift torches he and Connor held. "Above all else, the backfire must not be allowed to reverse direction!"

Hillary's entire body tensed as Ryan and Connor bent to touch the torches to the oil-soaked bundles of wood and dried coconuts positioned at intervals along the break. Flames immediately shot up into the air, and the men lifted their shovels to begin the task of extinguishing all but the front line of the blaze.

The lightning and thunder had tapered off, but not so the winds. They whipped the main fire into an even greater frenzy as it advanced upon Starcross. The smoke became heavier still and the air several degrees hotter. The heavens above the plantation grew increasingly lighter from the flames' glow, and the sounds of the coconuts exploding intensified, prompting Hillary to cover her ears with her hands in an effort to blot out the dreadful reminder of the fire's ravagement. She no longer cared about the din a moment later, however, as it began to dawn on her that the backfire was working.

The whole chain of events occurred with dizzying swiftness. The updraft from the main fire began pulling the deliberately set flames toward the larger blaze. Ryan and his men had managed by this time to secure a wide area of already scorched land behind the backfire, and it was now left to them to remain vigilant against any sparks or flying cinders that might ignite either the house or the surrounding greenery.

Within seconds, it became evident that the original blaze had been successfully diverted, for the flames began topping the trees in a circle about the clearing. Though Ryan motioned her back toward the house, Hillary gazed upward in fascination, and growing exuberance, as they were enclosed within a brilliant, wildly leaping ring of fire. It amazed her that she felt no fear. Glancing at Ryan, she sensed that he was every bit as confident as she that the danger had passed.

But there was still work to be done. The whalers continued to wield their shovels, pounding out stray bursts of flame as the blaze skirted about the firebreak they had made. Once he was satisfied that the house had been saved, Ryan gave the order for his men to retreat along the path to the fields, where they would be needed to ensure that the second break would be as successful as the first.

"Stay here!" he directed Hillary when she turned to follow them. She opened her mouth to argue, but he anticipated her defiance and cut her off with a terse, "Do as I say!" Her eyes flashed up at him reproachfully, but he was already turning away. She stared after him as he disappeared into the unscathed foliage guarding the entrance to the path.

Hillary released a long, ragged sigh and wearily gathered up her skirts. Drifting back to the house, she sank down upon the front steps, suddenly feeling quite drained. She closed her eyes and thought of Ryan and his men battling the flames again, a renewed heaviness closing about her heart when she reflected that the danger was far from over. There was still a chance the vanilla plants would perish in the fire, still a chance someone would be injured, or even killed.

Ryan. Throughout those terrible few moments following the roof's collapse, when the possibility of his death had flashed across her mind, she had felt almost as though her own life were ending.

She caught her breath upon a gasp, her violet eyes grew very round, and a warm flush stole up to her beautiful, smudged face. The realization of the depth of her feelings for Ryan Gallagher was a startling discovery—startling *and* alarming. She had never felt so strongly about anyone before, and it frightened her.

Her chaotic reverie came to an abrupt end when a

cold drop of moisture suddenly fell upon her hand. She jerked up her head in stunned disbelief, only to be pelted by several more raindrops as the storm finally broke. Thunder rolled and echoed, signaling the upcoming torrent. Within a matter of seconds, the heavens opened up and began drenching the earth with a downpour so heavy that the trees opposite the house were scarcely visible to Hillary's grateful eyes.

With an exclamation of joy, she flew down the steps and across to the trail that led to the fields. She was quickly soaked to the skin, but she did not care. She clutched her sodden skirts and hurried onward, anxious to see for herself how the cloudburst—a belated godsend, but a godsend nonetheless—was claiming victory over the fire.

Ryan stood in the pouring rain and exchanged a smile of mingled relief and irony with Connor. The crew of the *Falcon* leaned heavily upon their shovels and watched as the flames dancing about the perimeter of the fields were forever vanquished by the tropical deluge. Miraculously, the winds began to calm. The smoke rising from the smoldering earth no longer choked the air close to the ground, but instead dissipated until it was nothing more than a thin curl of steam reaching toward the sky.

"Better late than never, wouldn't you say, Captain?" quipped Connor, the rain streaming down his smoke-blackened face.

"I might just, Mr. Reid," Ryan murmured with another sardonic half smile on his own doused features. He seemed oblivious to the fact that they were standing about in the cold rain. As a seaman, he was well-accustomed to every kind of weather known to man. "Let's get the men inside that hut," he said, nodding to indicate the nearby, thatch-roofed building normally used as a schoolhouse. "I'll go back to the house and find what I can in the way of provisions. They'll need some nourishment after what they've been through, and the injured will have to be seen to right away."

He turned and began striding toward the path, only to catch sight of Hillary emerging from the trees. Her long hair was plastered about her head and shoulders, her gown clung immodestly to her supple young curves, and her wet skirts tangled about her legs to hamper her progress. Musing to himself that she looked much like a drowned kitten, Ryan was unable to suppress an appreciative grin as he hastened to meet her.

"Oh Ryan! Is it truly over? Did we lose any of the plants? Are the men all right?" she queried in a breathless rush when he grasped her arm and urged her back beneath the minimal shelter of the trees. Her stomach did a peculiar flip-flop as her eyes met his in the dim light, and she was sorely tempted to throw her arms about him and declare her undying gratitude for what he had done . . . and her profound relief that he was unharmed.

"It's over," he affirmed, his fingers tightening possessively upon her arm. "I need food and drink for my men, and something to tend their wounds."

"Of course!" Feeling unaccountably flustered, she turned away to head back down the path, then gasped as she was suddenly caught up in Ryan's arms. He bore her quickly toward the house, the two of them getting more drenched by the second. "I . . . I can walk, Captain Gallagher," she protested only half-heartedly. She secretly reveled in the feel of his strong arms about her, and she was once again rendered light-headed by his nearness.

"I was 'Ryan' only a moment ago," he lovingly

admonished. More than anything, he wanted to hold her close and kiss her until she begged for release, but he couldn't, at least not yet, for there were other matters to be seen to first. Before the night was through, he silently vowed, he would make her say the words he longed to hear.

Hillary was surprised to find her uncle and Tevaite waiting for them at the house. Denholm Reynolds embraced his niece as soon as Ryan set her on her feet inside the entranceway.

"We returned just as soon as it began to rain," he explained, his clothing almost as sodden as hers. Tevaite had already draped a blanket about his thin shoulders. He suddenly drew away and held Hillary at arm's length, his expression growing very stern. "I doubt if it will do any good to take you to task for coming back here, but I want you to know I am indeed quite angry with you. I can only thank God— and Captain Gallagher, I'm sure," he added, glancing past her to Ryan, "that nothing happened to you."

"I'm sorry, dearest Uncle, but I simply did what I thought was right," she replied earnestly. Her eyes glistened with tears as she reported, "Captain Gallagher and his men fought bravely to save Starcross. We owe them a debt of gratitude." She smiled and squeezed his frail hand before turning to the Tahitian woman at his side. "Please help me see to them, Tevaite. The kitchen was damaged by the fire and is no doubt flooding with water as we speak, but we should be able to find something for them to eat."

"Tehura is in the kitchen now," the older woman said, her dark gaze moving from Hillary to Ryan and back. "She gathers food and makes coffee while Mahi covers the hole to keep the rain out. I will get blankets

184

and medicines.''

A short time later, Hillary, Tevaite, Tehura, and Ryan were hurrying along the path to the hut where the exhausted men waited. The whalers were very appreciative of the bread, pork, and coffee spiced with rum. Several of the men had suffered burns on their hands and faces, which Tevaite tended, using a special salve and clean bandages. There were, thankfully, no serious injuries.

Hillary conveyed her gratitude to each of the men in turn as she offered them the food. Ryan was at her side, watching her with the crew and marveling at her fortitude—she had been through a lot the past few hours, but still she did not waver in her duties. His heart swelled with pride for both her courage and her beauty, and he grew increasingly impatient to be alone with her.

Tehura was put in charge of handing out the blankets. She smiled coquettishly at the whalers as she moved about the lamplit hut. The smile froze on her face, however, when her almond-shaped eyes fell on a slim, dark man in the corner. She gasped inwardly at the malignant gleam in his gaze, and she did not fail to notice the way he shook his head at her in a silent warning. The girl was too frightened to say anything to either her mother or Hillary, and so she merely turned away from the man and finished the remainder of her task in an unusually subdued manner.

The rains had slowed to a mere drizzle by the true nightfall. It was decided that Connor would take the men back to the ship, where only an anchor watch had been posted in the others' absence. Hillary insisted upon extending the hospitality of Starcross for the night, but Ryan argued, truthfully, that the whalers would feel ill at ease there and would much prefer the comfort of their own bunks aboard the *Falcon*.

And so it was that the men were soon climbing up into the wagons and mounting the horses, which had been brought back to Starcross by the natives. Ryan drew Connor aside before they left and said, "Don't look for me before morning. And thanks for all the help." His mouth curved into a sardonic grin as he added, "For devotion to service above and beyond the call of duty."

The black-haired man grinned back and nodded toward Hillary, who had changed into dry clothing and waited a short distance away on the steps. A hooded lamp burned from a post in front of the house, tossing light across the rain-soaked yard. "I can see why you've decided to give up your freedom," Connor told Ryan with a low chuckle. "She's a rare woman, that one. She'll not let you have your way too easily. It is my opinion that you need a woman who will stand up to you, Ryan Gallagher. Unless I miss my guess, you'll be getting exactly that!" He gallantly tipped his hat to Hillary, then swung up into the saddle and rode away into the misty darkness, the other men following.

Hillary's pulses began racing again as Ryan came toward her with slow, purposeful steps. She trembled at the look in his magnificent turquoise eyes—a look that was both sharply unnerving and absurdly thrilling.

"It's time we talked," he decreed in a quiet, resonant tone.

Feeling warm and breathless and not the least bit inclined to protest, she allowed him to take her arm and lead her inside.

VIII

Ryan pulled Hillary into the parlor and closed the doors. They were alone in the room, its rain-scented darkness adding to the mood of promised passion.

Hillary's air of compliancy vanished when she felt Ryan's strong fingers closing about her wrists and drawing her slowly toward him. Though she could scarcely make out his face as her eyes adjusted to the darkness, she was certain he was smiling that warm, enigmatic smile of his, the one that never failed to send her senses reeling.

Suddenly feeling very nervous and flustered, she murmured something unintelligible and hastily pulled her wrists free. Ryan made no move to stop her when she whirled about to light a candle. Her hand was shaking as she struck the match and held it to the wick, and it took her much longer than usual to nurture a flame. Once the room became bathed in the soft golden glow, she forced herself to turn back and face the man whose very touch set her blood afire. She trembled anew at the look in his smoldering, blue-green eyes, and a tingling warmth stole over her when his mouth curved into a smile that she mused could best be described as tenderly wolfish.

Swallowing hard, she desperately sought to regain at least some semblance of composure. She clasped her hands tightly together behind her back and said, "I . . . I have formally tendered my thanks to all but you, Captain Gallagher. Starcross would have perished if not for your efforts. And I . . . that is, my uncle and I, we . . . we owe you a debt of gratitude—"

"I don't want your gratitude." He crossed the space between them in two long strides, his hands moving upward to grasp her shoulders with gentle firmness. "Blast it, woman," he murmured, the loving amusement in his eyes and the affectionate tone of his voice belying his words, "we both know why I came." Lifting a hand to cup her chin, he shook his head and declared softly, "No, my love, I don't want your gratitude. I want *you.*"

Hillary's sparkling violet eyes grew enormous within the delicate oval of her face as the last of her defenses threatened to crumble. Never had she felt so . . . so *swept away* by anything or anyone! Ryan Gallagher was without a doubt the most overpowering presence ever to enter her life, and she was not at all certain how to cope with him *or* the feelings he evoked deep within her. She gazed up at him in helpless confusion, trying to think of what to say or do to resolve the turbulence of her emotions, a turbulence that had increased tenfold when she had seen him plunged into danger a few short hours earlier.

"Admit it, Hillary," commanded Ryan, his deep voice low and vibrant, his handsome countenance now appearing compellingly solemn in the soft candlelight. "Admit that you're mine. You know it's the truth. You've known it from the very first, just as I have." His arms slipped about her waist at last, and she drew in her breath upon a quiet gasp as he yanked her so close that her trembling curves were pressed intimately against his undeniably virile hardness. "I want to hear it from your own lips. Tell me you'll be my wife. Say it!"

"I . . . heaven help me, I . . . I don't know what to—" Hillary stammered breathlessly, then found herself abruptly silenced by the pressure of Ryan's warm mouth upon hers. His arms tightened about her with a fierce possessiveness, and his lips were bold and demanding, almost rough, as they drank deeply of hers. She moaned low in her throat, but it was a moan of passion, not protest. Desire coursed through her body like wildfire. Her arms crept upward to lock about the corded muscles of his neck, and she felt her feet leaving the ground as he lifted her higher within his fiery embrace. She returned his kisses with a fervency that sent his heart soaring and his own passion flaring to a dangerous level of intensity.

Completely lost in each other for the moment, they were unaware of one of the doors being eased open. They were equally oblivious to the light spilling into the room from the hallway to override the minimal glow of the candle's flame.

"It seems I have intruded," Denholm's voice suddenly drifted across to them.

The spell was broken. Hillary started guiltily and tore herself from Ryan in alarm, her beautiful face blushing crimson with embarrassment as she whirled to meet her uncle's unfathomable gaze.

Ryan, on the other hand, smiled across unconcernedly at the older man and responded, "A timely intrusion, however. Now that you're here, Mr. Reynolds, there is something of great importance I wish to discuss with you."

"And *I* with *you*, Captain." Denholm leaned heavily upon his cane as he made his way toward them. His gray eyebrows drew together in a frown of purposeful severity. "I am, of course, referring to the startling scene I have just witnessed taking place between you and my niece. Since I believe you to be a man of honor, Captain Gallagher, I am going to allow you the opportunity to explain your actions."

"Oh, Uncle, no!" gasped Hillary. Her wide, luminous eyes silently implored him to drop the matter, but he did not.

"Well, Captain?" he prompted.

"I can offer no particular explanation, other than to say that—" began Ryan, only to be cut off by the other man.

"Just as I thought!" Feigning an attitude of righteous anger, Hillary's uncle drew himself loftily erect and proclaimed in tight, clipped tones, "You, sir, shall do the only thing possible under the circumstances. You shall marry my niece!"

"What?" gasped Hillary in shocked disbelief. "You . . . you cannot mean—"

"I mean exactly what I say! You will marry at once!"

"But Ry . . . Captain Gallagher has—"

"Every intention of doing just that," Ryan calmly declared. He reached out and took hold of Hillary's arm, drawing her firmly back to his side. His eyes twinkled roguishly and a sardonic half smile played about his lips as he told Denholm, "It will give me the greatest pleasure to make Hillary my wife, Mr. Reynolds. And it might interest you to know that I had planned to do so all along."

"A likely story!" the older man snorted, playing his part to perfection. Inwardly, he was delighted to learn that Ryan Gallagher was every bit the man he had believed him to be. Though it now appeared his interference had been unnecessary after all, Denholm congratulated himself on having the foresight to keep an eye on the proceedings instead of following through on his announced intention of going up to bed.

"This is ridiculous!" cried Hillary. She tried to pull away from Ryan, but he held fast. Her eyes blazed resentfully up at him and across at her uncle in turn. "I will *not* stand meekly by while the two of you decide my fate! How dare you treat me as though I were nothing more than . . . than a child!"

"You are hardly that, my love," Ryan quipped softly.

"Why should you have any particular objections to the arrangement, my dear?" Denholm asked, favoring her with a fondly indulgent smile. "After all, since you have made it quite clear that Anthony Warren holds no claim upon your heart—"

"My feelings for Anthony have nothing whatsoever to do with this!" she retorted in exasperation. "You haven't even bothered to find out what I may or may not feel for Captain Gallagher! Why, we . . . we don't truly know anything about him! He's little more than a stranger to us, Uncle, and yet you are prepared—no, *anxious*—to see me wed to him!" She attempted to pull free again, but Ryan determinedly maintained his hold. She cast him a speaking glare before appealing in desperation to her uncle once more. "What happened here tonight need go no farther than this room. Captain Gallagher will be returning to his home soon, and there is no reason we cannot simply forget that this distasteful incident ever occurred!"

"Will *you* be able to forget it, Hillary?" Denholm suddenly challenged. "You are like a daughter to me, and I care more about your feelings than you think. That is why I must ask—can you honestly say you do not love Ryan Gallagher?"

Considerably taken aback by the question, Hillary could feel a dull flush rising to her face. Her amethyst gaze was filled with consternation as it shifted back and forth between the two men who stood patiently awaiting her answer. Her heart pounded erratically within her breast, and she was painfully aware of the way Ryan stared down at her in unspoken triumph. *What am I to do?* she mentally agonized. Since it was in her nature to be as truthful as possible, she gently cleared her throat and replied, "No, but . . . but I—"

"I rest my case and leave her in your hands, Captain," said Denholm, a strange little smile touching his lips. Without another word or a backward glance, he limped as quickly as possible from the room and closed the doors behind him.

"A wise and perceptive man, your uncle," murmured Ryan, chuckling softly. He took hold of Hillary's other arm as well now, and his gaze traveled over her beautiful, dazed features with deliberate boldness. "You'll never have cause to regret your decision, my love."

"It wasn't *my* decision!" she adamantly dissented, struggling weakly within his grasp.

"Oh, but it *was*," he insisted in a low tone brimming with loving amusement. His eyes glowed down at her disarmingly, and her feeble efforts to escape came to a sudden halt when he added in a voice scarcely above a whisper, "And what's more, my dear Miss Reynolds, it's a decision that ensures you a lifetime as the wife of a man who truly loves you."

Hillary stared up at him in wide-eyed stupefaction. *Had he really said he loved her?* Even if her benumbed mind could have conjured up a suitable response to his shocking declaration, she would have been unable to offer it, for he swept her exultantly into his arms and claimed the sweetness of her lips once more.

Passion flared between them, hotter than before, and it was quite some time before Ryan, employing every ounce of self-will he possessed, determinedly set a very flushed and breathless Hillary away from him. His voice sounded unusually harsh as he ordered her up to bed; she did not know that it was because he wanted her so much it pained him to let her go. She was feeling much too light-headed to think straight or to argue with him about anything, including the matter of a wedding he confidently asserted would take place two days hence.

The wedding guests began arriving shortly after noon. Denholm Reynolds, following what appeared to be an amazingly swift recovery from his long and debilitating illness, had accomplished a small miracle by arranging everything within a period of forty-eight hours. He had arisen the morning after the fire and set to work with a vengeance, anxious to see his beloved niece wed to a man he was now convinced was worthy of her. Satisfied that the young American would provide the strength and guidance Hillary required, Denholm told himself there was no longer any reason to worry about what would happen to her once he was gone. He would be leaving her in the capable—and loving, if he was any judge at all—hands of Ryan Gallagher.

Word had immediately been sent to Pastor Witherspoon, who had agreed to travel over from Moorea via the *Paradaiso* to perform the ceremony. Constance Bainbridge was only too delighted to serve as Hillary's attendant, though she did think it more than a little odd that the request came from Hillary's uncle instead of from the future bride herself. However, she and Donald presented themselves at Starcross on the day of the wedding with Pastor Witherspoon in tow, and they brought with them a special gift for the young woman who had proven such a good friend—a *tifaifai*, or patchwork quilt, made by the natives at Jade Point. The Tahitians had, ironically enough, inherited the occupation of quilt-making from the wives of New England whaling captains some years earlier.

Tahitian families, American whalers, British diplomats, French shopkeepers, and various others gathered on the fragrant, sunbathed grounds of Starcross to witness the marriage of Captain Ryan Gallagher and Hillary Reynolds. Minutes before the ceremony was to begin, an unexpected but entirely welcome guest appeared. Queen Pomare's ornately decorated coach, received as a gift from her British counterpart, Queen Victoria, sent a large part of the crowd scattering as it careened down the drive at a breakneck pace and came to an abrupt stop in front of the house.

A murmur rose from the startled assembly as the queen, dressed in a traditional, flowered gown reaching to her ankles, emerged from the coach. A tall and markedly stout woman of middle age, she was a much beloved personage in Tahiti. She was kind and gregarious, and though she no longer wielded any true power within the ranks of government, she still inspired a sort of regal reverence that would not be diminished.

"I have come to see wedding of Missy and the *Marite*," she announced in clear, ringing tones, referring to Ryan only as "the American." Smiling benevolently upon her subjects, she was escorted by one of her many companions to a high-backed chair set up with several others in the yard just beyond the partially reconstructed lower verandah.

Hillary, meanwhile, was blissfully unaware of the large number of people who had come to see her join her life with Ryan's. She remained closeted in her room, admitting no one but Constance and Tevaite as the fateful hour approached.

"Dear Lord, what am I doing?" she bemoaned aloud. Her voice held a note of rising panic, and her fingers trembled as she distractedly smoothed the gleaming white satin that fell in long, graceful folds from just below her breasts to the floor. The short, puffed sleeves were inset with lace, and the fitted bodice was trimmed with tiny seed pearls. Low and rounded, the neckline allowed a suitable yet tantalizing glimpse of her full young bosom. The gown had been worn by Hillary's aunt upon the occasion of her own wedding to Denholm Reynolds, and it had required only a few alterations by Tevaite's skillful hands to fit Hillary's more slender curves.

"Why, you're marrying the man you love!" Constance laughingly retorted. Her merriment vanished when she observed what appeared to be a shadow of uncertainty crossing the other young woman's face. "You *do* love him, don't you, Hillary?" she probed gently, her green eyes filling with concern as she rose to her feet and glided across the room to her friend's side. "When I asked earlier if you weren't perhaps rushing into this marriage, you told me—rather airily, I might add—that you had simply been swept off your feet by the man. Is that truly the case, my dear? You *are* marrying Captain Gallagher because you wish to do so, are you not?"

Hillary felt Tevaite's eyes upon her. The Tahitian woman stood near the dresser, her arms holding the wispy, scalloped veil that would be pinned within her young mistress's upswept ebony curls as the final touch to the bridal costume.

"I . . . of course," Hillary finally murmured, hoping her voice held more conviction than she actually felt. While it was true that part of her wanted to become Ryan Gallagher's wife, another part of her was absolutely terrified at the prospect. She still knew so little about him, and she was, after all, preparing to pledge herself to him—body and soul— for the rest of her life. Feeling trapped between her conflicting emotions, she was forced to admit to herself that she could not bear the thought of losing him. He had said he loved her—the memory of those words made her heart sing. Did she love him as well?

"Don't worry, my dear," said Constance with a bolstering smile and a quick, affectionate squeeze of Hillary's arm. "Every bride is a bit frightened on her wedding day. I daresay it would seem strange if she were not! And after all, yours *was* what one would call a whirlwind courtship." Her smile deepened until two engaging dimples appeared on either side of her mouth. "If you'll recall, I suspected there was something between you and Captain Gallagher when I saw the way the two of you looked at each other that day you came to Moorea. I suppose it isn't really all that surprising to learn you were swept off your feet by the likes of *him*. Why, if it were not for my deep and undying devotion to Donald, I myself might have been tempted to acquaint myself more thoroughly with the gallant captain!"

Smiling weakly, Hillary averted her gaze and distractedly smoothed a fold of white satin for what was quite possibly the hundredth time in the past hour. She was almost relieved when she heard Tevaite quietly proclaim, "It is time, Miss Hillary."

The veil was secured, the last-minute examination of the gown performed, and then Hillary found herself being whisked from the room by Constance and Tevaite to join her uncle. Denholm stood waiting at the foot of the stairs, his kindly face beaming up at her as she descended in a merciful daze. He reached for her arm and drew it through his, while Constance, taking her cue from the traditional wedding march being played only a little off-key on a pump organ borrowed from the seaman's mission in town, began moving through the front doorway with slow, measured steps. Tevaite drifted away, leaving Hillary and her uncle alone for a brief moment.

"He'll make you a good husband, my dear," Denholm reassured her. Smiling down tenderly at her beautiful, noticeably apprehensive features, he patted her hand and added, "Someday you'll understand." She raised eyes full of bewilderment to his, but he merely smiled again and led her outside into the sunshine.

Ryan was waiting for her beneath a canopy of gently swaying palms. There was only a hint of a smile on his ruggedly handsome face, but his blue-green eyes glowed with love and admiration as he watched her moving gracefully across the yard on her uncle's arm. Connor Reid, serving as his captain's best man, waited in place beside him. Pastor Witherspoon stood garbed in his best black suit, and he smiled warmly at Hillary when Denholm relinquished her into Ryan's care. Constance stepped forward to take charge of the bridal bouquet, and the ceremony began.

It was over almost before Hillary knew what had happened. Suddenly, Ryan was claiming her lips in the customary display of possession, though the kiss he bestowed upon her was much more passionate and lengthy than custom normally allowed. Hillary's head was swimming dizzily by the time he finally released her, and her cheeks flamed with embarrassment when she became aware of the knowing smiles and chuckles elicited by their ardent embrace. She cast her new husband a reproachful look as they turned to face the guests. He favored her with a brief, unrepentant grin before the two of them found themselves surrounded by a throng of well-wishers.

The *tamaaraa*, a traditional Tahitian feast, commenced immediately after the ceremony. Tevaite had overseen all the preparations, for the meal as well as for the entertainment to follow. She had selected a menu that included pig, fish, bananas, and breadfruit, all cooked in an underground oven in which hot stones had been layered with green leaves over the food and sealed with earth to cook for several hours. For dessert, there was *poe*, a flavorful dish made of papayas, taros, and bananas with sugar, vanilla, and coconut milk. A variety of drink was offered as accompaniment to the meal of celebration—coffee, tea, fruit juices, and for the more adventurous, *ava*, a highly potent and intoxicating drink brewed from the pepper root.

Hillary ate little. She sat at a table in the cool shade, flanked by her uncle on one side and her husband on the other. Her eyes strayed frequently to Ryan's face, but she hurriedly looked away whenever her gaze met his. Though musing that she should be relieved over the fact that he scarcely spoke to her, she was nonetheless plagued by something strangely akin to jealousy as he concentrated his attention on everything and everyone but his new wife. It was almost as if he were determined to force her to be the one to initiate any conversation between them, thought Hillary, her sense of disquiet increasing.

A special exhibition of wrestling, a much-loved and revered sport among the Tahitians for centuries, had been arranged as the first event to follow the meal. A dozen young Tahitian men, wearing only waistcloths, paraded slowly around the cleared area in front of the guests. They made loud, booming noises by striking their left arms with their right hands as they formed a wide circle. When they came to a stop, the wrestling began without delay, each man seeking any opponent who was convenient. The challenge was delivered by the contestants facing one another, lifting their hands to join their fingers together, and moving their elbows up and down. They then clutched one another and engaged in a fierce struggle of bronzed flesh and sinewy muscle until one of them was flung down. The Tahitian spectators broke into a sort of laudatory chorus whenever one of the wrestlers was thrown, while the other guests applauded politely.

Hillary was dismayed to feel a telltale blush rising to her face as she watched the performance. A sudden vision of Ryan's magnificent, undeniably virile body swam before her eyes. She remembered, with shocking clarity, the way he had looked the day at the bathing pool, and she couldn't prevent a silent comparison of his lean-muscled form with those of the young wrestlers before her now, a comparison in which he was the indisputable victor. Swallowing a sudden lump in her throat, she stole another surreptitious glance at him from beneath her eyelashes, only to find that his penetrating gaze was fastened upon her.

His eyes gleamed with amusement, and a faint, teasing smile touched his lips before he inclined his head to murmur close to her ear, "Perhaps you can teach me some of these wrestling maneuvers later when we're finally alone, my love."

Hillary gasped softly, her color deepening and a sudden warmth spreading throughout her body. Her mind raced to produce a suitable response. "I . . . I know nothing of them," she stammered as she looked away again, "save what I have witnessed upon a very few occasions. Even with the relaxed social structure here in Tahiti, females have never been allowed to participate in such activities."

"Then we shall have to remedy that, at least within the privacy of our nuptial chamber," Ryan decreed in a low, slightly husky voice that left little doubt as to his true meaning. He returned his attention to the performance, leaving Hillary to contend with all the turbulent emotions he had aroused within her.

The first exhibition ended soon thereafter, and the wrestlers took a bow before making way for the native dancers and musicians. The costumes of the men and women, fashioned of natural fibers and shells and flowers, were not nearly as brief as those worn by the young Tahitians who had performed the forbidden dances on Moorea. Three men pounded out a jolting rhythm on the drums, while two others played hand-carved bamboo flutes. Although the movements of the dances were fast and provocative, they were a good deal less so than what was required for the *upaupa* and *timorodee*.

The dancing had just begun when Hillary suddenly murmured an excuse and rose from the table. Having caught a glimpse of Anthony near the front of the house, she was anxious to speak to him before he left. She felt hurt that he had not yet approached her, but she told herself his reluctance to do so was understandable under the circumstances.

"Anthony," she softly called his name as she rounded the corner. Her mouth curved into a tentative smile when he turned to face her. Relieved to find a spark of warmth and no evidence of betrayal in his pale blue gaze, she gathered up her skirts and hurried forward to embrace him. "I was afraid you had forsaken our friendship, dear Anthony!"

"Never would I do that," he quietly assured her. He gave her a sad smile when she drew away to stand gazing up at him with wide, sparkling eyes. Dressed in a well-fitted dark serge suit and white linen shirt, he looked very distinguished and attractive . . . and *safe*. "It came as something of a shock, you know, to hear that you were actually going to marry that fellow. I suspected as much, though I didn't want to face it. Not that I believe you turned me down because of him, mind you," he remarked with a quiet chuckle of only slightly bitter irony. "But I now realize there was never a chance for me at all."

"I . . . I can't explain any of this," she told him with a sigh. "I'm as confused as anyone! It's all happened so quickly and—" She broke off when he held up a hand in an eloquent gesture of defeat.

"You owe me no explanations. You're married to him now, my dear Hillary, and I want to wish you both every happiness. Just remember what I said—if you should ever need me, for anything, you've only to send word." He smiled briefly again, but the smile did not quite reach his eyes. Without another word, he mounted up and rode away.

Hillary felt tears starting to her eyes as she watched Anthony go. Then, Constance was there beside her, placing an arm about her shoulders and urging her inside the house to change.

"That new husband of yours has expressed a very natural impatience to be off!" the other woman revealed with a laugh. "He charged me to see that you are ready to leave within the half hour."

"Leave?" echoed Hillary in bemusement, numbly moving up the staircase with the petite blonde.

"Yes, *leave!* Surely you didn't expect to spend your wedding night here at Starcross? No, my dearest friend, that simply would not do at all! Every newly married couple deserves the most complete privacy possible at such a time. Why, I can well remember my own wedding night! Donald and I—"

"But it's only mid-afternoon! and Ry . . . Captain Gallagher said nothing to me about spending the night elsewhere!" But then again, she added silently, she and her new husband had never discussed *any* details pertaining to their wedding night. She hadn't even seen him since the night of the fire.

"Then perhaps *Ryan* meant to surprise you. Whatever the case, you must make all haste to obey. You must at least start off by allowing him to believe he is your lord and master. Reality will intrude soon enough!" Constance declared with another soft laugh as she tugged Hillary inside the bedroom and closed the door.

Ryan was standing in the front entrance hallway with Denholm when the two women emerged a short time later. Tevaite and Tehura were waiting at the foot of the staircase as well, smiling up at Hillary as she came out onto the landing. Her heart pounded, and she hesitated to go any farther when she met Ryan's intense yet unfathomable gaze. To her eyes, he appeared more dangerously irresistible than ever before. Dazedly reminding herself that there was no longer any need to worry about resisting him at all, she gathered courage and descended the stairs.

Ryan's eyes glowed with approval as they swiftly traveled over her. She had exchanged the wedding gown for a simple dress of white *piqué* trimmed with pale yellow braid and fastened down the front with a row of matching yellow buttons. The veil had been replaced by a small, beribboned straw bonnet perched atop her cascading raven curls.

Almost before she knew it, Hillary was being embraced in turn by Constance, Tevaite, and Tehura as they bade her farewell and wished her much joy on her honeymoon. Denholm was the last to say good-bye, and his words touched her heart.

"If you find even half the happiness your aunt and I knew together, dearest niece, then you shall be happy indeed." He kissed her and smiled at her one last time, then watched as she was led outside and down the front steps by Ryan.

Hillary was surprised to discover that they were to leave on horseback instead of by coach or wagon. The guests were assembled in the yard and along the drive to see them off, and many of them called out felicitations—and a few teasing comments on the night ahead—as Ryan lifted his bride up onto the large chestnut stallion and mounted behind her.

"But, where are we going?" asked Hillary in a small voice, her head still awhirl. It suddenly occurred to her that she had forgotten to bring along any extra clothing or toiletries . . . or nightwear.

As if reading her mind, Ryan said, "Someplace near. Everything we'll need has already been arranged for." Clamping an arm about her waist, he pulled her back against him and urged the horse forward with a gentle nudge of his boots. The faces of the people who cheered them on their way became nothing more than a blur to Hillary as she rode before the man to whom she now owed her loyalty, her obedience, and her heart.

It wasn't long before Ryan was guiding the horse off the main road and along an overgrown path through the trees. Hillary caught sight of a small clearing ahead, where sunlight filtered softly downward to fall upon a simple, thatch-roofed hut nestled amongst greenery alive with fragrant bursts of color. The air, sweet and cool within the sheltered glen, was filled with the melodious chorus of birds and the gentle rustling of leaves, as well as the faint roar of the waves breaking on the coral reef in the near distance.

"Is this where we . . . where we're to stay?" queried Hillary, musing that it wasn't at all what she had expected. *Nothing* associated with Ryan Gallagher had been what she'd expected!

"It is indeed," Ryan confirmed in a lazy drawl. He reined the stallion to a halt in front of the hut and swung down, then reached up for her. "I thought we would much prefer this over a room in town or my cabin aboard ship."

"But who does it belong to? And how on earth did you find it?" Trembling a bit as his fingers closed about her waist, she found it increasingly difficult to meet his gaze. She hastily drew away from him when her feet touched ground.

"Your uncle suggested it. He believes as I do—we need time alone. And as for the owner, I recall Tevaite saying something about a cousin of hers who was 'persuaded' to visit family on Moorea for a few days. So you see, we *are* completely alone, Mrs. Gallagher," he finished with a slow, meaningful smile. His magnificent turquoise eyes were aglow with passionate intent as they fastened upon her.

Hillary's cheeks flamed and her eyes grew very round. She caught her breath as renewed panic gripped her. *Dear God, what had she done?* Why oh *why* had she allowed herself to be swept into marriage with a man who was little better than a stranger to her? After all, what did she truly know about Ryan Gallagher? Suppose he turned out to be a madman, or a pirate, or—heaven help her—a *bigamist!*

With such turbulent thoughts closing in on her, Hillary whirled about and instinctively sought an avenue of escape. Her desperately searching gaze yielded a narrow path winding through the trees beside the hut. Without pausing to consider either the wisdom or rationality of her actions, she gathered up her skirts and hurried across the clearing. She didn't see the look of tender amusement crossing Ryan's handsome face as she plunged into the green-mantled coolness. Her slippered feet flew along the ground while the shrubbery rustled about her, and her thick hair tumbled from its pins to cascade down her back in long, shimmering waves of midnight blackness.

A sharp cry broke from her lips when she reached the end of the path and nearly tumbled headlong into the glistening waters of a small tidal pool. She would have fallen indeed, if not for the unexpected support of Ryan's arm about her waist. He arrived just in time to catch her, and he gave a low, triumphant chuckle as he hauled her back against him.

"We'll return to bathe later, my love," he promised, the resonant, lilting quality of his deep voice sending a tiny shiver racing down her spine. "But for now, your bridal bower awaits." He quickly scooped her up in his strong arms, his gaze boring into hers and his mouth curving into a smile of mingled tenderness and desire.

Hillary felt all her resistance melting away, but she

managed to struggle a bit within his grasp as she protested in a quavering voice, "But we . . . we scarcely know each other!"

"A problem which shall soon be remedied," he quipped, flashing her another heart-stopping grin as he carried her back along the path. "A honeymoon is for the sole purpose of gaining knowledge, is it not?" His arms tightened possessively about her, and his eyes smoldered with a passion that would not be denied. "Be forewarned—I intend to discover everything there is to know about you. By the time the *Falcon* sails for New Bedford, you and I will have become well acquainted with each other, Mrs. Gallagher."

They had reached the clearing again by now. Ryan strode inside the hut with his momentarily speechless bride and set her on her feet. The door and windows were merely cutouts in the walls, so that the aromatic tradewinds wafted freely through the simple, two-room structure. There was very little in the way of furniture—in the front room, a short, round table laden with a few bowls, cups, and cooking utensils, a basket of foodstuffs, two woven coco frond mats on the rough wooden floor on either side of the table, and a large, handcarved *ti'i*, or religious statue, standing guard in one corner of the room just as it had for the owner's father before him. In the bedroom was a feather bed covered with, surprisingly, the quilt Constance and Donald had presented to Hillary earlier in the day. A trunk filled with clothing and other essentials rested beside the bed, and a single oil lamp hung from a beam overhead.

"Would you care for something to drink?" offered Ryan. Hillary started in alarm and spun about at the sound of his voice, for she had drifted over to the bedroom doorway to stand staring, wide-eyed and with increasing apprehension, at the big feather bed that had been carted down from Starcross the day before.

"No!" she virtually shouted, then colored in embarrassment. "I . . . no, thank you." Her violet gaze was noticeably troubled, and her beautiful face appeared so youthful and vulnerable to Ryan's eyes that he felt more than a twinge of guilt for having rushed her into matrimony. Yet, he silently reasoned with himself, the only alternative would have been to wait until his return to Tahiti, which in all likelihood would not have occurred for another year. And damn it, he loved her and wanted her more than he'd ever believed possible. A long wait would have put him through hell! No, he'd never have been able to rest, burning for her and at the same time agonizing over whether or not some other man had claimed her before he himself could return to do so. She belonged to him! And now that she was his wife, he'd have the assurance that she would be waiting for him.

"A little wine would do you good, my love," Ryan gently but firmly asserted, producing a bottle from the basket and pouring some of the red liquid into one of the cups, which had been carved from a coconut shell. Hillary gazed up at him wordlessly as he moved forward to press the cup into her hand. She astonished herself by taking it and draining it in a single gulp. A rosy flush stained her cheeks, and tears started to her eyes as the wine, stronger than what she was used to, seared its way down her throat. She raised a hand to her lips and abruptly pushed her way past Ryan, intent on fleeing outside. He caught her by the arm, however, and laughed softly as he forced her about to face him again.

Once before, when she had believed him to be amusing himself at her expense, Hillary had lost her temper and struck out at him. This time was no exception. Her emotions were strained to the very limit, and something deep within her snapped. She lifted her other arm, balled her hand into a fist, and began pounding at the steely hardness of his broad chest with all her might.

"Let me go, Ryan Gallagher!" she cried, her raven tresses swirling wildly about her face and shoulders as she frantically tried to pull free. "I'll not be the wife of any man who . . . who—"

"Who loves you?" he supplied in a low, vibrant tone. Disregarding her sudden aggression, he seized her about the waist and yanked her up hard against him, prompting her to gasp loudly and gaze up at him with eyes that were very round and sparkling like two fiery-hued jewels. "I do, you know. I love you more than life itself, and what's more, *you* love *me*, no matter how hard you try to deny it. But I'll not allow you to deny it after this day, sweet Hillary. It seems that I've already waited a lifetime to make you mine, and I'll be damned if I'll wait any longer!" She was given no chance to argue before he swept her higher in his masterful embrace and brought his warm, demanding lips crashing down upon hers.

Hillary moaned low in her throat as he kissed her with an all-consuming passion. His powerful arms were locked about her with such fierceness that she could scarcely breathe, but she was soon past caring . . . soon past any coherent thought whatsoever. There was only Ryan, only the spell of rapturous enchantment he cast upon her as his mouth branded her parted lips and his velvety tongue hungrily explored the sweetness within.

The kiss seemed at once endless and too brief. With

dizzying swiftness, Ryan lifted her as though she were a mere babe and bore her into the bedroom. Lowering her to the cushioning softness of the quilt-covered bed, he stretched out his tall, muscular frame beside her trembling curves, his lips reclaiming hers while his fingers began deftly liberating the buttons running down the front of her white *piqué* gown. Hillary gasped softly against his mouth as his hands brushed against her breasts, and it briefly entered the benumbed recesses of her mind to try to forestall his actions, but she hastily discounted the notion and gave herself up to wild, delectable assault upon her emotions as well as her flesh.

She was startled when he suddenly clasped her tight and rolled so that she was atop him. He immediately slipped the bodice of her gown downward, leaving her breasts protected only by the thin, delicate fabric of her chemise. Almost before she realized it, the chemise had also been dispensed with, joining the upper portion of her dress down about her waist and thereby baring her full young bosom for her new husband's pleasure.

And pleasure there was, with a more than equal share falling to Hillary. A delicious tremor shook her as his lips trailed a fiery path downward, and she stifled a cry when his mouth roamed across the pale, satiny roundness of her naked breasts before closing about one of the sensitive rosy peaks. Her fingers curled almost convulsively within his thick, dark brown hair as his hot tongue swirled about her nipple with tantalizing unhaste and his lips tenderly suckled. His knowing hands lightly caressed the graceful smoothness of her naked back, before delving beneath her breasts and gently lifting the beautifully fashioned globes even higher for the moist, evocative tribute of his warm mouth.

209

Hillary's ebony tresses fell about them like a curtain, and she gasped again and again at the exquisite torment Ryan was inflicting upon her with such sensuously beguiling artistry. Lost in a fiery haze of near painful ecstasy and disturbingly intense emotions, she felt as though drawn out of herself, as though she had entered a dreamworld where she had been transformed into this wildly yearning woman who could not seem to control her own raging passions.

Ryan finally rolled so that she was lying upon her back once more, and she did not even think of protesting when his hands moved to divest her of the remaining barriers of clothing. He impatiently tugged the gown, chemise, and petticoat from her body, leaving behind only the fine white stockings that were gartered midway up her shapely thighs.

She was only dimly aware of the cool rush of air upon her feverish body before her passion-blurred gaze made note of the fact that Ryan was standing beside the bed and peeling his own clothing from his body with an alacrity borne of much practice. It wasn't until she glimpsed the burning look in his blue-green eyes that she became truly conscious of her state of undress, and she felt herself crimsoning from head to toe before a small part of maidenly shyness returned and prompted her to tug an edge of the patchwork quilt over her nakedness. She hastily averted her gaze in the next instant when Ryan stripped the trousers down over his lean, hard-muscled hips, but she was given no further opportunity for modesty as he yanked the quilt away and brought his naked body down upon hers.

Hillary suffered a sharp intake of breath when bare flesh met bare flesh, and her violet eyes flew wide as she felt the undeniable evidence of Ryan's masculine desire pressing against her thigh. Trembling with a combination of apprehension and excitement, she entwined her arms about his strong neck and welcomed the loving pressure of his lips upon hers once more. He kissed her with an ever-increasing urgency, though he was employing every ounce of self-control he possessed to prolong the splendid agony. Concentrating on Hillary's pleasure instead of his own, he forced himself to proceed as slowly as possible.

"Oh, Ryan!" Hillary breathed in the next instant, for he had suddenly relinquished her sweet lips and begun nibbling his way down the silken column of her throat . . . down to the delectable fullness of her breasts, where he lingered for several long moments . . . then even farther downward. He seemed intent upon kissing every square inch of her pliant, womanly curves. Her head tossed restlessly back and forth upon the quilt as her senses reeled, and her fingers clenched and unclenched as a series of soft gasps escaped her lips.

Then, she was being turned facedown upon the bed, so that her backside could receive the same worshipful attention. She moaned quietly as Ryan's warm lips followed an imaginary path across her back and down her spine, and she blushed rosily when she felt him gently nipping at the pale, rounded cheeks of her bottom. He continued downward, until reaching the spot upon her slender white thighs where her stockings were still gartered. His fingers slipped beneath one beribboned garter and slowly began sliding the delicate cotton stocking from her shapely leg, his lips pressing a feathery kiss upon each expanse of satiny flesh he bared. By the time he had removed both stockings and turned her over to lie beneath him again, Hillary had been

211

rendered nearly mindless with passion and longing.

"Dear God, but you're beautiful!" Ryan whispered hoarsely against her lips. He swallowed her sharp gasp when his hand moved to the secret place between her smooth white thighs. His fingers gently parted the soft folds concealed within the downy triangle of black curls, and Hillary moaned as he bestowed a slow, expert caress upon the very center of her femininity. She clung to the bronzed hardness of his shoulders as if she were drowning, her thighs opening to him and her body instinctively arching upward. His other hand entangled within the fragrant mass of her long hair, and his mouth drank deeply of hers before returning to her breasts.

Just when Hillary was certain she could bear no more, Ryan positioned himself above her and gripped her buttocks with his two large hands. He lifted her slightly, his manhood easing within her honeyed warmth. A soft cry broke from her lips at the sharp pain, but the pain was almost immediately replaced by the most intense pleasure she had ever known. Ryan began a slow, careful rotation of his hips, tutoring her into the age-old rhythm of love, tenderly initiating her into the ultimate delights of the flesh.

The tempo of their loving quickly escalated as their passions soared heavenward in perfect unison. Hillary was scarcely aware that it was her own faint scream that reached her ears when a thousand bright lights exploded in her head. Ryan groaned softly and tensed above her in the next instant, and she experienced an unbelievably profound feeling of completion as his warmth filled her.

Seconds later, he rolled to his back and pulled her against him, one arm tenderly cradling her head while the other remained draped possessively across her bare midsection. His lips brushed lovingly across her slightly damp forehead, and she heard him release a long sigh of contentment as they lay together in the soft afterglow of their passion.

"My sweet love," murmured Ryan, holding her close. "I'm sorry if I hurt you, but I could wait no longer."

Hillary's head rested against his bronzed, softly matted chest, so that she could feel his deep voice rumbling pleasantly upward beneath her cheek. Her naked curves were fitted intimately against his hard-muscled leanness, but strangely she felt no inclination to draw away and cover herself. Reason slowly began returning to her as the debilitating languor wore off, and with it came a dawning realization of what had just happened to her . . . and the astounding knowledge of why she had been unable to resist.

She loved Ryan Gallagher.

Her luminous eyes grew very wide, and her heart began pounding erratically within her breast. She was forced to acknowledge the truth at last—*she loved him!* No matter how hard she had tried to prevent it, no matter how vigorously she had denied it, it had happened. She had fallen in love with the man who was now her husband.

"You're even more beautiful than I thought possible," his rich, mellow voice suddenly broke in on her startling reverie. He chuckled softly and trailed an appreciative hand along the silken curve of her naked hip. "Although, I do recall having been presented with an unforgettable glimpse of your charms that day at Starcross when you appeared like Venus rising from the water. I couldn't allow myself to think of it too often, else I'd never have been able to sleep, or eat, *or* keep my resolve to wait until the wedding."

Hillary could think of nothing to say in response. She was too dazed by her discovery to do anything other than lie still and quiet while she fought to regain control of her breathing. Her head was awhirl with all that had occurred within the space of only a few short hours. She was actually married to the rakishly handsome whaling captain who lay naked beside her, she had finally acknowledged the truth of her feelings for him, and his lovemaking had proven more tempestuous and thrilling, and more wickedly pleasurable, than she ever could have imagined!

So lost was she in her thoughts, that she was not immediately aware of Ryan slipping out of the bed. It wasn't until he was bending over her that she fully realized his warmth was missing.

"Wha . . . what are you doing?" she stammered breathlessly, her violet eyes wide and sparkling as she gazed up at him in puzzlement. He smiled enigmatically and lifted her in his arms.

"I promised you a bath, did I not?" He smiled again, gave her a long, lingering kiss, then began striding from the hut and toward the same narrow path where Hillary had made a last, desperate attempt to escape what she now realized had always been inevitable.

IX

Acutely conscious of Ryan's eyes raking over her naked curves with bold possessiveness as he carried her toward the pool, Hillary felt warm color staining her cheeks. In spite of the intimacy they had just shared, she found herself unable to meet his smoldering gaze. She could scarcely believe that the two of them had just consummated their hours-old marriage and were now wandering about completely naked in the broad daylight! Good heavens, she then mused, suppose someone came along and saw them?

When they reached the edge of the water, Ryan set her on her feet and held her at arm's length before him. She could not prevent her own arms from crossing protectively across her naked breasts, nor her eyes from straying downward to where his manhood sprang from a cluster of tight, dark brown curls. Her face flamed anew as she hastily averted her gaze.

"You've a perfect right to look upon your husband, Mrs. Gallagher," teased Ryan. A roguish smile lit his handsome countenance when he added, "Just as I've a perfect right to look upon you. And to do *this.*" Giving her no warning of exactly what he planned, he seized her about the waist, tossed her over his broad shoulder as though she were nothing more than a sack of meal, and started wading purposefully into the clear, sparkling waters of the tidal pool.

"Ryan! Put me down!" squealed Hillary, her long raven tresses spilling into the water as she squirmed and pushed against his naked back.

"Whatever my lady commands," he retorted, then proceeded to do just that—but not quite in the same manner she had intended.

A breathless shriek of protest escaped her lips when she suddenly found herself sailing backward through space, only to land bottom-first in the pool. She came flaring up to the surface a moment later, her ebony curls plastered across her stormy face. Hurriedly parting the curtain of streaming wet locks with her fingers, she fixed Ryan with a wounded glare and sputtered indignantly, "What a perfectly unchivalrous thing to do!"

"Yankee whalers are not known for their chivalry, remember?" he quipped with a mocking grin. He began advancing on her with slow, measured steps, the water closing about his trim waist. She eyed him mistrustfully and took a step backward, carefully finding her footing on the pool's sandy bottom.

"What are you doing? Don't come any closer!" He ignored her, a foreboding light of devilment dancing in his blue-green eyes as he kept advancing. Hillary, folding her arms protectively across her naked breasts once more, backed farther toward the center of the pool until the water reached to just below the full, rose-tipped mounds of flesh she was trying in vain to shield from her husband's searing gaze. "You . . . you keep away from me, Ryan Gallagher!"

"No." His mouth curved into a boyish, wickedly mischievous grin.

Hillary's eyes grew very wide. This playfulness he was exhibiting was a different, unfamiliar facet of his character, and one she wasn't at all certain she knew how to deal with. Her gaze anxiously scanned the surroundings before returning to fasten warily upon his predaciously smiling face.

"I thought you were going to let me bathe," she reminded him in a small voice, coming to a halt when the glistening, aquamarine water lapped at the bare smoothness of her shoulders.

"And so I shall. As a matter of fact, sweet bride, I shall perform the honors myself."

Suddenly, he lunged forward, seizing her about the waist and hauling her beneath the water with him. His strong arms imprisoned her, and he quickly turned so that he bore her weight upon his when the two of them went crashing down to the soft, powdery sand that formed the base of the secluded lagoon. He bore her back up to the surface in the next moment, allowing her only a single deep breath of air before capturing her lips with his.

Hillary melted against him, her heart soaring with the newly realized certainty of her love. Instinctively straining upward, she lifted her bare arms to wind them tightly about the corded muscles of Ryan's neck. She kissed him with an answering fire, and she soon grew dizzy with renewed passion as she reveled in the feel of his hard, naked body molded to perfection against her gloriously exposed curves.

She suffered an acute sense of loss and disappointment when he released her mere seconds later, but the disappointment turned to delight when, tugging her to more shallow waters, he bent and scooped up a handful of sand. He turned her about, swept aside her hair, and began gently smoothing the sand's soft grittiness across her shoulders and down the graceful curve of her back. Hillary caught her breath upon a gasp and trembled beneath his practical yet highly erotic ministrations.

"Is this how . . . how husbands bathe their wives in New Bedford?" she queried breathlessly.

"I've never had occasion to ask," he answered with a low chuckle. His fingers slowly spread the sand downward to where the delectable swell of her hips disappeared beneath the water's surface. "But I seriously doubt if they would have much opportunity to do so, given the climate in New England— particularly the climate *inside* the bedrooms," he added with another soft, resonant laugh. "The women there aren't, well, they're not exactly what one would term 'straightforward' regarding such things."

"You . . . you've met a great many women, haven't you?" Hillary couldn't resist asking, though she found it increasingly difficult to concentrate on the discussion as his fingers dipped below the water to stroke the satiny roundness of her buttocks. She stifled a moan and felt her knees weakening.

"I suppose I have." He turned her back to face him, and she saw that there was a strange half smile playing about his lips. Scooping up more sand, his hands began tenderly rubbing their way down toward her breasts. He was satisfied to note the telltale glow of passion on her beautiful face, and his piercing gaze bored down deeply into her wide, brightly shining one. "But this old sea rover never lost his heart until he met a beautiful, South Seas nymph with hair the color of a raven's wing and eyes that sparkle and flash like jewels held up to the sun. You're the only woman I've ever loved, Hillary, the only woman I will ever love."

She wanted to tell him that she had lost her heart as

well, but her lips would not form the words. Her head was spinning crazily, and she involuntarily clutched at his bronzed arms for support as his large hands glided across and all around her breasts. She bit at her lower lip, her eyes sweeping closed when his fingers lightly encircled the rosy peaks of her nipples. Then, his hands were smoothing down across the flat, silken planes of her belly . . . on to the apex of her shapely white thighs visible beneath the clear water. She could not prevent a soft cry from escaping her lips when he touched her there, and her fingers tightened about the steely hardness of his arms as his hands lingered for several long moments upon the velvety treasure between her legs.

Finally, he swept her up in his arms and lovingly conveyed her back across the pool toward the mossy bank. A glimmer of amusement briefly joined the fiery radiance of desire in his blue-green eyes as he smiled down wryly at her.

"I well remember what happened when I tried carrying you from the lagoon at Starcross. In the event you're tempted to employ that particular maneuver *this* time, my love, I give you fair warning that I will not be diverted from my purpose."

A shiver ran the length of Hillary's spine, but it was not due to any discomfort from being wet and naked. Indeed, she felt a splendid warmth stealing over her, and she drew a slightly ragged breath before replying with newfound boldness, "In truth, Captain Gallagher, it had not entered my mind to employ *any* maneuver of escape."

She was rewarded for her candor with a twinkle of his magnificent turquoise eyes and a heart-melting smile, swiftly followed by a thorough, impassioned kiss that continued even as he lowered her to the cool earth and covered her body with his own.

Ryan made slow, leisurely love to her there beside the pool, his hands and lips working together to bring her to the very pinnacle of desire and fulfillment. Gasping and moaning repeatedly at the wondrous things he did to her body, Hillary suffered no pain at all when he took her the second time. She responded to his lovemaking with all the fervor of her own, recently liberated passion, delighting him with her intrepid spirit and willingness to learn what he was only too eager to teach. Surrendering to the wild abandon calling her, she cried her husband's name aloud during the final blending of their bodies, and she obeyed without question when he instructed her to wrap her legs about his lean-muscled hips. Feeling that he had touched her very womb, she came perilously close to losing consciousness when the moment of completion occurred. She clung weakly to Ryan's virile, equally sated body as tremor after tremor of deep-seated pleasure shook her . . .

They did not return to the hut until darkness was beginning to cloak the luxuriant green countryside. Upon their arrival, Hillary was startled to find a platter of fruit, cheese, and freshly baked bread on the table. Her violet eyes grew wide and troubled, and she hastily clutched the towel, which Ryan had so thoughtfully snatched up on his way out with her earlier, more closely about her nakedness.

"Good heavens, I wonder who—"

"There's no need to worry, my love," he assured her, his chiseled lips curving into a smile of affectionately mocking humor. "Tevaite insisted upon being the one to deliver all our meals. It seems she didn't think Tehura could be trusted not to try to satisfy her natural, youthful curiosity about the progress of our honeymoon."

Hillary colored becomingly when she pondered

the possibility of what Tevaite might have seen—or heard—while bringing the food.

"Come," said Ryan, grabbing her hand and tugging her along with him to take a seat on the coco frond mats. His dark hair was still damp and curling rakishly about his sun-kissed forehead, and his superbly masculine form was clad in nothing more than a towel wrapped carelessly about his waist. Still feeling as if in a dream, Hillary knelt on the floor beside him and rearranged the folds of her own large cotton towel about her bare limbs. As she did so, the edges tucked above her bosom loosened and slipped downard, exposing the pale, rounded perfection of one of her breasts.

Hearing Ryan's soft groan, Hillary reflexively snatched the towel back up and turned her head to meet his gaze. What she saw reflected within the gleaming, aquamarine depths of his eyes prompted her to catch her breath and blush anew.

"I find I have a powerful hunger of a sudden," he confessed in a low voice hoarse with returning desire, his sinewy arms encircling her once more, "but it is a hunger that cannot be assuaged with mere food."

"But we . . . we have already—"

"And we shall do so again and again throughout these next few days," proclaimed Ryan, pulling her masterfully across his lap. He bent his handsome face close to hers and vowed, "I'm going to love you until you beg for mercy, until I hear your sweet lips speaking the words I long to hear."

"Then perhaps I should never speak them," whispered Hillary. Her eyes were aglow with all the love in her heart as she slowly raised a hand to his face and gently smoothed a tendril of damp hair from his forehead. "For I . . . I want neither mercy nor inattention from you." Ryan stared down at her intently, his eyes searching her face and finding the truth.

"Say it," he commanded quietly, his countenance growing very solemn while his eyes blazed with barely controlled passion. "Say it, Hillary."

She made him wait only a moment longer before declaring in a voice quavering with emotion, "I love you, Ryan Gallagher. I did not truly know it until today." She smiled up at him tentatively and repeated, "I love you."

With a low growl of triumph, he tightened his arms about her and claimed her lips in a fiercely possessive kiss that once again made her forget all else save him.

The evening breeze was warm and scented with the sweet, provocative aroma of gardenias and jasmine as it drifted leisurely through the trees. The moon, having already risen to greet the deepening twilight, cast its silvery luminescence upon the bewitching landscape and filled the hut with light and shadows. A lone bird trilled its plaintive lament in the near distance as the calm Pacific seas beat gently at the reef and the island settled into yet another star-filled night.

For Hillary and Ryan, the nightfall signaled not only the end of the day, but also the beginning of their new life together, a life they each hoped would hold boundless love and ecstasy and joy . . . and few storms to disrupt the enchantment.

With the dawn came a rude awakening for Hillary—in more ways than one.

The sun had not yet topped the mountains when she stirred softly in the bed beside a peacefully slumbering Ryan. Though her eyelids fluttered open, she lay suspended in the hazy world between sleep and wakefulness for several moments longer. Finally, she released a long sigh and began stretching lazily beneath the quilt, only to gasp at the sudden pain her actions caused. Her eyes flew wide as she was faced with the unpleasant discovery that her body was sore in places she hadn't even known existed.

Is it any wonder? a tiny voice deep within her taunted. Recalling with shocking clarity all that she and Ryan had done together, she groaned inwardly and colored hotly from head to toe. She sank low beneath the quilt, her naked curves making unintentional, yet highly stimulating, contact with her husband's hard warmth. A slow smile spread across his handsome face as he turned sleepily on his side and gathered her in his arms.

"Good morning, lady wife," he murmured, his eyes still closed. He pressed a wonderfully gentle kiss upon her temple while one hand crept upward to her breasts. She moaned softly as his warm, knowledgeable fingers caressed the rounded flesh he had repeatedly branded with his lips and hands throughout the magical night.

"Ryan!" Hillary protested weakly. Already growing light-headed and breathless, she forced herself to pull away. She hastily slid from his arms and held up the quilt over her nakedness, her long ebony tresses streaming about her face and shoulders in wild disarray. "Please, Ryan, I . . . I must look a sight!"

"That you do," he agreed with a wolfish grin. He attempted to pull her back down, then scowled in mock rebuke at her resistance. "Disobedience so soon, my love? I can see that you still have a good deal to learn about the execution of your 'wifely duties.' Perhaps we should begin the lessons *now*."

"Ryan!" she gasped out again when he suddenly

yanked her atop him. The quilt became entangled between them, a circumstance Hillary used to her advantage as Ryan momentarily concentrated his attention on tugging it free so that he could gain greater access to her delectable charms. She quickly rolled from the big feather bed, wincing at the shock to her aching muscles when her feet hit the floor. Losing her balance, she stumbled back against the trunk and grasped at the bottom edge of the unpaned window above it for support. She stood breathing heavily, her eyes appearing enormous within the delicate oval of her face when they traveled across to meet Ryan's amused gaze.

"Where the devil do you think you're going?" he lazily challenged, crossing his hands beneath his hand. "Get back in this bed, woman!"

"No!" She drew herself proudly erect and raised her chin in a gesture of wifely defiance, then was dismayed to feel herself blushing as she told him, "It may surprise you to learn, Ryan Gallagher, that even a bride requires a . . . a few moments of privacy!" Whirling about, she opened the trunk and began rummaging about in it for something to wear. She did her best to ignore her husband, whose eyes she could literally feel scorching over her naked back-side. Her hasty search yielded a small bag of toilet articles, a short-sleeved gown of pale blue dimity, and a thin, white cotton wrapper, which she hurriedly donned before turning back to face the man whose very gaze provoked a wealth of fiery sensations within her.

"Are you sure you don't want me to come along?" His gleaming eyes issued a silent challenge as his mouth curved into yet another sensuously persuasive smile. "After all, there should be no secrets between us now that we're man and wife." A dull flush rose to

Hillary's cheeks again as she looked away in confusion. Taking pity on her, Ryan chuckled softly and said, "Go on, my love. Only don't be long, else I'll begin to worry that you've changed your mind about anchoring yourself to a whaler, and a Yankee to boot!"

"Never," she earnestly proclaimed, her eyes sparkling with love. She flashed him a captivating smile, then left, heading back to the pool to bathe and dress. When she returned a short time later, her silken black locks had been tamed and fastened into a single long braid, and her shapely form was encased in the dimity gown. She had found no undergarments contained within the trunk, but she told herself, with an inward smile of wicked delight, that there would probably be little need for them—no need at all if the previous night was any indication of what the remainder of her honeymoon would be like.

Ryan took himself off to bathe soon thereafter, leaving her to face Tevaite alone when the older woman arrived with their breakfast.

"You and the captain are happy," said Tevaite as she padded noiselessly across the wooden floor with a fresh platter of food. Her words were not a question, but rather a simple statement of fact.

"Yes," Hillary admitted a bit shyly. She smiled at the woman who had always been so much more than a servant to her. "You were right, Tevaite—truth not spoken *is* still truth."

"Ah, then you have learned much already," pronounced the Tahitian, her brown eyes full of affection and approval as she set the platter on the table and turned back to her young mistress. The familiar, knowing smile lit her noble features when she added, "Your uncle will be pleased to hear your husband treats you well. As will Tehura. She was

225

much worried that her Missy would not like the way of love between a man and a woman."

A wave of embarrassment washed over Hillary. "You may tell Tehura—" she started to retort, then immediately changed her mind. "Please give my uncle my love, and . . . and tell him I am well." She moved forward to embrace Tevaite, who announced upon taking her leave that more food would be brought before sundown. Hillary waved at the older woman as she climbed back up into the wagon and guided the horse away from the clearing.

Ryan sauntered back inside the hut soon after the golden rays of the morning sun finally began filtering their way down through the trees to warm the thatch roof. Having washed and donned a clean pair of trousers, he had left the bronzed, smooth-muscled expanse of his upper body bare. He found his wife gazing out the window and munching rather absentmindedly on a piece of fresh coconut. Stealing up behind her, he surrounded her with his arms and molded the length of his splendid male physique against her voluptuous softness.

"I see Tevaite has already come and gone," he murmured against her ear. "Was it something she said that brought that faraway look to your beautiful eyes?"

"No," she replied with a soft laugh. Snuggling back against him contentedly, she released a sigh and revealed, "I was just thinking of all that's to be done before we sail for New Bedford. I give thanks for the fact that Uncle Denholm's health has improved so much these past few days. It would be extremely difficult for me to leave him if—"

"What are you talking about?" demanded Ryan, his rugged brow creasing into a frown.

"About the preparations for our voyage, of course.

Oh, I know you probably disapprove of my thinking about such practical matters while we're still on our honeymoon, but there are so many things to be seen to, and so little time. Since I've never been to New Bedford before, I shall have to rely upon you to—'' She broke off when he suddenly stepped back and spun her about to face him, and she stared up at him in wide-eyed bemusement as his darkening gaze filled with realization.

"I thought you understood, Hillary," he spoke in a low voice, his fingers tightening upon her arms. His handsome face looked very grim. "Damn it, but I thought you knew!"

"Knew what?"

"That you would not be coming with me."

Completely taken aback by his words, she stared up at him in stunned disbelief. *Not go with him?* Why, he couldn't mean it!

"I . . . I don't understand," she faltered, her violet eyes clouding with confusion as they desperately searched his for any sign of humor. There was none. She felt a growing sense of dread that he had indeed meant it, that he was truly planning to leave her behind in Tahiti while he sailed halfway around the world and back again. Or was it also possible that he did not intend to return at all? *No! Dear God, no!*

"Much as I would like to, I can't take you with me, Hillary. A whaling ship's no place for a woman. While I'll hate like the devil being parted from you, it will only be for a few short months. And when I return, it will be for good."

"You . . . you actually expect me to sit and wait patiently while you go back to New Bedford?" She jerked free of his grasp and took several, furious steps before whirling back around to confront him. Her eyes flashed their brilliant amethyst fire as she pointedly recalled, "I told you, Ryan Gallagher, that I would *not* marry a man who left me behind while he went traipsing about the world!"

"I won't be 'traipsing about the world,' as you so charmingly put it." He gave her a warm, conciliatory smile, determined to remain calm and reason patiently with her. Slowly crossing the distance between them, he placed his hands upon her shoulders soothingly and said, "For a bark, the *Falcon* is a speedy vessel. We should be able to reach New Bedford well before the end of summer. I give you my word I'll not remain there one moment longer than what is required to attend to certain matters of business—and a few family matters as well—and then I'll be on my way back to you."

"Why did you marry me if you had no intention of taking me with you?" she demanded accusingly, her eyes now glistening with hot, bitter tears. "You were in such a hurry to wed me and bed me, Ryan Gallagher, and yet you never bothered to inform me of the fact that I would scarcely be a bride before I became a . . . a sea widow!"

"A sea widow?" echoed Ryan, then chuckled quietly and shook his head. "No, my love, you'll not be a widow. I make you a solemn vow that I'll return to you—and that I'll be very much alive."

"How can you know for certain?" she retorted, the pain in her heart fueling her sense of betrayal as her world came crashing down upon her. Gone was the spell of enchantment that had cradled her since she had realized her love for Ryan. "Why, anything could happen to you during the voyage, or even after you arrive in New Bedford! You might very well decide to forget all about your wife in Tahiti. You might—"

"I love you, Hillary," he reminded her, his tone

edged with an encroaching sharpness. "I'll not forsake our love, no matter what happens." She tried to pull free, but he held fast. "I never meant to deceive you. You must believe that. And as for my eagerness to 'wed you and bed you' before I sailed, you must surely realize that my haste was prompted by my feelings for you. It was only natural that I wanted to know you were mine before I left."

"If you truly love me, you'll take me with you!" she challenged. "If you truly loved me, you'd not be able to leave me behind; you'd not be able to bear the thought of our separation!"

Ryan's hands relaxed their grip on her shoulders as he sighed in growing exasperation. He turned away, raked a hand through his damp, sun-streaked hair, and muttered a curse beneath his breath before rounding on her again.

"I *do* love you, blast it! Do you honestly think I *want* this separation? Nothing would give me greater pleasure than to have you with me, but it's impossible."

"Why? Other wives have sailed with their husbands. Whaling captains have been bringing their wives with them to Tahiti for years! Why shouldn't *I* go with *you*?"

"Because a whaling ship is no place for a woman!" he firmly reiterated. "It doesn't matter what other captains have done—I'll not have *my* wife sharing such close quarters with two dozen of the roughest men on the face of the earth. I'll not have you exposed to the dangers, to the heat and the cold and the storms. No, Hillary, you'll stay here. I'll rest easier knowing you're safe and being looked after by people who love you."

"Looked after?" she indignantly repeated, her violet eyes ablaze. "I'll have you know that it has not been necessary for anyone to *look after* me for several years now! I am a grown woman, Ryan Gallagher, and I—"

"The matter is settled!" Ryan abruptly cut her off, his tone one of unyielding authority. His eyes glittered down coldly into the stormy loveliness of her upturned features, and there was a forbiddingly set look about his handsome face as he said, "In three days' time, the *Falcon* will be sailing for New Bedford—*with no women aboard*. Since my presence will be required during the last hours of fitting her for the voyage, you and I have little time left to us. And I intend to make every moment count!"

He reached for her, but she nimbly eluded his grasp and flew across to the doorway, where she whirled back around to utter in a voice choked with emotion, "You . . . you have no right to treat me this way! Though I love you, I cannot and *will not* meekly submit to you in this! If you care so little for me that you can leave me for . . . for God only knows how long, to return to your home and your family without me, then our marriage was a mistake!" Dashing with angry impatience at the tears coursing down her flushed cheeks, Hillary drew a ragged breath and feelingly proclaimed, "I'll not allow you to break my heart any more than you have already done!" With that, she spun about to take flight, desperate to escape the presence of the man who only the day before had brought her such happiness, but who now had shattered that happiness with what she perceived to be a cruel betrayal of her love.

Ryan, however, closed the distance between them with lightning-quick speed. His hand shot out to seize her wrist, and a sharp gasp broke from her lips when he yanked her back and swiftly bent to hoist her upon his broad shoulder.

"Let me go! Put me down!" she tearfully raged, her bare feet kicking and her fists beating at the bronzed hardness of his naked back as he wheeled about and began striding toward the bedroom with her. "No more, damn you, no more!"

"You're mine, Hillary! You're my wife, and you'll do as I say!"

"No! I will not be your wife; I will not love you if—"

"You will!" he ground out. He flung her down roughly upon the bed and stood towering ominously above her while she struggled into a sitting position.

Her eyes were wide and sparkling with mingled fury, anguish, and a touch of fear as she met his dangerously smoldering gaze. But the pain in her heart made her reckless. Rising up on her knees, she lifted her chin in a gesture of scornful defiance and lashed out, "I should have known you didn't truly love me! I should have known you were no different than the others of your kind! You care only about your own selfish desires! Anthony tried to warn me about you from the very beginning, but I wouldn't listen! Had I married him instead, I would never have found myself *abandoned* with such callous disregard for my—"

Suddenly and without warning, Ryan breathed a savage oath and toppled her backward in the bed. His tall, powerful frame crashed downward to imprison her startled softness, one arm clamping like a band of iron across her waist. She gasped out a protest as his other hand shot purposefully downward. Rolling off her for one brief moment, he tossed her full skirts up about her waist, fully exposing the flawless symmetry of her lower body. Her silken flesh was laid bare for Ryan's hot caress, and he did not hesitate before taking advantage of her lack of undergarments.

His fingers stroked her quivering thighs, searing a relentless path upward.

"No!" Hillary cried breathlessly, refusing to surrender in spite of the responsive passion already flaring to life within her. "No!" Flailing and squirming and pushing violently against him, she was alarmed to feel him rolling to his back, to feel herself being held captive atop him.

Abruptly jerking her arms behind her back, he effectively imprisoned both of her wrists with one of his large hands. A sob of helpless fury escaped her lips as his fingers delved within the rounded neckline of her bodice and ripped the delicate cotton downward in one swift motion, but her anger turned to irrestrainable desire when his lips began roaming feverishly across her naked bosom. He tugged her suddenly pliant body farther upward upon his, so that the satiny, rose-tipped fullness of her breasts was positioned even more conveniently for his hungrily adoring mouth.

Hillary moaned low in her throat as his velvety tongue flicked tantalizingly across one of her pert nipples. She arched her back, her entire body feeling as if on fire when his lips closed about the quivering peak and drew it within the warm cavern of his mouth. He sucked demandingly upon the delicate morsel of femininity, sending a delicious shiver coursing down Hillary's spine.

"Oh, Ryan!" she murmured brokenly, her voice sounding foreign and distant to her ears. She was glad when he released her wrists, for she felt an urgent need to thread her fingers within the damp thickness of his hair, to boldly clutch his mouth even closer to her breasts. Her long braid of hair fell forward across her shoulder, and her head tossed restlessly above Ryan's as her breath came in short, quiet gasps.

She was hardly aware of the moment when his hands slid down over her curves and beneath her hips to unfasten his trousers, but she was made acutely conscious of his actions when the length of his aroused manhood suddenly came into contact with her own naked flesh. Inhaling sharply, she felt her passions careening wildly upward as Ryan gripped the delightful roundness of her bare bottom with his strong hands and brought the very center of her womanhood sliding erotically back and forth across his warm hardness.

Just when she was certain she could bear no more, Ryan lifted her hips and eased her down onto his rigid member. She nearly fainted with relief and longing and near painful ecstasy as he sheathed himself within her soft passage, and she glorified in the irresistible mastery of her body as he moved deep within her. His lips traveled back to her breasts while she clung weakly to his shoulders, his fingers tightening possessively about her buttocks while she rode atop him and instinctively matched the age-old, rapidly escalating rhythm of his loving.

Hillary screamed softly when, a brief moment after Ryan, she reached the very summit of passion's splendor. Feeling completed satiated and thoroughly overwhelmed by what she had just experienced, she collapsed upon her husand and sought to regain control of her riotously irregular breathing. Ryan gently pulled her down beside him and held her within the warm security of his arms.

He was the first to break the silence. "Damn, my love, but you are able to infuriate, incite, and exhaust me more than any woman I've ever met!" His deep voice was compellingly vibrant as it slid over her, and she could not prevent a soft smile from touching her lips.

"Oh, Ryan," she sighed, her eyes aglow with love and her beautiful face still lightly flushed. "Why is it you are so arrogant and overbearing at times, and so tender and charming at others?" She nestled contentedly against him and sighed once more, feeling not the least bit annoyed with him for having ruined her gown.

"Perhaps to keep you spellbound," he retorted with a low chuckle, his fingers tracing a repetitive path upon her arm.

Neither of them spoke again for several long seconds. Finally, Hillary rose up on one elbow and cast him a saucy smile. "I suppose you see *now*, Ryan Gallagher, why I cannot allow you to sail without me!"

"What do you mean?" His brows drew together into a faint frown, and his blue-green eyes kindled with more than a touch of suspicion.

"Why, only that since you have so generously 'enlightened' me, you cannot possibly expect me to return to darkness for so many months!" She blushed a little as she said it, but her gaze did not fall before the intensity of his. "How am I to endure—"

"Blast it, woman, our abstinence will be no easier for me to bear," he growled, pushing her head back down to rest upon the gleaming, rock-hard breadth of his chest.

"Come now, Ryan, why should you allow this foolish obstinancy of yours to make us both miserable?" Her voice was both softly pleading and confidently insistent. "Take me with you. I swear I won't be any trouble. A wife's place is at her husband's side, is it not? And I'm a good sailor. I was never once seasick when I came from England—"

"No."

"But neither of us wants this separation! It doesn't make any sense for us to be apart and lonely when we can be together. I know Tevaite can manage things without me for a while, and—"

"No."

Hillary sighed heavily. Then, deciding to employ another strategy, and armed with a new feeling of power, she began pressing a succession of feathery, alluring kisses across Ryan's chest and up along his neck. Her naked breasts swept provocatively against his side, making her tingle and making his desire for her flame anew in spite of the fact that he had scarcely recovered his energy from the most recent, tempestuous union of their flesh.

"You can't truly mean to do without me for months on end, dearest husband," she whispered when her lips reached his ear. Her voice was breathless and innocently seductive, and she punctuated her words with a light, teasing exploration down toward his reawakening maleness. In answer, Ryan flipped her unceremoniously onto her back, placed his own body atop hers once more, and imprisoned her hands above her head. A mocking smile played about his lips while his eyes glistened with amusement.

Hillary's face burned as he said, "While I would not normally be immune to such blandishment, sweet vixen, I'm afraid such tactics will avail you nothing in this particular case. As I told you before, the matter is settled."

"But—"

"*It is settled.* You're not to mention it again, understand?" Scowling down at her for effect, he did not allow her time to reply before his lips descended upon hers and silenced, at least momentarily, any further argument she might have offered.

Hillary's last coherent thought was that although he might consider the matter settled, she most certainly did not. She would have to think of some other means of persuasion. One way or another, when the *Falcon* sailed for New Bedford, the captain's wife would be aboard!

X

Although Ryan's refusal to discuss the matter of the voyage was always in the back of Hillary's mind, the remainder of the honeymoon was nonetheless idyllic for her. The hours sped past in a never-ending whirl of passion and enchantment, so that by the time Ryan took her back to Starcross, she was more than ever determined to prevent their separation.

Depositing her upon the front steps of the house that sunswept morning, he gave her one more highly intoxicating kiss before reluctantly setting her away from him and announcing that he would return before nightfall to bid her a last farewell. She watched him ride away, her mind already racing with a turbulent jumble of plots and schemes to ensure her presence aboard the *Falcon* when it weighed anchor the next morning. Once he had disappeared from view, she whirled about and went in search of her uncle.

Denholm Reynolds was much relieved to see the glow of happiness on his beloved niece's face. He was taking breakfast on the upper verandah when Hillary rushed across to embrace him, and he smiled across at her as she sank down onto her knees beside his chair.

"I take it there are no regrets on your part, my dear?" he softly queried, his eyes alight with fond amusement.

"None, Uncle," she answered without hesitation, her own eyes sparkling with joy. In the next instance, however, a shadow of disquiet crossed her features, and Denholm frowned in growing concern as he watched her rise to her feet and wander over rather distractedly to the carved-railing.

"What is it, Hillary?"

"It's Ryan," she disclosed with an audible sigh, turning back to face him. Sudden tears glistened in her eyes. "Oh Uncle, he intends to sail for New Bedford without me! He insists I remain and wait for his return, and he . . . he refuses to listen to reason!"

Denholm felt a sharp twisting of his heart. *No!* He had counted on Gallagher taking her away before . . . he had counted on her absence, on her being comforted and cared for by her husband. He now belatedly lamented the fact that he had not questioned him more closely, that he had not exacted a promise from him. He could tell the young captain the truth, but there was no assurance . . .

Hastily concealing his own distress at the news, he calmly prompted Hillary to tell him everything. He proved a sympathetic listener to her plight, and she was somewhat surprised to learn that he was just as anxious as she that Ryan not be allowed to leave her behind.

"Then you must help me think of some way to be aboard the *Falcon* when she sails!" she pleaded, kneeling beside him once more. Her eyes shone up at him earnestly as she took his hand between hers. "Please know that I would not think of leaving you if you were not well on the road to recovery. But, if I *can*

238

somehow manage to go with Ryan, it will only be for a few months. I promise we shall return to Starcross as soon as possible!"

"Your place is with your husband, my dear, no matter where he decides to settle," Denholm gently reminded her. He smiled again and patted her hand. "Indeed, I would not want it any other way." Retrieving his cane from the other side of his chair, he slowly stood and limped across to gaze out pensively upon the plantation's luxuriant grounds. Several long moments passed before he pronounced with a faint smile, "I think I know of a way to get you aboard Captain Gallagher's ship."

"You do? Oh Uncle, how?" Hillary asked eagerly, her gaze full of renewed hope.

"It will require Tevaite's help, of course, and the aid of several others she can be trusted to enlist. You will have to act quickly, and take every care to avoid detection."

"I will do anything necessary!" she assured him. "Please, Uncle, tell me of the plan!"

"It's very simple, my dear. We shall make use of a time-honored custom," he mysteriously declared, then proceeded to explain. Hillary listened intently, her confidence of success growing with each passing second.

True to his word, Ryan returned to Starcross just as the last golden rays of the sun were fading softly into the deep blue of the gathering twilight. With almost rough impatience, he drew Hillary into the parlor and closed the door. He swept her up against him and kissed her until they were both light-headed and breathlessly yearning for more.

"Would that I could stay long enough to hold you

close to my heart once more, to gaze upon your beautiful, naked body one last time," Ryan murmured in a voice brimming with raw passion as he tore his lips from hers and buried his face in the fragrant silkiness of her hair. His mouth possessed hers again before he solemnly vowed, "As God is my witness, my love, I'll come back to you. And when I do, I'll never leave you again!"

"Oh, Ryan!" she choked out, despising herself for deceiving him, yet knowing she had to do so. She forced herself to behave as though this were truly the last time they would see each other for months, and silently prayed that he would forgive her when he discovered the truth. "I love you! Please, my darling, never forget that I love you!" She clung to him in very real worriment, the tears coursing down her beautiful face as she kissed him with a vehemence that made it necessary for him to summon every ounce of self-control in order to finally set her away from him.

"I'll write to you," he promised, his magnificent, blue-green gaze burning down into her sparkling amethyst one, "though there's no way of knowing how long it will take for my letters to reach you. If anything should happen, if you should need to get word to me in a hurry, you've only to contact the American consul here and he'll see that I receive the message." Hillary, feeling miserable and guilty, made one last desperate attempt to change his mind.

"Ryan, please take me with you! I've spoken to Uncle Denholm, and he agrees that I should not remain behind! I could be ready to go in a matter of minutes. I could—"

"No, my love." He bent and gently brushed her cheek with his warm lips, then smiled down at her with such tenderness and love and desire that she found herself unable to look into his handsome countenance any longer. She was left pale and shaken when he strode from the house to charge her uncle with her care, and the sound of hoofbeats rapidly fading into the distance thundered in her ears long after there was silence.

It was close to midnight by the time the two outrigger canoes sliced through the dark, moonlit waters of Papeete's harbor. Hillary crouched low in the narrow hull of one of the vessels fashioned from a hollowed-out tree trunk, while in front of her half a dozen Tahitian women giggled and chattered softly amongst themselves at the prospect of the adventure that lay before them. Mahi and one of his many nephews paddled the canoe ever closer to where the *Falcon* lay anchored for her last night in Tahiti. The other canoe held an equal number of women, all of whose assistance had been secured by Tevaite, and all of whom had visited men aboard the whale ships before.

Hillary adjusted the knitted cap upon her head, making certain her raven tresses were securely concealed beneath its slightly scratchy protection. Dressed in a pair of heavy cotton duck trousers that were a trifle too fitted across her hips, an old flannel shirt with the too-long sleeves rolled up to free her hands, and a seaman's jacket that virtually swallowed the upper half of her body, she looked much like a child playing at dress-up in an older brother's clothes. Her stomach was churning nervously as she gazed at the ominous bulk of the ship ahead, but she sternly cautioned herself to remain calm and to follow the scheme her uncle and Tevaite had concocted for her benefit. If all went as planned, she mused, then her presence aboard the ship would not be detected until the *Falcon* was a good day out of Papeete. *If all went as planned . . .*

"We are there, Missy," Mahi whispered behind her. He and his nephew skillfully guided the canoe alongside the ship, and the women began calling out gaily to the few men on deck. Since it was customary for the natives to bid departing whalers farewell—a custom sometimes allowed by a ship's captain, sometimes not—the crew of the *Falcon* found nothing unusual in the fact that several of the local women had ventured out into the harbor in the middle of the night to see them off. One of the men hastened below to the forecastle to inform his comrades of the occurrence, while the others yelled a boisterous welcome to the women and tossed down the rope ladder.

Hillary sat very quietly and still as the women shinnied up the ladder, each of them taking along a bottle of *ave*. Within seconds, the deck was alive with sounds of laughter and the music of an accordion, and several lanterns were brought up to light the festivities.

It was no wonder that the captain, disturbed by the revelry while below in his quarters, suddenly appeared on deck and demanded an accounting. "Mr. Reid, what the devil is the meaning of this?" Ryan gruffly asked his first mate, who had arrived upon the scene mere seconds before him.

"It's a celebration of sorts, Captain," Connor supplied the obvious. His golden eyes were full of amusement as he met Ryan's piercing gaze. "Do you want me to have the women removed, sir?"

"No, Mr. Reid, that won't be necessary." The merest hint of a rueful smile tugged at Ryan's lips. Why shouldn't the men enjoy their last hours in this paradise? he mentally reasoned with himself. It would be their last chance for relaxation until they reached New Bedford. Merely because he was feeling wretched and empty inside didn't mean everyone else aboard should have to suffer. *Hillary*. Dear God, how he missed her already! "The women can remain for an hour—no longer," he decreed, his voice ringing out with unquestionable authority. His words were met with cheers and whistles from the crew, who threw themselves into the spirit of the celebration with even more abandon.

Hillary, holding her breath as she listened to the sound of her husband's voice, heard him murmur something to Connor before going below again. She was so preoccupied with thoughts of what his reaction would be when she made her presence aboard ship known to him that she started in alarm as Mahi suddenly touched her arm.

"Come, Missy," he whispered. "It is time." Nodding in silent understanding, she waited while he and a man from the other canoe climbed up the ladder to the deck. She took up the small carpetbag she had brought with her, then grabbed hold of the rope and swung herself up from the canoe. The two Tahitians stood planted above with their arms folded negligently across their naked chests, their bodies concealing Hillary from view as she made her way carefully to the top of the ladder and climbed over the railing to drop down onto the ship's deck. She had worn men's clothing so that she might blend in with the other whalers if seen, but it now appeared her disguise had not been necessary after all.

Pausing a moment to cast a furtive glance toward the spot where several of the women were dancing within a large circle of men, she began creeping stealthily toward one of the whaleboats on the starboard side. Gaining confidence that she had been unobserved, she reached the boat and lifted the heavy canvas tarpaulin covering it. She quickly tossed her carpetbag inside and scrambled into the musty darkness after it. Landing with a jolt, she winced at the pain in her knee and shifted about to try to find a more comfortable position on the hard wood. The music continued uninterrupted, as did the raucous laughter.

She had done it! She was aboard Ryan's ship! Silently congratulating herself and the others on the successful execution of her uncle's plan, Hillary tugged the cap from her head and smiled triumphantly. If she could just remain hidden for the next several hours, she would then be where she belonged —at her husband's side. She was certain he would not turn the ship around and sail back to Tahiti once they were a good day's distance away. She was convinced that, given enough time, she could make him see that she had done the right thing.

He would be furious at first, she told herself with an inward sigh. He would in all likelihood threaten to put her ashore on the first inhabited island they came to! But, recalling her uncle's parting words of encouragement to her, she held fast to the belief that her love for Ryan, and his for her, would overcome any feelings of anger and betrayal.

"Always follow your heart, my dearest Hillary," Denholm Reynolds had advised her. There had been a certain air of resignation about him, a noticeable sadness about his eyes, which Hillary had naturally attributed to her going. He had embraced her and smiled down into her tear-streaked face before adding, "When two people love each other, nothing else matters. Your Aunt Louisa and I were never meant to be parted—neither, I believe, are you and Ryan. Never forget that you owe your first allegiance

244

to him."

Tevaite and Tehura had shed tears upon saying good-bye, and the older woman had repeated an old Tahitian blessing—*ia mania te miti*—which translated "let the sea be calm." Knowing Tevaite as she did, Hillary was aware that her friend had meant it figuratively as well as literally.

Reflecting upon the fact that she would not be returning to Starcross for a long time, she closed her eyes and battled a sudden wave of homesickness. She listened to the accordion's jubilant melody, her heart pounding as she once again thought of Ryan. Whatever lay ahead for her, she would be sharing her life with the man she loved. And that was indeed the only thing that truly mattered . . .

The minutes stretched into hours. Mahi and the others had long since gone when, lulled by the gentle rocking motion of the ship, Hillary drifted off into a dream-filled sleep.

She was brought forcibly back to consciousness some time later by the shouts of men and the sounds of footsteps rumbling across the deck. Cautiously lifting an edge of the tarpaulin, she was surprised to see that it was still dark. She felt drugged from her all-too-brief slumber, and it took several moments for her searching gaze to find Ryan. He stood tall and commanding upon the quarterdeck, his first mate at his side. She was afforded a clear view of him, for a lantern had been suspended from a hook within the skylight, and its comforting light shone upward brightly through the multipaned glass.

"Stand by to weigh anchor!" Connor Reid sang out, obediently relating the captain's orders to the crew. "Shake out the main!" The activity on the deck intensified as the sails were unfurled and the anchor winched upward from the deep turquoise waters of the harbor to rest within its proper place at the bow of the ship. Hillary watched in fascination as men scrambled high into the seemingly tangled mass of rigging strung from the bark's three masts. There was no government pilot aboard this time—the authorities had reluctantly given way to Ryan's contention that enough damage had already been done to his vessel.

In no time at all, the *Falcon* was gliding through the pass in the reef and heading for the open sea. Ryan, serving as navigator and pilot himself, set a southeasterly course and handled the wheel with an easy confidence borne of many years' practice. The warm tropical wind proved cooperative as it billowed the sails and stretched the canvas tight before it.

Fearing detection if she dared to press her luck too far, Hillary ducked back beneath the tarpaulin. She was engrossed with thoughts of Ryan as she had just seen him—vigorous and handsome and vibrantly alive, looking even more magnificent than ever. Her cheeks flamed when a shockingly vivid memory of the way he had looked when frolicking naked with her in the tidal pool suddenly crept into her mind. Releasing a long sigh, she shifted restlessly about in the boat and tried to think of some way to help the time pass more quickly as the strengthening waves of the Pacific crashed against the ship's tub-shaped hull.

The hours crawled by as night became morning and morning lengthened toward noon. Reflecting that she had never been more uncomfortable in her life, Hillary repositioned herself yet again and drew off her jacket. The increasing heat and stuffiness inside the whaleboat, caused by the sun's merciless rays beating down upon the tarpaulin, made it difficult for her to breathe. Her head began to reel dizzily, and she was plagued by a sharp thirst. She opened her carpetbag and drew out the food and drink Tevaite had packed for her. Realizing that she had little appetite, she set aside the food and drank some of the coconut milk.

Panic rose within her a short time later as a very real lack of oxygen threatened to send her slipping back into unconsciousness. She hastily lifted an edge of the tarpaulin and inhaled deeply of the fresh, salty air. Though she had vowed to remain hidden until nightfall, she knew she could endure the oppressive darkness inside the boat no longer. She had to get out!

Having made her decision, Hillary wasted no time before pulling on the knitted cap and stuffing her hair underneath it once more. She pulled on her jacket, slid up to the prow, and eased her head from beneath the heavy canvas. Blinking rapidly against the almost blinding sunlight, she spied a handful of men moving about the deck. Her gaze traveled across to the quarterdeck and the companionway that led to the captain's quarters. Ryan was apparently below, for she saw that another man had taken his place at the wheel.

Oh Ryan, I pray your anger with me is swift and easily forgotten! she silently beseeched. Hoping that he would be the first man aboard to see her, for she certainly didn't relish the thought of a confrontation with his crew as an audience, she intended to try to make her way down to his cabin without arousing the suspicion of any of the men on deck.

"It's now or never," she murmured to herself, then climbed carefully from the whaleboat and found her footing on the deck below. She knelt and peered from behind the boat, satisfied to note that her movements had evidently gone unobserved. Taking a deep

247

breath, she drew herself up to her full height and moved away from the boat. She forced herself not to hurry as she crossed the short distance to the companionway. Tossing one last surreptitious glance over her shoulder, she raised a foot to step downward into the narrow passage.

"What've we got here?" a man suddenly growled behind her. Hillary gasped as she felt his hand closing about her arm. She was yanked about to face him, and her violet eyes widened when she saw that it was a slim, coarse-featured man with dark hair who stood glowering down at her menacingly. The man looked vaguely familiar to her, and yet it soon became apparent that he did not recognize her in her present attire. "A stowaway, is it? I'll show you what we do with stowaways on the *Falcon*, you skulkin' little bastard!" His fingers clenched with brutal force upon both her arms as he began hauling her toward the nearby railing.

"No!" Hillary choked out, struggling frantically within his cruel grasp. "Let me go!"

"If you want to call yourself a whaler, you'll damn well have to earn your berth!"

The other men on deck came running to see what all the commotion was about. Several of them laughed to see what they believed to be a fresh-faced young shaveling about to be taught a well-deserved lesson, and one whaler even stepped forward to help Hillary's captor subdue her.

"Stop it! Please, you . . . you don't understand!" she cried. "I'm not—" The breath was knocked from her body as she was lifted and bent roughly facedown over the hard wooden railing. Her eyes were full of terror as she found herself staring down into the churning depths of the Pacific.

"Give 'im the heave-ho, Peale!" one of the

onlookers shouted eagerly.

"Aye, Peale, let 'Master Scutter' have a taste of the sea!" the man beside him seconded.

"Send the babe swimmin' back to his mother! Why, I'll wager he's never done an honest day's work in his life—just look at the size of that rump!" another whaler observed with a derisive snort of laughter.

Hillary was growing faint as the blood rushed to her head. *Dear God, did they truly mean to cast her overboard?* Desperation gave her strength. Flinging her head up, she thrust her upper body wildly backward. The men holding her were taken by surprise, so that she was able to free one of her arms long enough to bring her fist swinging forcibly against the face of the dark-haired man who had first grabbed her, the one the others had called Peale.

"Why, you—" he snarled, rubbing at the coarse, reddened flesh of his cheek. His eyes gleamed murderously as he jerked her forward and twisted her arm behind her back, then forced her head down and clamped an arm about her neck. She cried out in pain and struggled with all her might against such harsh treatment. In the midst of her futile efforts to escape, the stocking cap was suddenly torn from her head. Her long hair tumbled free, streaming down about her face and shoulders in a shimmering mass of midnight-black curls.

"Damn, but it . . . it's a woman!" one of the whalers gasped out in startlement. All of them fell into an awestruck silence, their eyes widening and their mouths agape.

"What the devil is the meaning of this?" Ryan's voice suddenly cut across the deck. Hillary's backside was turned toward him, and she was surrounded by the men. "Mr. Peale, release that man at once!"

"But Captain, it—"

"Do as I say, blast you!"

Hillary nearly collapsed with relief as Peale's punishing grip upon her relaxed. She hurriedly straightened and spun about, her face flushed and her entire body trembling. The whalers stepped reverently away, so that Ryan's gaze finally lit upon his wife's beautiful countenance.

"Hillary?" he breathed, his eyes widening in stunned disbelief as he stood just beyond the entrance to the companionway. He and Connor had been going over some charts in his cabin when he'd heard the laughter and decided to investigate. His jacket had been discarded, his sleeves rolled up negligently to his elbows, and his shirt unbuttoned almost to his waist. To Hillary, he had never looked more rakishly attractive . . . nor more dangerously forbidding. His handsome face had become a mask of barely suppressed fury, and his eyes virtually singed her with their glittering, blue-green intensity.

"Ryan! Oh Ryan, I had to—" she blurted out, only to break off when he began striding toward her at a slow, deliberate pace. Keeping a tight rein on his emotions, he did not trust himself to look at her again. His narrowed, smoldering gaze fastened instead on the surly features of Peale, and his blood boiled as he recalled the fact that the man's arms had been locked about his wife only moments before.

"I'm awaiting your explanation, Mr. Peale!" Ryan ground out. He stood towering above Hillary, and she could literally feel the hot rage emanating from his body. She swallowed hard and stared down at the well-maintained deck.

"We was just dealin' with a stowaway, Cap'n," muttered Peale.

"It so happens you were 'dealing with' my wife!"

pointed out Ryan, his tone low and seething with fury. The savage light in his eyes struck fear in the other man's heart, though Peale would not show it.

"We didn't know it was a woman, Cap'n!" one of the other men hastened to reveal. "We was only plannin' to put a little scare into—"

"Man or woman, stowaway or not, I'll remind you that it is *not* up to the crew of this ship to decide what is done!" His fierce gaze traveled over the faces of the men, their eyes falling guiltily before his. Only Peale continued to meet his gaze squarely, and Ryan battled the urge to pound his fist into the man's face. "You've wasted enough time, damn it—get back to work, all of you!" he commanded, his voice whip-cord sharp.

Several of the men stole one last look at Hillary before taking themselves off. She raised her eyes to find Peale's dark, unsettling gaze upon her, and then he, too, was gone. Left alone with Ryan, she fought down the cowardly temptation to throw herself upon his chest in a fit of weeping and beg for mercy. She suffered a sharp intake of breath when she finally gathered enough courage to look up at him again, for the man she loved had become a stony-faced stranger.

Without a word, he seized her arm in a bruising grip and led her across the deck to the companionway. She wisely chose not to resist. Her pulses raced alarmingly, and she stumbled more than once as he pulled her down the dimly lit steps.

Connor jumped to his feet when the door to Ryan's cabin suddenly crashed open. He stared in amazement at Hillary as she was flung inside.

"Mrs. Gallagher?"

"Leave us, Mr. Reid!" directed Ryan. Gripping the edge of the door while his first mate obediently beat a hasty retreat, he slammed it after Connor, then rounded on Hillary and gave vent to his explosive temper at last. His hands shot out to close upon her shoulders and yank her forward, his head lowering until his fury-tightened face was almost touching her pale, visibly apprehensive one. "What the devil are you doing aboard this ship?"

"I . . . I'm going to New Bedford with you!" she gasped out, blanching inwardly at the raw anger in his gaze. She had thought herself fully prepared for his wrath, but *this,* this white-hot rage of his, overpowered all her defenses.

"The hell you are!"

"I had to do it, Ryan! Both of us would have been utterly miserable, and for no good reason!"

"How exactly *did* you do it?"

"I sneaked aboard last night, when the women were . . . were entertaining your men," she disclosed in a small voice. "I stayed hidden in one of the whaleboats until I couldn't stand it any longer, and then I climbed out and was on my way to see you when Peale caught me and accused me of being a stowaway! He and the others were threatening to toss me overboard when you came up on deck!" she finished in a rush, her words almost tumbling over one another.

"You *are* a stowaway and I ought to toss you overboard myself!" Ryan ungallantly bit out. Suddenly releasing her shoulders as if the contact had burned him, he wheeled away from her with a blistering curse. "You certainly played your part to perfection last night, didn't you?" His deep voice was edged with bitter sarcasm. Pacing furiously back and forth, he went on to recall, "You had me believing you'd accepted the situation. You deceived me well, my love, particularly when we said our good-byes!"

"I didn't want to deceive you! But you wouldn't

listen to me; you wouldn't think of anything but that . . . that damnable male pride of yours!" Her own rising temper made her forget her fear of him. Stalking forward, she installed herself firmly in his path and planted her hands on her hips. Her eyes flashed their brilliant amethyst fire as she tilted her head back and confronted him with a renewed burst of spirit. "It may surprise you to hear this, Ryan Gallagher, but you married a woman with a brain! If you had wanted a simpering little idiot who would never cross you, never challenge you, and never be anything or do anything other than what she was told, then you have every reason to regret your choice of a wife!"

"The only thing I regret is that I trusted you to keep your word!" thundered Ryan.

"I never gave you my word that I would remain behind! I never told you I would wait for you in Tahiti!"

"Perhaps not, but you damned sure never told me you were planning to stow away on my ship, either!" He could not seem to prevent his hands from straying upward to grip her arms, and he ground out another savage oath as his fingers tightened upon her soft yet unyielding flesh. "Was your uncle in on this as well?"

"It was his idea. But he only helped me because I pleaded with him to do so! As I told you before, he believed in the separation no more than I. It would not have been necessary for any of us to deceive you if only you had listened to reason!" She gave a defiant toss of her head, sending her ebony curls bouncing riotously across her shoulders and down her back. "In any case, I *am* here with you, and I cannot in all honesty say I am sorry for my actions!"

"Despite the fact that by doing so we would lose

another day while waiting for the tide again, I am sorely tempted to turn the *Falcon* around and sail her straight back to Tahiti," he avowed, his demeanor suddenly becoming one of deadly calm. Several conflicting emotions played across his handsome, sun-bronzed countenance as his eyes bored down into Hillary's.

"Why, that . . . that would be ridiculous! Your men would very likely be driven to mutiny if you did such a thing!" She stared up into his face closely for a number of seconds, then released a sigh. Her lips curved into a tentative smile, her hands moved to rest upon his partially covered chest, and her tone became conciliatory when she said, "Oh Ryan, why don't you simply accept the fact that I'm here, that I'm going to New Bedford with you, and that the voyage will be so much nicer with your wife—"

"It isn't a question of accepting the fact that you are aboard, Hillary. What's at issue here is your disobedience and how I'm going to deal with it."

Hillary stared up at him blankly. Was he saying he had definitely decided not to take her back to Tahiti? And what exactly did he mean by *dealing* with her disobedience?

Both questions were answered in the next moment, though not quite as she would have wished. Her husband suddenly picked her up and bore her into the adjoining stateroom. Most of the space was taken up by a three-quarter bed, fitted with gimbals so that it would remain upright even with the heavy roll of the ship, and it was upon the bed's firmness that Ryan deposited his momentarily speechless burden.

"You shall spend the remainder of the day in contemplation of your folly," he dispassionately proclaimed, his eyes gleaming dully. "Perhaps by nightfall, I will have found it in my heart to forgive you."

"What?" breathed Hillary. She scrambled to her knees in the bed and faced him with an expression of wide-eyed disbelief. "Is your arrogance truly such that you will not even *try* to consider my feelings in this matter? For heaven's sake, Ryan, I only did what I believed, and still believe, to be the right thing! Why, I thought—"

"No, Hillary, you did not think at all. Call it arrogance if you will, but a man must be master of his own household. Heed me well, my love—you *will* learn to obey me, even if I have to turn you across my knee and beat you into submission!" At the moment, he looked entirely capable of carrying out the threat. Hillary instinctively edged backward in the bed, her eyes round as saucers and her heart pounding wildly.

"You . . . you wouldn't!" she stammered breathlessly.

"I would." Casting her one last scorching look, he spun about on his booted heel and was gone, slamming the door behind him. Hillary heard the sound of the key turning in the lock an instant later, then the sound of Ryan's footsteps as he strode from the cabin and back up the companionway to the deck.

Feeling thoroughly wretched, she heaved a ragged sigh and collapsed back wearily upon the bed. She lay there for a long time, staring up at the beamed ceiling and despondently reflecting upon her quarrel with Ryan. What had happened to the man she loved, the man who had treated her with such tenderness and playfulness on their honeymoon? Her eyes filled with tears of self-pity, resentment, and more than a touch of remorse, and she soon surrendered to the almost painful urge to cry. The gimbals squeaked softly as the bed followed the rocking of the ship, but she was oblivious to both the noise and the motion.

Finally, she dragged herself from the bed and made her way across to the washroom/privy located in a separate compartment off the stateroom. She filled the porcelain bowl and splashed water across her face, then impulsively decided to draw off all her clothes and scrub herself from head to toe. Feeling somewhat invigorated afterward, she hurried back into the stateroom and knelt to search through the small chest of drawers opposite the bed, hoping to find another set of clothing to put on.

There was a sudden rattling in the lock. Hillary started in alarm. Leaping to her feat, she scarcely had time to snatch up one of Ryan's shirts and drape it across her nakedness before the door swung open.

"One of the men retrieved—" Ryan was stating with cold aloofness, only to fall abruptly silent when his eyes fell upon his wife's scantily clad form. Sunlight, streaming in from the portholes, filled the room and lit her thick, raven tresses with touches of golden fire. The shirt she clutched to her breasts reached to just above her knees, and covered only a small portion of her glorious body. Ryan's memory was well able to supply his brain with the knowledge of what was concealed.

"Oh, you brought my . . . my things," faltered Hillary, the direction of her gaze indicating the carpetbag he held in one hand. Her cheeks were flaming, and she was surprised to realize that she felt awkward and shy at standing so revealed before her own husband. But, she then dazedly thought, he seemed almost as though a stranger to her now. "I . . . I was trying to find something to wear."

Ryan said nothing in response. A telltale muscle twitched in the tanned ruggedness of his left cheek, and his darkening gaze seemed at once unfathomable and full of torment. He tossed the carpetbag on the bed, devoured Hillary with his eyes once more, then staunchly turned away.

"There is food and drink on my desk. You may have the use of the cabin, but do not leave these quarters."

She was tempted to call out after him, but she did not. Alone again, she released an uneasy sigh and allowed his shirt to slip to the polished wooden floor. She opened her carpetbag and drew out her gown of creamy white muslin—the same one she had been wearing on that fateful day when Ryan Gallagher had first come into her life.

Her spirits plummeted again, and it was all she could do to pull on the dress and braid her hair. Drifting out into the main cabin, she forced herself to eat a little of the ham and beans. The meal was barely palatable, but she washed it down with strong tea.

She wandered about the room for a while, absently scrutinizing the books, charts, and other items cluttering up every inch of space and then some. Growing increasingly restless, she glanced up at the skylight, then pulled a book from one of the shelves and sank down onto the horsehair sofa. Try as she would, however, she could not focus more than passing attention on the well-worn pages. Releasing yet another sigh, she closed her eyes and eventually fell into a troubled sleep.

The cabin was bathed in darkness when Hillary awoke. Her eyes flew back up to the skylight, where she caught a glimpse of a star-filled sky above the mizzenmast and its rigging. Though she had no idea what time it was, she realized she must have been asleep for hours. And Ryan had still not returned.

She could bear the nerveracking tension between them no longer. Something had to be done!

She gathered up her skirts and hurried across to the door. Surprised to find it unlocked, she eased it open and slipped out quietly into the companionway. Ryan would no doubt be up above on the quarter-deck, she thought. He would have no choice but to speak to her if she confronted him in front of the crew. She didn't care if he ranted and raved at her, even if he struck her, for such a response would still be preferable to the awful, icy indifference he was displaying toward her now.

Quickly climbing the steps, she was met by a rush of cool air when she emerged upon the deck. She inhaled deeply, her eyes scanning the deck and making note of the fact that the men assigned to the night watch were busy changing the sails to match the shifting of the wind's course. The sounds of their activities combined with the gentle slapping of the becalmed seas against the sides of the ship.

Hillary looked to the quarterdeck, then frowned when she saw no sign of her husband. There was only Connor Reid and a much younger man, the two of them silhouetted against the moonlit horizon as they talked. Where was Ryan?

Swiftly abandoning the notion of returning to the loneliness of the captain's quarters, she set out across the softly rolling deck. She was intent upon either finding Ryan or, at the very least, spending a few moments gazing out upon the sparkling waters of the Pacific and enjoying the feel of the whispery, salt-tinged breeze against her face. Unaccustomed to spending so much time cooped up indoors, she reveled in her freedom, however brief it might be.

Suddenly, there were shouts of warning. A startled

Hillary jerked up her head just in time to see a large block and tackle swinging out from a carelessly tied boom high in the rigging and hurtling down through the night air straight toward her. Although it dawned on her in that split second of time that she was in danger, she was nonetheless unable to move. It was as if she had become rooted to the spot, and she could do nothing more than gaze upward with wide, terror-filled eyes as the deadly apparatus bore down upon her.

"Hillary!" It was Ryan's voice calling her name, though she had no time in which to realize it. The next thing she knew, she was being knocked violently aside by someone. She slammed down upon the deck, where she lay stunned and gasping for breath. An instant later, the block and tackle smashed into the very spot where she had stood. There was a loud, accompanying crash as wood splintered everywhere.

"Dear God, Hillary, are you all right?" Ryan demanded hoarsely, his voice full of raw emotion. He sprang up from the deck and hastened to her side. Falling to his knees, he cradled her in his strong arms, his handsome face revealing the most profound worry he had ever experienced. "Hillary, can you hear me? Hillary!" Her eyelids fluttered open, and she tried to sit up, only to fall weakly back against him as her head swam dizzily.

The crew had scrambled down from the rigging by now, and they crowded about, their faces tight with anxiety. Connor pushed his way through and, hastily sizing up the situation, bellowed out, "Stand back, damn it, stand back!" With the utmost care, Ryan lifted Hillary in his arms and transported her back across the deck. Connor, who was close on his heels as he carried her down into the cabin and laid her gently upon the sofa, hurried to light a lamp.

"Are you feeling any pain, my love?" Ryan asked, dropping down on one knee beside her again. He passed his hands over her in a quick yet expert examination, searching for any perceptible signs of injury. Her vision was still somewhat blurred, but it began to clear while she was gazing up into his somber features.

"I . . . I don't think so," she replied, her voice a trifle unsteady. "I may be a bit bruised come morning, but I don't feel any pain right now. Only a strange numbness."

"It's a wonder you weren't killed," Connor told her with a crooked smile. "If Ryan hadn't come above and seen you when he did—well, let's just give thanks he did." Hillary returned his smile with a rather tremulous one of her own before he excused himself and returned above to investigate precisely why the mishap had occurred.

As soon as Connor had gone, Ryan sat down beside Hillary and pulled her into his lap. She was only too happy to rest within the warm circle of his arms, and for the first time in what had seemed to be an excruciatingly long day, her heart soared with the certainty of his love.

"There was a moment there when I thought I'd lost you," he confessed in a low, vibrant tone, pulling her even closer. "My heart stopped when I saw you standing there with that damned block about to hit you. Why the devil didn't you try to get out of its way?"

"My legs refused to move! It was as if I suddenly stood suspended in time, as though I were somehow taken out of myself to witness the event." She raised her face to his, and he saw that there were tears swimming in her beautiful violet eyes. "I went up on deck to find you, because I couldn't bear to have you angry with me any longer!"

"Oh my sweet Hillary," murmured Ryan, a wonderfully tender smile touching his lips as he lifted a hand to her cheek, "don't you realize yet that I love you more than life itself? You were right, you know," he then admitted, his eyes brimming with an endearing mixture of self-reproach and amusement. "It *was* my damnable male pride that stood between us. I would never have forgiven myself if you had been hurt. Blast it, but I was just so furious with you for disobeying me, for taking it upon yourself to decide what was best for us!"

"Oh Ryan, it *is* best, isn't it?" she insisted, resting her head upon his shoulder again. "It was wrong of me to deceive you, but I didn't know what else to do. I've never loved anyone before, and I couldn't bear the thought of losing you. Though you insisted we would only be apart for a few months, I envisioned a thousand different things that could prolong your absence—or even prevent your return altogether. Foremost was the thought of you at home with your family. I know they must love you very much, and you them, and it would be only natural for you to feel torn between—"

"You're wrong there, my love," he firmly dissented. "While it is true I hold great affection for them, my love for you is by far the strongest. I would have allowed nothing to keep me from your side!"

"Yet you were willing to return to New Bedford without me," she countered with a frown of remembrance.

Ryan sighed heavily. "Only because I believed you would be safer, and happier, waiting for me in Tahiti."

"Why, how could I possibly have been happier

without you?'' challenged Hillary, tilting her head back to meet his gaze once more. "And how could you know for certain that I would have been any safer at Starcross than here aboard the *Falcon* with you?" She smiled up at him softly, her glistening violet eyes reflecting all the love in her heart. "Whatever happens, I am where I belong."

"Much as I hate to admit it, I do not possess enough strength of will to send you back," Ryan murmured huskily. His piercing, blue-green gaze raked over the entrancing loveliness of her upturned features. "Damn it, woman, I've been on fire all day, ever since I came in and saw you standing there with nothing more than my shirt covering those beguiling curves of yours!" He gave a low groan of mingled defeat and desire as he brought his mouth crashing down upon hers. Thrilling to the onslaught of his passion, she entwined her arms about his neck and eagerly parted her lips for his sweetly demanding kiss.

Rising to his feet with her moments later, he began moving toward the stateroom, only to come to an unexpected halt before reaching the doorway. He tore his lips from Hillary's and muttered a curse. She stared up at him in bewilderment.

"Ryan? What is it?"

"Tradition demands my presence at the officers' table," he regretfully disclosed, scowling darkly. "Besides which, you are no doubt still feeling the effects of that near-disaster on deck. It would be unforgivably selfish of me to—"

"To leave me now," she finished for him, her voice low and breathless and her eyes aglow with an undeniable invitation. Her mouth curved into a slow, alluring smile as she boldly declared, "The only effects I am feeling at this moment, Captain

Gallagher, are the ones *you* have brought about!"

Ryan, his pulses racing even more wildly than before, favored his wife with a long, intense look full of such warmth and hunger that she felt positively branded by his eyes.

"Tradition be damned!" he triumphantly decreed, then carried her into the other room and slammed the door shut with his booted heel.

XI

The next few weeks were full of happiness and adventure for Hillary as Ryan set about sharing his life with her.

The day after the *Falcon* sailed from Tahiti, he took time out from his busy schedule to show her around and explain the inner workings of a whale ship. She had never before been particularly interested in either ships *or* whaling, but she suddenly found herself wanting to know everything she could about both.

They began the tour on the main deck, where Ryan first pointed out the tryworks, a large brick stove located amidships and which, he told her, was used for cooking the oil out of the blubber once it had been stripped from the whale and cut into chunks of a size to fit in the iron pots. The deck was sheathed fore and aft with thin pine lumber to protect the main planks while the work was done, and a portion of the railing there was movable for the "cutting in" to be done.

"It must be terribly unpleasant work," mused Hillary, wrinkling her nose at the lingering smell of oil.

"Unpleasant perhaps," Ryan conceded with a low

chuckle, "but extremely profitable." Taking her arm, he leisurely guided her farther toward the bow. The wind tugged at her braided hair and whipped her full skirts about her legs as she strolled beside him. She was wearing one of the other three dresses she had been able to stuff into the carpetbag, a simple blue cotton with short puffed sleeves and a demurely rounded neckline. Acutely conscious of the way the crew stared at her as she traveled across the deck, she found herself wishing she could have drawn on the old trousers and jacket instead. Never in her life had she felt so conspicuous!

Ryan led her over to the hatchway that opened into the forecastle. He did not take her down into the crew's quarters, but he allowed her a close glimpse of the triangular-shaped space wherein were two tiers of narrow bunks forming a semicircle right at the bow of the ship. The cool air smelled of stale oil, mildew, and pipe smoke, and there were no windows or portholes to allow either fresh air or sunlight inside—the only way to do so was to leave the hatchway open. Hillary was relieved to straighten and breathe deeply of the sea air once more.

"How on earth do so many men manage to live in such a small space?"

"They spend as little time as possible down there," answered Ryan. "In fair weather, they take all their meals on deck. And they pass their off-duty hours up here as well, unless, of course, rain or storms force them below."

"But what is there for them to do when they're not working?"

"The same things you'll be doing," he replied with a wry smile. "Reading every available book, washing and mending clothes that never seem to last until the next port of call, writing letters to loved ones at

266

home. Most whalers become scrimshanders. I've seen them spend hour upon hour carving whalebone into rolling pins, corset husks, jagging wheels, chess sets—whatever they set their minds to."

"Uncle Denholm had a beautiful piece of scrimshaw once," recalled Hillary. "It was a hunt scene, etched into a large fragment from the jawbone of a sperm whale. He presented it to Queen Pomare as a gift not long after he came into possession of it." Her eyes clouded with a touch of sadness as she thought of her uncle and her adopted homeland, though she did her best to smile and make light of the memory. "I've always wanted to see exactly how someone creates such a masterpiece, and now it seems my curiosity will be satisfied at last."

His perceptive gaze missing little, Ryan clasped both of her hands with his and quietly reassured her, "He'll be fine, my love. The months away will pass quickly."

His concern touched her heart, and she was truly comforted by his words. She slipped her arm through his and smiled up at him as she asked brightly, "What will you show me next, dearest Captain?"

They walked back across the deck, past the tryworks and over to the companionway that led down into the galley. Finding the burly cook busy with his preparations for the noon meal, they did not remain long. Ryan pointed out the passageway off the galley where the officers' quarters and mess quarters were situated, then gestured toward another doorway and told her the room was where some of the ship's stores were kept. Hillary gathered up her skirts and held fast to his hand as he led her down still more steps.

"The *Falcon* don't deserve to be no hen frigate," Josiah muttered to himself in disgust as they left him to his salt beef and potatoes. Like most other ship's cooks, he resented the presence of a female in his galley—particularly if it was the same female who, if the talk he'd heard was true, had used her wiles on one of the best whaling masters the world had ever known in order to convince him to give up the sea!

Sourly musing that the only thing worse than a woman aboard was a cockroach, the black-bearded giant tossed a handful of salt into the huge pot filled with boiled potatoes and took great pleasure in pretending they were a certain young female's backside as he whipped at them with a long wooden spoon.

Blissfully ignorant of the cook's thoughts, Hillary stood beside her husband in the cool semidarkness of the hold. She felt a wave of nausea at the pungent odor emanating from row upon row of casks filled with sperm oil.

"You've already met Ewan, the ship's cooper," said Ryan, nodding at the large, powerfully built man who came forward to greet them.

"Mighty glad to have you aboard, ma'am," he told Hillary with open sincerity, his amiable manner belying his brawny appearance.

"Why, thank you, Ewan." As she smiled back at him warmly, her eyes were drawn down to the bucket of water he held in one immense hand.

He grinned when he noticed the direction of her gaze. "It's part of my job, ma'am, watering the casks. The water, you see, soaks into the slats and makes them swell. That way, they don't leak, and the Captain here doesn't kick my—" He broke off at the sound of the captain clearing his throat, then reddened guiltily when it dawned on him that his customary rough language was not fit for a lady's ears. It had been a long time since he'd been in the presence of a woman of quality, a woman like the captain's wife. "Begging your pardon, Mrs. Gallagher, ma'am," he sheepishly proclaimed, "but I'd best be getting back to my work." He nodded in turn at her and Ryan before hurriedly taking himself off.

"Ewan's a good man," Ryan opined with a low, indulgent chuckle. He tucked Hillary's arm through his again and told her, "It may interest you to hear, my love, that we've taken a total of more than two thousand barrels of oil this voyage. Add to that a more than decent quantity of ambergris and know that the *Falcon* is carrying a rich cargo indeed."

Hillary didn't need to ask what ambergris was, for she had once seen some of the soft, black, evil-smelling substance while at the market in Papeete. Found only in the bowels of sick whales, it hardened, faded, and began to exude a surprisingly pleasant smell upon exposure to sun and air. Ambergris, she recalled, was extremely valuable, since it was in much demand as a fixative for perfume, and also as a spice in the Far East.

"Will the men make a great deal of money?" she asked. "I would hope so. It must be terribly difficult to be away from home for years at a time."

"Each man has a lay in the venture. If any man's work was above average, he'll be promoted to a better share. As for being away from home, you must remember that whaling is a way of life in New Bedford. The men who choose the sea accept the inevitability of long periods of absence, as do their wives and families." Turning to lead her up from the hold, he was puzzled when she suddenly held back. "What is it?" he demanded, viewing the look of wide-eyed startlement on her beautiful face.

"Why, I . . . I could have sworn I saw something very much like a cat!" exclaimed Hillary. Amusement flickered briefly over Ryan's sun-bronzed features.

"If what you saw did indeed resemble a cat, then it was probably Dammit. Of course, it could also have been one of the rats he—"

"*Dammit?*" she echoed, not at all certain she had heard him correctly.

"The ship's cat," explained Ryan, a disarming grin tugging at the corners of his mouth. "A powerful and dedicated feline who keeps the rat population within reasonable bounds."

Tempted to ask him how the cat had come by such an unusual name, Hillary instead kept silent on the subject, for it wasn't really too difficult to imagine.

Ryan soon returned to his duties on the quarterdeck. Hillary wandered about in the windswept sunshine for a while, until it was time to go below and eat. She dined in the mess quarters with Ryan and the ship's officers. It was her first meal with them, for she had taken breakfast in the cabin. In the beginning, only Connor was brave enough to engage her in conversation, but it wasn't long before the other young men at the table joined in.

The captain himself spoke little, though his gleaming turquoise gaze missed nothing. He was surprised at the powerful surge of jealousy rising within him as he watched his wife's beautiful, animated face while she talked and laughed with the men and he viewed the responsive warmth and admiration filling their gazes. Swearing inwardly, he mused to himself that he couldn't very well keep her locked in his quarters until they reached New Bedford, no matter how much it annoyed him to see the way the eyes of his men followed her everywhere. Damn, but having her aboard was going to be both a blessing and a curse!

As the days wore on, however, he found that Hillary's presence was making the voyage the most peaceful and cheerful one he had ever known. She had soon won over all but the most hard-hearted of the crew—Josiah still treated her with barely concealed hostility, and there were a few others who remained adamant in their belief that a whaling bark was no place for a woman. But the majority of them were glad to have her aboard, for she treated them with respect and kindness. Although they never forgot she was the captain's lady, they found themselves telling her of their lives, of their families, and of their dreams.

There was another benefit as well, one that affected both master and crew of the *Falcon*. Particularly to those who had sailed under his command before, it seemed that Captain Gallagher was something of a changed man. His humor, it was generally agreed upon, had improved greatly, for he did not thunder curses and threats at them with quite as much regularity as before. And though he still demanded they fulfill their duties with just as much discipline and hard work as ever—tarring and tending the rigging, patching and mending sails, swabbing the deck and companionways, and other such tasks associated with the continual maintenance and upkeep aboard ship—he apparently did not feel the need to drive them quite as relentlessly as in the past. Perhaps it was because he was relying upon their own eagerness to reach home; but whatever the case, they grew increasingly grateful for the fact that the captain's young bride had been foolhardy enough to stow away.

Ryan, on the other hand, noticed a marked difference in the attitude of his crew, and he commented on it one evening when he and Hillary were closeted alone in his cabin. He was at his desk, making an entry in the ship's log by the light of a whale oil lamp, while she sat on the sofa frowning over the sewing in her lap. Attempting to mend a tear in her best muslin gown, she was noticeably discontented with her needle's progress.

"I'll see what I can do about getting you a sewing machine when we call at the Juan Fernández Islands," offered Ryan, smiling across at her. Her brow immediately cleared, and she laughed softly as she put aside the dress and rose to her feet.

"Oh Ryan, that would be wonderful! I didn't want to say anything, since it is, after all, my own fault, but I was beginning to worry about the regrettable state of my 'trousseau.' I should really like to look my best when I meet your family. It certainly wouldn't do for them to believe me a penniless *vahine* with nothing more than three tattered gowns to her name!"

"Whatever you're wearing, they'll believe you to be the loveliest and most adorable *vahine* they've ever seen, just as I have from the very first." His eyes were brimming with loving mischief as he unbent his tall frame from the chair. Favoring her with a mock scowl, he grumbled, "It seems you have also enchanted every blasted man aboard this ship! Never have I seen them so conscious of their appearance or their manners. Damn it, woman, you've turned an entire crew of able-bodied seamen into a bunch of lovesick fools!"

"Quite the contrary, my dearest captain!" she retorted, smiling up at him saucily. "I am of the opinion that they are merely grateful to have a sympathetic listener to their tales of *your* tyranny!"

"Tyranny?" he echoed, his scowl deepening.

"Yes, tyranny! Why, one of the main arguments you used against my coming along was that you did not want me exposed to the company of some of the 'roughest men on the face of the earth,' remember? However, I have found all but a very few of them to be decent, hardworking men who care a great deal about their families. Perhaps they were only 'rough' because you did not treat them with enough respect!"

"Respect?" The scowl became a grin of teasing irony. "Do you realize, my love, that you are talking about the same men you yourself once referred to as 'scoundrels,' as 'degenerate whalers,' as—"

"Yes, but that was before I knew them!" Hillary protested with a defiant toss of her head. Folding her arms across her breasts, she went on to add, "I thought *you* a scoundrel, too, especially that day when your unmitigated arrogance was the cause of poor Anthony's heat exhaustion!"

"Come now, sweet wife, would a true scoundrel have toiled beneath the hot sun all day as I did to help you with the harvest?" Ryan mockingly challenged.

"As a means to an end, yes!"

"Well, it worked, did it not?" he countered with a soft, unrepentent chuckle, rounding the corner of the desk at last. Hillary's violet eyes grew very wide and luminous as she gazed up into his devilishly handsome features, and she felt the familiar weakness stealing over her when his hands reached for her.

"Have you . . . finished your entry?" she asked breathlessly, referring to the log book still open on his desk.

"I've not yet begun," he murmured with a roguish twinkling of his eyes. Hillary's cheeks flamed at his meaning, but she was not afforded the opportunity to chastise him for his wickedness, for in the next moment he caught her up against him and captured her lips with the demanding warmth of his.

That night, like many previous nights, held a

bounty of rapturous enchantment for the captain and his lady. Ryan had taught Hillary much in the weeks since they had sailed from Tahiti—and she had taught him much as well. She had become increasingly emboldened, even going so far as to take the initiative upon more than one occasion, something she couldn't help musing would probably be quite a rarity among the stiff and proper wives of the plantation owners back on Moorea. All except Constance of course, whom she was certain frequently delighted Donald with her incorrigible nature.

Hillary was thinking only of Ryan, however, as her naked body lay entwined with his upon the gently swaying three-quarter bed. Moaning softly when his lips began wandering, she then elicited a moan from him as her fingers lovingly smoothed across his bronzed hardness. His warm mouth and velvety tongue worked their oh-so-sensuous magic upon the rose-tipped fullness of her breasts, before trailing a fiery path downward and soon provoking a series of soft, feverish gasps and tremors of irrestrainable passion.

She offered a breathless protest when he suddenly drew away, but her protest became yet another moan of tempestuous desire as he turned her gently over onto her stomach and set about worshiping the neglected curves on the opposite side of her captivating form. Her hands clenched within the softness of the pillow when she felt him sweeping aside her hair and following the curve of her spine with his wonderfully persuasive mouth. Rosy color flooded her face when he lingered at her derriere, his lips tenderly nipping and his hot, moist tongue saluting the delectable roundness with light strokes that traveled downward across her pale, silken thighs.

Her hips moved restlessly beneath the exquisite torment of his caress, and she was so overwhelmed by the sensations he had created within her that it took a moment for her to realize he was slowly drawing her upward to her knees upon the bed.

The unspoken question in her mind was answered in a highly satisfactory manner when his large hands gripped her hips and pulled her back into his embrace. She cried out softly as his manhood sheathed expertly within the welcoming pliancy of her feminine passage. Straining weakly back against his steadying warmth, she followed his lead while the sweet agony of their union, a union of their spirits as well as their flesh, prompted such a floodtide of love and passion deep within her that she felt certain she would faint with the sheer intensity of it all.

And indeed, she came very near to losing consciousness when their lovemaking culminated in the most glorious fulfillment only the truest of lovers can ever know. Afterward, Ryan stretched out upon the bed and pulled her close. She smiled softly to herself as she listened to the rapid beating of his heart, and to the ceaseless creaking of the ship's timbers. And when she finally drifted off into a deep slumber of utter contentment, her dreams were filled with visions of a tall, handsome scoundrel with laughing blue-green eyes who swept her up in his arms and carried her off into the clouds.

The *Falcon* encountered few storms while on the way to her first port of call, the Juan Fernández Islands off the west coast of Chile. There was, however, a particularly bad night when the waves ran almost as high as the masthead and battered the ship with merciless force. The swelling sea splashed over the deck and threatened to drag the men back into its churning depths, while the howling winds tore at the rigging and ripped the sails. Laboring and rolling violently, the ship rode like a whale herself above the white-foamed mountains of water.

The only thing to do was furl all sail and keep her running before the dreadful gale. Ryan stayed on the quarterdeck throughout the long, crashing night, praying that the still largely uncharted Pacific would not send up a patch of atolls or reefs to tear the ship asunder. Hillary lay alone in the stateroom, listening to the terrible din from above and fervently wishing her husband had allowed her to remain at his side. She was more frightened for him than for herself, and it was only because she realized it would add to his worries that she did not surrender to the urge to drag herself from the bed and battle her way up the companionway to the deck.

The morning after the storm was amazingly calm and clear. There was a great deal of cleaning and patching and pumping to do, but the ship had miraculously come through it all intact. As Ryan later commented to Hillary, the *Falcon* was nigh on to thirty years old and hadn't bowed to defeat yet.

There was a different kind of storm brewing between Hillary and Josiah. For the first several weeks, she had avoided him as much as possible, enduring his highly dissociable manner toward her without complaint. There finally came a day, however, when she decided it was time to force a confrontation and resolve the issue once and for all.

It was a balmy Sunday in June, and the men were "knocking off" as they were allowed to do only on the Sabbath and certain holidays. After Ryan led them in prayers and read a few passages from the well-worn pages of the ship's Bible, the crew spent

276

the remainder of the day either lounging about on deck or simply lying in their bunks. Some of them tended to personal tasks such as trimming their hair and beards, while others played checkers and cards, or even pitched peas for both amusement and profit.

Singing old ballads of the sea was also a favorite pastime of the homesick whalers, and this particular, temperate Sunday evoked a wave of nostalgia. Hillary felt tears starting to her eyes as she stood within a hard-found patch of shade nearby and listened to an especially poignant tune called "A Soldier's Gratitude," which related one man's thoughts of home. She found the most stirring ballad, however, to be the one that followed. Entitled "Loss of the *Albion*," it detailed a shipwreck that had claimed some fifty souls in 1822:

> *Come all you jovial sailor boys,*
> *And listen unto me,*
> *A dreadful story I will tell,*
> *Which happened on the sea.*
> *The loss of the* Albion *ship, my boys,*
> *Upon the Irish coast,*
> *Where most of her crew and passengers,*
> *Were all completely lost . . .*

Hillary finally wandered across the deck, raising her face to the sun and letting the wind have its way with her unbound hair. Her thoughts turned, with their customary frequency, to Ryan. Wishing he could be abovedecks enjoying the pleasant afternoon with her instead of down in the hold inspecting the oil casks with Ewan, she released a sigh and turned back toward the quarterdeck.

The smell of Josiah's cooking drifted up from the galley to be borne aloft upon the breeze, prompting her to wrinkle her nose at the unmistakable aroma of "lobscouse." The thick, unappetizing stew, Connor had informed her upon the occasion of her first reluctant taste of it, was made by taking hardtack and a thick grease referred to as "top of the pot," and boiling it with molasses and water. Potatoes were sometimes substituted for the grease if Josiah had not recently boiled any salt pork and skimmed off the fat. It wasn't at all difficult for Hillary to understand why the crew could be seen fishing for their meal in desperation whenever they heard lobscouse was going to be the main course. She smiled to herself in anticipation of the men's reaction when the telltale aroma reached their noses.

It was then that the notion suddenly hit her.

If Ryan and the crew were going to be subjected to lobscouse that night, perhaps she could make their lot a trifle more bearable by baking something for dessert. She was a more than adequate cook, though she'd had little opportunity to hone her talents while aboard the *Falcon*. Her specialty was a coconut cake that had been praised not only by her uncle, but by Queen Pomare herself. The recipe, her own creation, employed a combination of English and Tahitian culinary traditions. She was certain the men would appreciate the small gesture of goodwill, and the thought of cooking for her husband appealed to her.

But what about Josiah? her mind's inner voice queried.

"Josiah will have little choice!" she decreed aloud. Musing that it was high time the irascible cook accepted the reality of her presence aboard ship, she marched determinedly to the companionway and down the steps.

Josiah's back was turned toward her as she came to stand just within the almost stifling warmth of the galley. Proudly lifting her head, she had just opened her mouth to address him when he growled, "Haul your black-hearted carcass out of here, damn it!"

Hillary's mouth fell open and her eyes grew round as saucers. Immediately following upon the heels of startlement, however, was righteous indignation.

"I beg your pardon?" she icily demanded.

The perpetually ill-tempered giant wheeled about at the sound of her voice, and the thunderous expression on his face deepened. "Not *you*," he snarled, *"him!"* He jerked his head toward the hefty, yellow-eyed tabby who was lying in wait near the stove, ready to pounce on any stray morsels of food that might find their way to the floor. Hillary's gaze, following the direction of the cook's murderous glower, lit with understanding and amusement when it fell upon the cat.

"Are you cursing him, or merely calling him by name?" she challenged Josiah with good-natured sarcasm. Undaunted when he responded with nothing more than another scowl, she stepped farther inside the galley and calmly announced, "I have it in mind to bake a coconut cake, Josiah. I know where to find the stores of fresh coconut, but would you be so kind as to tell me where I may find—"

"You may be the captain's wife, but I'll not have you flitting about in *my* galley!"

"I was under the impression that this vessel belonged to my husband's family," Hillary countered with a brief, meaningful smile, then sighed audibly and folded her arms across her breasts. "You may rest assured, Josiah, that I have no intention of usurping your position aboard this ship. I wish only to intrude long enough to bake a cake, and I would be grateful indeed for your forbearance and cooperation."

"If there's any baking to be done aboard the *Falcon,* I'll be the one to do it!" he stubbornly insisted. He surprised both Hillary and himself when he suddenly relented enough to add, "Even if I was to let you make your blasted cake, them skirts of yours would no doubt flail against the fire whenever this old bark took it in mind to ride the waves. And *I'd* be the one to catch the devil from your husband if you was to come to harm in *my* galley!"

"Well then, if my skirts are the only obstacle, I can very well remove them!" Hillary blithely suggested, her violet eyes sparkling with merriment.

"Remove them?" rumbled Josiah in stunned disbelief. His scowl grew even darker as it occurred to him that the captain wouldn't take kindly to finding his wife half-naked in the galley with another man. As much as it galled him to admit defeat, he muttered a foul imprecation beneath his breath, then virtually roared, "Make your blasted cake! Only don't go blaming me when you swoon from the heat!"

"You forget, Josiah, I lived in the tropics before marrying Captain Gallagher. I daresay I would be able to endure a good deal more warmth than you." This she said with an engagingly mischievous smile, and the cantankerous seaman was dismayed to find the corners of his mouth twitching upward in response. He covered the near disaster with a loud cough and turned back abruptly to his lobscouse.

"There's sugar and flour in them barrels by the stove," he gruffly announced, "and anything else you'll need, well, tell me what it is and maybe I can tell you where to find it. Maybe not!"

"Thank you, Josiah," murmured Hillary, suppressing another smile. Congratulating herself on the small victory, she tied on one of the cook's stained but freshly washed canvas aprons and set to work.

It took her most of the afternoon to bake four cakes—she had decided it would take at least that many in order for everyone to receive an adequate portion—but she deemed her efforts well worth it when she viewed the expressions of delight on the faces of Ryan and his officers. Josiah had taken it upon himself to serve the dessert, and he looked none too pleased to find the cake receiving such notable attention. He stood behind Ryan at the head of the table, his black-bearded features reflecting an air of injured pride.

"Josiah, you've outdone yourself this time!" pronounced Connor, quickly downing another forkful of the sweet concoction.

"You've been holding out on us, you old pirate!" the young second mate accused with a teasing grin.

There were several other such comments, though Ryan said nothing. He merely smiled, his irrepressibly twinkling gaze shifting from Josiah to Hillary. A dull flush rose to the cook's face as his lips compressed into a tight, thin line.

"It truly *is* a delicious cake, Josiah," Hillary said pointedly, her eyes conveying a silent message to him. She smiled brightly as he favored her with a deep frown of mingled suspicion and bafflement. "Perhaps you can show me how to prepare one sometime in the near future." Disregarding the knowing amusement in her husband's eyes, she smiled up innocently at Josiah again and took another bite of the cake.

Her magnanimous gesture threw the hardened old cook into a quandary. While he didn't want it known that he'd broken his own rule and allowed a female in his galley, neither did he want to take credit for something he hadn't done. But how the hell was he going to set the matter straight without losing face?

Though he'd never let on, he was touched by Hillary's unexpected generosity and regard for his feelings.

"Mrs. Gallagher made it." There, he'd said it. And the devil with everyone knowing!

"What? You're saying you—" began Connor, only to be cut off by Josiah's deep growl.

"Damn your eyes, Mr. Reid, you heard me! I said the captain's wife made the blasted cake! Now finish it off before I throw it to the sharks!"

No one dared say a word after that. Connor and the other officers exchanged speaking looks. Only a faint curving of Ryan's mouth gave evidence of his enjoyment of the situation. Josiah subjected Hillary to a long, scrutinizing stare before nodding down at her curtly and taking himself back into the galley to do his duty by the rest of the men. He steeled himself for the certainty of their reactions when they tasted the cake and then learned who had made it.

Later, Ryan and Hillary were taking a turn about the moonlit deck together when the now infamous subject of the coconut cake surfaced once more.

"I do believe, Mrs. Gallagher, that you've finally discovered the way to a certain old sea dog's mercenary heart," Ryan drawled lazily. His arm tightened about her waist as they paused at the railing and gazed outward upon the calm Pacific seas.

"How did you know I was the one who—"

"Because in all the years I've known Josiah, he's never once thought to use a coconut for anything other than its milk." He gave a low chuckle before confessing, "And besides that, I caught a glimpse of you in the storeroom when Ewan and I came up from the hold."

Hillary laughed softly and replied, "I don't believe

282

he's half as toughened and hard-hearted as he wants us all to believe. He reminds me of my father, actually. *He* was also fond of pretending to care nothing for those around him, even his own wife and child. But we were not so easily fooled," she recalled with a sad little smile.

"You know, my love, that's the first time I've heard you speak of your family," observed Ryan. He pulled her back against him, his strong arms enveloping her from behind. "How did you come to be living with your uncle in Tahiti?"

"My parents were both killed while traveling on the Continent when I was twelve. I lived with my mother's sister for nearly four years thereafter, though most of that time I spent away at school. Finally, Uncle Denholm and Aunt Louisa sent for me. I discovered upon my arrival in Tahiti that they had been trying for years to convince Aunt Marian to let me come." She paused and released a sigh before remarking, "It seems she feared I would be eaten by cannibals! She was, I think, equally worried that her young and impressionable niece would be unduly influenced by what she referred to as Tahiti's 'deplorable lack of moral structure.'"

"And were you?" teased Ryan, his arms hugging her even closer.

"Of course! Why, I must have been, for I married *you*, did I not?" she parried, then sighed more dramatically. "Aunt Marian will no doubt believe her worst fears have been realized when she hears I have married a notorious sea captain!"

"And a Yankee to boot," he obligingly added in a deep, resonant tone brimming with humor. A companionable silence fell between them. Only those members of the crew assigned to the evening dogwatch were up on deck. The wind felt refreshingly cool as it caught the distinctive, tangy scent of the ocean and carried it across the ship. A thousand twinkling stars set the night sky aglow.

"It's as though we were sailing the heavens instead of the sea," Hillary murmured softly, her beautiful violet eyes mirroring the sky's brilliance.

"I've my own bit of heaven right here," declared Ryan. He bent his head to tenderly brush the smoothness of her cheek with her lips. Oblivous to the presence of the crew, Hillary pivoted within his embrace and returned the favor with a sweetly provocative kiss that made them both yearn for more.

As Ryan took her arm and began leading her toward the companionway, she was plagued by a sudden uneasiness. She glanced quickly to her left and found Peale's gaze fastened upon her. His dark eyes appeared hooded and strangely menacing, and she caught her breath at the slow, derisive smile that touched his weathered lips. Although tempted to inform Ryan of the man's unspoken insolence, she decided against it, for Peale abruptly turned away in the next instant. It wasn't the first time she had been aware of his eyes following her with such disturbing intensity, but she had always told herself it was of no real signficance. Perhaps she *should* mention it to Ryan . . . , she mused distractedly.

The matter was soon forgotten, however, as she and her husband went below and slipped away into that special world inhabited only by the two of them, a world of both fiery passion and endearing tenderness, a world where, for a few short hours, they felt as though they were indeed sailing the heavens.

XII

They sighted the Juan Fernández Islands less than a week later. Located off the west coast of Chile, the trio of islands was traditionally the first port of call visited after leaving behind the whaling grounds of the South Pacific, as well as the last port of call before rounding Cape Horn and sailing homeward through the waters of the Atlantic. Conversely, the ships would usually set a course for Juan Fernández after successfully braving the storms of the Cape on their way to the Pacific.

Given her first glimpse of Mas-a-Tierra, the island Ryan had already identified for her as the nearest and most important, Hillary found it difficult to understand why it was considered such a welcome landfall. It appeared quite rugged and forbidding to her eyes, rising as it did like a deep blue cloud out of the sea, with its mountains surrounded by mists. Having earlier been informed of the fact that the population was of a considerably small number, she shivered a bit and reflected that she could well understand why so few chose to call it home.

Upon closer inspection, however, her opinion became more favorable. She smiled when she caught sight of the seals and sea lions lazily sunning themselves on the island's rocky shores, and she was pleasantly surprised to note several goats, sheep, and cattle grazing over a green-mantled valley she had not been able to see from farther out at sea.

It wasn't until the following morning, however, that she finally set foot on Mas-a-Tierra. While the *Falcon* lay anchored in Cumberland Bay, Ryan, Hillary, Ewan, and Josiah traveled ashore in one of the boats. Their destination was a quiet agricultural and fishing village called San Juan Bautista, the only settlement on the entire island. Though it consisted of little more than a small wharf and a few simple wooden structures, it was able to provide desperately needed fresh water and provisions for the ships calling there.

"Once we've seen to that sewing machine, I'll take you to visit Robinson Crusoe's cave," Ryan told Hillary as Ewan and Josiah rowed the boat to shore.

"Robinson Crusoe's cave?" she echoed in puzzlement. "But I . . . I thought Defoe's book was a work of fiction!"

"It was, though it chronicled the true story of a Scotsman named Selkirk. It was here on Mas-a-Tierra that Selkirk was marooned for several years. The islanders insist upon every visitor seeing his cave," he finished with a wry grin.

Hillary's legs felt shaky when, a few minutes later, she stepped onto dry land for the first time in weeks. She was immediately surrounded by a group of curious and welcoming residents, many of whom were Spanish settlers. There were a surprising number of children about, and she smiled warmly at them as Ryan took her arm and led her toward the center of the village.

She was amazed when their hour-long search

through the handful of stores yielded a sewing machine. Though a trifle rusty from the sea air, it was in otherwise excellent condition. Ryan also purchased several bolts of warm woolens and heavy cottons for her, as well as a sturdy pair of boots, a fur-lined cloak, and various other necessities for the cold weather awaiting them on their journey southward to Cape Horn. Hillary was overwhelmed at their good fortune in finding everything, so much so that she shocked the watchful islanders by impulsively throwing her arms about her husband's neck in gratitude when they emerged from the last well-stocked establishment. Laughing at her blush when she realized her actions had attracted quite an audience, Ryan placed an arm about her shoulders and bore her away with merciful swiftness.

It was still before the hour of noon when they set forth on their expedition to the cave. Arranging with one of the local fishermen and his sons to transport them there, Ryan pointed out to his eagerly attentive wife the sights he had first seen more than sixteen years ago. The boat's route took them past cliffs that dropped hundreds of feet directly into the sea. Wild mountain goats grazed high on the cliffs and along the mountain ridges. The island's highest peak, Cerro Yunque, dominated the scenery at all times, even as the boat traveled around Point San Carlos to Puerto Ingles, where there was a gently curving inlet with a rocky beach. They soon entered a tiny cove at the inlet's eastern side, beneath an overhanging ledge and a natural bridge. After the boat was maneuvered toward a small promontory, Ryan disembarked and reached for Hillary. She shuddered involuntarily at the many crabs and starfish lining the shore, but she staunchly lifted her skirts and picked her way carefully across the beach.

"The cave's only a short distance," Ryan assured her. He clasped her hand and urged her up a steep hill. Hillary was surprised when, upon reaching the summit, they found a green, treeless valley where more cattle and sheep were grazing.

"Why, it looks exactly like a pastoral scene in England!"

"I wouldn't know about that, but there *were* some English families living here at one time." He smiled and tugged on her hand again. "Come on. It's only a little farther now."

She couldn't help but be a trifle disappointed in the cave, for it wasn't anything like she had imagined. Created by some overhanging rocks, it was very shallow and contained nothing to evoke the presence of a Robinson Crusoe. There was a narrow, crystal-clear stream nearby, with a colorful array of water lilies blooming along its banks. Ryan led her over to it, then pulled her down to sit with him on the cool grass.

"When I first came here, I was only fifteen," he quietly reminisced, surrounding her with his arms. "My head was filled with grandiose ideas and dreams back then, exactly the sort favored by a boy on the very brink of manhood." His eyes filled with amusement at the memory, and a brief smile of irony lit his face. "I believed myself ready to conquer the world."

"And did you?" asked Hillary, tilting her head back to gaze up into his ruggedly handsome features.

"In some ways, I suppose," he replied with a soft chuckle. "I had to do a lot of growing up first. A young greenhand who had never ventured farther than five miles from home during the first fourteen years of his life couldn't help but find himself matured by the sights and experiences awaiting him at sea. That first voyage alone, I saw dozens of whales breeching in the frigid waters of the Okhotsk Sea off Siberia, found myself awestruck at the tropical splendor of the Sandwich Islands, and damn near broke my neck taking giant turtles just off the shore of the Galapagos."

"It must have been very difficult for your parents to let you go at such a tender age."

"Perhaps for my mother, but my father was delighted that I was finally sailing off to follow the family's whaling tradition. Even if they had harbored any misgivings, I'm sure they were both somewhat consoled by the fact that I was serving under my father's brother the first time out." He paused for a moment and chuckled again.

"I take it you enjoyed being on your uncle's ship?" queried Hillary, smiling at the light of merriment in his eyes.

"Enjoyed?" he repeated, then shook his head. "Hardly that. Uncle Seamus was a black-hearted old devil with flaming red hair and a temper to match! He ruled his crew with an iron hand, and he was even rougher on me, determined as he was not to show any favoritism. But I was a brash young hellion back then and equally determined to do what I could to flout his authority. I was totally unimpressed by his lofty position, as well as by the fact that he was in essence my benefactor, so I would lie in my bunk at night and think of devious ways to avenge myself."

"Were you ever brave enough to actually do anything?" she challenged, musing to herself that it was difficult to imagine him at fourteen. He was such a strong figure of authority now that she couldn't summon a mental image of him as anything less.

"It took a while to gather the courage, but one night I finally decided I'd had enough. I sneaked into his cabin, took his favorite pair of trousers, and used a red-hot poker to burn tiny holes in the back seam. When he came abovedecks the next morning, the first thing he did after assembling the crew was to march forward, lift the hatchway, and bend over to make an inspection of the fo'c's'le—he was strict about enforcing the rule of no spirits aboard. The seam of his trousers gave way with a loud tearing noise, and the men broke into laughter. Uncle Seamus was nearly purple with rage as he rounded on us. The look on my face must have given me away, for he started chasing me around the deck, yelling curses at the top of his lungs and threatening to hang me from my thumbs high in the rigging. After that, he seemed to ease up on me a bit. I think he respected me for standing up to him at last, even in that small way.''

"I shall keep that particular incident in mind should I ever feel I am losing your respect!'' teased Hillary. She sighed and leaned back against him. "Indeed, from what you have just told me, I am of the opinion that you are very much like your Uncle Seamus. You can be extremely overbearing at times, Ryan Gallagher!''

"You may be right there,'' he allowed with a crooked grin. "I've never been one to quibble. Whatever I set my mind to doing, I did. If there was something I wanted, I simply went after it and made it mine. 'Failure' was a word never mentioned amongst the Gallaghers, you see.''

"So, my dear captain, is that why you married me? Because you did not want to admit to failure?'' she accusingly demanded, her violet eyes aglow with loving mischief.

"You *did* present me with the greatest challenge I'd ever known, my love,'' he retorted. A disarming grin tugged at the corners of his mouth, and his blue-green gaze traveled swiftly over her in a gesture of critical assessment. "However, it wasn't necessary for me to marry you in order to prevent failure. If I had only been desirous of adding you to my list of conquests, I would have done so," he asserted, a teasing light dancing within his eyes.

"Why, of all the arrogant, unscrupulous, egotistical—" Hillary sputtered in mock indignation. She pushed away from him and attempted to rise, but he merely laughed and sent her tumbling back onto the sweet-smelling grass. Struggling to escape, she gasped when he suddenly locked his arms about her and rolled so that she was beneath him. "Ryan! Someone will see us! The fisherman—"

"Has strict orders to wait for us on the beach. And there's no one else about for miles."

He smiled down at her wolfishly, and she swallowed hard before forcing herself to protest, "But it's getting late and . . . and Ewan and Josiah will be expecting us back . . ." Her voice trailed away into nothingness when Ryan's lips began nibbling along the silken white column of her throat. Moaning softly, she wound her arms about his neck and was rewarded for her willingness to surrender when his mouth captured hers in a deep, rapturous kiss that sent her desire flaring upward to meet his.

He was soon leading her back into the semi-darkness of the cave. Feeling deliciously wicked, she laughed when he pulled her down onto the cool earth and impatiently tossed her muslin skirts above her head. Her laughter quickly turned to gasps of impassioned delight as he slipped his warm fingers into the waistband of her drawers and yanked the lacy cotton undergarment downward, then set about masterfully teasing and stroking her satiny flesh until she was certain she could bear no more.

"Oh! Oh, Ryan!" she whispered feverishly, her fingers tightening upon the hard-muscled expanse of his broad, linen-clad shoulders. He swept aside her skirts and hungrily claimed her lips with his once more, and it was only moments later that he unfastened his trousers and brought his manhood gliding expertly within her honeyed warmth. She moaned and strained upward to meet his thrusts, her shapely limbs wrapping about his waist and her soft cries urging him onward until the wildly tempestuous blending of their bodies soared to its inevitable and highly satisfying conclusion . . .

If the fisherman and his sons noticed the telltale grass and dirt stains on the back of Hillary's cream-colored dress when Ryan assisted her into the boat again, they wisely kept their observations to themselves. The return trip to San Juan Bautista was achieved in near record time, for Ryan had promised to increase the boat owner's compensation if he could get them back in time to have dinner at the village's lone restaurant.

The "restaurant" was in actuality little more than a shack, but as Hillary soon discovered, it offered mouth-watering meals and wine of surprising quality. The main course was *langosta*, a large crayfish similar to the lobster, yet without any pincer claws. Its meat was succulent and flavorful, and Hillary amazed herself by the quantity she ate.

They returned to the ship in the early afternoon. Ewan and Josiah had seen to the transfer of the provisions and water to the *Falcon*, and they were waiting at the wharf to row Hillary and Ryan back out to the ship. Shading her eyes against the bright sunlight, Hillary reluctantly bid farewell to the island, a faint blush rising to her cheeks when she mused that she would of a certainty never forget

Robinson Crusoe's cave. Realizing that it was the first time in weeks she and her husband had shared such blazing intimacy in something other than a bed that swayed and rocked the entire time, she suppressed a giggle and dreamily wondered if marriage to Ryan Gallagher would always be so exciting.

The *Falcon* began the journey southward to Cape Horn the following morning. The sun shone intermittently throughout the day, while the calmness of the sea near the Juan Fernández Islands soon gave way to great swells that signaled the fact that the ship had entered the cold, turbulent Humboldt Current. Running from the antarctic to the equator, the current was nearly always accompanied by a bone-chilling southerly wind.

Hillary was grateful to escape below. She wasted no time in setting to work making the warmer dresses she would need. The sewing machine needed only a little oiling, and it wasn't long until the first project, a gown of soft green wool, was well under way in the lamplit confines of the captain's cabin.

She spent the majority of that day, and each day thereafter, bent over her sewing, and as a result saw little of Ryan. The increasing difficulty of the voyage required his presence on the quarterdeck a good deal of the time. He was often too weary at night to do anything more than collapse upon the bed and drift off into a few hours of deep and dreamless sleep.

Changes in temperature became more apparent with each passing day, and the whalers soon exchanged their lightweight clothing for that more suited to a cold climate. There was a repeated shifting of the wind now, while the periods of bad weather occurred with more and more frequency. Some days saw heavy gales battering the ship, and Ryan once again cursed the fact that they would be rounding the Horn during the summer months—actually winter there in the southern hemisphere—when conditions were at their worst. Chunks of ice had already been sighted in the frigid seas that seemed to take perverse pleasure in cradling the ship in a lull one moment and tossing it relentlessly about the next.

Hillary sat talking with Connor in the mess quarters one evening when the *Falcon* lay in one of those all-too-brief periods of calm. They sat gratefully sipping at steaming hot mugs of Josiah's bolstering, thick-as-mud coffee. Ryan was in his station on the quarterdeck, but he had insisted that his first mate take a well-deserved break and go below.

"Why, I've seen it so cold at the Horn that ice crackled from the rigging and wool blankets actually froze in the fo'c's'le," Connor related at her prompting. "Icebergs are always a danger—not all surprising when you realize you're as close as anyone can get to the South Pole. And a ship can be up against a head-on storm within minutes. When those winds come howling down from the Andes and the deck is suddenly buried under a mountain of green water, you pray for deliverance and ask yourself why you were ever dimwitted enough to think you wanted a life at sea!"

"Then why haven't you given it up?" Hillary asked with a slight frown of bemusement.

"I will someday, if I live long enough to make the choice," he answered with a crooked grin, his golden eyes twinkling across at her. "Maybe if I had a wife like Ryan's, I'd consider letting myself be anchored."

"Surely a man like yourself has someone special

waiting for him somewhere," she insisted. "Perhaps even *several* someones!" She saw that her remark had hit close to home when a sudden shadow crossed his attractive face.

"No, only one," he murmured, his eyes clouding with remembrance. Hillary wanted to ask him more about the mysterious lady in question, but she decided not to press the issue. In the next instant, he returned to the subject of Cape Horn and the perils awaiting them.

"I guess I shouldn't be filling your head with all this talk of storms and ice. While it won't be a pleasant journey, there's truly no need to worry," he hastened to reassure her. "That husband of yours is the best master I've ever seen. He's piloted the *Falcon* around the Horn a dozen times before, and you can bet he won't be taking any chances with you aboard."

"I know," she murmured, sipping at the coffee again. She released a sigh as she lowered the mug back to the table, and her own gaze grew noticeably troubled. "To tell the truth, I'm more than a little concerned about him, Connor. He's driving himself so hard." Indeed, she added silently, it was as if he had become yet another person of late, one who could scarcely eat or sleep or think of anything else save his duties as master of the *Falcon*.

"Like any captain worth his salt, he holds himself solely responsible for the lives of everyone on his ship," explained Connor. "And he knows how anxious the men are to reach New Bedford, so he's trying to pick up speed wherever he can. It's only when sailing homeward that haste enters into a whaler's life—at any other time, it would be his undoing." He finished off the last of his coffee and excused himself, promising to do his best to persuade

Ryan to come below for at least a few minutes' respite from the inclement weather.

The *Falcon* continued to fight her way southward through the turbulent seas. Then, one bleak afternoon brought with it the first glimpse of the black, menacing cliffs of Cape Horn off the ship's starboard bow. By nightfall, the ocean and wind and heavens had conspired together to release their hellish wrath upon the defenseless ship, and the storm Ryan had been fearing was upon them at last.

The winds roared at nearly a hundred miles per hour, the waves towered fifty feet into the sky, and severe squalls of hail and sleet blasted the deck. The men were forced to face away from the gusts in order to breathe as they desperately scrambled about to haul in the ice-coated canvas.

The wheel plunged against the lashings that bound it. Ryan and Connor battled to hold it against the force of the storm, but it repeatedly tore itself from their grasp, its spinning stokes threatening to break their arms before they could seize it once more. Mountains of water crashed vengefully over the deck until it was as high as their waists, its greenish, phosphorescent wake heaving far astern.

Ryan had banished Hillary to his quarters at the first sign of trouble. She knelt upon the bed, watching with terror-filled eyes as the water, pouring in at both the companionway and skylight, filled the stateroom. Already two feet high, the level rose with each frantic plunging of the ship.

"Dear God!" she breathed in horror, more frightened than she had ever been before. Could it be that the ship was sinking? Were she and Ryan and everyone else destined to end their lives this very night?

Ryan! He had made her promise to stay below no matter what happened, but she could no longer sit and wait while the seas raged above. If there was any possibility at all that the *Falcon* would succumb to the storm's fury, then she had to be with him! She had to see him before—

"Oh Ryan!" she whispered, her voice breaking. Already well-bundled against the cold, she took a deep breath and lowered herself from the bed. She shivered violently as her booted feet disappeared into the icy depths of the water, but she did not waver in her purpose. Flinging an oilcloth slicker about her shoulders, she pulled a battered sou'wester low upon her head and made her way through the cabin. She pulled with all her might upon the door, but it refused to budge until another huge wave crashed over the deck and sent a torrent of water sluicing down the companionway.

Hillary staggered back and clutched at the sofa behind her for support as the door gave way beneath the water's force. Determinedly regaining her balance, she propelled herself out into the companionway and up the steps.

"Keep those pumps manned!" Ryan thundered to the wearying crew as, unbeknownst to him, his wife began stumbling and pulling her way across the storm-lashed darkness of the deck. "We'll ride it out yet! Hold fast, damn you, hold fast!" It was almost impossible for him to be heard above the rumble of the sea and roar of the wind, but the men took courage from the sight of their captain's defiant stance at the wheel.

To Hillary, it seemed to take hours for her to reach

his side. She was forced to grip the railing in order to keep from being either blown or swept back into the churning, heaving waters that flung the ship about with unrelenting ferocity. Hurtled forward by yet another violent motion of the ship, she grasped at Ryan's arm, a sharp cry bursting from her lips.

He swung about and caught her just in time. Another man quickly stepped to take his place beside Connor at the wheel. Hillary cried out again as Ryan's hands closed with punishing force about her arms, and she paled at the absolute savagery of his features, revealed by the glow of the lighted binnacle near the helm.

"Damn it all to hell, why aren't you down below?" he bellowed, the rain and sleet and sea spray pelting down across his own hat and slicker.

"Oh Ryan, I couldn't stay down there! I was afraid I'd never see you again!" she shouted back hoarsely. Her eyes burned terribly, and she felt chilled to the bone. She didn't understand how Ryan or any of the men could keep their balance on the slippery, wind-ravaged deck, for her own legs refused to hold her weight. Ryan clamped an arm about her waist and held her up against him, his expression still tight lipped and furious but his fiery gaze softening when he viewed the heartfelt alarm in her wide, glistening eyes.

"We'll not let the Horn beat us!" he decreed with an unnerving confidence that gave her hope. "And you'll not be rid of me so easily, Mrs. Gallagher!" he added with a brief, endearingly rakish smile. "Now get below and stay there this time!" He turned to give her over into the care of Connor, but disaster struck before he had done anything more than turn back to the helm.

A gigantic wave, almost twice as high as those that

had been battering the ship for the past several hours, suddenly rose up to smash over the port bow. Snapping the foremast in two as though it were a mere twig, the wall of water splintered one of the whaleboats and carried away everything on deck that was not securely lashed down. In its wake, the ship was left listing at a dangerous angle to the starboard side, and the lines of the broken mast threatened to bring the other two masts and their rigging crashing down as well.

Hillary was nearly torn from Ryan's side as the *Falcon* lurched and swayed. Connor and the other man lost control of the wheel, and it spun round with terrifying freedom before they could wrestle it to a stop. Ryan quickly dragged himself and Hillary back to the helm and commanded at the top of his voice, "Cut away the mast! Cleave those lines, men!" The crew hurried to grab their axes and do his bidding, for they knew as well as he that the ship would be lost if another wave took them before they had freed and tied off the rigging.

Ryan abruptly relinquished his hold on Hillary, charging the first mate to take her below while he himself resumed control of the wheel.

She refused to go with Connor, however, resisting his efforts and adamantly proclaiming, "No! I will not sit alone and meekly wait to see whether we are to live or die!" Her words struck a responsive chord within Connor. He knew it was mutiny to disobey his captain's orders, but he couldn't bring himself to force her below when there was a very real possibility the ship would not make it through. Wrapping an arm about her shoulders, he nodded down at her in silent understanding and pulled her back to watch with him behind the helm.

The crew worked feverishly to cut away the broken

mast. More than once, a man had to be rescued when the sea tried to drag him from the deck. Finally, the lines were all cut and the portion of the mast that had crashed down through the starboard railing was heaved overboard. Ryan battled to right the ship, his efforts impeded by the howling winds and towering swells.

Then, ever so slowly, the remaining masts began pointing back up toward the sky. Hillary felt her pulses racing as she watched her husband, his eyes gleaming with unconquerable spirit and his handsome face set in lines of a determination that would not be denied, and she thought her heart would burst with love and pride. She knew in that moment that the master of the *Falcon* had won.

Although the storm continued to rage through the night, the ship prevailed against it. By dawn of the following day, the worst had passed and the crew set about repairing the damage as best they could. Ryan set a course for the Falkland Islands, more than three hundred miles northeast of the Horn, and finally allowed himself to be relieved at the helm in order to go below for a much-needed rest.

It was the first time he and Hillary had been alone together, at least while conscious, in days. She had returned to the stateroom soon after he had brought the ship under control the night before. Having fallen asleep in spite of her resolve not to do so, she was just beginning to stir when he entered the cabin and waded through the few inches of water still covering the floor.

"Ryan?" she called softly, sitting up in the bed and sweeping the tangled ebony locks away from her face. She had changed into dry clothing before lying down, but the damp and the cold still made her shiver. She felt warmed by Ryan's weary smile as his

300

tall frame filled the doorway.

"You are truly a sight for sore eyes, my love," he remarked, his deep voice sounding noticeably fatigued. To Hillary, he appeared younger and more vulnerable than the dauntless sea captain whose gallantry and expertise had saved a ship and its entire crew from a watery death mere hours earlier.

Returning his smile with a tender one of her own, she scrambled from the bed and helped him draw off his wet things. Within minutes, he was stretching out upon the bed and drawing her down to lie close beside him.

He released a long sigh and closed his eyes, then murmured, "Remind me later, Mrs. Gallagher, to beat you for disobeying me again."

"But Ryan, I—"

"*And* to bring Connor Reid up on charges of mutiny," he added with a suspicious-sounding gruffness.

She rose up on one elbow and peered closely down into his unfathomable countenance, but he refused to open his eyes or give her any indication of whether or not he truly intended to carry out his threats.

"It isn't fair to blame Connor!" she vehemently protested. "Why, he couldn't very well—"

"Shut up, woman, and let me get some sleep!" he growled. Glimpsing a telltale twitching of his lips, Hillary smiled to herself and lay back down.

Watching as the albatrosses wheeled and dipped in the wake of the ship, Hillary became aware of a new smell to the wind. It was a distinct, sweet scent, and she frowned in puzzlement while inhaling deeply in an attempt to identify it.

"It's the Falklands you're smelling," Ryan pro-

301

vided with an indulgent grin. He reached out and drew her back to stand with him at the wheel. "They may be rugged, but they're covered with shrubs and grasses that give off a fragrance like no other. We ought to catch sight of them soon." Hillary drew the fur-lined cloak more closely about her, for the strong, northwesterly wind seemed determined to send her hastening below again.

"You've been there many times before, haven't you?" she asked, staunchly trying to prevent her teeth from chattering.

"Yes, but never with a 'lame duck' before," he commented wryly, referring to the damage sustained by the *Falcon*. "We'll be able to get her repaired at Stanley."

"Are we going to stay long then?"

"As much as a week, I'm afraid. It depends on how many other ships have suffered the same fate." He chuckled quietly as he wrapped an arm about her shoulders and pulled her close. His blue-green eyes were brimming with fond amusement beneath the brim of his hat. "You look half-frozen, my love. Why don't you go below and wait? It will be another hour or more before we drop anchor."

"Oh, very well," she reluctantly agreed, wanting to stay with him yet forced to concede the fact that she would probably be stiff as a board from the cold if she dared remain abovedecks any longer. She quickly brushed Ryan's cold lips with hers and scurried back across the quarterdeck.

A short time later, the "land ho" call was sounded by the lookout. The horizon ahead was marked by misty silhouettes of the hills of the main island of East Falkland. At first, the coastline was only a slender ribbon of gray beneath the cloudy skies, but as the *Falcon* cut through the icy waters and closed the distance, it developed into a formidable array of cliff faces and dazzling, white sand beaches. The rich green expanses of the grasses Ryan had mentioned to Hillary contrasted sharply with the sand, and still farther inland could be seen a veritable patchwork of reds, greens, grays, and buffs.

Hillary had returned to the quarterdeck by the time they entered the waters of Port William, the outer harbor to the town. There was as yet no sign of Stanley as Ryan guided the ship through a narrow waterway that opened up into another harbor, but upon passing through these last narrows, the town suddenly unfolded before Hillary's pleasantly surprised eyes.

Built across a gently sloping hillside that ran all the way down to the shoreline of the almost landlocked harbor, Stanley was a charming collection of neat rows of white cottages and other light-colored structures, which, once again, contrasted with the dark gray ridges that formed the tops of the slopes behind the town. There were a few piers and jetties in front of the town at the water's edge, and a railed-in dockyard where the Union Jack flew above a number of government buildings. Almost at the exact center of the town, and readily identifiable from the harbor, was a large stone church and clock tower.

Hillary was delighted to learn from Ryan that they were to take rooms ashore for the duration of their stay. By late afternoon, he had made all the arrangements for the ship's repairs and was leading his wife through town to the hotel, located past the church on the main road.

Marveling at the unexpected size and prosperity of Stanley, Hillary gazed about with avid interest while Ryan briefly explained the settlement's origin and history as a British colony. Most of the island's inhabitants were sheep farmers, for the animals thrived in the cool, oceanic climate. Although there were a variety of businesses in town, it was the Falkland Islands Company that employed the majority of the population. The Company, its interests mainly in sheep and the thousands of wild cattle that roamed East Falkland, had been incorporated and granted a Royal Charter by Queen Victoria more than six years earlier.

"But the most profitable trade in the Falklands right now is the one dealing in ship repairs," opined Ryan. "There isn't much of a bargain to be found when their services are required," he added with a faint, sardonic smile. "It's going to cost like the very devil to have the *Falcon* made seaworthy again, though I was able to make them promise to finish the work by the end of the week."

"What about Connor and the others? Where are they going to stay for the next four days?"

"There are several establishments in town that cater to single men. Only those men daft enough to bring their wives along on a voyage put up at the hotel," he told her with an unrepentant grin.

Hillary affected an indignant air and retorted, "You should count yourself fortunate, Captain, that you do not tumble into a cold, empty bed every night like those men who are not *daft* must do!"

"Perhaps I should at that," teased Ryan, slipping an arm beneath the edge of her cloak and about her waist. "Although I think of you as a good deal more than just a bed warmer, my love." He emphasized this last by moving his hand downward to bestow a wickedly playful smack upon her backside. She gasped and colored, then hastily glanced about to make certain no one had seen.

The Eagle Hotel proved to be a comfortable, two-storied stone structure, which had provided many a homesick seaman, and his wife, with food and lodging. The rooms to which the proprietor showed them were spacious and warm—they seemed a palace after the tiny stateroom aboard the *Falcon*.

Hillary thoroughly enjoyed their stay in the Falklands. Since Ryan was gone much of each day, making certain the repairs were being carried out to his specifications and helping Josiah see to the purchase of the fresh meat, vegetables, and other provisions the waterfront market offered, she occupied her time by exploring the town's many shops. It snowed a little every afternoon, but never enough to do anything more than leave a thin coating that quickly melted; indeed, it was not nearly as cold as she had expected, for the daytime temperature was usually above freezing. The winds were ceaseless and unvarying, their persistence and strength her only true complaint of the weather.

The nights were heavenly. She and Ryan would lie together in the big, four-poster bed and snuggle down beneath the mountain of quilts. Sometimes they made splendidly tempestuous love, sometimes they simply talked, but they always fell asleep in each other's arms.

Their last night in Stanley found Hillary waiting alone in the snug warmth of the hotel room. The sun was already sinking low upon the horizon, and still Ryan had not returned. She released a sigh and wandered restlessly toward the window again, staring out at the darkening street below.

Acting on a sudden impulse, she whirled about and flung her cloak about her shoulders. She blew out the lamp before sweeping from the room and down the stairs. Smiling to herself, she emerged from the hotel and turned her steps toward the waterfront, following the same path Ryan took when he returned at the end of each day. She would intercept him, and perhaps the two of them could enjoy a last stroll about the town, though the temperature would of a certainty begin to plummet soon with the advent of nightfall.

There were few people about at such a late hour. Hillary fastened the hood of her cloak more securely about her head and gave silent thanks for the fact that Ryan had insisted upon purchasing her even warmer boots and stockings. She was unaccustomed to the cold after living in Tahiti for the past five years, but she had adapted quite well. It was a miracle that neither she nor anyone else had contracted pneumonia after the soaking they had received while rounding the Horn, she reflected with an inward sigh.

Traveling past the church and its clock tower, she thought she heard someone call her name. The sound was strangely muffled. She frowned in puzzlement and looked about, then concluded that she must have been mistaken, for the area in which she stood appeared deserted. The church itself was dark and its wide double doors closed. The only light came from the windows of the surrounding buildings, which were also shut tight against the cold.

"Oh Ryan, where are you?" Hillary murmured under her breath. She was beginning to regret her impulsiveness, but she turned about and went on her way, her steps quickening as she moved farther down the hill.

Suddenly, a dark figure loomed up from an alleyway to her right. She had no time to cry out before she was seized and pulled roughly into the black, narrow space between the buildings. A man's arm tightened about her, threatening to crush her with its brutal force, while an equally cruel hand clamped across her mouth. Dimly aware of the strong smell of spirits, she struggled for breath and fought against a wave of sheer, debilitating panic.

Dear God, help me! her mind screamed. She clawed at the man's hand and twisted violently against his arm. Unable to see his face behind her, she struck out blindly, her hands doubling into fists in an effort to land a blow that would make him release her. He seemed oblivious to her struggles, for his arm suddenly jerked up from her waist so that his fingers could close ruthlessly upon the fullness of her breast.

Hillary moaned in pain and outrage. She began fighting him like a tigress, her increased vehemence surprising him long enough for her to wrench free and hurl herself from the alleyway. Her unknown assailant lunged forward and grabbed at her skirts, his hand twisting within the woolen fabric to jerk her back. She whirled about and caught him on the side of the head with her fist. He cursed loudly, his grip on her skirts relaxing as he staggered back into the alleyway.

Drawing in a ragged breath, Hillary started running. She could think only of getting away. Her skirts flew about her booted ankles as she raced down the empty street. She tossed a wide, terror-filled glance over her shoulder, then came hurtling up against someone whose hands shot out to grip her arms.

"No!" she screamed, instinctively struggling within his grasp without looking at him.

His fingers tightened, and he gave her a brisk shake as he demanded, "Hillary! Hillary, what is it? What happened?" Her eyes filled with recognition as she raised them to his face at last.

"Ryan!" she cried brokenly. Hot tears suddenly spilled over from her lashes to course freely down her cheeks, and she sobbed with relief while her husband's strong arms enveloped her. "There was a man . . . by the church. It was too dark to see his face. He . . . he grabbed me and—" She broke off as Ryan abruptly pulled her back to search her face with his penetrating gaze.

"Dear God, did he hurt you?" His deep voice was raw with emotion, and his eyes gleamed with savage fury at the thought of the man who had dared to lay hands on her.

"No!" she gasped out, vigorously shaking her head in denial. "I was able to get away before he . . . before he—"

Ryan suddenly swept her up in his arms and carried her swiftly toward a nearby boardinghouse. Striding inside, he left her in the care of the proprietress, an older widow who had befriended him when he had stayed there some years earlier. He paused only long enough to tell Hillary that he would be back for her soon, then took himself off to try to find the man who had attacked her.

Nearly a full hour had passed by the time he returned. His efforts had met with little success. He had questioned a number of people who lived in the area of town where the attack had occurred. An elderly shopkeeper and his wife recalled having seen someone fitting Hillary's description walking past the church at the time in question, but they had seen nothing of the man. Ryan found no sign of her assailant, and no one who had witnessed the attack.

Realizing it would do little good to contact the authorities with such a regrettable lack of evidence, he thanked the widow for her help and took Hillary back to the hotel. He immediately bundled her into bed and refrained from scolding her for wandering about alone at night. Though he was still filled with a smoldering rage for what had happened to her, he did not mention the incident again. Hillary was grateful for his tender solicitude, and she finally drifted off to sleep while cradled within the warm, loving security of his arms.

The attack seemed like nothing more than an awful nightmare to her when she awoke the following morning. She had managed to banish it to the back of her mind by the time the *Falcon* weighed anchor and set sail from Stanley.

The natural beauty of the island's rugged, rocky coast was revealed beneath the rarity of sunny skies as Hillary stood on the quarterdeck and watched in fascination when the rocks suddenly came alive with the dark brown forms of hundreds of fur seals and sea lions.

"There used to be quite a number of sealers calling at the Falklands," Connor supplied as he came to stand at the railing beside her. Smiling at the noisily awakening creatures in the near distance, he added, "I can't say I'm sorry they don't come with as much regularity nowadays. I've always been sort of partial to seals—perhaps because they're such lively little rascals."

"They *are* appealing, aren't they?" agreed Hillary, her sparkling gaze drawn to where a group of them slid from the rocks to begin porpoising in the turbulent waters. Another stretch of wild, unspoiled coastline soon yielded an unbelievably large colony of penguins. "Good heavens, there must be thousands of them!" Some of them waddled comically high upon the rocks and along the shore, while others, sighting the ship, plunged into the sea.

"Did you know they were once actually hunted for their oil?" remarked Connor, folding his arms across his chest. "Of course, it didn't require much of a search to find them. The seal hunters built corrals and herded the penguins into them, then proceeded to club and boil them down in try-pots much like ours."

"Oh, Connor, that's horrible!" exclaimed Hillary with a stricken look on her beautiful countenance.

"There's no telling how many millions were killed," he said grimly, obviously in accord with her feelings in the matter. The *Falcon* rounded another point, and Connor's golden eyes sighted something else he thought would prove of interest to Hillary. "See that wreck over there?" He nodded to indicate the remnants of a ship on the sea-lashed rocks below the cliffs. As Hillary's gaze followed his, he told her, "It's no secret that more than one vessel has fallen prey to deliberate wrecking in these waters. The cargo can fetch a high price, and the timber from their hulks is always in high demand."

"But who would do such a thing?" she queried, finding it difficult to believe anyone would be so greedy as to purposely cause the destruction of a ship.

"Some say it's arranged by the very men who repaired them, angry over not having received full payment. Others claim the crew is often to blame, particularly when they are reluctant to sail round the Horn in a vessel they consider unseaworthy. Whatever the case, the—"

"If you've finished with your fascinating lecture on the Falklands, Mr. Reid, perhaps you'd consider getting back to your duties as first mate of *this* vessel!" Ryan's deep, commanding voice suddenly rang out behind them. Hillary spun about and smiled fearlessly in response to the mock scowl of anger on his handsome face.

"If the captain of this ship would do the honors, then the generosity of the first mate would not be required!" she retorted, her violet eyes dancing with amusement. There was an answering glow in Ryan's gaze, and his scowl deepened for effect as he strode forward. Connor chuckled and obediently took himself off to resume his work.

"Are you questioning my authority yet again, Mrs. Gallagher?" challenged Ryan in a low tone brimming with humor. He took her arm and tucked it firmly within the crook of his.

"Not at all, Captain Gallagher," she dutifully murmured, though an impudent light still lurked within the sparkling amethyst depths of her eyes. Ryan's features finally relaxed into a smile, and he laughed softly as he turned back to the railing with her.

"Far be it for me to scold Connor, when I myself am so tempted to forgo my duties and spend all my time with you," he declared in a rich, mellow voice that made Hillary tingle as its resonant tones washed over her.

She released a sigh and said, "Oh, Ryan, will we always be this happy? Sometimes I think it's all too good to be true, and I can't help but worry that things will change when we reach New Bedford. Suppose your family truly disapproves of me; suppose—"

"You're my wife, and as such they will welcome you into the family. I have no doubt that my mother, my brother, *and* my sisters will do so quite willingly. They can't help but love you," he assured her once more.

Hillary wanted to believe him, yet she still felt a nagging uneasiness. Telling herself that it was perfectly natural to feel somewhat nervous when faced with the prospect of meeting one's in-laws for the first time, she sighed again and curled her fingers more tightly about her husband's arm. They watched together as the *Falcon* left the Falklands behind and sped homeward in the icy Atlantic.

XIII

It was a late summer's day in New Bedford, Massachusetts. Hailed as the new "Capital of Whaling," the city that lay on the west bank of the Acushnet River had wrested the title from Nantucket some years earlier by refitting its cargo ships as whalers, by having the good fortune to possess a larger and better harbor, and by exhibiting a more vigorous spirit that allowed it to make the whaling industry second only to that of cotton in the New England economy. Nowhere else could be found a more intriguing combination than New Bedford's population offered, particularly on such a pleasant, sunny afternoon. Cannibals from Africa and the South Seas stood chatting together at street corners, Quaker merchants strutted around in their tall beaver hats and swallow-tailed frock coats, newly arrived greenhorns anxious to go "a-whaling" stood gawking at the ceaseless bustle, men who had already earned the distinction of being called whalers returned to the waterfront to receive their share of the profit, and a crowd of friends and relatives gathered along the wharves to greet the shipload of tired, homesick voyagers who had been absent for three years.

Hillary knew a great deal about New Bedford already, for Ryan had spoken of his home with increasing frequency during the last few weeks of the voyage. She was aware of the fact that whale oil was even used as currency, especially when it came to paying the schoolteachers and ministers, and that the city was one of the wealthiest per capita in the entire world. Oil and whalebone were used in lamps and corsets, perfumery and soaps, caps and sewing machines, and the head of a sperm whale contained an oil that was refined into a superb candle wax; one good cargo alone could be worth nearly a quarter of a million dollars. She had learned many other things as well: New Bedford had a fleet of more than three hundred whaling ships, it was a thriving place that boasted of twenty thousand or so residents, and more Quakers than not lived there.

It seemed that nearly everyone depended on the taking of whales for his livelihood. Men who never went to sea drove wagons and carts loaded with oil casks to the warehouses, worked in blacksmith shops to forge the harpoons and lances, made and repaired the sails, toiled in coopers' shops and carpenters' shops and candle factories, ran the hardware stores and mercantiles that supplied the ships and their crews, and were occupied in every other line of business even remotely connected to whaling.

New Bedford men are born with the fever of the sea in their veins, Ryan had told her. Hillary wondered if it were true, if the city would turn out to be every bit as obsessed with whaling as he had made it sound.

Under a full sail and before a brisk northwesterly wind, the *Falcon* almost flew across the choppy waters of Buzzards Bay. She raced in between the Clark's Point Light and the rocks, past Palmer's Island, making straightaway for the crowded wharf and the promised welcome of yet another home-coming.

Hundreds of tall masts of both ships and barks fringed the harbor's skyline. The cluttered docks were piled high with hundreds of wooden casks and with ship's rigging, crates of provisions, and equipment of all kinds. Dock hands were tossing forkfuls of wet seaweed over the barrels of whale oil to keep them moist and prevent leakage of their precious contents. There were always ships tied up at the wharves, either unloading or preparing for a voyage, and always smaller vessels darting in between with supplies. The heavy, sweet smell of oil filled the air.

Hillary stood beside Ryan on the quarterdeck and gazed with widened eyes upon the busy scene before her. It had been years since she had seen so many people and ships and industry in one place. The noise of it all was carried upward on the cool, salty breeze as a waiting shoreman caught the lines and the *Falcon* was finally tied up at her home port.

"There they are!" proclaimed Ryan, lifting his arm in greeting toward the crowd while his other hand tightened upon Hillary's arm.

"How on earth can you spot them amongst so many others?" she wondered aloud. Her apprehension was increasing by the second, and she desperately wished she had been able to wear something a bit more stylish than the simple, dark blue wool dress she had made during the last leg of the voyage. Her violet gaze grew even more troubled when she noticed that the greater majority of ladies on the wharf were attired in fine silks, satins, and velvets, and that their skirts were bowed out and made very full by the use of crinolines. She had not bothered with corsets or hoops since leaving England, and the necessity to readopt the custom before reaching New

Bedford had never occurred to her.

"Come on, my love. Tradition demands that the ship's master be the first to go ashore." Ryan flashed her a bolstering smile, then drew her arm possessively through his and led her across to the lowered gangplank. She was acutely conscious of the hundreds of pairs of eyes watching them, and she could have sworn she heard more than one gasp of surprise amidst the din that rose from the crowd. She and Ryan were surrounded by a veritable horde of welcoming townspeople the moment they stepped ashore, but he expertly began maneuvering them through the crowd to where his mother and sisters were waiting.

The crew of the *Falcon*, meanwhile, raced from the ship into the receptive arms of their own friends and families the very instant Connor gave the order of dismissal. Their first visit ashore would be to one of the many barbershops for a bath and a haircut, then to an outfitter's store for a new suit of clothing— "shore clothes"—that did not reek of oil and the lingering stench of the forecastle. Hillary caught a brief glimpse of Josiah and Ewan, who were both so tall they towered above the rest of the crowd, before Ryan urged her along toward the three women who stood waving from their post near a carriage and horses.

"Ryan! Oh my dear son!" the oldest of the three cried as she hastened forward to embrace him. Momentarily drawing away from Hillary, Ryan caught up his mother in his arms and kissed her warmly.

"The wayward scion of the Gallaghers returns at last!" he declared with a laugh. No sooner had he set the petite, silver-haired woman on her feet again than he quickly caught up his two beaming sisters in turn and kissed them as well. Smiling happily, he grasped Hillary's arm again and pulled her back to his side. His turquoise gaze was aglow with loving pride as he announced, "This is Hillary, my wife."

"*Your wife?*" Three pairs of eyes widened in stunned disbelief. Ryan's mother compressed her lips into a tight, thin line and slowly transferred her gaze to Hillary, her light gray eyes fixing the younger woman with a look so cold that she actually felt chilled. Ryan's sisters gaped at her as though she had suddenly sprouted an extra head.

"Hillary, this is my mother, Priscilla, and my sisters, Gillian and Erin," said Ryan, smoothly continuing with the introductions.

"I . . . I'm very pleased to meet you. Ryan has told me so much about you," Hillary declared with a tentative smile, doing her best to ignore the heavy tension in the air. Though she had expected them to be taken aback at the news, she had not expected this glaring animosity to which they were subjecting her.

Gillian, the eldest sister, was a younger replica of her mother, both in physical appearance and demeanor. Hillary judged her to be in her mid-twenties. Erin, on the other hand, seemed to be exhibiting more curiosity than anything else. No more than fifteen, she was a blue-eyed brunette who promised to blossom into a real beauty someday. All three were very attractive, and the resemblance to Ryan was immediately noticeable, though he stood more than a foot taller.

"Well, this is a . . . surprise, my dear," Priscilla Gallagher murmured with a forced smile that did not quite reach her eyes. She regally extended a hand and took Hillary's in a grip that was so limp and of such brief duration it was barely cordial. "My son did not tell us he planned to marry," she said with an obvious edge to her voice, her gaze shifting significantly back to Ryan.

"It is highly doubtful any announcement of my intentions would have reached you before the deed was done," he quipped, his mouth curving up into a sardonic half smile. "I met Hillary while in Tahiti. We've been married only a short time."

"In Tahiti?" the older woman in deep emerald velvet repeated. "I see." On her lips, those two words seemed to convey a good deal.

"Welcome to New Bedford, Hillary." This came from Gillian, who reluctantly stepped forward to offer her own hand. She made no attempt to infuse warmth into her greeting, nor to conceal her low opinion of her new sister's appearance as her gray eyes swept disdainfully over Hillary's unadorned wool gown and windblown hair. Her own, impeccably styled gown was of pale yellow silk, and her tawny curls were swept high upon her neck and topped with a beribboned satin bonnet.

"Thank you, Gillian," Hillary murmured. If not for Ryan's arm about her, she would have been sorely tempted to flee back up the gangplank and into the sanctuary of the ship's cabin.

"Are you *truly* his wife?" Erin blurted out, eyeing Hillary with both suspicion and youthful inquisitiveness. The girl's plump, immature curves were encased in rose-colored foulard, while her thick hair, much the same shade of brown as Ryan's, had been plaited and pinned up on either side of her head.

"She is indeed," Ryan answered for her. There was a certain tightness about his mouth now, and a hard gleam had crept into his gaze. He tugged Hillary even closer and declared firmly, "I know my marriage has taken you by surprise, but the fact remains that Hillary is my wife now. As such, I

318

expect her to be accorded the respect and affection due her."

"Of course, Ryan," his mother concurred, another cool smile touching her lips. Neither Gillian nor Erin offered a reply, the two of them staring long and hard at Hillary. Though she raised her head proudly and met their gazes without flinching, inwardly she was a mass of raw nerves.

"Where is David?" Ryan suddenly asked, his eyes hastily scanning the crowd for any sign of his brother.

"I'm afraid he is . . . well, he was involved in an accident while making an inspection of the refinery last week," disclosed Priscilla, a shadow of maternal pain crossing her features at the memory. "The doctor said his recovery will require at least a month's time. Poor David was quite distressed to hear that he must neglect his duties for so long, but I know he will begin to rest easier now that you are home to take care of things. He—"

"Ryan!" an unmistakably feminine voice rang out. "Oh Ryan, you're home at last!"

Hillary turned with the others to see a tall, willowy vision in blue satin bearing down on them. Young and beautiful in a thoroughly aristocratic sort of way, the blonde held her lace-trimmed parasol in one hand and swept up the hem of her full, flounced skirts away from the oily planks of the wharf with the other. Her green eyes were shining brightly as she approached, and it was clear that her smile was meant only for Ryan.

"Oh no, it's Alison!" breathed Erin. Her widened gaze flew from Hillary, to her brother, then to her mother and sister. Both Priscilla and Gillian wore noticeably troubled expressions, while Ryan gallantly did his best to conceal his displeasure at seeing

319

Alison Bromfield again.

Watching while the tall blonde made her way through the outer fringes of the crowd, Hillary became aware of a sudden tenseness to Ryan's muscular frame. She raised her eyes to his face in puzzlement, only to experience a sharp twinge of uneasiness when she glimpsed the set look to his sun-bronzed features.

"Ryan! My darling Ryan!" cried Alison, then startled everyone by throwing her arms about his neck and straining upward to press a highly enthusiastic kiss upon his unwilling lips.

Hillary gasped and numbly took a step backward. Ryan's arm slid hastily from about her waist, and he brought his hands up to seize Alison's gloved wrists and force her arms from about his neck. She was smiling unrepentantly for her boldness as he ground out, "Save your kisses for someone who wants them, Alison!"

"Come now, Ryan, I thought we settled all that three years ago," she replied with a throaty laugh. She gazed up at him coquettishly from beneath her eyelashes and affected a seductive pout. "Don't tell me you're still going to be difficult about things, my darling. I've missed you terribly and I know how anxious you must have been to get home to me!"

"To get home, yes, but not to you." He wasted no more time before possessively draping an arm about Hillary's shoulders again and informing Alison, "I've brought my wife with me."

Hillary once again found herself the recipient of a glare, though Alison's was ten times more heated and venomous than the others had been. Her head was reeling from what she had just witnessed, as well as from what she had heard—*my darling Ryan,* Alison had called him—and she wondered if her husband's

320

relationship with the woman had been as intimate as Alison's words and actions implied.

"You lie!" the stormy-faced blonde seethed, rounding on Ryan with her green eyes ablaze. "This is some cruel jest of yours, isn't it?" she demanded. "You're trying to punish me for—"

"No, Alison, it's no jest. Hillary and I were married in Tahiti," he disclosed, his manner aloof yet not unkind. While it was true that Alison Bromfield was a coldhearted, selfish witch, he had no wish to hurt her. He had fancied himself in love with her once, many years ago, only to discover her true nature and break things off before promising her marriage. She had continued to insist that they belonged to each other, even going so far as to orchestrate an embarrassingly melodramatic scene in front of everyone on the day of his departure three years ago.

"But you . . . you couldn't have . . . why, you are betrothed to *me!*" Her pale, aristocratic features became suffused with hot color as she turned her vengeful wrath upon Hillary, who could only gaze up at her in stunned disbelief. *"You* did this, you little slut! You tricked him into marrying you somehow, didn't you? Did you—"

"That's enough, Alison!" Ryan's deep voice, whipcord sharp, cut her off. Striving to control his temper, he decreed, "You will never address my wife in such a manner again, do you understand? If you feel the need to blame anyone, look to yourself!"

"My dear Alison, perhaps you should—" Priscilla tried to intervene.

"You can't let him do this!" cried Alison, her eyes glistening with tears as she seized the older woman's arm in a desperate grip and implored her to help. "You must make him see that he can have no other wife save me! Why, everyone knows we were to be married!"

"I've business to attend to," said Ryan coldly, turning his back on Alison and escorting Hillary to the waiting carriage. Gillian and Erin, painfully aware of the attention Alison had attracted, were only too happy to follow after them. Priscilla gently disengaged her arm and gave the distraught blonde a faint, sympathetic smile.

"I'm sorry you had to learn of it this way, Alison. It would have been easier for us all if we had been warned first. But do not despair, my dear. We shall talk later." She did her best to smile once more, patted the younger woman's arm consolingly, then moved away to join the others.

Alison Bromfield's blazing green eyes filled with murderous intent as she stared after the Gallaghers. Ryan would be made to pay for his betrayal of her! And she would think of some way to make that black-haired little strumpet he had married pay as well!

You think it's settled, don't you, Ryan Gallagher? she silently raged. Well, it is not! No man treats me so shamefully and gets away with it—no man!

Ryan, meanwhile, helped his mother up beside the others in the carriage and told Hillary, "I'll join you at home as soon as I can." His heart twisted at the pain and confusion in her eyes, but he told himself explanations would have to wait until later. Mentally cursing Alison for her untimely theatrics, he looked to his mother and declared in a low voice full of meaning, "I leave my wife in your care, Mother."

"We shall see that she is made comfortable, my dear," Priscilla quietly assured him. "Please, do not let your business keep you too long, for David will be very anxious to see you, as will the children."

"Children?" echoed Hillary, her eyes flying back

322

to Ryan's face. Dear Lord, was there something *else* he had forgotten to mention to her?

"Jimmy and Bridget," Erin obligingly supplied. "They belong to David and Cara." Her childlike gaze fastened on her new sister-in-law with unnerving intensity as she spoke.

"Oh, I . . . I see," Hillary murmured, dismayed to feel the hot color staining her cheeks.

Ryan raised his hand to her in farewell as the carriage drove away, but she did not respond. She was feeling utterly miserable, and her turbulent thoughts were preoccupied with all that had occurred since he had led her ashore. Alison's furious, scornful words still rang in her ears. Why oh why hadn't Ryan told her about the woman waiting for him in New Bedford?

The air grew heavy with an even more powerful mixture of aromas as the carriage traveled away from the wharves and up Johnnycake Hill. The warehouses along the waterfront were laden with sandalwood and tea waiting to be sold to the wealthy merchants and shipowners, the candle-making factories gave off the distinctive scent of spermaceti, while the musky odor of ambergris, which would be shipped to the perfumeries of London and Paris, was carried high upon the salt-tinged breeze.

The sound of the iron-rimmed wheels of the horse-drawn carriages rattling over the cobblestone streets added to the din created by the clanging and clattering of the smithies, riggers, and cooperages. Human voices—predominantly masculine—were raised in song and command, in conversation and laughter, and in ceaseless discussion of a business centered almost wholly upon a mighty, mystical beast of the sea.

The route of the Gallaghers' carriage led them past

streets lined with the sailors' boardinghouses, many of which were operated by the widows of whalemen. There were the counting rooms of the shipowners and the shops of the outfitters, as well as the taverns and grog shops into which ambled men of more than a dozen different nationalities. Also located on the busy avenues that sloped down to the waterfront were the banks, law offices, insurance establishments, oil refineries, rope factories, and the shipping offices where young men eager to become whalemen flocked to sign the formal Whalemen's Shipping Paper, a contract whereby they agreed to perform their duties in consideration for a lay in the resulting profits of the voyage.

Hillary was only dimly aware of the sights, sounds, and smells of the whaling capital, but she was acutely conscious of the three pairs of eyes that shifted her way with discomfiting frequency. There was no mistaking the disapproval in their gazes. Their decidedly unwelcoming behavior both disturbed and baffled her. She wondered if perhaps it stemmed from Ryan's involvement with the woman called Alison. Whatever the case, she told herself in a renewed burst of spirit, she would not allow them to intimidate her as they seemed so set upon doing. Forcing a smile to her lips, she remarked in a clear, steady tone, "New Bedford is very much the way Ryan described it to me. The weather here is very pleasant this time of year, isn't it? It's a good deal cooler than in Tahiti, of course, but—"

"Are you a *kanaka?*" Erin demanded abruptly, utilizing the whalers' often derogatory term for a crew member from the South Pacific.

"I beg your pardon?" responded Hillary in puzzlement.

"I believe Erin is trying to ascertain if you are a

native of Tahiti," Gillian interpreted rather loftily.

"My home was originally in England, but I have lived with my uncle in Tahiti for the past five years," Hillary calmly replied.

"Oh. Then I take it you are part Tahitian?" queried Ryan's mother, her pale gray eyes flickering pointedly over Hillary's black hair and lightly tanned skin. It was obvious from the tone of her voice that the possibility of her new daughter-in-law's mixed heritage did not give her pleasure.

"No," answered Hillary, determined not to take offense yet unable to keep a certain sharpness from her own voice. Her violet eyes flashed a bit as she went on to proclaim, "But I consider myself a Tahitian. It would be of great benefit to the world if more of us were like the gentle, unselfish people who inhabit the islands there."

"Would it indeed?" was Priscilla's only reply, spoken with a significant lack of enthusiasm.

Hillary lapsed into silence once more. Despondently musing that things were going to be even more difficult than she had imagined, she settled back against the cushioned leather seat with an inward sigh and tried to focus her attention on the passing scenery. But Alison's face swam before her eyes, and she could not shake the memory of the familiar kiss the woman had bestowed upon Ryan's lips.

The carriage had now entered an entirely different portion of the city. On the hill behind the waterfront, well away from the bustling confusion and the smell of oil, were the mansions of the shipowners and merchants. Beautiful and well kept, these spacious, multistoried houses were embowered in green foliage, their trees and lawns and fragrant gardens bordering New Bedford's principal streets. The quiet gentility of this particular area of town contrasted sharply with the waterfront, so much so that more than one returning seaman had declared that strolling up the well-shaded avenues was very much like taking a trip to the country.

The mansions perched high above the city were visible tributes to gambles that had paid off. A whale ship owner risked thousands of dollars on each venture, for there was always a possibility that a ship might disappear off Cape Horn, or that a cruise would turn up few whales and thereby bring in little or no profit at all. As Hillary soon discovered, the luck of the Gallaghers' had been consistently good.

Their home was among the largest and finest in all of New Bedford. The grand white structure sprawled across several acres of lawns and gardens, and the entire grounds were surrounded by a spectacular wrought iron fence sporting emblematical harpoons that proudly attested to the fact that the estate belonged to a whaling family.

The interior of the mansion proved to be even more sumptuous than the outward appearance had led Hillary to believe. Although she received only a brief glimpse while being led inside and up the winding staircase, what she saw was enough to make her realize that the Gallaghers were quite wealthy, even wealthier than her own father's family had been. The stairs were carpeted in a deep, lustrous shade of blue, and a crystal chandelier of immense proportions was suspended from the rafters high above the marble-tiled entrance foyer. A number of richly framed portraits lined the gleaming, oak-paneled wall beside the staircase.

"This particular room has been used by my son since he was a boy," Priscilla told Hillary, leading her to the uppermost reaches of the house. She turned the ornate brass knob and swung open the door. A faint smile of remembrance touched her lips when she recalled, "He insisted upon being as close as possible to the stars." The smile quickly faded again, and she swept across to throw open the double windows. "I'm afraid it's a bit musty right now, and there may not be quite enough room for the two of you, but—"

"It's a perfectly charming room!" pronounced Hillary, her eyes sparkling with delight. The walls were papered in a tiny floral print blending cream and gold, the polished wooden floors were covered with an assortment of brightly colored, hand-woven rugs, and the carved cherry furniture smelled pleasantly of lemon and beeswax. An embroidered white coverlet had been spread upon the tall, canopied bed that was nestled in one corner of the sun-filled room.

"I shall send Agnes up with some tea. We do not dine until eight," said the older woman as she sailed back toward the doorway. She paused and fixed Hillary with a considering look. "You will no doubt wish to rest now."

"Yes, I *am* feeling a bit tired," Hillary admitted with a smile of genuine warmth. She tried to hide her disappointment when Priscilla did not reciprocate but merely nodded wordlessly and left, closing the door behind her.

Her silken brow creased into another frown of disquiet as she began wandering about the room. She soon stood beside a second set of windows, only to discover that they were actually doors that opened out onto a railed perch atop the house. Though she did not yet know it, the "widow's walk" was where the women of New Bedford watched for the familiar, square-rigged sail that announced the return of a whaling husband or son or other loved one.

Hillary opened the doors and stepped gratefully out into the fresh air and sunshine. Her gaze traveled across the rooftops of the other mansions, and down the hill toward the waterfront, where the fascinating panorama of the harbor, the ships, the sky, and the ceaseless activity of the whaling industry was laid out for her inspection.

"Oh, Ryan," she sighed, her fingers curling about the sun-warmed iron railing. How was she going to endure the next several weeks in such a hostile atmosphere? The situation was only going to worsen when his family learned he was planning to return to Tahiti. Would they try to prevent him from leaving?

Her troubled thoughts inevitably returned to the tall blonde who had greeted Ryan with such bold familiarity at the wharf. What exactly had the woman been to Ryan? Had they truly been betrothed to each other?

These and a thousand other questions ran together in her mind. She longed to be aboard the *Falcon* again, to be back where she and Ryan had shared so much love and laughter. A sudden wave of homesickness brought tears to her eyes, and she wondered what her uncle and Tevaite were doing at that very moment, if they were perhaps thinking of her as well. She had left two letters, one in San Juan Bautista and the other in Stanley, to be delivered to her uncle by ships planning to call at Papeete, but there was no way of knowing if he had received them yet.

Battling the urge to throw herself on the bed and cry until she could cry no more, Hillary turned and slowly drifted back inside. A knock sounded at the door moments later, and she hastily composed herself before answering it.

"The mistress said I was to bring you this," announced the plump, rosy-cheeked young woman who stood holding a silver tray laden with tea and sandwiches. She smiled shyly up at Hillary, whose features immediately relaxed into an answering smile.

"Thank you." Hillary opened the door wider and stood aside while the young woman hurried to set the tray atop a round table near the windows.

"My name's Agnes, ma'am," the copper-haired little maid said, smoothing her apron down over her gray cotton dress as she turned back to Hillary. "If there's anything else you need, just ring." She smiled again and added, "I hope you'll be very happy here, Mrs. Gallagher."

"Thank you very much, Agnes. But please, call me Hillary. It might get terribly confusing to have two Mrs. Gallaghers under one roof," she declared with a soft laugh.

"Oh, but there are *three* of you!"

"Three?"

"Yes, ma'am. There's you and the mistress and Miss Cara. She's Mister David's wife. They live with those two little scamps of theirs in the west wing. Why, there'd be no laughter in this house at all if it weren't for Mister David and his family!" Agnes eagerly disclosed, her brown eyes sparkling.

"Perhaps I'll get to meet them at supper this evening."

"Only Miss Cara. The children go to bed early, and Mister David's still confined to his bed. He was in an accident, down at the refinery, and I hear his leg's burned pretty badly."

"Burned?" echoed Hillary.

The little redhead nodded and revealed, "One of the planks he was standing on gave way and he fell. His poor leg came right up against one of those great cauldrons of oil, still hot enough to melt the flesh."

329

Hillary shuddered at the thought.

The highly informative Agnes took her leave soon thereafter. Sinking down onto a velvet-upholstered chair, Hillary poured herself a cup of tea and sat back with a sigh. A faraway look came into her eyes as she thought of Starcross again. Remembering how Tevaite's attempts at making tea were never too successful, in spite of all the years Denholm Reynolds had given the Tahitian woman proper instruction, she smiled wistfully. That smile was the first thing Ryan noticed when he swung open the door and stood framed in the doorway.

"Well, it's clear to see you were thinking of me!" he quipped, his handsome face alight with a disarming grin as he stepped inside and closed the door again. He tugged the hat from his head and tossed it to land atop the washstand, then shrugged out of his jacket. His eyes made a swift, encompassing sweep of the room before he pronounced, "Things have changed little since I was here last. I'm glad we'll be using this room—it's by far the most private."

"Your mother told me it's been yours since you were a boy," murmured Hillary, her manner still preoccupied as she set the cup back on the tray and rose to her feet.

"Did she also tell you how I used to sneak out of bed at night and spend hours out there?" he asked with a low chuckle, nodding toward the widow's walk. "She tried to convince my father that it was too dangerous for me up here, but he insisted I be allowed to stay. I think he understood how I sometimes needed to escape these four walls and sit out under the stars." He came forward to press a kiss upon her lips, but she surprised him by drawing away.

"Ryan, I . . . I want to know about Alison."

His dark brows knit into a frown, and his mouth tightened into a thin line as he moved slowly past her to take a stance at the windows. When he finally spoke, his voice was low and edged with annoyance at the recollection of Alison's behavior.

"Alison Bromfield and I were once . . . seeing each other. The relationship was fortunately short-lived."

"Were you in love with her?" Hillary couldn't refrain from asking. She scrutinized his reaction closely, a sharp pang of dismay coursing through her when she observed what she believed to be a look of pain crossing the rugged perfection of his face.

"I thought I was at the time. Our families have known one another for years, and I cannot deny that it would have pleased them greatly for us to marry. But then I discovered, quite by accident, just how capricious and self-centered the beautiful Miss Bromfield really is. That was several years ago, and I have done nothing to encourage her since," he honestly declared, his somber gaze meeting and locking with Hillary's. "The regrettable little scene you witnessed today was nothing more than yet another desperate attempt of hers to rekindle something that never should have been."

"But if you've told her you no longer care for her, then why does she still publicly maintain the two of you are . . . *were* to be married?"

"Because Alison Bromfield has never been denied anything she's wanted!"

"She certainly made it clear that she still wants you!" parried Hillary. Though she despised herself for sounding like a jealous wife, she could not deny that a jealous wife was precisely what she was.

"Just as I made it clear that there's only one woman I want—you." He reached for her and pulled her close, his arms folding her tightly against his lean-muscled hardness. "Blast it, Hillary, I've never loved anyone before you!"

"Oh Ryan," she sighed, then inhaled deeply of the clean, masculine scent of him. Her voice quavered somewhat as she asked, "Why didn't you tell me about her before now?"

"For the simple reason that you drove her completely from my mind!" His lips curved upward into a soft smile, and his eyes glowed with a tender light. "I've thought of nothing but you, my love, since that first day I set eyes on you in Papeete." His powerful arms tightened about her until she could scarcely breathe, but she did not feel at all inclined to protest. "I suppose I *should* have remembered to warn you about Alison," he continued, "but, damn it, I didn't want to add to the anxiety you were already feeling about our arrival here. You seemed troubled enough about my family's acceptance of you."

"With good reason," she murmured, a telltale catch in her voice. Ryan's hands moved to take a firm but gentle grip upon her arms, and he drew her away slightly so that his penetrating, blue-green gaze could search her face.

"What is it, Hillary? Has anyone said or done anything to—"

"No, of course not!" she hastened to assure him, telling herself it was not a *complete* lie. She had no desire to spoil his homecoming, nor to create a rift between him and his family. "It . . . it's simply that the news of our marriage came as such a shock to them," she said, quickly looking away.

"I know. But they'll soon get used to the idea." Apparently satisfied with her answer, he pulled her back into his warm embrace. "By the time we sail for Tahiti again, they'll be just as sorry to see you go as they will me," he insisted, dropping a kiss upon the top of her head.

Though Hillary seriously doubted such a thing would ever come about, she did not say so. She released another sigh before raising her head from Ryan's chest and gazing up at him with a rather tremulous smile.

"Do you suppose, Captain Gallagher," she asked quietly, her luminous violet eyes issuing a silent invitation, "that we might pretend, if only for a while, that the two of us are still aboard the *Falcon* instead of within the confines of your ancestral home?"

Ryan's eyes gleamed down at her in return, and the irresistibly roguish smile she loved so well tugged at his lips. His deep voice was brimming with mingled amusement and passion as he replied, "If what you're asking is whether or not I would allow the fact that we are under the same roof as my family to prevent me from carrying you over to that bed and doing what I've been thinking of doing all day, then the answer is most definitely *no!*"

Hillary laughed in delight as she was suddenly tossed over his broad shoulder and spirited across the room to the canopied bed, where she was tumbled backward to land with an unceremonious bounce atop the embroidered coverlet. Ryan's body quickly covered hers, and his mouth descended upon her parted lips with a fierceness that made her tremble. Growing light-headed as a result of the liquid fire of passion he sent coursing through her veins, she moaned softly and entwined her arms about the corded muscles of his neck.

"Mister Ryan?" a feminine voice suddenly called out from the other side of the door. A loud, insistent knock soon followed. "Mister Ryan?"

"What the devil—" Ryan ground out, his handsome countenance reflecting almost savage displeasure at the interruption as he raised his head and glared toward the door.

"It sounds like Agnes," whispered Hillary.

"Who the hell is Agnes?"

"One of your mother's maids!" Suppressing a giggle at the thunderous look on his face, she hastily pushed him away and scrambled down from the bed. Ryan muttered a curse and drew his tall frame upright, then stalked to the door and flung it open.

"What is it?" he demanded gruffly.

The hapless little maid crimsoned and blinked rapidly up at him. She swallowed hard before stammering in a small, breathless voice, "Why, your . . . your mother, sir . . . she said I was to tell you that Mister David is waiting to see you." Her brown eyes, round as saucers, traveled past him to where Hillary stood smiling near the bed.

"Thank you, Agnes," said Hillary. Agnes gave her a quick, nervous smile in return, then whirled about and fled back down the stairs. Ryan chuckled and turned back to his wife.

"Well, my love, it looks as though our own 'business' will have to wait until later," he reluctantly conceded, his mouth curving into a wry grin. He moved forward to rest his hands upon her shoulders as he avowed in a low, vibrant tone, "And we *shall* complete it tonight, Mrs. Gallagher." The smoldering light in his eyes left little doubt that he fully intended to make good his vow at the first available opportunity.

"Is that a promise or a threat, my dearest captain?" teased Hillary. She was rewarded for her impertinence with a quick kiss and a hard, playful smack on her bottom.

334

"Both!" he retorted, then took himself off to see his brother. He had already learned the full details of David's accident, but he was anxious to judge for himself if the eldest Gallagher male's recovery was proceeding as quickly as could be hoped.

Once Ryan was gone, Hillary rang for Agnes again and requested that hot water be brought for a bath. She spent the next hour and a half scrubbing the last effects of the voyage from her skin, washing her long raven tresses and drying them before the fire she had started, and arraying herself in the most becoming gown she owned. Of a deep lavender wool challis, it fit her supple curves to perfection and highlighted the unique color of her eyes. Though not nearly as fine and fancy as that worn by the other Gallagher women, she was satisfied with her attire and was confident that her husband would be pleased as well.

Ryan *was* pleased, and he proudly led her down the winding staircase and into the dining room just as the massive grandfather clock in the entrance foyer began to chime the hour of eight. He had exchanged his own sea-swept clothing for a well-fitted black suit and white linen shirt, which had been awaiting his return within the mirrored wardrobe in his room. It was the first time Hillary had seen him in anything other than his usual "sea togs," and she could scarcely believe the elegantly attired gentleman beside her was the same man who had been so at home on the quarterdeck of a whaling bark.

The dining room was exquisitely decorated in crimson and gold, and light from yet another crystal chandelier filled every corner of its rich interior. A long table, its polished surface covered with a spotless, lace-edged white tablecloth, rested amidst the very center of the grandeur and offered seating for a dozen on velvet-cushioned chairs. The table glistened with fine bone china, eating utensils of solid silver, and leaded crystal goblets, while the food was served on silver platters by a small army of uniformed servants.

Fortunately for Hillary, the evening meal was traditionally a silent affair in the Gallagher household. She was therefore spared the necessity of answering the barrage of questions that might otherwise have greeted her, though she was, once again, very much aware of the frequent, examining looks cast her way by Priscilla, Gillian, and Erin. Flanked by Ryan on one side and David's wife, Cara, on the other, she ate little and was relieved when Priscilla finally stood to lead everyone into the parlor.

The parlor, as it turned out, was nothing like the rest of the house. Hillary was amazed to discover the Oriental decor of its rather smallish confines. She did not realize that Priscilla Gallagher's parlor was very much like those of other whaling wives. Both exotic and elegant, it reflected a lifetime of adventure and romance and travel.

A peacock table sat in the very middle of the room, surrounded by half a dozen Chinese Chippendale chairs that were ribbon-backed and upholstered in a rich yellow Chinese brocade. A matching settee and wing chair were nestled before the fireplace, where a marble mantel sported a pair of old rose Canton vases with ornate, fretwork handles. The draperies were especially impressive, for they were also of a deep yellow brocade and cascaded all the way from the tops of the high windows to the Brussels-carpeted floor. The walls were covered in a pattern of wide yellow bands alternating with green.

The room was filled with a wide assortment of treasured mementos, collected by three different generations of Gallaghers. A magnificent portrait of a handsome yet stern-faced whaling master hung above the mantel, and next to the portrait was a delicate piece of needlework that celebrated the appropriate message of Psalms 107:23-24. Hillary stepped forward to read the words. Ryan moved to stand beside her while the other women sank down upon the Chippendale chairs.

"They that go down to the sea in ships, that do business in the great waters; these see the works of the Lord, and his wonders in the deep," she softly repeated to herself.

"My grandmother made that more than fifty years ago," Ryan told her. "And the portrait of my father was painted shortly after my birth."

"David once tried to convince me that *he* had painted it!" Cara recalled with a quiet laugh. "Of course, we were only children at the time." Her deep blue eyes sparkled at the memory, and a becoming flush rose to her cheeks. An attractive woman with honey-colored hair, she was nearer Gillian's age than Hillary's, and possessed of a gentle, compassionate nature that had made Hillary warm to her from the first moment they had been introduced to each other.

"I'm looking forward to meeting your husband and children," Hillary declared earnestly as she turned to Cara.

"I'm afraid I'm to blame for the fact that you've not yet done so," the other woman admitted with an apologetic smile. "David was naturally quite anxious to meet you, but I thought it best, for his sake as well as yours, to wait until tomorrow to take you round to see him. His fever was up again today, you see, though he did insist upon taxing his strength by talking business with Ryan," she revealed, a faint look of sisterly reproach in her eyes as she glanced at the tall culprit at Hillary's side. "Jimmy and Bridget wanted to come and make your acquaintance this afternoon, but I would not let them. I thought they might be . . . well, I wasn't sure you were quite up to that particular ordeal on your first day here!" she finished with another smile.

"'Ordeal' is precisely the term I would have chosen," Ryan affectionately teased. Grasping Hillary's arm, he led her over to the settee and took a seat with her upon its yellow brocade cushions.

"Jimmy and Bridget are exceptionally well-behaved children," his mother pronounced with a stern frown in his direction.

"It isn't at all surprising to hear you say that, Mother," Erin suddenly piped up, "for we all know you care more about *them* than you do any of the rest of us!" The pain and jealousy in her voice was apparent. Just when Hillary was tempted to give the fifteen-year-old a sympathetic smile, however, the girl rounded on her and rudely demanded, "Are you by any chance carrying my brother's child? I sincerely hope not, for we've more than—"

"Erin!" Ryan sharply admonished.

"Why should you rebuke her when she is only asking what is on the minds of us all?" challenged Gillian. "You and Hillary *were* married in something of a hurry, were you not? It is only natural that we should wonder if—"

"That's enough, damn it!" Ryan's eyes glowed with a fierce light as his gaze raked over the faces of his mother and sisters. "I expected my wife to be met with respect when I brought her home to my family—not with insults! If you cannot bring yourselves to treat her with the same civility you

338

would show any other guest in this home, then perhaps we should make arrangements to stay elsewhere!"

"Oh Ryan, no!" breathed Cara, looking quite distressed.

"Come now, my dear son, there is no reason to take offense at what is, after all, only youthful curiosity," Priscilla insisted with a conciliatory smile. "You must surely realize that the news of your marriage has taken us somewhat by surprise. Though I must admit their methods lack refinement, Gillian and Erin are merely anxious to learn all they can about their new sister."

"There are certain things that concern no one save myself and my wife!" Ryan tersely decreed. Hillary remained silent beside him, and she felt as though a knot tightened within her stomach.

"Nevertheless, you must try to be patient with us," his mother requested with an indulgent glance at each of her daughters. "You have been away for a long time. I think a certain period of adjustment is called for, don't you?"

"Please, Ryan," murmured Hillary. Her violet eyes were glistening softly as she placed her hand upon his arm and gazed up at him in silent entreaty. His angry features visibly relaxed, and he covered her hand with his own before turning back to his mother.

"We'll forget this bit of unpleasantness," he granted. "But I will not tolerate any further discourtesy to my wife!"

Gillian lifted her chin in a gesture of haughty defiance, Erin fell mulishly silent, and Cara still looked terribly ill at ease. Priscilla merely smiled at her son again and began regaling him with all that had happened to their family, their business, and their acquaintances during his long absence.

Hillary was very glad when he finally stood and announced they were retiring for the night. She was grateful for Cara's bolstering smile as they left the room, and she did her best to ignore the way Gillian's eyes, more so than those of Priscilla and Erin, followed her with such purposeful steadiness.

Once he had led his wife into their room and locked the door, Ryan set about keeping the promise he had made to her earlier. In no time at all, Hillary found herself being disrobed with an utterly beguiling urgency. She eagerly assisted Ryan in drawing off his own clothing, then gasped in delight when he lifted her high in his arms and bore her to the canopied bed once more.

His lips claimed hers while his knowing hands began the delectably tortuous exploration of her satiny curves. Not to be outdone, her own fingers paid rapturous tribute to his hard, splendidly virile form. Passions flared and quickly escalated, so that when their bodies finally came together as one, it was with a loving fierceness that was almost violent.

Afterward, when their breathing had become less labored and their heads had begun to clear somewhat, they spoke of what had happened in the parlor that evening. Ryan was the first to mention the unpleasant incident.

"I'm sorry Gillian and Erin behaved so badly toward you, my love," he said as he tenderly smoothed a damp tendril of midnight black hair from her softly glowing face. "I don't know what came over them. From what I recall, they never used to be so ill-mannered."

"It doesn't matter, Ryan," replied Hillary, knowing very well that it did. "As your mother pointed out, this is a difficult time for everyone right now. I'm sure everything will be fine." She hoped her words held more conviction than she actually felt.

"Everything had better be," he murmured with a frown. "At least Cara hasn't changed. And there's no doubt in my mind that the children will adore you." He gave a low chuckle and shifted his muscular frame farther downward beneath the covers. Since Hillary's naked curves were pressed close to his equally bare hardness, she had no choice but to reposition herself as well, though she didn't mind in the least.

"What is your brother like?" she asked, snuggling contentedly against him.

"David's one of the finest men you'll ever meet. He's very much like our father, actually," declared Ryan, a faint smile of remembrance touching his lips, "except when it comes to the sea. His first voyage took place two years before mine. Upon his return, he startled everyone by announcing that the experience had convinced him that he was meant to be a shore-going Gallagher instead of a whaling one. And that's exactly what he became. He knows the business better than anyone now."

A companionable silence fell between them after that. A short time later, just when Hillary had begun to suspect that Ryan had fallen asleep, she was surprised to feel him sliding from the bed. Her eyes were wide and full of puzzlement as she watched him pull on his trousers in the dim glow of the lamplight.

"Ryan? What are you doing?"

Instead of answering her directly, he moved back to the bed and suddenly lifted her, covers and all, in his strong arms. She was about to ask him where he was taking her, when the need to do so vanished. She smiled as he opened the glass doors and carried her out onto the widow's walk.

The moon's silvery radiance set the night sky

aglow. The lights of the city and the harbor twinkled in the near distance, and the circling beam of the Clark's Point Lighthouse cast its benevolence far and wide. Tinged with the scent of wood smoke and flowers, the cool breeze tugged at Hillary's gloriously disheveled locks as Ryan held her tightly against him and gazed up at the stars.

"Some things never change," he observed in a low, vibrant tone that sent an appreciative tremor coursing through her. A captivating smile lit his handsome, sun-bronzed features, and his magnificent blue-green eyes glowed when he looked down at his wife and declared, "I love you, Hillary Reynolds Gallagher."

"And I love you," she answered softly, her own eyes sparkling with sudden tears of happiness. She rested her head on his shoulder and gazed heavenward. What did it matter if anyone else approved of their marriage? She was loved by the most wonderful man in the world, a man who was both tender and strong, a devilishly irresistible man who was possessed of a romantic spirit that thrilled and enchanted her . . . a man who took her to look at the stars.

XIV

"Is *that* Uncle Ryan's lady?" a towheaded, freckle-faced boy of four blurted out as Hillary entered the dining room the following morning. Ryan was close behind her, and he confirmed his nephew's suspicions before Cara could scold the irrepressible tyke for his rudeness.

"That she is, Jimmy," he said with a nod. He slipped an arm about Hillary's waist and pulled her over to where the youngest Gallagher sat attacking a plateful of sausages and poached eggs. "This is your Aunt Hillary. And this rapscallion," he told Hillary as he playfully lifted a hand to ruffle the youngster's hair, "is James Ryan Gallagher." He then smiled affectionately across at the six-year-old girl seated to Jimmy's right. "Good morning, Bridget. I should like to introduce my wife to you."

"How do you do, Aunt Hillary?" the dark-haired Bridget inquired politely. Her manner was quite formal and ladylike for one so young, but Hillary glimpsed a telltale spark of merriment in her wide-set green eyes.

"Very well, thank you, Bridget. I'm so pleased to make the acquaintance of you both," Hillary proclaimed with a warm smile that included Jimmy as well.

Ryan gallantly held the chair opposite Bridget's for her while he cautioned with a mock scowl at the children, "Don't be deceived, my love. These two are infamous for their shenanigans and tantrums!"

"Oh Ryan, you'll have Hillary believing they're totally lacking in manners or guidance!" Cara protested with a gentle laugh. Hillary smiled and assured her she would disregard his disobliging comments. Gillian was the only other person present at the breakfast table, and it seemed she was doing her best to ignore everyone else as she sat quietly sipping her tea beside Cara.

"Where are Mother and Erin this morning?" Ryan asked his sister. He helped himself to a generous portion of the eggs while Hillary did the honors of pouring their tea.

There was a long silence before Gillian finally answered. "I believe Mother has taken to her bed for the day, and Erin has already breakfasted." She cast Hillary a cold, meaningful look, then returned her attention to her tea.

"Priscilla suffers from frequent headaches, I'm afraid," explained Cara, with only a hint of disapprobation in her voice. She smiled at Hillary again and queried, "What are you and Ryan planning to do today?"

"Why, I . . . I'm not quite sure," replied Hillary, glancing inquisitively at her husband.

He flashed her a quick grin before informing Cara, "After taking my wife on a whirlwind tour of the shops, where I intend to see that she is bedecked in the finest frippery New Bedford has to offer, I must return to the shipping office and set about bringing some semblance of order to the place. David may have been absent for only a week, but the resulting confusion and disorganization make it appear as though the business had been neglected for at least a month."

"Surely you're not going to take *her* to the office with you?" demanded Gillian, glancing sharply toward Hillary. None of the Gallagher women had ever been allowed in the shipping office, for it was always filled with young men who displayed rough manners and employed extremely vulgar language.

"No, Gillian, I am not," Ryan answered in a low tone, his penetrating turquoise gaze fastening upon her attractive yet overly proud features. She flushed uncomfortably and looked away.

"Father's leg is burned, you know," Jimmy suddenly felt the need to impart to Hillary. She quickly transferred her widened gaze from Gillian to the engaging little boy with the dancing blue eyes.

"I know, and I was very sorry to hear about the accident," she solemnly declared. "It must have been very difficult for you all."

"Why no, only for Father," Bridget interjected with a deep frown of puzzlement at her new aunt. "It was *his* leg that got burned, not *ours*."

"Mother says you are going to see him today. Are you going to ask to see his leg, too?" Jimmy was curious to know. "You ought to. It looks very much like a roasted—"

"Jimmy!" Cara sternly called him down after somehow managing not to choke on the hot tea she had just sipped. Coloring in embarrassment, she hastened to tell Hillary, "It seems he's developed a rather morbid fascination with such things. I don't quite know how to handle it, and David indulges him shamelessly." She released a faint sigh of wifely exasperation while Hillary suppressed a smile and

Ryan gave his nephew a conspiratorial wink.

Immediately after breakfast, Ryan led Hillary back up the staircase and into the west wing of the house, where David and Cara had lived during eight years of an exceedingly happy marriage. Ryan's older brother sat propped up in a massive oak bed in a sunlit room filled with deep hues of gold and emerald. The patient's bed was conveniently situated beside a pair of wide, multipaned windows, and the patient himself was staring rather disconsolately outward when Ryan's knock interrupted his reverie.

Hillary was startled to hear a voice so much like her husband's calling out for them to enter, and she was even more surprised when her eyes fell on David Gallagher for the first time.

The resemblance between the two brothers was remarkable. David's eyes were almost the same striking blend of green and blue as Ryan's, his nose and mouth and chin were of the same chiseled appearance, and his height and physique, at least as far as Hillary could discern from his position in the bed, were also similar to Ryan's. But, whereas Ryan's dark hair was streaked with gold, David's was essentially one shade of burnt almond; whereas Ryan's gaze was always filled with an irrepressible light, David's looked much more settled. And though Hillary knew them to be separated in age by only two years, she found herself musing that the difference appeared even greater. David Gallagher was a handsome man indeed, she mentally concluded, but he did not possess the same vibrancy of spirit as his dashing, adventurous younger brother.

"Well, it's about time someone got around to introducing me to my new sister-in-law!" David proclaimed with a quiet chuckle as Ryan led his wife across the room. He eased himself farther upright in

346

the bed and smiled up at Hillary amiably. "You're even more beautiful than Ryan said. I suppose I'll have to offer my apologies for accusing him of gross exaggeration!"

"I'm so pleased to meet you," Hillary told him with an answering smile, her violet eyes sparkling with genuine warmth. She was wearing the same lavender gown she had worn the night before, and her luxuriant ebony curls were arranged upon the nape of her neck in a simple yet highly becoming chignon.

Ryan slipped a possessive arm about her waist, and there was an unmistakable note of pride in his deep voice when he remarked to his brother, "I told you she was special, didn't I?"

"Yes, and so did Cara." He winced at a sudden twinge of pain as he attempted to shift his injured leg slightly. It was heavily bandaged and lay atop the covers while the rest of his body was tucked beneath one of his mother's handmade quilts.

"It pains you greatly, doesn't it?" Hillary asked softly, her eyes full of sympathy. "One of the children at Starcross was burned while playing too near a cook fire last year. We tried everything to alleviate his pain, but it wasn't until Tevaite—the woman who has managed my uncle's house for a number of years—used a poultice of ground coconut, boiled chestnut leaves, and lime juice that he was afforded any relief."

"It sounds a good deal more agreeable than the treatment prescribed by the doctors here," opined David, frowning darkly when he thought of how his beloved wife had to change the dressings three times a day and apply a distastefully pungent ointment that made his leg feel as though it were on fire. "Perhaps I should try and persuade Cara to try your Tahitian remedy." His brow cleared in the next instant, and he smiled again as he reached for Hillary's hand and spoke sincerely, "I want you to know that we're all very glad to have you here. Personally, it's a great relief to see that my brother had the good sense to find himself a wife like you!"

"Thank you," she murmured with a soft laugh, finding herself charmed by yet another Gallagher male. If only the women of the family could be so congenial, she mused wistfully.

She was soon riding beside her husband in the carriage as its wheels rolled down the sloping, cobblestoned street toward the area of the city where the most fashionable clothing shops were situated. The morning passed in an enjoyable, dizzying whirl of fittings and decision making and wonderfully impulsive purchases. Though Hillary laughingly protested against such extravagance, Ryan was determined to buy his wife anything and everything she so much as *appeared* to like. The only purchases she herself insisted upon making were gifts for her uncle and friends back in Tahiti.

By the time the church bells tolled the hour of noon, Captain and Missus Gallagher had collected so many boxes that the coachman had to be dispatched back to the mansion with them. Ryan and Hillary strolled farther down the hill to one of New Bedford's finest restaurants, where they shared a leisurely meal and pleasant conversation about the city and its history. Afterwards, they climbed back up into the waiting carriage once more and traveled the short distance to the bustling activity of the waterfront.

"I'll try to be home before nightfall," Ryan

promised when the coachman pulled the horses to a halt before a large brick building just off the wharves. Above the door hung a wooden sign upon which the name Gallagher was printed in big, bold letters.

"Pray, my dear captain, do not concern yourself about me," replied Hillary, her eyes alight with merriment as he stepped down from the carriage and turned back to say good-bye. "I've plenty to do, what with sorting through everything you bought for me today!"

"Nevertheless, if you should feel the need for company, I'm sure Cara would be delighted to let you look after Jimmy and Bridget." His mouth curved into a wry grin, and his gaze brimmed with mischievous humor. Pausing to give her one last kiss, he then strode up the steps and disappeared inside the shipping office where so many other Gallaghers had gone about conducting the business of whaling.

Minutes later, as the carriage was rattling back up Johnnycake Hill, Hillary's attention was suddenly captured by a building she hadn't noticed the day before. It was a simple, whitewashed structure that looked very much like a church to her interested gaze. She quickly bade the coachman stop, then climbed down without waiting for assistance and moved forward to take a closer look. Standing upon the lower step, she glanced up to note the words that had been carved above the building's wide double doors: *Dedicated in May, 1832.*

"Hil . . . Mrs. Gallagher?" a familiar masculine voice spoke behind her. She spun about to see that it was Connor Reid who stood smiling at her with his hat in his hand. Like Ryan, he had exchanged his sea attire for that more suited to life on shore.

"Why, Connor! What a pleasant surprise!" she

declared earnestly. "What are you doing here?"

"I always pay a visit to the Whaleman's Chapel after a voyage," he replied, his gaze flickering over the structure before them. "It's become sort of a tradition with me."

"The Whaleman's Chapel," murmured Hillary, looking up at it again as well.

"The Seaman's Bethel, actually," Connor amended with a brief smile. "Have you been inside yet?"

"No. I was on my way back to the Gallaghers' when I happened to see this place," she explained, nodding toward the chapel.

"Well, if you can spare the time, my dear Mrs. Gallagher, why not do me the honor of coming inside with me?" he gallantly suggested, an endearing twinkle in his golden eyes.

"Only if you'll cease addressing me in such ridiculously formal terms!" she retorted, smiling companionably as she took his arm. He chuckled and led her up the steps.

Inside, the walls of the bethel were lined with memorial plaques bearing the names of whalemen who had been lost at sea throughout the past thirty years. Hillary could not help but feel saddened as she read several of the inscriptions—*carried overboard by the line, and drowned*; *fell from aloft, off Cape Horn*; *towed out of sight by a whale*—and noted the mostly youthful ages of the victims.

"I knew some of these poor fellows," revealed Connor, his darkly attractive features bearing an unusually grim expression. "I guess I come here because it serves to remind me what a lucky devil I am to have made it home safely once more."

"I can well understand that," Hillary said quietly. She was about to turn away when her gaze happened to fall upon a familiar name. Her eyes grew very wide and her heart pounded as she read aloud, "Seamus Donnelly Gallagher. Born August, 1792—died March, 1849. Killed by a sperm whale."

"Ryan's uncle," Connor confirmed as he stood just behind her and gazed over her shoulder at the plaque. "He was attempting to rescue his men after a whale stove in their boat off the Gilbert Islands."

"What a terrible way to die," murmured Hillary.

"Not for a whaler. Like any good soldier, a whaleman would choose to die in battle if he got the choice."

Hillary was glad when they emerged into the warm sunshine once more. She stood upon the top step with Connor for a moment before returning to the carriage.

"I hope you'll come to visit us soon," she told him, then couldn't resist adding, "It would be so nice to see a friendly face!"

"Are you having trouble with Ryan's family?" he asked, his eyes full of genuine concern. When Hillary nodded in wordless affirmation, Connor smiled in understanding and remarked, "It's no secret that Priscilla Gallagher tends to rule the household with an iron hand. And Erin no doubt fancies herself all grown up by now. Gillian . . . well, Gillian can be difficult, to say the least."

"You sound as if you know them well."

"I do. The friendship between our families goes back more than a hundred years. Of course, the relationship became somewhat strained there for a while when Gillian and I broke off our engagement, but—"

"You and Gillian?" Hillary breathed in surprise.

He nodded and said, "It was a long time ago— four, maybe five years. I'm surprised Ryan didn't tell you about it."

"No, he . . . he never mentioned it." She wanted to ask Connor to elaborate upon the subject, but she told herself it wouldn't be right to pry. It was difficult for her to imagine the easygoing whaler beside her being paired with the cold and haughty Gillian. Realizing that the coachman was probably beginning to wonder if she was ever going to leave, she smiled once more at the man who had become a good friend and told him, "Thank you very much for showing me the chapel. And please, Connor, do call on us soon."

Escorting her down the steps, Connor assisted her up into the carriage, then lifted a hand in farewell as she rode away. He pulled his hat low upon his head as he turned back toward the Seaman's Bethel, only to draw up short as his startled gaze fell upon a very pretty young woman who was just about to enter the building. Her manner of dress bespoke her faith, for she wore a familiar Quaker costume—a bonnet of gray satin showing a ruffled cap of sheer lawn underneath, a simple dress of gray cotton with a white kerchief crossed in front and tucked in at the waist, and an unfringed shawl of white silk. Although her attire met the strict requirements of an outwardly "plain" appearance, it was of the best quality.

Connor Reid felt his pulses quicken, and his heart pounded fiercely within his breast. The terrible ache deep within him intensified until he thought he could bear it no more. He swept the hat from his head again and hurried up the steps.

"Bethany?"

She gasped at the sound of her name on his lips. Though she had come to the chapel hoping to find him, it was nonetheless a benumbing shock to be faced with the reality of his presence there. She had waited so long! For the past three years, she had prayed for his safety, had yearned for his return, and had longed to hear him speak the words he had sworn in anger never to speak again.

"Connor!" Bethany Roberts breathed. Battling the tears that had suddenly sprung to her eyes, she turned slowly about to face him at last. Her heart rejoiced when she met his gaze, for she discerned something within the smoldering golden depths of his eyes that told her his love for her had not died. Praise God, it had not died!

"You're even more beautiful than I remembered," murmured Connor, his voice low and hoarse with emotion. His eyes raked hungrily over her, drinking in the sight of her delicate, heart-shaped face, her wide, china blue eyes, the honey-colored curls peeping from beneath the stern bonnet, and the soft, womanly curves that he had burned to mold against his hardness from the first moment he had seen her standing beside her father in front of the Meeting House.

"And thee . . . thee is more handsome," she breathlessly reciprocated, her gaze falling before his as a maidenly blush rose to her cheeks. Connor stepped closer, gazing down upon her with eyes full of unspoken passion.

"Have you been well, Bethany?" he asked, his voice scarcely above a whisper. "Have you . . . married?"

"Oh Connor!" she cried out softly, the glistening tears spilling over from her lashes as she raised her eyes to his once more. "Thee knows I can love no other!"

That was all he needed to hear. He took her arm and led her inside the chapel so they could speak more privately. Telling himself he and his beloved had wasted enough time, Connor vowed to do everything in his power to see that they wasted no more.

The Gallagher mansion was already filled with the lilting strains of violins and the brilliant radiance of a dozen chandeliers by the time the guests began arriving.

Hillary stood with Ryan in the splendor of the ballroom. It was the first time she had set foot inside the room, and her violet eyes were filled with appreciative awe as she scrutinized the elaborate furnishings. The walls were covered in a flocked and gilded paper of crimson and gold, while the floor was tiled with gleaming white marble. A long, lace-covered table had been set up near the garden doors and generously laden with every manner of drink and other refreshments. Five musicians sat playing a waltz within a crimson-draperied alcove in one corner of the room, and it was not long before the tastefully opulent scene came alive with conversation and laughter and dancing.

Ryan had been pleased to learn of his mother's plans to formally present his new wife to their extended family and friends. He believed Priscilla Gallagher's intentions to signify that she had accepted her new daughter-in-law and was willing to make that acceptance publicly known. Hillary, on the other hand, had been able to summon little enthusiasm for the upcoming event, for she could not shake the suspicion that Priscilla's motives stemmed from something other than a desire to show any sort of approval for her son's wife.

Neither Ryan's mother nor his sisters had treated her with anything more than the barest civility throughout her first three days in New Bedford. There had certainly been nothing to indicate that their feelings for her had undergone a miraculous transformation of some kind—quite the contrary. Though she was reluctant to believe such a thing, she could not help but think the Gallagher women would always look upon her as an outsider, as someone who had dared to capture Ryan's heart and turn it from them. She knew she was innocent of this last, for she had done nothing to try to lessen her husband's regard for his family. In truth, she had refrained from telling him of the many remarks full of spiteful meaning that both Gillian and Erin had conspired for her to overhear. She had done her best to ignore them, but she feared she would not always do so. Her temper had already flared to a dangerous level more than once; if they persisted in their unwarranted, dissociable behavior toward her—

"Would you grant me the honor of this dance, my love?" asked Ryan, his wonderfully deep and resonant voice breaking in on her unpleasant reverie.

"You do *me* the honor, sir," she replied with a playfully coquettish smile. She was delighted when he returned her smile with a roguish one of his own and swept her out onto the dance floor with him. One powerful arm folded her close while his other hand clasped hers, and he began whirling her about expertly in the graceful movements of the waltz while a great many pairs of eyes followed them.

"Have I told you yet, Mrs. Gallagher, how beautiful you look tonight?"

"Yes, Captain Gallagher, but I should be delighted to hear you say it again!" She laughed softly, her eyes shining brightly as he willingly complied. Her ball gown—one of several Ryan had insisted upon purchasing—was fashioned of white tarlatan with a number of flounces and delicate rosebud trimming. The fashionably low neckline hugged the smoothness of her shoulders and the satiny swell of her bosom, and the voluminous skirts were made even fuller by the crinoline she wore beneath them. Her lustrous raven tresses had been parted in the middle and swept upward, with two long curls left hanging down over her left shoulder.

"I hope you paid very close attention when being introduced to the three hundred people here tonight, for you'll no doubt be called upon to recite their names at the close of the evening," teased Ryan, who looked breathtakingly handsome in his evening clothes. Hillary felt both jealous and proud as she glimpsed the numerous admiring glances he received from the ladies, young and old.

"There are only *two* hundred, and I shall be more than happy to recite their names if you agree to do so as well!" she saucily retorted. Ryan chuckled and whirled her round even faster.

"No matter their names—you have captured their interest like no other woman in this room. After all, it isn't every day one of New Bedford's own brings home a bride from the South Seas."

"I was beginning to think you'd forgotten you *have* a bride," she commented, pointedly reminding him of the fact that she had seen little of him the past two days. He had been occupied down at the waterfront until late each evening. If it had not been for Cara and the children, mused Hillary, she would have been quite lonely indeed.

"Never that," he assured her with a soft smile, his gaze smoldering with the promise of passion. "I'm sorry we've had so little time together of late. David's absence from the office has made things a great deal more difficult than I expected."

"I know, and it's all right, Ryan, truly it is. It's just that . . . well, I do miss being with you during the day. I can't help remembering how often I was afforded the pleasure of your company when we were aboard the *Falcon*."

"It won't be long, my love," he promised, his eyes gazing deeply into hers as the music rose to its inevitable finale. "We'll soon be starting a new life back in Tahiti, where you and I will have all the time in the world to become 'reacquainted.'"

Hillary sighed happily at his words, her violet eyes sparkling up at him. She leaned closer into his masterful embrace while he swung her about until she was breathless.

Once the waltz had ended, Ryan took a negligently possessive hold upon his wife's arm and led her through the crowd to where his mother stood talking amidst a group of friends. Priscilla Gallagher, looking quite attractive in a dress of mauve patterned silk, smiled when she glanced up to note the approach of her tall, handsome son. She was preparing to excuse herself and move forward to speak to him, when her eyes were suddenly drawn past him to the doorway.

Alison Bromfield was making her entrance at last. At her side was her father, an elderly, bespectacled gentleman with sparse gray hair and a perpetually scowling face to match his acerbic disposition. Ebenezer Bromfield had made his fortune in shipping, not whaling, and it was generally agreed upon that the sharp-tongued old miser cared for two things and two things only—his money and his daughter. He had seldom, if ever, denied Alison anything. Although he had spared little kindness for his late wife, he had lavished attention on their only child. Thus, she had grown into a spoiled, pampered, and exceedingly selfish young woman who was accustomed to getting whatever her heart desired. And her heart desired Ryan Gallagher.

"Why Alison, how good of you to come!" declared Priscilla, sweeping past Ryan and Hillary to greet the tall, imperious blonde. "And Ebenezer, it has been much too long since you have graced this house with your presence," she cordially remarked to the man she had known for nearly forty years.

He took her proffered hand and brought it up to his cold lips, then grumbled, "Don't like to get out in the night air, you know!"

Priscilla responded with a coolly indulgent smile, while Alison ignored her father and demanded of Ryan's mother, "Did you tell him I was coming?"

"Why no, my dear, I . . . I thought it best not to do so."

"Good," purred Alison, her lips curving into a slow, well-satisfied smile and her green eyes full of a scheming light. She looked resplendent in an extremely low-cut gown of emerald satin. Her shimmering blond curls had been fashioned into an elaborate style high upon her head, and a magnificent cluster of diamonds rested in the hollow of her white throat. Her smile grew mockingly triumphant as her gaze suddenly encountered the piercing, blue-green intensity of Ryan's.

Hillary felt her husband's fingers tightening upon her arm. Wondering why he had suddenly stiffened beside her, she glanced up at him in puzzlement, only to inhale sharply upon discovering that his handsome face had suddenly become a tight mask of barely concealed fury. Her own eyes hastily followed the direction of his, then grew very wide at the sight of the bold, arrogant blonde who had created such a disagreeable scene at the wharf—the same young woman who had once held, if only briefly, Ryan's affections.

"What the devil is *she* doing here?" he muttered beneath his breath.

"I . . . I suppose she was invited. After all, her family and yours are still on good terms, are they not?" Hillary pointed out, forcing a smile to her lips. Doing her best to disguise the awful feeling of dread that had sprung to life within her, she lifted her head proudly and said, "We should bid them welcome, Ryan."

"Welcome?" he echoed in disbelief, then shook his head. "No, my love, I'll not—"

"For your mother's sake," she insisted, her eyes soft and pleading as she raised her face to his once more. "They are guests in her home, and it would distress her greatly if we did not greet them as we did the others." Reluctantly acknowledging the truth of her words, Ryan heaved a disgruntled sigh and escorted her the short distance to the doorway.

"Good evening, Ebenezer. Alison," he formally declared once he stood beside his mother. A smile of mingled pride and relief was evident on Priscilla's face, though the smile faded somewhat when Ryan drew Hillary closer and announced, "Ebenezer Bromfield, I'd like to present my wife, Hillary."

"How do you do, Mr. Bromfield?" she asked politely.

"So *you're* the chit he married!" Ebenezer rudely growled, fixing her with a decidedly rancorous glare. His yellowish brown eyes narrowed as they subjected her to a swift, critical appraisal. "You look different from the way Alison described you," he pronounced with yet another scowl. He refused to so much as acknowledge Ryan's presence. As far as he was concerned, the second son of Kevin and Priscilla

Gallagher had betrayed his beloved daughter. Although there had never been a formal engagement between them, their eventual marriage had been understood. And Ebenezer would never forgive *or* forget the dishonor Ryan Gallagher had brought upon the Bromfield name.

"And I believe *you*, Miss Bromfield, have already made the acquaintance of my wife," Ryan told Alison with a meaningful, tight-lipped expression. Evidently not the least bit affected by Ebenezer's purposeful inattention, he settled his coldly glittering gaze on the old man's troublesome daughter.

"Of course," Alison murmured with icy composure, though her green eyes blazed with enmity as she looked at Hillary. "I'm *dreadfully* sorry, but it seems I've forgotten your name."

"It's Gallagher," Hillary impulsively retorted. "Hillary Gallagher." Ryan stifled a chuckle, while his mother could not prevent a faint smile from briefly touching her lips. Even Ebenezer's inimical gaze appeared to soften slightly.

Alison's gaze, however, filled with even more venom.

"I hope you don't mind, *Mrs. Gallagher*, if I claim Ryan as my partner for the first dance," she uttered with a catlike smile as she inserted herself on his other side and boldly slid her hand up his arm. "You see, it's *long* been a tradition with us."

"I've started a new tradition," Ryan countered tersely, his eyes boring into hers.

"Come now, my dearest son, you and Alison are old friends. Surely it would do no harm for the two of you to dance together?" urged Priscilla, favoring them both with a benignly maternal look.

Unhappily aware of the fact that neither she nor Ryan had any choice in the matter, Hillary battled another wave of jealousy and forced a smile to her lips. She endeavored to keep her tone casual as she said, "Please, Ryan, do take Miss Bromfield out onto the dance floor. I don't mind in the least, and besides, I should like to find Cara and have a word with her."

Ryan stared closely down into her upturned, only slightly flushed countenance for a moment before reluctantly leading a haughtily smirking Alison away. Hillary stared after them, watching as her husband took his former lover into his arms and began whirling her about with an easy, masculine grace of movement.

"They make such a striking couple, do they not?" Priscilla Gallagher pointedly remarked to Ebenezer as she cast Hillary a look full of not-so-subtle meaning.

"That they do," Alison's father was forced to admit, though his blood boiled anew when he thought of how, by all rights, his daughter should have been the one being honored as Ryan Gallagher's wife that evening.

Gratefully spying Cara near the refreshment table, Hillary excused herself and made her way across the ballroom. Her gaze frequently drifted back to light upon Ryan and Alison, and no matter how hard she tried, she could not shake the inexplicable apprehension she felt as she watched the two of them dancing together.

Cara, attired in a becoming gown of cream-colored taffeta, smiled warmly when she caught sight of Hillary. She immediately gathered up her skirts and glided forward to say, "I hope you're enjoying the festivities, my dear. We've not had anything this grand in ages!" She laughed softly, her deep blue eyes aglow with obvious pleasure. "David isn't the least bit sorry he had to miss it—you see, he isn't overly fond of balls or

361

parties or anything that requires him to smile and be charming for hours on end!''

"The effort *does* begin to wear on one after a while, doesn't it?'' Hillary responded with an answering smile. "All the same, I wish David had been able to attend. And Jimmy and Bridget as well.'' She had grown very fond of them in the short time she had been in New Bedford, and they of her.

"So do I. But they'll adore hearing all about it in the morning.'' Her own gaze was drawn to Ryan, though she hastily looked away again.

"Alison Bromfield is very beautiful, isn't she?'' Hillary murmured a bit disconsolately as she noted Cara's actions.

"I suppose most people find her to be so,'' allowed Cara. Her blue eyes shone with kindness and understanding as she added, "But those of us who know her true nature find her beauty much diminished.''

"I wonder if Ryan does.''

"Ryan cares only for you, my dearest Hillary,'' Cara gently asserted. "Why, it's been obvious to everyone here tonight that he has eyes for no one save his wife!''

Hillary wanted to believe her, but the sight of Ryan gazing intently down into the pale, aristocratic loveliness of Alison Bromfield's face provoked a wealth of renewed disquiet within her. She willingly accompanied Cara out into the garden for a welcome breath of fresh air a moment later. Although her spirits lifted a trifle once she had escaped the noise and warmth of the ballroom, they would no doubt have plummeted again if she had been privy to the conversation taking place between her husband and his beautiful dancing partner . . .

"Come now, Ryan, the very least you can do is

grant me a few minutes of your time!" insisted Alison, affecting a childish pout that some men would no doubt consider appealing. "After all you have put me through—"

"Any so-called 'heartbreak' you have suffered has been brought about by no one but yourself, Alison," he ruthlessly parried. "It will serve no purpose for us to engage in a private discussion."

"How can you be so cruel? I only want to talk to you! Once you have heard what I have to say, you can naturally do whatever you think best about the situation."

"What situation?" he demanded in a low voice edged with anger. "If you mean my marriage to Hillary, then you can damn well save yourself the trouble of trying to get me to listen to you!"

"Please Ryan, *please* come outside with me for a moment," she now pleaded, her eyes glistening with the tears she was so adept at summoning. "More than anything in the world, I want us to settle this matter between us, to make peace between our families and—"

"All right, Alison," Ryan finally capitulated with a deep frown. "But whatever it is you have to say, you'd better say it quickly and have done with it." Hoping that once he had listened to her the matter would indeed be settled once and for all, he swung her about in the last movements of the dance and visually searched the room for Hillary. He recalled having seen her talking with Cara near the refreshment table, but there was no sign of her now. Frowning again, he led Alison across the room and through the open glass doors that led out into the spacious, immaculately groomed gardens.

They soon paused beside a huge oak tree surrounded by a charming, whitewashed bench. Alison sank down upon the bench and gracefully arranged her emerald satin skirts about her, then smiled winningly back up at Ryan and asked, "Do you remember the day you did this?" She lifted a gloved hand to trace the heart-embowered "R.G. and A.B." that had been carved into the tree by Ryan some twenty years earlier. "You swore to love me always."

"What is it you want to say?" he impatiently prompted, his handsome face looking quite grim in the light given off by a dozen lanterns placed strategically throughout the gardens.

"Why don't you sit here beside me?" she suggested, her lips curving up into an unmistakably inviting smile. "I always find it difficult to talk to someone who stands glowering down at me from such a great height."

"Enough of this nonsense, Alison," he coldly decreed. "I've a wife to get back to, remember? A wife I happen to love—"

"Of course I remember!" she hotly exclaimed, his words sending her explosive temper out of control. Dropping all pretense of politeness at last, she abruptly rose to her feet once more and hissed, "You should never have married her, Ryan—not when you knew *I* was waiting for you at home! You had no right to do it! You had no right!"

"I had every right in the world." His deep-timbred voice was dangerously low and level, and his eyes gleamed with a foreboding light as they met the blazing fury of hers. "I tried to make you understand how things stood between us before I left, but you refused to listen. That was always your trouble, Alison—you never bothered to listen to what you had no wish to hear. As a result, you caused everyone, including yourself, unnecessary anguish."

"You cannot have so easily forgotten what we

meant to each other!"

"I've forgotten nothing. But the most vivid memories I have of our mercifully brief time together are of your lies and deceptions."

"You belong to *me*, Ryan Gallagher! You've always been mine and you always shall be! God help that little whore you married, for I swear I'll make her—"

"Shut up, damn you!" Ryan ground out, his own temper flaring to a perilous level of intensity. His fierce gaze burned down into Alison's as his hands shot up to close about her arms in a forceful, almost bruising grip. "You're not going to do one blasted thing to hurt my wife, do you understand? If you make any attempt at all to cause her pain or embarrassment, then *you'll* be the one who needs God's help! Heed me well, Alison, for I'll not tolerate any more of your loathsome, outrageous tactics to regain something that was in truth never yours!"

"It *was* and still *is!*" she vehemently dissented. Desperate to make him admit he still loved her, she brought her hands up to clutch at the front of his white linen shirt while straining upward against him and pressing her mouth to his.

Hillary's eyes widened in stunned disbelief when they traveled across to where her husband and Alison Bromfield were locked in what seemed to be a mutually passionate embrace. Drawing in her breath upon a startled gasp, she came to a sudden halt on the path just beyond the shadow of the oak tree's far-reaching branches.

"Hillary? What is it?" Cara asked with a slight frown of bemusement. The two of them had just that moment returned to the house from a brisk walk along the outer fringes of the garden. "Is some-thing—" There was no need to inquire further, for

365

her own gaze finally encountered the distressing evidence of Ryan's entanglement with Alison. "Oh no!" she breathed in shocked amazement.

"Oh *yes!*" Hillary choked out. Torn between the desire to storm forward in righteous indignation to demand an accounting of her husband's contemptible behavior and the desire to whirl about and flee the heartbreaking sight altogether, she found she could do neither. She could only stand and watch while her world came crashing down about her.

Ryan, astonished by Alison's bold assault, finally managed to seize her wrists and force them roughly down to her sides. Glaring down at her murderously as he sought to control the violent impulses surging within him, he had done no more than open his mouth to offer her a dire warning against further theatrics when he became aware of the two women who stood watching nearby.

"Hillary? Hillary, what are you—" he started to demand, only to break off and mutter a blistering curse as she suddenly took flight. He flung Alison away from him and gave chase.

Choking back a sob, Hillary raced blindly back through the doors and across the crowded ballroom. She was oblivious to the curious stares and murmured exclamations of surprise that followed her, for she could think of nothing but what she had just witnessed. The tears were streaming down her face by the time she broke from the gaiety of the ballroom and began stumbling up the stairs, her full, crinolined skirts impeding her progress so that Ryan was able to catch her before she had gone far.

He grabbed her arm and forced her to a halt as he demanded, "Hillary! Damn it, Hillary, what the devil do you think you're doing?"

"What the devil am *I* doing?" she seethed,

rounding on him with her violet eyes ablaze and a fiery color staining her cheeks. "How *dare* you, Ryan Gallagher! How dare you stand there kissing that woman and then behave as though *I* were the guilty party!"

"I wasn't kissing her—she was kissing *me!*"

"A likely story, Captain Gallagher!"

"If you'll just allow me to explain, I—"

"No explanations are necessary! Cara and I both saw you with that . . . that she-cat!"

She furiously wrenched her arm from his grasp and started up the stairs again, then gasped as Ryan suddenly jerked her back and ground out, "Blast it, woman, you *will* hear me out!" He seized her about her slender, corseted waist and slung her over his broad shoulder. Her hooped skirts and petticoats swayed and bounced as he swiftly carried her up the remaining steps to their bedroom. Slamming the door behind him with his booted heel, he set her on her feet once more and said in an attempt to reason with her, "I went out there with Alison because she said she wanted to talk, and because I—"

"Because you wanted to steal a few moments alone with your *paramour!*" she wrathfully finished for him. Her lustrous mane of hair had come unpinned as a result of his manhandling, and the raven locks now tumbled wildly about her face and shoulders. The delectable swell of her breasts heaved above the low, rounded neckline of her white gown. "The two of you couldn't even control your . . . your passions until you were alone! Oh no, you had to make a public spectacle of yourselves; you had to—"

"The 'spectacle' to which you refer was neither public *nor* of my doing! I was putting an end to the discussion between Alison and myself when she suddenly took it into her head to kiss me. If you had bothered to observe more closely, instead of flying off the handle and jumping to all the wrong conclusions, then you'd have noticed my unwillingness to participate in the blasted 'spectacle'!"

"I was a fool to believe you when you said your love for her was a thing of the past!" she proclaimed bitterly, her pain and anger making her irrational. "Oh Ryan, why did you have to lie to me? Why did you—"

"I have never lied to you, Hillary. Not about this, not about anything," he declared in a dangerously low tone. His blue-green eyes were smoldering as he stood towering above her, and if Hillary hadn't been so infuriated herself she might have taken warning from the telltale muscle twitching in the bronzed ruggedness of his left cheek.

"I don't believe you! You truly *are* a scoundrel, Ryan Gallagher, and I never should have married you!" She spun about as though she could not bear to look at him any longer. The tears burned against her eyelids as she tightly closed her eyes and uttered brokenly, "Why don't you go to her? If your . . . your lust for Alison Bromfield is so strong that it impels you to make a fool of me in front of all your friends and family, then you can just . . . just return to the garden and . . . and be with *her!*"

"If I feel the need to slake my *lust*, as you so charmingly put it, then I can damn well do so *here!*"

Hillary whirled about to face him again. A strangled cry of alarm broke from her lips as his hands suddenly closed upon the soft, bare flesh of her shoulders. She tried to fight him off, but to no avail. He easily bore her downward to the rug in front of the fire, the flames of which Agnes had dutifully nurtured a short time earlier.

"No! No, damn you, no!"

Ryan paid no heed to either her furious struggles or her tearful protests. Her refusal to listen to him, her willingness to believe him guilty, had both wounded and enraged him. Driven by a fierce desire to remind her that she was his and would always be his, he set about to do just that—in the most effective way he knew how.

Imprisoning her body with his, he captured both of her wrists and forced them above her head, then held them there with one large hand. Hillary's eyes grew very round as his other hand moved to the decolletage of her gown, and she gasped when his warm fingers dipped beneath the layers of tarlatan and fine white cotton. With one impatient tug downward, he freed her breasts.

"No!" she choked out again, still tormented by the vivid memory of his lips pressed against Alison's. Bringing both of her knees upward and twisting her body in one violent motion, she succeeded in sliding from beneath him as he was forced to release her long enough to keep from crashing backward against the red-hot andirons of the fireplace. She had no sooner scrambled upright, however, than his hand shot out to entangle within her skirts. He swiftly rose to his feet before her, his arm closing like a band of steel about her waist and hauling her roughly to him.

"Let me go! You've no right to touch me, not when you've—"

"You're mine, Hillary! *Mine!*"

She pushed futilely against the unrelenting hardness of his chest as he forced her back against the floral-papered wall and yanked up her flounced skirts and lacy, beribboned petticoats so that they were bunched about her waist.

"No!" Her face crimsoned and her pulses raced when she felt his fingers insinuating themselves

369

between her thighs, then slipping within the edges of her open-leg drawers. Inhaling upon another gasp as he bent his head and branded her naked breasts with his lips and tongue, she suddenly found herself unable to do anything more than cling weakly to his shoulders. A powerful tremor shook her and a soft moan escaped her lips when his demanding fingers began caressing the delicate flower of her womanhood. Her legs threatened to give way beneath her, and she would have fallen if not for the support of his arm about her waist.

"Damn it, Hillary, you know I love only you!" Ryan murmured hoarsely as his lips traveled hungrily upward from her breasts to her mouth. She swayed against him, her arms lifting of their own accord to entwine about his neck while he kissed her with an almost savage ardency that served to further arouse her already tumultuous passions.

Moments later, just when she was certain she could endure no more of the delicious agony, Ryan withdrew his hand from the convenient opening of her lace-edged drawers and deftly unfastened his trousers. With captivating mastery, he lifted her slightly and then brought her down upon his hard, throbbing manhood.

She moaned low in her throat and clasped him more tightly, feeling as if she would surely faint with the forceful, near painful ecstasy that seized her. His hands gripped her buttocks as he pressed her back against the wall once more, and she strained instinctively upward against him, her skirts softly rustling as they slid across the floral wallpaper. The fire crackled and hissed, but the only sounds Hillary was aware of were those of her heart pounding in her brain and her breath coming in a series of short, quiet gasps. Her hips followed the wildly evocative rhythm of Ryan's, until the passions deep within her soared heavenward and she cried out at the glorious feeling of completion. Dazed and breathless, she leaned back against the wall, while Ryan's entire body tensed in the next instant and he, too, was left weakened and struggling for breath.

He wordlessly drew her back down before the fire, stretching out his tall, muscular frame upon the rug and cradling her in his arms while they both stared pensively into the bright, dancing flames. Finally, Ryan sighed heavily and declared in a low, vibrant tone, "I love you with all my heart. Alison Bromfield means nothing to me—nothing."

More than anything else in the world, Hillary wanted to believe him. He *must* be speaking the truth, she told herself. If he really did still care for Alison, then what purpose would it serve for him to try so hard to convince her otherwise?

"Oh Ryan," she murmured, the tears starting to her eyes once more as she pressed even closer to his hard warmth, "I . . . I know I shouldn't have behaved the way I did, but it's just that I couldn't bear to think that you still loved *her!* I love you so very much, and it hurt terribly to see the two of you . . ." Her voice trailed away into nothingness as she released a pent-up, slightly ragged sigh of her own.

"Whatever else I may have done, my love, I've never found it necessary to lie to anyone, and most particularly not to you. Alison is obviously determined to stir up trouble, even though I made it quite clear to her that it will avail her nothing." He paused for a moment and tenderly brushed her forehead with his warm lips, then chuckled quietly, his eyes gleaming with wicked amusement as his thoughts turned to a different subject. "The way we resolve our differences almost makes a heated argument worthwhile."

Hillary blushed anew and retorted, "I would much prefer for us to do our 'resolving' without first having to cause each other so much pain!"

"What's a little pain compared to—"

"Please, Ryan," she pleaded, suddenly growing serious once more. "Promise me you won't go near Alison Bromfield again." There was a discernible catch in her voice, and Ryan felt a twinge of guilt when he thought of what she must have suffered upon witnessing Alison's damnable kiss. Though she had been too quick to judge him, he told himself she had more than paid for her mistrustfulness.

"I promise, my love." He gently cupped her chin and lifted her face for his kiss, and she soon forgot all about Alison or anyone else . . . there was only Ryan.

XV

"Miss Gillian said I was to fetch you right away, ma'am!" related Agnes. She colored rosily as her curious gaze was drawn past Hillary to where the covers lay in a wildly disheveled heap upon the big, four-poster bed. More than once since their arrival at the house a week ago, she had heard Mister Ryan and his beautiful young bride laughing together behind the closed door of their bedroom, and her cheeks had burned as all manner of wicked thoughts as to what they might be doing on the other side of that door had popped into her young, highly impressionable head.

"Did Miss Gillian happen to say what she wished to see me about?" Hillary asked with a faint, puzzled frown. Gillian had spoken no more than a dozen words to her since the night of the party. What could she possibly want?

"No, ma'am. She said only that she wanted me to fetch you. She's waiting down in the parlor, looking mighty pleased with herself about something, if I do say so! Mrs. Gallagher's gone out with Miss Erin, and I think Miss Cara and the children are still out in the kitchen making cookies."

"Thank you, Agnes," she murmured as the pert

little maid glanced toward the bed once more and then left.

Hillary reluctantly put away the letter she had been writing to her uncle. She had still received no word from him, and though she told herself his letters might very well have been lost even if he had written, she could not help worrying that something might have happened to him or someone else back home at Starcross.

Gathering up the full skirts of her blue-and-white-striped silk dress, she strolled from the room and down the stairs. Gillian, waiting for her sister-in-law in the parlor just as Agnes had said, immediately rose to her feet when Hillary entered the room.

"I have a message for you from Ryan," the eldest Gallagher daughter loftily announced, her gray muslin gown almost a perfect match for her eyes. Her tawny curls were fashioned into a rather severe style for one so young, and Hillary was once again struck by what appeared to be Gillian's intention to look like a younger version of her mother.

"A message?" she echoed with a slight frown. Absently musing that Gillian did indeed look a trifle smug about something, she moved farther into the bright, yellow-hued room and asked, "What is it?"

"He sent one of the men from the shipping office round with it. It seems Ryan wants you to meet him there at the office in half an hour."

"That's odd," Hillary murmured, half to herself. She glanced toward the window, only to note that the late afternoon sun was already sinking low upon the horizon.

"Why should you consider it odd?" Gillian coolly challenged.

"Well, I . . . I suppose because Ryan has never asked me to meet him anywhere before, and most

374

particularly not down at the waterfront. I wonder why he—"

"If you're *afraid* to go alone, perhaps I should accompany you," the other woman offered, though she did so with noticeably ill grace. She released a faint sigh of exasperation and added, "I would not have thought you so weak spirited. After all, you *did* sail all the way from Tahiti as the lone woman amongst a shipload of men, did you not?"

Hillary tried not to take offense, but there was a certain edge to her voice as she replied, "It is not fear that causes my reluctance, Gillian, but rather puzzlement. I can think of no reason why Ryan should wish to have me meet him at the shipping office."

"Then I take it you are simply going to ignore the message?"

"Why should it be of such interest to you?" Hillary couldn't refrain from querying.

"It isn't. Not in the least," Gillian declared with an indifferent shrug of her shoulders. She resumed her seat on the yellow brocade settee and took up her embroidery once more, apparently dismissing Hillary and the matter of Ryan's message from her mind.

Hesitating only a moment longer before making her decision, Hillary swept from the parlor and back up the staircase to fetch her bonnet and shawl. She did not see the way Gillian watched her as she hurried across the entrance foyer to the front door, nor did she see the malignantly triumphant smile that touched Gillian's lips once she had gone.

Recalling the fact that Priscilla and Erin had taken the carriage, she set off down the hill on foot. She was in truth relieved to escape the house for a while, and she looked forward to the walk. The inactivity of the past few days had taken its toll, for she had begun to feel decidedly restless. Of course, the main cause of her uneasiness was Ryan's family, who still treated her very much as an outsider. To make matters worse, ever since the night of the dance, it seemed that Priscilla introduced Alison Bromfield's name into the conversation at every opportunity—always when Ryan was absent from home, of course.

Good heavens, if they are so disapproving of me now, how are they going to react when they learn of Ryan's plans to abandon New Bedford and the whaling business and live in Tahiti? she asked herself with a deep, inward sigh. So far, Ryan had told only David, who had expressed regret for his brother's decision but had also promised support.

Soon, Hillary was passing the Seaman's Bethel. She thought of Connor Reid and wondered if he and his young lady, whoever she was, had managed to work things out between them. She still had not questioned Ryan about Connor's broken engagement to Gillian. She would have to remember to do so later that evening when they were finally alone.

The air became noticeably cooler as the night grew nearer. Hillary pulled the fringed woolen shawl more closely about her shoulders and quickened her steps. She noticed that there were few people about at that hour of the evening, and only a handful of carriages had passed her since she had left the Gallagher mansion behind.

Things changed, however, as she approached the waterfront and headed in the direction where she knew the buildings housing the Gallagher Shipping Office and Counting Rooms to be located. There were more and more people about—mostly men—as well as a good many more conveyances, though these were predominantly public carriages and supply wagons.

Once again, she was prompted to wonder why Ryan had summoned her to the office where he had been working well past eight o'clock most evenings. She began to doubt the wisdom of her decision to walk, for she became aware of the many avidly curious glances being directed her way as she began marching briskly past the area reserved for the taverns.

Darkness was rapidly enclosing the city now. The waterfront saloons were already filling with the sounds of masculine curses, songs, and laughter, as well as with the smells of smoke and strong spirits and salty, unwashed bodies. Later, crowds of men would burst from the taverns and roll toward the docks, singing at the tops of their lungs in celebration of a completed voyage, or roundly cursing the prospect of a sailing day.

A slim, dark-haired man with coarse features and strangely hawkish eyes stood within the open doorway of the Spouter Inn—perhaps the most infamous of the taverns—and leaned back negligently against the weathered frame. He scowled out upon the darkening streets as the revelry in the room behind him grew increasingly clamorous. Feeling restive and craving some action of some kind, be it a fight or a woman or whatever else he could get mixed up with, he muttered a curse and set forth from the tavern. He hadn't gone far when his sinister gaze fell upon the young woman of obvious quality who was hastening toward one of the side streets leading to the wharves. Recognition flickered in his dark eyes.

"Well, well, if it ain't the captain's lady herself," Peale murmured to himself with a low, malicious chuckle. More than a little curious as to why Ryan Gallagher's wife was wandering about alone on the waterfront, he turned up the collar of his seaman's coat and tossed his cigarette to the cobbled street below his feet. His thin lips curled into a predatory smile as he turned to follow her.

Plagued by a growing uneasiness, Hillary cast a quick glance over her shoulder. Her heart began pounding erratically when she spied a lone, dark figure following only a few feet behind her. A hat was pulled low upon his head, and his face was effectively concealed by the collar of his coat, but there was something about him that seemed oddly familiar. Suddenly reminded of the nightmarish attack that last evening in Stanley, she snapped her head back around and fought down a rising sense of panic. She could literally feel the man growing closer.

She felt almost giddy with relief when she spied the well-remembered outlines of the shipping office ahead. Gathering up her skirts, she practically raced across the last remaining distance, and she did not look back as she climbed the steps and entered the safety of the building.

Pausing for a moment beside the closed door to catch her breath, she became aware of the fact that there seemed to be no one else about. The very long, outer room, usually oveflowing with prospective whalers, was deserted. The only light came from within another room to her immediate left, so she turned her steps in that direction and softly called out, "Ryan?" She heard what sounded distinctly like an oath just as she reached the doorway, followed by the readily identifiable sound of boots connecting with a bare wooden floor. Ryan's handsome, thunderous features suddenly loomed menacingly above her.

"What the devil are you doing here?" he demanded, his hands shooting out to close tightly about her arms.

Hillary was stunned by his inexplicable anger. Her

eyes were very wide and luminous as she tried to explain, "Why, I . . . I thought you—"

"Damn it, woman, don't tell me you came down here *alone* at this time of day?" he ground out as his fiercely gleaming eyes made a quick, encompassing sweep of the outer room. Without giving her the chance to answer, he started hustling her back toward the main entrance. "I want you to get back in that blasted carriage and take yourself home where you belong! I thought you understood that you were never—"

"But Ryan, I . . . I didn't come in the carriage!" she breathlessly informed him, resisting his efforts to evict her. "I walked."

"You *what?*" He came to an abrupt halt and hauled her in front of him, his eyes burning down into hers. "Blast it all to hell, Hillary, don't you realize what might have happened to you? Decent women don't walk the streets of New Bedford alone at night, and they damned sure don't do so on the waterfront!"

"While I most assuredly had no desire to be mistaken for anything other than a 'decent' woman, Ryan Gallagher, I did have a desire to follow *your* instructions!" she indignantly parried, her eyes flashing their brilliant amethyst fire up at him. "I walked because the carriage was not available, and while I admit it was probably not the wisest course of action, I only wanted to meet you here at the hour you had indicated in your message to me!"

"What are you talking about? What message?"

"The one delivered to the house by one of your employees!"

"I sent you no message."

Hillary stared up at him in speechless bewilderment. She closely scrutinized his face, only to read the

379

truth in his penetrating, blue-green gaze.

"But Gillian . . . she said you—"

"Gillian," murmured Ryan, the sound of her name on his lips holding evidence of realization and a growing fury. His hands slid from Hillary's trembling arms at last. He turned away and swore, then ground out, "I warned her, damn it! I told her *and* Erin what I'd do to them if they dared to cause trouble!"

"Oh Ryan, why would she do such a thing? What could she possibly hope to gain by sending me down here like this?"

"I don't know. But I'm damned sure going to find out!" he vowed in a low tone seething with vengeful anger.

In spite of the malicious and childish prank Gillian had played on her, Hillary felt a tremor of fear on her sister-in-law's behalf. She was all too familiar with Ryan's temper.

"What are you going to do?" she asked quietly, her eyes shining with concern.

"Though I am sorely tempted to give the over-grown brat the thrashing she deserves," he confessed with a grim, tight-lipped expression, "I suppose I'll have to settle for making good on my threat to cut off her allowance for the duration of our stay. You see, until David is well enough to return to his duties here, *I'll* be the one controlling the purse strings!"

Still feeling confused and dismayed by Gillian's actions, Hillary released a sigh and drew her shawl back up about her shoulders.

Ryan frowned thoughtfully and moved back to tower above her once more. He reached for her, his hands closing with gentleness about her arms this time as he said, "I'm sorry, my love, that you had to be the one to bear the force of my anger. But you should have known better than to come down here alone like this. Dear God, when I think of all that could have happened to you—" He broke off and drew a ragged breath before somberly commanding, "I want you to promise me you'll never come near the waterfront again unless I am with you."

Hillary's thoughts were suddenly drawn back to the man who had apparently been following her, and an involuntary shiver ran the length of her spine. She battled the urge to tell Ryan of the incident, for she knew he would only grow angry again and would no doubt scold her all the more. Besides, she mentally reasoned with herself, no harm had been done. She had suffered nothing more than a few moments of anxiety.

"Very well, Ryan," she agreed, her eyes very round as they met his. He pulled her against him and enfolded her supple, silk-covered curves within his warm embrace.

They left the office soon thereafter. Ryan led her down the steps and up the side street toward the corner where it was his habit to hail a carriage every evening after work. Neither he nor Hillary noticed the man who stood watching them from the shadows nearby.

Peale waited until they had climbed up into a carriage before he stepped from the cloaking darkness onto the lamplit walk. He stared after the carriage for several long moments, his coarse features displaying a mixture of rancor and lustful intent as it rolled out of sight.

He had heard talk lately—talk about a rich and powerful young lady who had put it about the waterfront that she just might be looking for someone to 'persuade' Ryan Gallagher's wife to depart New Bedford and get herself back to Tahiti where she belonged. There was also talk that this particular lady might be willing to pay as much as a thousand dollars for this 'persuasion.' With that kind of money being mentioned, more than one down-on-his-luck sailor had expressed interest in the rumored scheme, but nothing had been settled as yet.

Peale decided there and then that he would be the one to do the lady's dirty work for her. After all, he recalled with an ugly curl of his lips, he'd had such doings with the high and mighty Mrs. Gallagher before. Only *this* time, he silently vowed as his dark eyes narrowed and filled with a malevolent light, he wouldn't be drunk.

This time, I'll finish what I started in the Falklands! he silently vowed. With that thought in mind, Peale turned his steps back toward the Spouter Inn, where he knew he stood a good chance of learning more about the mysterious lady's plan.

Ryan and Hillary, meanwhile, were at that moment alighting from the carriage, which had just pulled up before the Gallagher mansion. They fell into silence as they entered the house, though Hillary cast her husband several worried glances. She dreaded what was to come, and she fervently hoped he wouldn't require her presence during his chastisement of his sister.

Gillian, however, was nowhere to be found. Ryan combed the house for her, only to have one of the maids belatedly inform him that Miss Gillian had gone out for the evening. Hillary, wandering into the parlor while he was searching upstairs, encountered Priscilla and Erin, who had just that moment returned from their own unusually late outing. Ryan's mother immediately demanded to know what in heaven's name had occurred to make her son so angry, for she could not help but hear his deep-timbred voice echoing throughout the rooms above them as he roared Gillian's name.

"I'm afraid Gillian . . . did something—" Hillary reluctantly started to explain, only to be interrupted by Erin.

"Did something?" she eagerly probed. Her blue eyes were glimmering with hopeful mischief as her dark curls bounced about her head. "To *you?*"

"What precisely is my daughter accused of doing?" Priscilla stiffly demanded before Hillary could respond to Erin's less than congenial question.

"She relayed a message that had, in fact, not been sent," Hillary calmly revealed at last.

"Is that *all?*" the older woman countered in icy tones of disbelief. "Why should Ryan be so incensed over such an inconsequential matter?"

"Because *your daughter*, madam, could very well have been responsible for a grievous harm done to *my wife* this evening!" Ryan answered from the doorway. His mother and sister stared up at him with more than a touch of wide-eyed apprehension as he moved to Hillary's side. "Rest assured that Gillian will be made to pay for her despicable little prank!"

"Come now, Ryan, you know how high-strung our Gillian is," Priscilla sought to reason with him. "Things have been very difficult for her since your father died, and I'm sure you wouldn't—"

"Things are about to become a hell of a lot *more* difficult for her!" he mercilessly shot back, his magnificent turquoise eyes ablaze.

"Ryan, please," murmured Hillary. She raised a hand and gently rested it upon the tense, granite hard muscles of his arm.

He covered her hand with his and told his mother, "Gillian will have to learn that she cannot play games with the lives of others!"

"How do you know for certain that she is to blame for this . . . this misunderstanding?" Priscilla demanded. "Perhaps the fault does not lie with Gillian at all!" This last she said with a narrow, meaningful look toward Hillary. "Perhaps it's time you realized, my dearest son, that it is not right to forsake the family and friends who have loved you and remained loyal to you during all your years at sea!"

"Yes, perhaps you should remember that *we* knew you long before *she* did!" Erin seconded with a significant look of her own.

"That's enough, damn it!" snapped Ryan, his voice whipcord sharp. Hillary was acutely conscious of the effort it was costing him to maintain control over his flaring temper, and her fingers tightened upon his arm. When he spoke again, it was with deadly calm. "Hillary is my wife. She is a part of this family now. I thought I had made it quite clear that she was to be treated as such." He paused for a moment while Priscilla and Erin stared up at him speechlessly, their faces displaying a combination of obstinancy and resentment. "I suppose now is as good a time as any to inform you of my plans. Maybe you'll be more inclined to make the best of things if you realize you may never see us again."

"Never see you again?" gasped Priscilla. "What do you mean?"

"As soon as David's recovery is complete, Hillary and I will be returning to Tahiti. I've already made arrangements to sell my share of the business to David and Cara."

"You're actually going to *live* in Tahiti?" asked Erin, apparently believing her long-idolized older brother had taken complete leave of his senses.

"Dear God, you . . . you can't be serious!" Priscilla Gallagher stammered in horrified disbelief. She sank down weakly onto one of her Chinese Chippendale chairs and raised a visibly unsteady hand to the lace at her throat. "Why, both your father and your grandfather lived in this house . . . you were born in this house. You . . . you can't really mean to turn your back on everything three generations of Gallaghers have worked so hard to build; you can't mean to abandon the business that has been the lifeblood of this family for so many years!"

"I'm not turning my back on the achievements of the Gallaghers—I'm merely setting out to achieve something of my own. You know as well as I do that David is more than capable of running the business. And I've already recommended that Connor Reid take my place as master of the *Falcon.*"

"*Connor Reid?*" Priscilla echoed with unmistakable disaffection. "How can you even think of giving that man command of one of our ships after what he did to your sister?"

"He didn't do anything to her," Ryan firmly dissented. "Gillian admitted she did not truly care for him, remember? Being the honorable man he is, Connor would have gone through with it if she hadn't given him his freedom. Neither one of them truly desired the marriage—it was pressed upon them by you and Father, and by Connor's family as well."

A knock sounded at the front door while Ryan was speaking, and Hillary was only too willing to go to answer it. When she returned to stand framed in the parlor doorway a moment later, Connor Reid was at her side. His unexpected appearance evoked a different reaction from each of the three Gallaghers within the room. Priscilla's attractive countenance became suffused with a dull, angry color, Erin gave him her best imitation of a flirtatious smile, while Ryan chuckled and murmured with a crooked grin of

385

appreciative irony, "Speak of the devil . . ."

"It seems I've interrupted something," Connor perceptively observed.

Priscilla subjected him to a cold glare as she abruptly rose to her feet and directed Erin, "Come, my dear!" The plump little brunette was obviously tempted to disobey, so her mother took her by the arm to forcibly lead her away. Priscilla Gallagher paused in her retreat long enough to tell Ryan, "We shall talk more about your ridiculous plans later! I cannot believe you are truly so selfish that you would shirk your duty to your family!" With that, she swept regally from the room, pulling Erin along with her.

"I'm sorry, Ryan. I didn't mean to intrude upon a family discussion," said Connor. He was well aware of how unpleasant such "discussions" in the Gallagher household could be.

"To tell the truth, I was glad of the interruption," Ryan confessed with another low chuckle. He smiled down ruefully at Hillary as she returned to his side. "It seems, my love, that we're not destined to enjoy a very peaceful existence during our stay here. If it were not for David and Cara, I'd damn well leave and—"

"No, Ryan, don't talk of doing something you'll only regret," she bade softly, her violet eyes full of understanding. "The situation may not be as we wish, but surely we can endure things for a little while longer." And let's just hope the situation doesn't get any worse, she added silently. Turning back to their guest, she smiled and gestured toward the settee. "Please have a seat, Connor. I'm so glad you finally came to call on us."

"This isn't entirely a social call," he admitted. He returned her smile with a brief one of his own, waiting until she had taken a seat in one of the chairs before he sank down upon the brocade-cushioned settee.

Ryan sat next to his wife and asked the man who had been his friend since boyhood, "Well, what is it? Is there some kind of trouble with *your* family as well?"

"No. I think they've finally given up on me," Connor replied with a faint, mocking grin. There was a troubled look in his golden eyes, and an uncharacteristic air of indecision about him. "It's Bethany," he finally disclosed.

"Bethany?" repeated Hillary.

"The woman I'm going to marry," supplied Connor.

"So she did indeed wait for you," Ryan murmured, pleased to learn he had not been mistaken about the young woman.

"She waited. But her father still refuses to give us his blessing. He insists I'll never be anything but wild and fickle hearted."

"Oh Connor, why would he think such a thing of you?" Hillary questioned, her eyes aglow with both sympathy and puzzlement.

"Because I was betrothed to Gillian when I fell in love with Bethany."

"Bethany is a Quaker," Ryan explained quietly. "Her father considers a betrothal to be almost the same as a marriage. He believes Connor behaved dishonorably, even though Gillian broke the engagement only a short time later."

Hillary frowned thoughtfully as she contemplated all that she had just heard. Her gaze traveled back to Connor, who sat looking as though he were still trying to make a decision about something.

"Does he also disapprove of the fact that you do not

share their faith?'' Hillary asked him, then was surprised when his darkly attractive features relaxed into a genuine smile of amusement.

"No. You see, I happen to be a Friend myself," he told her, referring to the fact that he was a birthright member of the Society of Friends—known as Quakers to those outside the faith. "A backslid one, I'll admit, but not a total apostate. It seems that Jacob Roberts is perfectly willing to accept a son-in-law who has drifted away from the Inner Light, but not one whom he believes to have acted as little better than an adulterer. Mind you, I never spoke of my love for Bethany until Gillian had dissolved the 'understanding' between us, but Jacob maintains that it makes no difference. And he knows I cannot deny falling in love with his daughter before I was free."

"What are you planning to do now?" Ryan queried. A frown of concern creased his sun-kissed brow as he settled back in the chair and looked at his friend. "Does she still refuse to marry you without her father's permission?"

"No," Connor answered with a heavy sigh. "That's why I needed to talk to you. I needed someone's advice, for I'll be damned if I can make any sense of what's going on in this blasted head of mine!" He muttered a hasty apology to Hillary for his language as he flung himself from the settee and stood beside the fireplace. Bracing a hand on the cool marble of the mantel, he expounded in a low tone brimming with raw emotion, "Bethany has agreed to elope with me. She claims to be willing to risk alienation from her family, to risk ostracism by the close-knit circle of friends she has been a part of all her life. I should be the happiest man in the world, but, God help me, I'm not!"

Though Ryan appeared somewhat bemused by the

other man's predicament, Hillary's beautiful eyes filled with comprehension. She chose her words carefully as she said, "It would be very difficult for her, Connor, being cut off from her friends and family. I'm afraid your being away at sea would prove to be an almost unbearable hardship for her, for she would miss the comfort of her family even more at such a time."

"I know," he reluctantly concurred, releasing another deep sigh. "I suppose I just wanted to hear someone put into words what I'd already realized. Or maybe I wanted someone to talk me into saying the devil with everything else and taking what I wanted while I had the chance!"

"That wouldn't be fair, Connor, either to Bethany or yourself," Hillary gently asserted. Connor nodded in silent agreement.

"But neither would it be fair to allow the love you bear for each other to wither and die as though it had never been," insisted Ryan. Although a man of honor himself, he had seldom let anything or anyone stand between him and whatever he'd set his mind to having.

"I know that, too," Connor murmured, looking more troubled than ever. "Something's got to be done. I just haven't figured out what."

He stayed only a few minutes longer, then took his leave with the announced intention of thinking the whole thing over again. Hillary remained preoccupied with thoughts of Connor's plight, and thoughts of Gillian's mischief, throughout the evening meal. Afterward, she and Cara sat together in the parlor while Ryan kept his mother in the dining room for a few moments of private "discussion."

"Hillary, I hope you don't mind if I . . . well, if I try to explain a bit about Priscilla and the girls,"

Cara hesitantly declared.

"No, of course not. In fact, I would be grateful for any insight you could offer."

"It might help if you knew how difficult these past several years have been for them. I don't suppose Ryan has told you much, has he?" she asked, though it was clear she already knew the answer. Smiling as Hillary shook her head in affirmation, she remarked, "He and David are very much alike in that respect." Her countenance grew solemn once more, and a faint sigh of remembrance escaped her lips. "While Priscilla has never displayed an outwardly cheerful disposition, she did not become quite so unapproachable until after the death of her husband. They were very happy together, in their way, and even though he had spent the majority of their married life at sea, he was an important part of this family. Everything revolved around him—everything. Kevin Gallagher was a man who was truly loved and revered by his wife and children. His homecomings were always a cause for great celebration."

"Ryan said David is very much like their father."

"He is," Cara agreed with another brief smile, her eyes softly aglow. "David was a desperately needed source of strength when Captain Gallagher caught a fever and died here in this very house. Ryan was away at the time, and he didn't learn of his father's death until nearly six months later. It hit him very hard, just as it did Gillian and Erin. Gillian, in particular, had always adored Kevin. I doubt if she would have turned out quite the way she did if her father had been at home more during her childhood. She needed a strong hand, which was something Priscilla, in spite of her stern demeanor, never provided. Perhaps because Gillian was such a favorite of Kevin's,

Priscilla never gave her the same measure of discipline she gave her other children."

"And yet, I understand that both of Ryan's parents did their best to arrange Gillian's marriage to a man she did not love," said Hillary, referring to what she had learned of Connor Reid's past involvement with Ryan's sister.

"Yes, but they only did so because they thought it best for her. I know it sounds rather coldhearted, but it wasn't, not really. Neither Connor nor Gillian resisted their efforts, at least not at first. They had known each other since childhood, and while no one could claim theirs was a love match, it was generally acknowledged that the two of them would deal famously together. But then . . . well, then Gillian decided she would rather not marry at all, and Connor, as it turned out, had already fallen in love with someone else."

"It seems that Priscilla blames Connor for what happened, for she treated him very badly when he called here earlier this evening."

"I suppose she felt she had to blame *someone*. She had wanted to see Gillian settled with a man from a 'suitable' family, and the connection between the Reids and the Gallaghers was a long and amiable one. Gillian had never expressed an interest in any man before Connor returned home from a voyage some five years ago and suddenly started courting her. He was lonely and yearning for a home and family of his own, and Gillian was someone he could be himself with. David knew their relationship was doomed from the start—he tried to tell Priscilla and Captain Gallagher so, but they refused to listen."

"Was Ryan away from home during this time?" asked Hillary, then inwardly mused that his absence would have been unlikely, since Connor had served as his first mate for a number of years.

"No, but he said very little on the subject. I suppose because he is himself so independent, he was loath to interfere. I do recall, however, that he advised both Connor and Gillian not to allow themselves to be rushed into anything. That seemed an odd bit of advice, coming from Ryan, since he has always been more than a little impetuous. And yet, even as a boy, he was always so sure of what he wanted."

"He hasn't changed," Hillary murmured with a soft laugh.

"No, I can tell he hasn't." Cara smiled affectionately at her and asked quietly, "You love him very much, don't you, my dear?"

"More than I ever believed possible. And I wish there were some way I could ease the tension our marriage has created." Her violet eyes clouded with renewed disquiet, and she sighed before adding, "Now that his mother knows of our plans to settle in Tahiti . . ."

"Then your plans are definite?"

"Yes."

"But what if Ryan should change his mind? What if he decides to remain here in New Bedford?" Cara then questioned. She still found it difficult to believe that a man whose entire life had been spent around the business and adventure of whaling would be content to settle in a place she had always heard described as unbearably hot, rife with cannibals, and lacking in any sort of decorum or refinement.

"Change his mind?" echoed Hillary. It was obvious that she had never even considered such a possibility. "I don't think there's any likelihood of that."

"Perhaps not. But family ties can be very strong, even if the family seems to be forever at odds with one

392

another." Her features relaxed into a smile once more, and her eyes were full of sisterly benevolence as she leaned forward to pat Hillary's arm. "I just don't want to see you hurt or disappointed. As David said after telling me of Ryan's plans, it can be very hard for a man to leave behind an old way of life, particularly when it's been more or less ingrained within him from birth."

Although Hillary returned the other woman's smile and sincerely thanked her for her concern, she could not help but be troubled by Cara's words, for they had planted a tiny seed of doubt in her mind.

Ryan entered the parlor at last, only to report that his mother had already retired for the night. Cara stayed a few moments longer, then took herself upstairs as well.

Doing her best to forget about the last, unsettling part of her conversation with his brother's wife, Hillary moved to Ryan's side and asked, "Your mother is still very upset, isn't she?"

"She'll get over it," he grimly asserted, his eyes glinting dully at the recollection of the unpleasant little scene that had just been enacted in the dining room. A brief smile touched his lips as he told Hillary, "Why don't you go on up to bed? I expect Gillian will be home soon, and I don't think you want to be present when—"

"I most certainly do not!" she hastily assured him, her thick ebony curls straining against their pins as she shook her head. "But please, Ryan, do try to control your temper. You can be quite intimidating when you're angry!"

"Really? Then why is it, my love, that instead of quaking with fear as a dutiful wife should, you always fling the gauntlet right back at me?" he demanded wryly, his turquoise gaze alight with loving amusement.

"Because, my dearest captain, *I* am not the mousy, spineless little creature you thought you were marrying, remember?" she retorted, tilting her chin upward in a mock gesture of defiant pride.

Ryan gave a low chuckle and yanked her masterfully against him. "I never believed you anything other than what you are—a headstrong, willful, beautiful, damnably desirable little witch who enrages me one minute and sets me on fire the next!" Hillary shivered in delight as he encircled her with his strong arms and claimed her lips with his. When the kiss finally ended, she found herself spun about and sent off to bed with a playful smack upon her bottom and a promise that she *would* be disturbed when her husband came up later.

She had already drifted off to sleep by the time Ryan finally slipped into bed beside her. Awakened by the warmth of his body, she released a sigh of utter contentment and turned into his welcoming embrace. Though he offered her no details regarding his confrontation with Gillian, he did mutter something about hoping *his* offspring were all of the masculine gender.

Meanwhile, not far from the Gallagher mansion, Connor Reid stood holding his own beloved close to his heart within the darkened interior of the Roberts' kitchen. Bethany was crying softly as she clung to him. Her gleaming, red-gold tresses streamed freely across her trembling shoulders, for she had been in too much of a hurry to don the cap and bonnet she had snatched up on her way to meet Connor.

Although he had mentioned the possibility of an elopement to Ryan and Hillary, Connor had not revealed his plans to take Bethany from her home that very night. He realized now that it was because, deep within him, he'd known all along he couldn't go through with it. He loved Bethany more than anything, and because of his love for her he could not condemn her to a life of loneliness and shame.

"But why, Connor? Why did thee change thy mind?" she murmured brokenly. "I thought thee loved me; I thought—"

"I *do* love you!" he whispered fiercely, his arms tightening about her as though he would never let her go. "As God is my witness, I love you more than I've ever loved anyone!"

"Then why does thee say we cannot be married?"

"I'm not saying we won't ever be together, only that we'll have to think of some way to win your father's approval first."

"But this morning, thee talked only of tonight, only of—"

"I know." His golden eyes looked deep into the wide, glistening blue depths of hers as he tenderly cupped her chin and tilted her face upward. "It was wrong of me to ask you to turn your back on everything you hold dear, wrong of me to expect you to live the kind of life you'd be living if you went against your own principles and beliefs. I know, Bethany, for I've come to realize that I still hold those same principles and beliefs within me. I thought I had left it all behind me, but I haven't. It's as much a part of me as it ever was."

"Oh Connor!" Bethany smiled up at him joyfully through her tears, and Connor Reid knew with a certainty that his patience and honor would be rewarded. "Thee has truly listened to the voice in thy heart at last?"

"Yes, my darling," he answered, gently folding her

against him once more, "I guess I have."

Suddenly, the soft glow of a lamp filled the kitchen. Bethany started guiltily and pulled away from Connor just as a deep, familiar voice rumbled out, "I beg thy forgiveness for eavesdropping, daughter, but it appears thee and Friend Reid have something to say to me." Jacob Roberts, a large man with graying brown hair and a thick yet neatly trimmed beard to match, stood gazing across at the two lovers in somber expectation.

"Father, I . . . that is, we . . ." Bethany stammered breathlessly.

"What she's trying to tell you, sir, is that we were planning to elope tonight," confessed Connor, meeting the older man's penetrating gaze without flinching. "It was my fault—Bethany didn't really want to marry me this way, but I talked her into it. I was planning to take her away and—"

"Then why are thee still here?" queried Jacob, only the faintest glimmer of telltale humor in his eyes.

"Because I decided it wasn't right. I'm sorry, Mr. Roberts. I'm sorry for a good many things, but most of all for all the pain I've caused Bethany. I love her more than life itself, but I . . . I won't rob her of the chance for a happy future."

"Father, please!" implored Bethany as she hastened to his side and took one of his hands between both of hers. "I love Connor, and he has turned back to the Light! He has—"

"I know, daughter." His stern features relaxed into a smile as he admitted, "I heard. I saw thee stealing from thy room, and I thought it best that I see why thee was so impatient to come downstairs at such a late hour." He looked to Connor, and his expression grew solemn again. "Thee could have taken my daughter from me, but thee did not. Thee chose the path of righteousness, and for that I am truly thankful." He cast a tenderly paternal look upon Bethany once more before proclaiming to Connor, "Thee has proven thy worth to me, and to God, Friend Reid. If thee still wishes to marry my daughter, thee has my permission to do so."

"If I still wish—" Connor echoed in stunned disbelief, only to break off when the realization of Jacob's words sank in.

Pausing just long enough to press a jubilant kiss upon her father's bearded cheek, Bethany flew across the room and back into Connor's outstretched arms.

Their love had been tested . . . and had triumphed.

XVI

The wedding of Connor Reid and Bethany Roberts took place in the early afternoon hours of a beautiful Saturday—called "Seventh-day" by the Quakers—in August. The ceremony was accomplished with both the simplicity and dignity so esteemed by the Friends, who placed more value on the sacrament of marriage than perhaps any other religious group in the country.

The Meeting House was filled to overflowing as friends and family of the happy couple gathered to celebrate their eternal union. The wedding guests, shown to their seats by the ushers Connor had appointed, sat waiting on the unadorned wooden benches in silent expectation. The parents of the bride and groom were soon led to the bench that was closest to the front of the large, candlelit room.

Finally, the bride and her bridesmaids appeared at the back, their arrival followed closely by that of the groom and his groomsmen. Bethany and Connor looked at each other and smiled, their eyes aglow with love. Connor's gaze filled with unmistakable tenderness and admiration as it flickered over his future wife. Bethany's gown was a simple but elegant concoction of white satin. Her beautiful, red-gold hair was pinned securely at the nape of her neck, and she wore nothing upon her head save for a small square of lace that Connor had given her nearly five years earlier.

Connor looked quite handsome in a black suit, his face appearing tanned and healthy above the collar of his white linen shirt. Bethany felt as though her heart would burst with all the love and joy welling up within her, and she did not hesitate before taking Connor's arm and walking up the center aisle with him.

The bridesmaids and groomsmen slowly filed two by two after them, then stood waiting at the front while Connor and Bethany went to their seats between their parents. The Meeting House remained hushed and silent for several long moments. Then, the bride and groom rose and faced each other, joining right hands as they spoke the solemn words—only before God and the witnesses present—that would forever bind them together as man and wife.

"In the presence of the Lord and of this assembly, I take thee, Bethany Roberts, to be my wife, promising with divine assistance to be unto thee a loving and faithful husband until death shall separate us."

Bethany earnestly pledged to do the same as his wife, and the two of them sat down together. Ryan and one of the other groomsmen brought forth a small table and set it before the newly married couple. On the table was the marriage certificate, which both Connor and Bethany signed. Bethany's father then stood and read the certificate to all present, after which the assembly fell into another period of silence. Several Friends felt compelled to rise long enough to speak a spiritual message to wish

Connor and Bethany success in their marriage and happiness in their lives. Finally, another Friend stood and suggested that the wedding company withdraw from the Meeting House.

The reception was held on the grounds of the chapel. A number of tables and chairs had been set up beneath the trees, and the guests were met with a veritable feast as they left the Meeting House and mingled with one another in the cool shade.

Hillary strolled outside with Cara to wait for Ryan. In spite of her friendship with Connor's parents, Priscilla had refused to attend the wedding, and she had stubbornly forbade either Erin or Gillian to go as well. Only Erin had been disappointed; Gillian had coldly professed a dislike for such sentimental gatherings. In truth, however, she had wanted to avoid any further unpleasantness between herself and her brother, whom she had sworn never to forgive for what she had perceived to have been his cruel and humiliating treatment of her. Not only had he made good his threat to cut off her allowance, but he had also made it painfully clear that he would not hesitate to turn her over his knee and administer the thrashing he believed she deserved if she dared to cause trouble between himself and his wife again.

Ryan and Connor remained just within the doorway of the Meeting House for a few moments as Bethany was laughingly spirited outside by her bridesmaids. After offering his friend heartfelt congratulations and best wishes, Ryan grinned broadly and announced, "It's official, *Captain* Reid. You're the new master of the *Falcon*. You're to set sail at the end of the month."

"Dam . . . I mean, do you really mean it?" his former first mate blurted out, unable to believe so much good fortune had come his way all at once. As

Ryan nodded to confirm it, Connor dazedly realized that the two things he had wanted most in the world were now his—Bethany, and command of the *Falcon.*

"I met with the board this morning, and David signed the papers just before I left the house. So it seems, Captain Reid, that you are finally getting all that you deserve."

"Thanks, Ryan. Thanks for . . . well, for everything," said Connor as he took his friend's hand in a firm grip and shook it.

"You've earned it," Ryan insisted. He clapped the other man companionably on the back before the two of them went to join the celebration.

Locating his wife after a brief search, Ryan took her to meet the bride. Hillary was delighted to find Bethany every bit as warm and sweet as she had hoped Connor's beloved would be, and her violet eyes were sparkling with tears as she embraced the groom and told him, "I wish you much happiness, dear Captain Reid." She smiled with genuine affection as he thanked her and leaned down to brush her cheek with his lips. Cara related her own best wishes to the newlyweds, and then Ryan led both women over to a group of friends a short distance away.

Hillary's eyes widened in surprised dismay a few minutes later when she looked up to see Alison Bromfield alighting from a carriage. Though it was not at all unusual for many friends and acquaintances of the couple to attend the reception and not the ceremony—particularly if they were not of the same faith as the couple—it was a bit out of the ordinary for them to do so when they had not been invited.

"*Dearest* Connor!" Alison gushed as she sailed forward with her gallant young escort in tow.

Dressed in an elaborately frilled and flounced, *decolleté* gown of peach-blossom silk, and wearing a gaily feathered hat atop her blond ringlets, she looked conspicuously out of place amongst the predominantly Quaker gathering. "I'd heard you were to be married today, and I thought it only fitting that I come and offer you my *sincerest* felicitations!"

"Thank you, Miss Bromfield," Connor stiffly replied. Wondering what had prompted the usually less than friendly Alison to bother herself with attendance at his wedding reception, he took note of the way her gaze sought out Ryan. A sharp feeling of dread gripped him, but he concealed his disquiet and calmly presented Alison to his new wife and in-laws.

After enduring the introductions with noticeable impatience, Alison made straightaway for Ryan. Her companion, a tall, slender man with wavy brown hair and a perpetually bored expression on his aristocratic features, followed leisurely in her wake.

"Good day to you, Captain Gallagher!" she proclaimed with a mischievously enticing smile, her green eyes narrowing up at him. Hillary's cheeks flamed, and her entire body tensed as she sought to control a fresh wave of jealousy and anger.

"What are you doing here?" Ryan demanded in a low and deceptively level tone. His hand tightened upon Hillary's arm, while a wide-eyed Cara took an instinctive step backward. The others in the group had already drifted away, for most of them were familiar with Alison Bromfield and had no wish to bear the sharpness of her tongue.

"In case you've forgotten, Connor Reid is an old friend of mine! I've known him nearly as long as you have. Why shouldn't I want to congratulate him on his marriage?"

"Since it appears you've already done just that,

why don't you and your friend be about your business!''

"You've no right to tell me what to do, Ryan Gallagher! You're not *my* husband, remember?'' Alison parried with biting sarcasm. She finally turned her venomous gaze upon Hillary and said, "Really, my dear, perhaps you should endeavor to educate *dear* Ryan on the finer points of how to treat women he has loved and lost!''

"Lost?'' Hillary repeated ever so quietly, her violet eyes flashing with evidence of her own rising temper. "If my husband has lost anything, Miss Bromfield, you can rest assured that it was purposely done.''

Alison's only response was to glare at her all the harder. The corner's of Ryan's mouth turned up into an appreciative expression of humor. Cara blanched inwardly at the verbal battle taking place, for she was made uncomfortable by conflict of any kind.

The rather foppish young man serving as Alison's escort, only one of a large number of admirers she favored with her company whenever it suited her to do so, looked even more bored and sniffed, "Let us leave this place, my dear Miss Bromfield. Surely we may find more interesting pursuits with which to occupy our time.''

"An excellent suggestion,'' Ryan concurred with a faint, mocking smile. He turned his smoldering gaze back upon Alison and rigidly decreed, "You are indeed going to take your leave now, for I'll not allow you to do anything to spoil Connor's happiness!''

"As I said before, my darling Ryan, you possess neither the privilege nor the power to prevent me from going *where* I wish and doing *what* I wish!'' she countered with a haughtily defiant toss of her head. Her eyes glimmered with a malicious light as she suddenly rounded on Hillary again and demanded in a ringing voice that was easily heard by the entire assembly, "Tell me, *Mrs. Gallagher,* is it true that you hail from Tahiti? The women there still consider it a great honor to . . . well, to *expose* themselves to our gallant boys from New Bedford, do they not? Why, isn't it true that they actually swim *naked* out to the ships and—"

"Alison!" Ryan tersely cut her off. His blue-green eyes were ablaze as he took a menacing step toward her, but she merely flashed him a contemptuous smile. Though Hillary could feel her face burning as a chorus of startled gasps followed Alison's words, she lifted her head proudly. She was painfully aware of the shocked and curious stares being directed toward her by the Quakers, and she glimpsed Connor's visibly enraged features out of the corner of her eye.

"And isn't it also true," Alison continued, "that they still worship *graven images* there and still make human sacrifices to—"

"Damn you!" Ryan ground out. Hillary clutched at his arm in an effort to hold him back, for he appeared to be surrendering to the temptation to forcibly remove the malevolently troublesome Alison from the premises. Alison's aristocratic young squire, suddenly looking anything but bored, showed his true colors and hastily retreated a few steps in fear that he would be called upon to defend his ladylove against the tall, muscular whaler who appeared entirely capable of snapping him in two.

"Please, Ryan, don't!" pleaded Hillary. She was relieved when, after several tense moments, he successfully mastered his explosive fury and drew up before laying hands on the triumphantly smirking blonde. Hillary smiled up at him gratefully, then stepped forward herself. Lifting her head unashamedly once more, she met her adversary's gaze squarely and declared in a clear, steady tone, "Yes, Miss Bromfield, Tahiti *is* my home. While it is true that the Tahitian culture differs greatly from yours, it is *not* true that the people there are any more heathen or immoral than a great many of their 'civilized' counterparts!"

"Come now, my dear," Alison responded in a voice dripping with further sarcasm, "surely you aren't presuming to compare *us* to those savages you have lived amongst for—"

"The only savages I ever encountered there had come from other parts of the world."

"Indeed? Tell me then, Mrs. Gallagher, are you by any chance including *whalers* in that ridiculous assessment—*New Bedford* whalers?"

"Yes, Miss Bromfield, I am," Hillary replied without hesitation. She could hear the sudden murmur that rose from the crowd of onlookers standing nearby. "As a very wise and very dear friend once saw fit to remind me, there are both good and bad among *all* men."

"And among all *women*," Ryan added pointedly. He moved to Hillary's side once more and placed a protective arm about her shoulders. "You're not welcome here, Alison," he quietly reiterated. "Your little plan has backfired, for you've succeeded only in making a fool of yourself."

"You're the only fool here, Ryan Gallagher!" she spat at him. Her fury-heightened color deepened as her virulent gaze sliced to Hillary, then back to Ryan. "It won't be long before you realize just how much of a fool you really are!" With that, she whirled about and flounced away amidst a flurry of peach-blossom silk, with her cowardly swain trailing close behind.

Connor was the first to break the heavy silence that

hung in the warm, sweetly scented air after their departure. Determined to deny Alison Bromfield the satisfaction of ruining the festivities, he called out to Ryan, "Perhaps, Captain Gallagher, it's time I told everyone about your wedding gift!" All eyes turned to Connor, and he smiled broadly as he disclosed, "Bethany has gone and married herself a whaling master!"

His declaration was greeted by a renewed burst of congratulations and best wishes, and it wasn't long before nearly everyone had put the recent unpleasantness from their minds. They returned to the joyful business at hand—celebrating the beginning of a new life for Connor and Bethany.

On their way home later, Ryan comforted his wife with the reassurance that Alison would not be inclined to repeat such unsuccessful tactics, while Cara cheerfully asserted that anyone even remotely familiar with Alison's ill-behaved ways knew better than to lend any credence to whatever she said.

Although Hillary promised to try to forget about what had happened, she found that she was unable to do so. There was something about Alison Bromfield, something in the woman's eyes, that made her think Alison was capable of causing far more serious trouble than the mischief she had brewed thus far.

"I'm not at all certain David would approve of something so . . . well, something quite so frivolous!" Cara remarked with a rather self-conscious laugh. She held the morning dress of fine French cambric before her again and critically examined her reflection in the shop's large cheval glass. "What do you think?" she asked Hillary.

"It is my opinion that David will like it very much

indeed," Hillary replied, her violet eyes sparkling across at the other woman as she came to stand beside her. "It's a lovely dress, Cara, and will be even more so when worn without a crinoline or a great many undergarments."

"Why, Hillary!" breathed Cara in shocked disbelief. She blushed rosily and stammered, "I . . . I couldn't possibly think of . . . of going about like that!"

"You could wear it when you're alone with your husband," Hillary suggested with a teasing smile. "I'm sure he would be delighted. After all, his leg is improving very rapidly now, is it not?" A significant twinkle was evident within the bright amethyst depths of her gaze, and Cara blushed again. Hillary laughed softly and remarked, "One of the first things I intend to do upon my return to Tahiti is get rid of these dreadful corsets and hooped petticoats, and slip into a *pareu!*"

"A what?" Cara asked in bafflement.

"A *pareu*," repeated Hillary. "It's actually nothing more than a piece of cloth that is wound about the body and knotted. It's very comfortable, and completely unrestricting, as well as being perfectly suited to the climate."

"Good heavens!" Cara's blue eyes grew very wide as she then queried, "Do you wear so . . . so little all the time?"

"No," Hillary admitted with another laugh. "Only when I'm working about the house or in the fields."

"But, don't you have servants?"

"Yes, of a sort. But things are very different there. Everyone must lend a hand in order for Starcross to survive. Although Tahiti is a paradise, life there presents a considerable challenge for those of us who run the plantations."

"I see," Cara murmured politely, though she didn't really see at all. Since she had spent the entirety of her life in New Bedford, she knew little of the outside world. She had never been terribly curious to learn more, for everything she cared about was there in the city that lay on the Acushnet River.

They left the shop soon thereafter and began strolling down the uncrowded, sun-warmed walk toward the milliner's establishment. Cara was already regretting her impulsive purchase of the morning gown, though Hillary continued to assure her that David would approve. Neither one of them noticed the two large, burly men who had suddenly begun following them.

"Are you sure it's her?" Josiah doubtfully asked the man striding along beside him. His black brows drew together in a frown as he stroked his beard and looked uncomfortable.

"It's her, all right," Ewan insisted. "Now come on, damn it! It won't hurt to say hello, will it? From what I've heard, the captain's family didn't take too kindly to him bringing her back with him. Seems to me she'll be mighty glad to see a friendly face or two."

"All right, all right!" grumbled Josiah. In truth, he was every bit as anxious as Ewan to find out how the captain's lady was faring. Though he would never admit it to anyone, he had grown rather fond of her. After all, she *was* the first and only female he had ever allowed in his galley.

The recipient of this dubious honor was at that moment preparing to enter the millinery shop with Cara. Hillary had done no more than gather up her full skirts to step through the doorway, when a ramshackle-looking coach suddenly came rattling around the corner and drew to an abrupt halt immediately behind her. She and Cara both turned at the sound, only to watch in startled disbelief as two men burst from the coach and lunged for them.

"Dear God, what—" Cara gasped out. A filthy hand was clamped across her mouth, and she slumped in terror against the man who started dragging her toward the coach.

"Not that one, you stupid bastard! The black-haired bitch is the only one we want!" growled the second man, who was being met with unexpectedly forceful resistance from Hillary. She squirmed violently and flailed at him with her fists, and she managed to twist her head about so that she could sink her teeth into the hand across her mouth. Her assailant swore and jerked his hand away, at which time Hillary drew in a ragged breath and screamed.

Help arrived sooner than she had hoped. Josiah and Ewan, who had started barreling down the walk at the first sign of trouble, wasted no time in laying hands on Cara's and Hillary's would-be abductors. Ewan literally tore the man till holding Cara away from her and sent him crashing back against the red brick wall of the millinery shop. Josiah bodily lifted Hillary's attacker and flung him to the ground, then lifted him again by the front of his coarse flannel shirt and dealt him a bloodying punch to his unguarded face.

"Josiah!" Hillary whispered in amazement as she stumbled back against the building. Her gaze flew to Cara, who had unfortunately somehow managed to insert herself between Ewan and the other man. The man took advantage of Cara's terrified confusion, for he seized her and thrust her forcibly against Ewan. A breathless shriek escaped Cara's lips as Ewan, surprised by the villain's strategy, instinctively steadied her. The man flung himself back into the coach, and the driver snapped the whip above the horses' heads.

The man's comrade, meanwhile, grew desperate when he saw the coach rolling away without him. Pulling a knife from within his boot, he slashed wildly at Josiah. The blade glinted in the sunlight for an instant before slicing down into the corded flesh of the black-bearded cook's left arm. Josiah muttered an oath and grabbed at his arm. Hillary cried out and rushed to his side as the man with the knife ran after the coach and managed to get himself inside it before it disappeared down a side street.

"Oh Josiah, your . . . your arm's bleeding very badly!" Hillary gasped out. She bent and hastily tore a strip from her petticoat, then wrapped it about his wound. "We're got to get you to a doctor right away!"

"I don't need no doctor!" Josiah irritably dissented.

"Got any idea who those scuttling cutthroats were?" Ewan quietly asked his friend as Hillary moved to comfort a badly shaken Cara.

"No, but I sure as hell aim to find out!" He breathed another curse before he and Ewan turned back to the women.

"Are you all right, ma'am?" Ewan's question was obviously meant to include both of them, but Hillary was the only one to answer.

"Yes," she said, placing a supportive arm about Cara's trembling shoulders. "We're fine. Thank God you came along when you did!"

"Oh Hillary, what . . . what could have prompted those . . . those awful men to do such a thing?" Cara gasped out in dazed horror.

"I don't know, Cara. I don't know." She swallowed

hard, and tears sprang to her eyes as she turned back to the two burly whalers. "How can we ever repay you for what you did? If you hadn't . . . hadn't—"

"Why, ma'am, your husband would have had us drawn and quartered if we'd stood by and let you get taken!" declared Ewan, making light of what they had done.

"We ought to go tell the captain, just in case those ugly bas . . . those blackguards take it in mind to try something else!" Josiah ground out. Hillary's gaze clouded with worriment as she glimpsed the bright red stain spreading across the makeshift bandage on his arm.

"We shall do just that, Josiah, but not until after we've had a doctor look at your arm!" she firmly decreed. She gave Cara over into Ewan's care and charged him with seeing Ryan's sister-in-law home in the Gallagher carriage. Then, she slipped her arm through Josiah's uninjured one and teasingly challenged, "There was a time when you'd probably have been glad to see me spirited away, wasn't there?" Josiah's lips twitched, and his eyes filled with begrudging admiration for her indomitable spirit.

"You're a feisty one, Mrs. Gallagher," he gruffly proclaimed. "A right feisty one!" She smiled up at him and led him away to hail a carriage.

Two hours later, she and Josiah finally arrived at the Gallagher Shipping Office. Josiah insisted upon waiting in the crowded outer room while Hillary saw her husband alone first. She raised her hand to knock upon his door, but her hand paused in midair when she heard a familiar, decidedly feminine voice from within. Her eyes grew round as saucers, and her heart twisted painfully within her breast.

Alison! There was no mistaking that voice. Alison Bromfield was in Ryan's office!

Hillary swung open the door and swept inside with a vengeance. Alison and Ryan were alone, and they stared at her in astonishment as she virtually slammed the door behind her.

"Wha . . . what are *you* doing here?" Alison breathlessly demanded, her surprise obviously much greater than Ryan's. She had been seated in a chair opposite his desk, but she now rose abruptly to her feet.

"I might ask you the same thing!" retorted Hillary, her violet eyes ablaze as they raked over the other woman.

"Blast it, Hillary, I thought I told you not to come down here anymore!" Ryan angrily reminded her. He rounded his desk and strode forward to confront her. "What the devil do you mean, storming in here like that?"

"I'm sorry, dearest husband, if I *disturbed* you!" she proclaimed with bitter sarcasm, not the least bit intimidated by the fact that he was towering ominously above her. "I had no idea you were entertaining old friends this afternoon!"

"It so happens that Alison and I are discussing an important business matter!"

"Business?" Hillary echoed in obvious disbelief. Her jealousy and sense of betrayal had driven all thought of the attempted kidnapping from her mind. Fresh tears stung against her eyelids, and she fairly trembled with the force of her anger. "You lied to me, Ryan Gallagher! You promised me you would have nothing else to do with her!"

"That's enough, damn it!" His own eyes filled with an answering fire as his hands shot out to close with bruising force upon her shoulders. "And lower

413

your voice! Do you want every blasted man out there to hear you?'' he added curtly, jerking his head in the direction of the outer room.

"Why shouldn't they hear?" Alison interjected with a scornfully complacent smile. "After all, the whole town will know sooner or later, won't they? Poor Ryan, you cannot hope to keep the truth about your disastrous marriage a secret forever!"

"Shut up, Alison!" he snapped, then told Hillary more evenly, "I'm sorry if it appears I broke my promise, but—"

"Appears?" She gave a short, humorless laugh, her eyes flashing up at him resentfully. "Are you offering *that* particular excuse again, the one wherein you claim that appearances are oh-so-deceiving?" She knew she was allowing her turbulent emotions to provoke her to irrationality once more, but she could not seem to help it.

"I'm not offering any excuses at all," he declared in a dangerously low tone. His own eyes were glinting dully now, and there was a foreboding tightness about his handsome, sun-bronzed features as his hands dropped from her shoulders. "As I said, Alison and I are conducting business."

"I thought you allowed no women in this office!" she caustically parried. Her eyes narrowed and filled with unavoidable suspicion as she looked at Alison and challenged, "I was not aware, Miss Bromfield, that it was your custom to personally handle your business affairs!"

"Oh but it *is*, my dear, especially when the *affairs* concern Ryan!" the tall blonde retorted archly, casting a meaningful smirk in his direction before her disdainful gaze traveled back to Hillary. "And we were having a pleasant discussion indeed before we were so rudely interrupted! It is beyond my comprehension how Ryan can abide such a shrewish, overly possessive—!''

"Blast it, Alison, I said that's enough!'' Ryan ground out as he shot her a quelling glare. His emotions warred within him as he struggled once again to maintain control over his flaring temper. Seizing hold of his wife's arms, he demanded, "Just what the devil *are* you doing here?''

"What difference does it make?'' countered Hillary, her violet eyes clouded with pain. "I arrive to find you closeted—*alone*—in your office with the woman you swore never to see again, and all you can say is that you had business to conduct!''

"For the simple reason that it's the truth. Damn it, woman, if you haven't learned by now that I—''

"The only thing I've learned, Ryan Gallagher, is that you . . . you are not to be trusted!''

"Hillary, I'm warning you!'' he seethed, his fingers biting into her flesh.

"And *I'm* warning you!'' she flung back at him as the hot tears finally began spilling over from her lashes. "Don't lie to me anymore, Ryan Gallagher! If you want to be with . . . with *her*, then at least tell me the truth so that I can—'' She broke off with a gasp as he gave her a decidedly ungentle shake and appeared to be battling the temptation to do a good deal more than that.

Hillary felt something within her snap—something that had nothing whatsoever to do with Ryan's manhandling—as the lingering, traumatic effects of the attack upon her and Cara combined with the equally disturbing emotions brought about by the discovery of Alison Bromfield in Ryan's office.

"Let go of me, damn you!'' she raged. Then, with swift and unexpected vehemence, she twisted free of Ryan's grasp and dealt him a stinging blow across his handsome face. She wrenched open the door and sped from the room, her silken skirts and lace-edged petticoats flying up about her trim, booted ankles as she rushed headlong past the startled eyes of the men in the outer room. She was too distraught to notice Josiah, who scowled worriedly and was about to follow after her when he caught sight of her husband.

Hillary disappeared outside just as Ryan stalked from his office and thundered, "Hillary! Damn it, Hillary, come back here!" Oblivious to the group of whalers and would-be whalers who were providing an audience for this fascinating display of marital strife, he muttered a blistering oath and headed for the door to give chase. When he finally emerged into the bright sunshine, it was only to see his wife riding away in a hired carriage.

"Begging your pardon, Captain," Josiah suddenly spoke behind him, "but—"

"What the devil do *you* want?" Ryan demanded fierily as he wheeled about to face the burly cook. His smoldering gaze filled with recognition, and he released a long, pent-up sigh. "What are you doing here, Josiah?"

"I came with Mrs. Gallagher," the older man answered gruffly. "I didn't think you'd want me to be letting her come alone. And after what happened to her and the other—"

"What the bloody hell are you talking about?"

"Those bastards who tried to—" Josiah started to reply, then broke off and asked with another fierce scowl, "Didn't she tell you?"

"Tell me *what*, damn it!" Ryan growled in furious bewilderment.

"Two men tried to snatch her and your brother's wife—tried to snatch them right off the streets, they did. Ewan and me saw what was happening and jumped in, but we . . . well, we wasn't able to catch the oily bastards! They got away in a coach.''

"Were either of the women hurt?" Ryan demanded in a deceptively level tone, his handsome countenance becoming a mask of white-hot fury.

"Didn't seem to be," Josiah answered with an accompanying shake of his head. "The other one looked to be pretty shook-up, but your little lady kept a cool head. You'd have been right proud of her, Captain."

Ryan swore again as he wondered what could have prompted the attempted abduction. He thought of the men who had dared to attack Hillary and Cara, and his eyes glowed with a savagely vengeful light as he asked in a low, simmering tone, "Did either you or Ewan get a good look at their faces? And what about the coach? Is there any chance you'd be able to—"

"It all happened too damned fast," Josiah reluctantly disclosed as he shook his head once more.

"What was that?" Alison suddenly queried as she swept forward to join them outside. Feigning only mild interest, she smiled coolly and asked, "Did I hear you say something has happened?"

"It's nothing that concerns you, damn it!" Ryan tersely declared. Infuriated by the way she had purposely goaded Hillary a few moments earlier, he frowned darkly and told her, "Go home where you belong, Alison. Tell your father I'll see that he gets his share of the profits in the next day or so." As usual, Ebenezer Bromfield had invested a small amount in the Gallaghers' ventures—a very small amount, since he had little regard for the business of whaling.

"But Ryan, my dear, perhaps there's something I can do—" she sweetly offered.

"You've done enough, Alison," muttered Ryan,

his fiery, blue-green gaze shifting back to where he'd last seen Hillary riding away in the carriage. "You've done quite enough!"

Priscilla Gallagher's treasured grandfather clock —which had, appropriately enough, been brought from Europe by her grandfather a century ago—had just begun chiming the hour of six o'clock in the evening when Hillary finally returned home. Feeling tired and dispirited, she moved with heavy steps toward the staircase, only to find her path suddenly and quite effectively barred by Ryan.

"*Where have you been?*" he ground out. His handsome features were contorted with barely suppressed fury, and his eyes were virtually shooting sparks as he stood looming over his recalcitrant wife.

"Nowhere," she evasively murmured, refusing to meet his gaze.

"Damn it, Hillary, I spent the entire afternoon looking all over town for you, and I've been waiting *here* for over an hour! Now I demand to know where the devil you've been!"

"I . . . I needed to be alone. I went for a walk." She had dismissed the carriage soon after leaving Ryan's office. And though she had walked until she could walk no more, she had found that it hadn't helped— she still remembered Ryan's broken promise, and she still felt as though she had been betrayed.

"For a walk? Dear God, woman, don't you realize how worried I've been about you?" After what Josiah had told him, he had been tormented with visions of a second attack. He had set out to find her right away, not only to ensure her safety, but also to try to explain about Alison.

"Mother, is Uncle Ryan going to yell at Aunt

418

Hillary for a long time?" Jimmy asked loudly, his childish voice drifting outward from the parlor.

Cara could be heard shushing him, at which time Bridget chimed in, "Grandmother says Uncle Ryan and Aunt Hillary are not com...com...*combatible!* Is that true, Mother?" the six-year-old demanded to know.

Cara's face flamed, for she was painfully aware of the fact that Ryan and Hillary were right outside the room and could no doubt hear what the children had said. Lowering her own voice to an undertone, she threatened both of her little darlings with an early bedtime if they did not keep quiet and turn their attention back to the new books their grandmother had just given them. Then, she hurried to close the parlor doors so that, even if Jimmy and Bridget surrendered to further bursts of curiosity, they would not be overheard.

Ryan and Hillary, meanwhile, stood silent and still at the foot of the staircase. Ryan stared long and hard at his wife, while her eyes remained stubbornly downcast. Finally, his gaze softened, and he quietly muttered a curse before reaching out and drawing her close. Though she did not resist, she was stiff and unyielding as she came against him.

"I heard about what happened. Why the devil didn't you tell me?" he gently scolded.

"Because you were *occupied* when I came to do so!" she recalled, her weary voice holding unmistakable evidence of her lingering pain and bitterness. She fought back a fresh wave of tears as her head rested against Ryan's broad chest.

"I told you the truth, Hillary," he reiterated, his arms tightening about her. "Alison came to the shipping office to discuss a matter of business. Ebenezer usually sends his solicitor, but it seems the man's gone up to Boston for a few days. Though she did make an attempt to turn the visit into a social call, I would not allow her to do so. As a matter of fact, we were just concluding our discussion when you arrived."

"Then why did you act so guilty when I—"

"Guilty? Hardly that, my love. I was just so surprised to see you, and, damn it, I was angry with you for disobeying me again!"

"I didn't come there alone. Josiah was with me. He . . . he was injured while helping me."

"Injured?" he repeated with a frown. "He didn't tell me he'd been hurt. I spoke with him right after you left the office." He sighed heavily, and his voice was tinged with huskiness as he said, "If I'd only known what you'd been through, I . . . well, I wouldn't have blown up at you the way I did."

"Oh Ryan, I never really had the opportunity to tell you *anything* before you started ranting and raving at me!" she insisted, raising her tear-streaked face to his at last.

"I suppose I did rant and rave a bit, didn't I?" he conceded with a soft chuckle. His eyes glowed with a captivating radiance as they gazed deeply into the sparkling amethyst depths of hers. "But I seem to recall a certain beautiful, tempestuous young woman who burst into my office without warning, then proceeded to rake me over the coals in front of another woman who no doubt enjoyed the spectacle very much indeed! And knowing Alison as I do, the news of our 'matrimonial discord' will probably be all over town by this time tomorrow!"

"I don't care!" Hillary proclaimed defiantly. "She can say whatever she likes, just as long as I know she truly means nothing to you! Oh Ryan, she *doesn't* mean anything to you, does she? I mean, you . . . you really *are* telling me the truth about her, aren't you?"

There was such a vulnerable, entreating look on her face that Ryan felt the last vestiges of his anger evaporating. He smiled down at her tenderly and declared, "I love only you, Mrs. Gallagher. I'll do whatever it takes to convince you of that."

"Then do you promise—*again*—to have no further contact with Alison Bromfield?" she obstinately persisted.

"If the contact is at all avoidable, yes. Hell, sweetheart, I couldn't very well throw her out of the office today!" he remarked with another low, disarming chuckle.

"I would have been more than happy to perform the honors myself!" retorted Hillary.

"I'll bet you would at that!"

In the next instant, Hillary found herself being thoroughly kissed by her maddeningly irresistible husband. She moaned softly and wound her arms about his neck, her lips parting beneath his . . .

Cara, aware of the lengthening silence on the other side of the parlor doors, mistakenly believed that Ryan and Hillary had taken their quarrel upstairs. She therefore opened the doors with the intention of taking Jimmy and Bridget back to the west wing of the house. The two children scampered from the parlor ahead of their mother, only to draw up short at the astonishing sight of their Uncle Ryan holding their Aunt Hillary so tightly they were sure she would be flattened.

"Golly Moses, Uncle Ryan, you shouldn't ought to—" Jimmy started to adominish with precocious, four-year-old severity.

"James Ryan Gallagher, not another word!" exhorted Cara, coloring with embarrassment as she hastily averted her gaze from the entwined lovers.

"Come along, the both of you!" she told her children, then quickly herded them down the hallway that led to the kitchen.

Ryan, who had refused to let his blushing wife go even after they had been caught in the midst of their embrace, was about to resume the pleasurable blending of their mouths when his mother and youngest sister suddenly came sailing down the stairs together. They, too, appeared quite shocked by the "public" display of affection taking place at the foot of the staircase.

Priscilla drew herself rigidly erect and charged, "My dear son, could not you and your *wife* at least have had the decency to wait until you were alone for such . . . such—"

"It's called kissing, Mother," quipped Ryan, a devilish twinkle in his blue-green eyes. "I know you're familiar with the custom, madam—I believe myself to be perfect evidence of such knowledge."

His words elicited a giggle from Erin, but it was obvious that Priscilla did not share her daughter's amusement. Hillary's cheeks flamed as she groaned inwardly and pushed against Ryan. He reluctantly released her at last, then turned to face the two women who had by this time descended the remaining steps.

"I should like to have a word with you in the parlor, if you do not mind," his mother solemnly requested of him, her icy gray gaze purposely excluding Hillary.

"Of course," he readily agreed, though he grasped his wife's hand and started leading her toward the parlor with him.

"No, Ryan, I . . . I've things to do upstairs," Hillary told him, anxious to excuse herself from what she suspected would be yet another unpleasant confrontation. She smiled up at him and added, "Besides, I would welcome the chance to rest before supper." Relieved when neither he nor anyone else objected, she beat a hasty retreat up the stairs.

Once in the room she and Ryan shared at the very top of the house, she rang for Agnes and began undressing. She was glad of the fire's warmth, for there was a chill in the room, in spite of the fact that it was still early in the evening. Slipping on her wrapper and knotting the sash at her waist, she wandered over to the window and gazed outward as twilight crept upon the city.

Reflecting that Alison Bromfield had disrupted her happiness—if only briefly—yet again, Hillary sighed and reached up a hand to absently finger the curtains. Her troubled thoughts drifted back over all the startling events of the day.

Why had those men tried to abduct her? Could it have been because they harbored some sort of grudge against the Gallaghers—or even against Ryan in particular? Or was it possibly because they had hoped somehow to profit from the abduction? Whatever the case, she gave silent thanks once more for the fact that Josiah and Ewan had come along in time. She would never forget what they had done for her and Cara.

"Would you be wanting your bath now, ma'am?" Agnes suddenly queried from the doorway. Though she had knocked lightly first, apparently her young mistress had been too lost in thought to hear.

"Yes, thank you, Agnes." Hillary smiled at the petite redhead, then released another sigh as Agnes hurried to do her bidding.

A short time later, the ornately decorated, metal hip bath had been set before the fire and filled with steaming hot water. Hillary waited a few minutes for the water to cool somewhat, then eased herself down into its soothing warmth. Taking up the cake of lavender-scented soap and the sponge Agnes had provided, she scrubbed at her naked body until her skin was pink and glowing. She was in the process of rinsing away the last of the soap when Agnes returned with yet another large kettle of hot water.

"I thought you might welcome a bit more," the little maid explained with a congenial grin. She padded her hand with a piece of toweling from the kitchen and tipped the bottom of the kettle up to carefully add the water to the bath.

Without warning, the door swung open behind her, and the sudden rush of cool air made Hillary shiver and sink lower into the water's warmth. She folded her arms across her breasts in an instinctive reaction to the unexpected intrusion, and her eyes grew very round when she heard Ryan drawl lazily, "It seems I've come at a decidedly opportune moment."

Agnes, meanwhile, drew in her breath upon a startled gasp and flushed crimson to the very roots of her copper hair. Shocked and embarrassed at being in the same room with a man and his naked-as-the-day-she-was-born wife, the little maid very nearly dropped the kettle into the bath water. She hastily regained control of it, set it on the floor beside the tub, dipped a quick curtsy to Hillary, cast another wide-eyed look at Ryan, then fled the room in a whirl of gray skirts and starched white petticoats. Ryan laughed softly as the door closed resoundingly after her.

"Oh Ryan, you . . . you shocked poor Agnes terribly!" Hillary breathlessly exclaimed, her violet eyes glimmering with wifely reproach.

"Then poor Agnes will simply have to accustom

herself to the fact that you've a husband who will not let anything, including the state of his wife's dress— or *undress*, as the case may be—keep him from this room when it is his desire to enter it!'' he decreed with another low chuckle.

He sauntered closer to where she still sat in the tub, and Hillary could not fail to notice the direction of his burning gaze as it lit upon the glistening swell of her naked breasts above her crossed arms. A warm flush stole over her, though her heightened color, unlike Agnes's, had nothing whatsoever to do with embarrassment.

"I . . . I did not expect your discussion with your mother to end so soon,'' she murmured in a small voice.

"It wasn't much of a discussion, really. She tried a new tactic to persuade me to abandon my 'disastrous' plans to settle in Tahiti, but her efforts met with no more success than her previous ones.'' He negligently folded his arms across his chest and stood staring down at her with unnerving—and highly stimulating —intensity as the firelight played across the rugged planes of his sun-bronzed features.

"What exactly was her new . . . tactic?'' Hillary asked with another shiver. Her long hair was tied high upon her head with a red velvet ribbon, and the shimmering ebony curls appeared almost blue-black in the fire's soft glow.

"She insisted I must provide Jimmy with the same opportunity given me by my Uncle Seamus—to serve as cabin boy under my command. And since it will be at least another nine or ten years before my dear nephew is of an age to go to sea . . .'' There was no need to finish the sentence, for the implications were clear. His lips curved into a slow, tenderly mocking smile, and his eyes took on even more of a beguiling gleam as he said in a low tone brimming with humor, "I'm sure that water is beginning to get cold by now, my love."

Hillary's face grew rosier, and another shiver ran the length of her spine before she replied, "Yes, it . . . it *is* turning a bit chilly." Her eyes widened as she watched Ryan unfold his arms and reach for the large, thick towel Agnes had draped across a chair to warm before the fire.

"Stand up," he commanded softly. Not in the least bit inclined to disobey, Hillary rose to her feet in the hip bath. Her wide, luminous gaze met and locked with Ryan's, and she slowly uncrossed her own arms from against her naked breasts. Standing proud and unashamed before her husband, she was rewarded for her boldness when he stepped forward and willingly performed the task of drying her glistening, gloriously revealed body.

With tantalizing unhaste, he brought the towel smoothing gently across the satiny curve of her shoulders . . . down along the graceful curve of her back . . . across the entrancing roundness of her buttocks and her pale, quivering thighs . . .

The soft glow of passion filled Hillary's violet eyes, and a delicious tremor shook her. She caught her breath upon a gasp when Ryan suddenly straightened again and transferred his loving attentions to her breasts. Her knees grew perilously weak, and she caught at her bottom lip with her teeth to stifle a moan when the towel was rubbed lightly over each satiny, rose-tipped globe . . . downward across the silken smoothness of her belly . . . then further downward to the beckoning triangle of black, velvety curls between her thighs . . .

"Oh!" she gasped out as the softness of the towel was suddenly replaced by the demanding warmth of

426

her husband's fingers. Her eyes swept closed, and her hands instinctively clutched at the support of his broad shoulders. She held tight to him while her head swam dizzily and her passions went careening wildly upward. Then, before she quite knew what was happening, Ryan swept her from the tub and lowered her gently to the rug in front of the fire.

Warmed by the heat emitted from the flames dancing beneath the mantel, as well as by the flames her beloved had so skillfully created within her, Hillary remained happily oblivious to the encroaching chill in the room. She moaned low in her throat when Ryan, having quickly discarded his own clothing, brought his hard, lean-muscled flesh into extremely pleasurable contact with her womanly softness. His lips descended upon hers with an enchanting mixture of tenderness and urgency.

"Oh Ryan! Ryan!" she breathed a few moments later, her head tossing restlessly to and fro as his mouth began trailing a searing path downward. His sensuously persuasive lips traveled from where her pulse beat so alarmingly in the hollow of her throat to where her beautiful, firm breasts, turned a soft golden hue by the firelight, seemed to be inviting his caress.

His warm, eagerly obliging mouth first pressed a succession of light, provocative kisses across the tops of her breasts, then dipped lower so that his velvety tongue could flick erotically across the sensitive, rosy flesh of her nipples. She cried out softly and threaded her fingers within the thickness of Ryan's sun-streaked brown hair, and her entire body trembled as she instinctively strained upward. While his lips paid loving tribute to her breasts, his hands explored the secrets of her curves. His warm, questing fingers prompted her to moan and gasp anew when they searched out the feminine treasure concealed beneath the petals of softness at the apex of her supple thighs.

By the time his lips finally returned to drink deeply of the sweetness of hers once more, she was almost totally incapable of coherent thought, for the wild yearnings had built to a fever pitch deep within her. Ryan prolonged the splendid agony no longer. He positioned himself above her and gripped her hips with his two large hands, then brought his masculine hardness sheathing expertly within her silken, honeyed warmth. When he began a slow, evocative rotation of his own hips, Hillary clung to him as if she were drowning, and her shapely limbs tightened about him as their passions soared heavenward in the firelight. The ultimate blending of their bodies proved even more rapturous and richly satisfying than either of them could have hoped . . .

Later, after the bath water had grown quite cold indeed, they stood together on the widow's walk and gazed up at the first twinkling stars of the night, just as they had done upon several other occasions. That particular night, however, was different—or at least it seemed so to Hillary. In spite of the wondrous ecstasy she and Ryan had shared only a short time earlier, she became aware of a vague sense of uneasiness. Though she told herself it was undoubtedly prompted by what had happened to her and Cara, she could not shake the strange, inexplicable feeling of anxiousness.

"Well, my love, I suppose we'd best make an appearance downstairs," murmured Ryan. Like her, he was already dressed for the evening meal. He pulled her back against him, his strong arms encircling her from behind as his magnificent turquoise gaze drifted leisurely over the darkening landscape below.

"Oh Ryan, must we? I'd much rather stay out here with you," she confessed. She sighed and snuggled contentedly back against him, determinedly banishing all unpleasantness from her mind.

Her husband's eyes lit with a roguish twinkle, and his deep voice was laced with sardonic amusement as he replied, "I'm willing to risk further disapproval if you are. I doubt if we could shock them any more than we already have!"

Hillary laughed softly and drew him back inside.

XVII

David Gallagher was elated to be getting out of the house at last. The doctor had granted him permission—albeit reluctantly—to accompany the rest of the Gallaghers to the picnic being held that day at the home of Cara's parents. It had been more than three weeks since his unfortunate encounter with the boiling hot cauldron of whale oil, and he had begun to fear he could not endure so much as another day of the boredom and inactivity forced upon him.

Cara and the children were nearly as excited as he, for though he was normally an even-tempered and fair-minded man, his restiveness had made being in his company something of a trial. But his leg was now pronounced free of infection and healing nicely, and they all knew it would not be long before he would be able to resume his duties at the shipping office.

The day promised to be a pleasant one. The brilliant blue canvas of the summer sky was dotted by only a few wispy clouds, while a cool, gentle breeze rustled the leaves of the maple and horse chestnut trees that lined the avenues on the hill above town.

It was only mid-morning when David and the

eight other Gallaghers, attired in their most comfortable yet undeniably elegant clothing, set out for the picnic. Jimmy and Bridget chattered animatedly, Priscilla gazed indulgently upon her grandchildren, Gillian looked completely disinterested, Erin smiled secretively to herself in anticipation of the many flirtations she intended to conduct, while Cara and David happily surveyed the passing scenery and exchanged comments about what their eyes beheld.

Hillary, glad to be riding beside Ryan in a second carriage, raised her face toward the sun's warmth and inhaled deeply of the sweetly scented air. She was looking forward to the picnic at Cara's childhood home very much. Her spirits were high, and she felt certain that the day would turn out to be as enjoyable as she hoped. Ryan apparently shared her enthusiasm, for he turned and flashed her a boyish grin, then drew her arm possessively through his.

There were a good many carriages rolling along the cobbled streets that morning, and most of them were also headed for the Ludlows' mansion a few miles outside of town. More than two hundred people had been invited to the affair, and it was expected that nearly all of them would attend. Not only was the Ludlows' country estate a lovely, peaceful place far from the bustle of the city, but the Ludlows themselves—Captain Horatio Ludlow and his wife, Susan—were renowned for their warm hospitality.

Hillary was delighted to find their destination every bit as beautiful as Cara's description had led her to believe it would be. The mansion itself was a sprawling, Colonial-style structure with massive white columns and a front verandah larger than the entire lower floor of the house at Starcross. There were blazes of color everywhere, for the three-storied building was surrounded by all kinds of trees and flowering shrubs and other greenery. The large, circular drive in front of the house was already crowded with carriages. The liverymen were busy tending to the horses, all of which would be sheltered in the Ludlows' stables for the duration of the all-day picnic.

Cara's parents stood waiting on the verandah to greet their arriving guests. Hillary gathered up the skirts of her white, embroidered muslin gown and smiled at Ryan, who swung her down effortlessly from the carriage and escorted her up the front steps of the house. It seemed she was to be introduced to the Ludlows even before they had bid either their daughter or their grandchildren or any of the other Gallaghers welcome. Though she did not know it, Ryan was merely following the old New England custom of presenting an unfamiliar guest first.

"Welcome to our home, my dear!" Susan Ludlow proclaimed once Ryan had made the introductions. Her kindly features were wreathed in a truly welcoming smile as she took Hillary's hand between both of hers. A slender, dark-haired woman of slightly less than average height, she was approaching fifty years of age but looked ten years younger. Her balding, blond-haired husband towered above her. Well over six feet in height, Horatio Ludlow was one of the tallest men Hillary had ever seen.

"It's about time we got a look at the little girl who married the *second* best whaling master New Bedford's ever seen!" the retired captain remarked in a deep, booming voice that evoked images of what he must have looked like standing on a quarterdeck and thundering orders to the men below.

"Second?" echoed Ryan, casting the older man a good-naturedly challenging frown.

433

"The truth hurts, doesn't it, my boy?" Horatio retorted with an answering twinkle in his eyes. He and Ryan chuckled in unison and shook hands.

Ryan took Hillary by the arm and led her into the house while Jimmy and Bridget, nearly bursting with impatience, were finally set free upon their grandparents. The children hurled themselves up the steps and into the outstretched arms of the delighted Ludlows. Cara gave a maternal shake of her head before she and David followed up the steps after their rambunctious offspring. Priscilla and Susan were soon greeting each other like the old friends they were, leaving Gillian and Erin to find their own way through the house and to the sight of the picnic behind the mansion.

Hillary was enchanted by the scene unfolding before her eyes as she and Ryan emerged from the house and stepped out into the sunshine once more. The spacious, gently rolling grounds were mantled in freshly cut grass and shaded by periodic groves of tall trees. A family of ducks glided peacefully across the waters of a small lake surrounded by half a dozen white, wrought-iron benches. It appeared that most of the guests had already arrived, for the area was alive with sound and movement. The ladies present were clad predominantly in white, and many of them twirled lace-trimmed parasols over their shoulders as they strolled leisurely about with their escorts. The men sported summer suits of lightweight serge, while the numerous children who laughed and scampered gaily about were attired in frilly dresses and short pant suits that could not possibly make it through the day without being torn or stained or both.

Although it was not yet noon, a few of the adults were helping themselves to food and drink at the linen-covered tables set up just beyond the wide, open doorway at the rear of the mansion. An additional table was laden with quilts for the guests to spread upon the ground and sit on, for the Ludlows' annual picnic was designated as an "informal" gathering of friends and family.

"Connor and Bethany are here," Ryan informed her, acknowledging Connor's wave with a smile and a nod. Hillary's eyes swiftly followed the direction of his gaze, and she smiled as well when she caught sight of the newlyweds sitting near the lake. She and Ryan moved to join them, while the remaining Gallaghers finally emerged from the house and began mingling with the other guests.

"There's no need to ask how married life is treating you!" Ryan commented with a broad grin as his former first mate stood to shake hands.

"No need at all," agreed Connor, grinning back.

"I am so pleased thee has come," Bethany said to Hillary, who sank down beside her on the quilt and settled her white skirts about her. "Connor has told me thee and Captain Gallagher are planning to return to Tahiti soon." She looked very fresh and lovely in her light gray dress and matching bonnet, and Hillary could not fail to notice the happy glow in her wide, china blue eyes.

"Yes, we hope it will be very soon indeed," she confirmed with a warm smile.

"Is it truly as lovely there as Connor says?"

"Perhaps you will be able to judge for yourself someday. If you could but persuade your husband to bring you with him when next he sails for the South Pacific—" Hillary suggested with a smile that was only half teasing

"Don't go filling her head with ideas!" Connor interrupted with a quiet laugh. He and Ryan bent their tall frames and took their places beside the women on the soft, shaded ground.

"Why not?" Hillary countered with playful defiance. "I myself can vouch for the benefits of sailing with one's husband!"

"Yes, my love, but there are few wives with your determination and sense of adventure," asserted Ryan. Amusement flickered briefly over his handsome face before he added, "Besides which, you spent only a brief time on board the *Falcon*. To participate in an entire whaling cruise would require two or three years' time at sea."

"I wouldn't mind," she stubbornly maintained, her violet eyes aglow as they met the dancing, blue-green depths of his. "I would prefer being away from home over being separated from my husband, no matter how long I had to remain at sea!"

"And no matter *how* much your husband objected to the presence of women aboard his ship!" he pointedly reminded her.

"A wife, my dearest captain, is not merely a *woman*," she insisted with a proud toss of her raven curls.

"Then what, may I ask, have I gone and married?"

Connor, exchanging a merry smile with his own wife, gently cleared his throat and sought to introduce another topic of conversation. Relieved when his efforts met with success, he and Ryan and their beautiful young wives settled into a pleasant discussion about the unusually cooperative weather and the remembered activities of summers past.

It was nearly an hour later when Ryan and Hillary took their leave of the Reids and went to join David and Cara, who were seated with some friends on the opposite side of the lake. Jimmy and Bridget were frolicking with several of their cousins all about the grounds they knew so well, though Cara kept a mother's vigilant eyes upon them while she talked.

"Well, Ryan Gallagher, what's this rumor I've heard about your plans to leave New Bedford for good?" a middle-aged man by the name of Ichabod Broome asked as they approached the group.

A faint, mocking smile touched Ryan's lips, but he waited until he and Hillary had taken a seat before answering, "It's no rumor, Ichabod."

Musing that he had been acquainted with Ichabod Broome for nearly twenty years and had never yet known him to utter anything worth hearing, Ryan was not surprised when all the man could respond with was, "Surely you're not serious?"

"Tell me, Ichabod, have you by any chance been talking to my mother?" Ryan sardonically challenged.

"To your mother?" The other man looked greatly baffled. "Why, no, no. Should I have been?"

"You *are* serious about this, aren't you?" another man joined in with a snort of disbelief. He turned to David and said, "Haven't you tried to talk some sense into this brother of yours? Whoever heard of a New Bedford whaling master going off to live on a—"

"Ryan has made his decision," David quietly but firmly cut the man off. His piercing gaze, so much like his father's, moved to encompass everyone in the group. "And whatever he chooses to do, he has my support, *and* my blessing." He glanced over at Ryan, and the two brothers nodded at each other in silent understanding.

Soon, the others in the group drifted away, leaving the four Gallaghers alone. Ryan and David fell into a discussion about business, while Cara and Hillary talked of many things. Time passed quickly as the sun rose overhead and the morning wore on.

Captain Ludlow startled his guests when he signaled the hour of noon—and hence the official commencement of the meal—by vigorously ringing a ship's bell he had attached to one of the trees near the house. Men, women, and children converged on the tables, filled their plates, then returned to the actual business of picnicking under the trees.

Hillary and Ryan now dutifully joined Priscilla and Gillian. Erin had taken herself off to eat with several other girls her age, while Cara, along with the aid of her father, urged David to go inside for a while lest he overdo things on his first day out.

Alison Bromfield arrived—late as usual—with her father just as the guests settled down to the meal. Her gaze immediately searched out Ryan, and her green cat's eyes literally came alive with vengeful mischief. Leaving the dour Ebenezer deep in conversation with Captain Ludlow, she sailed regally across the grounds to where the object of her selfish desire sat alongside his wife, mother, and sister near the lake.

"Alison, my dear!" Priscilla Gallagher exclaimed with obvious pleasure. She stretched out a hand in welcome when she saw the tall blonde, clad in a multiruffled gown of pale blue dimity, bearing down upon them. Ryan's handsome features grew taut with annoyance as he nonetheless rose gallantly to his feet. Hillary felt a dull flush rising to her face, and a sudden knot tightened in her stomach. Gillian smiled to herself in malicious amusement for the "interesting" scene she knew to be forthcoming.

"How nice to see you all again!" purred Alison, casting Ryan a narrow look full of nuance as she sank down oh-so-gracefully upon the quilt beside his mother. She favored Hillary with a smug, disdainful smile as she made a great show of settling her skirts

438

about her. "Such a lovely day, isn't it?" she airily remarked to no one in particular, though her gaze flitted coquettishly back up to Ryan.

"Is it?" he retorted coldly. He was about to resume his seat when he caught sight of Captain Ludlow motioning to him. Smiling down at Hillary apologetically, he said, "I'm sorry, my love, but I'd best see what Horatio wants. I'll only be a minute."

"But Ryan, what about your—" she started to question him about his untouched plate of food, only to break off when she saw that he was already striding away.

She was sorely tempted to go after him, for she did not relish the prospect of being left alone with the three women who had made no secret of the enmity they bore her, and the temptation intensified when Alison suddenly rounded on her and remarked in a tone laced with heavy sarcasm, "I *do* hope you and dearest Ryan were able to resolve your differences the other day, for I should hate to think a simple, perfectly *innocent* thing such as my visit to the shipping office was the cause of any estrangement between the two of you!"

"The 'differences' of which you speak were resolved later that same day," Hillary coolly informed her. "So you see, Miss Bromfield, there's no reason at all for you to flay yourself with guilt." Nor to congratulate yourself! she added silently. Aware of Priscilla's and Gillian's eyes upon her, she raised her head and squared her shoulders in an unconscious gesture of proud defiance.

"Oh, but I would never do *that,* my dear!" Alison sweetly reassured her. The haughty blonde's lips curved into another caustic smile, and her eyes gleamed with a purposeful light. "By the way, perhaps I should not make mention of it, but . . .

well, since you and Ryan *have* apparently come to an understanding about his past relationship with me . . ." She left the sentence hanging as she paused for a moment and busied herself with rearranging her skirts. Flashing a conspiratorial look at both Priscilla and Gillian, she then said to Hillary, "I should think you would at least make an attempt to control your jealous, possessive impulses long enough to realize that it is only natural for dearest Ryan and me to maintain the special friendship that our—"

"Friendship?" Hillary's violet eyes flashed, and a bright color stained her cheeks. "Let us be honest with each other, Miss Bromfield—you want my husband and will stop at nothing to get him! There are many reasons why I am anxious to return to Tahiti, and you are without a doubt one of them!"

"Then pray, *Mrs. Gallagher,* return to Tahiti, but leave Ryan in New Bedford where he belongs!" hissed Alison, her own eyes glittering belligerently. "No one wants you here, including Ryan's family!" she declared, then looked to Priscilla for confirmation.

"It's true," the older woman quietly verified. Her gaze was totally devoid of warmth as it fastened upon Hillary. "And in my opinion, it is both cruel and unpardonably selfish of you to have used your wiles to entice my son into abandoning his home, his family, and all that he has here, all that he and his father and *his* father before him worked for, in order to—"

"I did not *entice* your son into his decision!" Hillary denied in a low, furious tone as her temper flared to a dangerous level. "Ryan knows I would live with him anywhere he chose!" It was true. No matter how desperately she wanted to return to Starcross, she would not do so unless Ryan wanted to as well. He had become more important to her than anything or anyone else in the world. And as long as he returned her love, she could never think of leaving him.

"You'll live to regret it if you make him go!" Gillian piped up, her gray eyes narrowing venomously at her sister-in-law. "He'll leave you. He'll leave you and come back to us!"

Hillary bit back the retort that rose to her lips and rose abruptly to her feet. She would hear no more!

"Please excuse me," she requested with icy composure. "I believe it would be best if I joined my husband." Without waiting for a response, she turned upon her heel and started up the grassy slope to where Ryan and Captain Ludlow were still talking.

Suddenly, a breathless scream sounded behind her. She whirled about to see one of Cara's older nieces, who was crying and obviously distraught, wading into the lake. The girl came to a stop when she stood knee-deep in the water, amidst the cattails that grew within the shallow, marshy depths there at the opposite end of the lake. Her shrill, hysterical words struck fear in Hillary's heart.

"Jimmy! Jimmy, come up!"

Hillary wasted no time. Clutching at her skirts and racing forward, she had already plunged into the lake before anyone else could react. She took a deep breath, then dove in an attempt to find Jimmy. Searching near the spot where the girl stood calling out to him, she saw a dark form entangled within the cattails beneath the water's surface. She hurriedly swam closer, only to discover that it was indeed Jimmy. Her blood pounded in her ears as she worked to free him and get him to the surface.

She had just burst into the air with the unconscious boy in her arms when Ryan, finally reaching the lake as well, waded swiftly into the water to help her. Her long, sodden skirts were weighing her down, and she was struggling to catch her breath, but she managed to gasp out, "Take him!" Ryan snatched Jimmy from her weary grasp and hurried to place him face-down on the ground. Everything had happened so quickly that realization was just now beginning to dawn on the onlookers, who gasped in horror to see the pale, apparently lifeless form of Jimmy Gallagher being carried from the lake by his uncle.

Hillary staggered from the water at last, and she was grateful for the warmth of someone's coat about her shoulders as she fell to her knees on the ground beside Ryan. Whispering a fervent prayer, she watched, dazed and trembling, while he placed his two large hands on his nephew's back and literally pumped the water from the boy's lungs. After what seemed like an eternity, a cough broke from Jimmy's lips, and then another and another.

"Thank God!" Hillary breathed amidst a chorus of relieved sighs and growing murmurs of disbelief that the mishap could have occurred with so many people about. Rolling Jimmy to his back, Ryan lifted the boy in his strong arms and began carrying him toward the house.

Jimmy blinked up at his uncle in surprise and coughed again before demanding, "What happened to the duck I caught?" Before a quietly chuckling Ryan could answer, Priscilla seized her precious grandson from his arms and practically smothered the hapless four-year-old with kisses as she bore him away.

Hillary shivered as the cool breeze swept across her

thoroughly drenched form. Her white dress was plastered to her slender curves, and her long, wet hair streamed wildly about her face and shoulders. Several people commended her on her quick thinking and bravery, while others merely looked askance at her bedraggled appearance.

Ryan made his way back through the crowd and drew her close. His arms tightened about her with loving fierceness as he vibrantly murmured, "My sweet love, you are without a doubt the most beautiful and remarkable woman I've ever known!" She released a long sigh and closed her eyes, feeling safe and warm and contented within his arms.

"Come one. We've got to see about getting you into some dry clothes," he said when he reluctantly set her away from him a few moments later. His own clothing had received only a minimal soaking, though his polished knee boots were now caked with mud.

He kept an arm about her shoulders as he began leading her toward the house, and she sighed again before remarking, "I'm glad Cara didn't see what happened, though I suppose she'll never forgive herself for trusting that poor girl to look after Jimmy. He never should have been allowed near the water. And those of us who were so occupied with our own affairs should have paid a bit more attention to the children!"

"*Our* children, Mrs. Gallagher, will learn how to swim," Ryan firmly decreed. He smiled down at her before adding, "Of course, that shouldn't be too difficult, seeing as how they'll be living in such a warm climate."

A sudden shadow crossed Hillary's features as she recalled what Alison, Priscilla, and Gillian had said about Ryan's plans to leave New Bedford. Cara's words, though spoken in kindness, came back to haunt her as well.

"Ryan, are you . . . are you certain you want to live in Tahiti?"

"Abolutely. Why shouldn't I be?"

"Well, it's just that—"

"Has my mother said something to you? Or Alison perhaps?" he demanded with a frown of suspicion. Hillary's gaze fell before his, and she nodded. They had reached the mansion's back doorway by now, and there were still a number of guests wandering about the tables. "We'll talk about this later," Ryan promised after casting a quick look at the men and women who stood nearby.

Susan Ludlow came bustling forward at that point and immediately took charge of her drenched and disheveled young guest. Shooing Ryan away, she led Hillary up to Cara's old room on the second floor. A maid soon appeared with an armload of beautiful dresses, which she dutifully spread upon the coverlet of the bed for Hillary's inspection.

"Choose whatever pleases you, my dear!" urged the kindly Mrs. Ludlow. "I'm afraid the fit may not be perfect, but no matter—you will look lovely in anything!" She smiled and turned to leave, then paused in the doorway to announce, "I'll send one of the girls up with hot water right away, for I'm sure you must be feeling quite chilled!"

Hillary responded with a grateful smile of her own. She set about removing her wet garments as soon as the door had closed. Sweeping aside her tangled mass of hair, she reached for the buttons on the back of her gown. She sighed in exasperation when she encountered difficulty in unfastening them, for the fabric loops were uncooperative when wet, and she decided to wait and ask for assistance

444

from the maid who would soon be delivering the hot water. But when the door swung open mere seconds later, it was not the Ludlows' maid who stood framed in the doorway—it was Alison Bromfield.

"My, my, you *do* look a fright, Mrs. Gallagher," she drawled as she strolled inside the room and closed the door behind her.

"What do *you* want?" Hillary demanded sharply.

"Why, I have merely come to do you a favor," Alison replied, feigning a look of wide-eyed innocence.

"A favor?" It was obvious that Hillary did not believe her.

"Yes. You see, I was sent to tell you that an old friend is waiting for you at the side entrance downstairs. You'll find it just to the right of the staircase."

"An old friend?" echoed Hillary, frowning in puzzlement. "Who is it?"

"I've no clue as to his identity," Alison now responded with her usual haughtiness. "He merely asked me to convey the message to you."

She had already pivoted about and swept back to the door when a still bewildered Hillary asked, "But, why . . . why didn't he approach me when I was outside?"

"How should I know?" the other woman retorted with a slight, indifferent shrug of her elegantly clad shoulders. "Perhaps he merely wished to speak to you alone. That *does* appear to be his intent, does it not?" She gave a toss of her blond ringlets, then swept loftily from the room.

Hillary stared thoughtfully after her. An old friend, her mind repeated. Who could it be? The only friends she had in New Bedford—other than those present at the picnic—were Josiah and Ewan. It could be either one of them, or perhaps someone she knew from Tahiti . . . or even someone from England. Whatever the case, she decided, there was only one way to find out.

She completely forgot about her sodden clothing and hurried from the room. Cara, David, Priscilla, and Jimmy were all in the parlor downstairs, but they did not see Hillary as she reached the foot of the staircase and turned her steps in the direction of the side entrance.

Alison, however, did see her, for she was watching from her vantage point in the shadowed space beneath the stairs. Mentally congratulating herself on the way she had played her role to perfection, she also gave thanks for Jimmy's accident—it had made her scheme all the more easy to carry out. Her green eyes lit with a malevolently triumphant gleam, and she hummed softly to herself as she sailed back through the house to seek out Ryan once again.

Hillary, meanwhile, slipped quietly through the side doorway. Her violet eyes quickly scanned the narrow space between the house and the shrubbery, but she saw no one. Her silken brow creased into a frown of renewed bewilderment. In the next instant, she thought she heard someone, or something, rustling through the thick greenery. She spun about, only to feel a sudden, sharp pain at the back of her head. A soft cry broke from her lips as she crumpled to the ground, and she welcomed the blissful darkness that came up to meet her.

They had searched everywhere—every room in the house, every square inch of the grounds, even the outbuildings and the stables—but there was no sign of her.

There was no way of knowing exactly how long she had been gone, but her absence had first been noticed by one of the Ludlows' maids, who estimated that she had gone upstairs with the hot water some ten minutes after receiving her mistress's orders to do so. The maid had quickly returned downstairs to tell Mrs. Ludlow that the room was empty, at which time Susan had alerted Ryan. No one had seen Hillary leave, and no one could recall having seen anything unusual. There had been several carriages coming and going throughout the first half of the day, so that one more would certainly not have been noticed.

Ryan, who had wasted no time in organizing the men into groups to search the Ludlows' estate, now wasted no time in assigning them to scour various parts of the city. Captain Ludlow volunteered to contact the authorities, while Connor and a dozen other men were dispatched to round up other friends and acquaintances to join in the search.

Ryan's alarm and fury increased with each passing moment, but he did not panic. His many years at sea had prepared him well. But, though he was accustomed to dealing with tense situations such as this, he had never been so personally involved before, had never felt the awful, searing pain deep within his heart as he felt now.

Hillary. He loved her more than life itself. The thought of her in danger, in the hands of someone who might harm her, was almost more than he could bear. He would find her. He would find her, and he would kill the bastards who had taken her!

Recalling the abduction attempt that had occurred only a few days ago, he flung himself on horseback and rode off to find Ewan and Josiah. Perhaps they could remember something, anything, about that day and the two men who had attacked Hillary and

Cara. It was a long shot, but it was worth a try.

Slowly regaining consciousness, Hillary became aware of a foul, musty odor. Her eyes flew open at last, but it took several moments for her vision to clear enough for her to be able to view her unfamiliar surroundings.

She was lying on her side upon a dirty, hard, wooden floor, and she winced at the pain that shot through her head as she rose up to look around. The small room in which she was imprisoned was completely empty save for a few pieces of debris piled in one dark corner. The only light came from a narrow, grate-covered window high above, where the streaked and grimy panes of glass allowed little of the sun's rays to penetrate the hot, airless space.

Her eyes widened as her ears suddenly detected the not-too-distant sounds of ships' bells. She was somewhere on the waterfront!

Who had done this to her? And why? Dear God, why?

Ryan's handsome face swam before eyes, and she battled a sudden wave of panic. Did he know yet that she had been abducted? Was he perhaps already looking for her?

Oh Ryan! Ryan! her heart cried out to him in anguished silence as her eyes filled with tears.

Her thoughts were drawn back, just as Ryan's had been, to the terrifying incident that had occurred several days earlier. Was it possible that those same men were responsible for what had happened to her today?

She was so lost in her desperate reverie that she did not hear the door behind her slowly opening.

"Looks like you're comin' back to life," a familiar

voice startled her. She gasped and twisted about to see that it was one of her husband's own crewmen who stood there gazing down at her with dark, hawkish eyes.

"Peale!" she breathed in stunned disbelief.

"Well now, I wasn't real certain you'd remember me," the slim, coarse-faced man taunted with a sneer. "Seems to me you wasn't so friendly when we was all aboard the *Falcon* together!"

"Why . . . why did you bring me here?" demanded Hillary. Climbing to her feet, she battled a forceful wave of pain and dizziness.

"You'll find out soon enough," was all he would say. His lips curled scornfully once more as he told her, "This time, there ain't no place for you to run, *Mrs. Gallagher!*"

"What are you talking about?" She was more frightened than she had ever been, yet she was determined that he should not see any evidence of it. If she could somehow manage to stall him, perhaps she could think of a way to escape. Perhaps Ryan would have time to find her!

"That last night in the Falklands, remember?" His dark eyes gleamed with a fierce, baneful light, and his coarse features grew even uglier as he snarled, "You'd never have gotten away if I hadn't been drunk! No, damn you, I'd have—"

"Then it . . . it was *you!*" she murmured in dawning horror.

"It was me all right, *my lady*, and I aim to finish what I started that night!"

"But why, Peale? What did I ever do to you to make you want to . . . to hurt me?"

"You never did a blasted thing, damn you! Not a blasted thing!" he contemptuously spat at her. "You was always there, always laughin' and talkin' to the others, always struttin' about with the captain! *The Captain's Whore*, I called you! You're no better'n them other *vahines* back in Tahiti! That little friend of yours, she talked like you was a queen, but I wasn't fooled!"

"What friend?" Hillary demanded as a sudden suspicion crept into her mind. "Are you . . . are you talking about Tehura? Dear God, were you the one who—"

"I didn't do nothin' to her she didn't ask for! Just like I'm only gonna do to *you* what you asked for all those months aboard the *Falcon!*" Peale threatened. "All those months you wiggled those hips of yours and let that black, witch's hair of yours blow free in the wind! Yes, by damn, soon as I take care of business, you're gonna by *my* whore instead of the captain's!"

"No!" cried Hillary. His words drove her to an act of desperation. She hurled herself forward, frantically trying to push past him and flee. But Peale caught her and cruelly flung her back down to the hard floor, then pulled a knife and brandished it before her wide, terror-stricken eyes.

"Try that again, and I'll have to slit your throat!" He glared menacingly down at her for several long seconds, breathing heavily, before muttering a curse and slamming out of the room again. He called out to her from the other side of the bolted door, "If you scream, or try anythin' at all, there's a man out here with orders to kill you!"

Wondering if he was telling the truth about leaving someone to guard her, Hillary flew forward again and strained upward to peer through a hole that had been cut high in the thick, roughly hewn door. Her hopes fell when she spied the large, craggy-faced man sprawled across an overturned crate in the

450

semi-darkness of what appeared to be an abandoned warehouse. There were a few old barrels strewn about the large space, but little else.

Her heart heavy with despair, Hillary sank back down to the floor and closed her eyes. She was trapped. There was nothing she could do but wait . . . wait for the dreaded hour of Peale's return . . . wait for Ryan to find her before it was too late . . .

"We found him only yesterday," Ewan solemnly revealed. "From what we heard, he's been going around bellyaching about not being paid for his 'work.' We've been keeping an eye on him, hoping he'd lead us to whoever it was paid him—or didn't pay him—to snatch Mrs. Gallagher!"

"Damn them oily sons of bitches!" Josiah furiously growled. "I'll break them in two when I get hold of them!"

"It's not likely the same men were given the chance to try again," Ewan pointed out, still reeling from the news Ryan had just given him. "Maybe the man we found could shed some light on who might have—"

"Blast it, let's get going!" Ryan ground out. He burst outside into the sunshine once more, his handsome features a mask of savage fury and his blue-green eyes afire with a vengeful purpose. Ewan and Josiah were close on his heels, their own blood boiling at the thought of Hillary's abduction.

The three of them set off for the tavern where one of the men who had made the unsuccessful attempt to kidnap her was known to spend his days and nights of late. It was due to the disgruntled villain's loose tongue that Ewan and Josiah had been able to find him, for it seemed he had made no secret of his grievances with whoever it was that had hired him.

Ryan cursed their luck when they arrived at the tavern and discovered the man was not there. Although Connor, Captain Ludlow, and at least a hundred other men were out searching for Hillary, he feared she would not be found before coming to harm. Rage smoldered within him as he asked himself yet again who could possibly have taken her, and why.

Dear God, where is she? Please help me find her!

"Captain, that's him!" Ewan suddenly whispered beside him.

Ryan's piercing gaze shot across to the rough, unkempt man who had just that moment sauntered through the tavern's doorway. Josiah's eyes darkened, and he tensed as though planning to spring upon the man there and then.

"Not yet," Ryan cautioned with deadly calm. "Let's get him outside first." He slowly stood and moved with purposeful unhaste toward the doorway. Ewan and Josiah, following his example, casually rose from their seats at the table in one corner of the smoke-filled room and headed after him.

"What the—" the man rasped out when Ryan lifted a negligent hand to his shoulder. "Who the devil are you?" he grumbled, his bloodshot eyes narrowing up at the tall, grim-faced stranger.

"I'd like to have a word with you," Ryan disclosed in a low, dangerously level tone.

The foul-smelling man was about to tell him to go to hell, but then happened to notice the two large, burly seamen who had come to stand just behind Ryan. His eyes filled with dismayed recognition, for he remembered Josiah and Ewan from that day he and his cohort had botched the job of snatching young Mrs. Gallagher. He swallowed hard, and a shadow of alarm crossed his rough countenance.

"I . . . I ain't got nothin' to tell you!"

"Outside!" snarled Josiah. He struck even more fear in the fellow's evil, cowardly heart by touching a hand to the spot upon his arm where the man's knife had sliced into his flesh a few days before.

Ewan and Josiah stepped forward, and each of them took hold of one of the man's arms. He wisely chose not to resist as they led him outside and around to the narrow, filth-ridden alleyway at the side of the tavern.

"Who paid you to abduct my wife?" demanded Ryan.

"Your wife?" the man echoed, feigning ignorance. Damn, but it must be Captain Gallagher himself who stood there!

"Mrs. Gallagher," Ryan ground out, his turquoise eyes blazing down at the man. "The young woman you tried to kidnap last week!"

"I don't know nothin' about no kidnappin'!" he feverishly denied. Josiah's fingers tightened menacingly upon his arm.

"You'd better start talkin', you worthless bastard, else I'll have to make you! Now the Captain's wife is missing, and we want to know who the devil took her!"

"It wasn't me! I ain't been near her since—" the man blurted out, then suddenly realized he'd said too much.

"Who hired you to do it?" Ryan demanded once more, his eyes gleaming with bloodthirsty intent.

"I . . . I don't rightly know! I heard tell it was a lady, but I don't know her name and I never got a look at her! We was promised a lot of money by some man in right fancy longtops if we . . . if we took Mrs. Gallagher and shanghaied her aboard a merchant

453

ship bound for the South Seas. But we never got paid! I never got a cent of—"

"What about your partner? Would he be able to tell us the name of the 'lady' who arranged all this?" Ryan's eyes narrowed in growing suspicion as he thought of the one woman who wanted Hillary out of the way, the one woman who was no doubt willing to employ such despicable means to get what she wanted. *Alison Bromfield.* While it was true that his mother and sisters had exhibited nothing but a perplexing animosity toward Hillary, he did not believe them capable of this treachery against his wife.

"No. But even if he could've, he ain't here no more! He shipped out yesterday morning!"

His mind racing to hit upon the next plan of action, Ryan ground out a curse. Although he was tempted to confront Alison with his suspicions, he reluctantly conceded that it was best not to do so, at least not yet. He knew Alison, knew her well, and he could easily imagine the way she would vigorously deny any involvement and then call upon her doting father to back up her claims of innocence. Besides, if she had indeed paid someone else to do her dirty work, then there was a good chance she wouldn't even know where Hillary was being held prisoner. But if the scheme still involved a ship bound for the South Pacific, then the waterfront would be the natural—

"I did hear tell of a certain whaleman takin' up the job," the man suddenly revealed. Desperately hoping to save his own skin, he told himself it might help if he were to come clean and spill all he knew.

"A whaleman?"

"I don't know what outfit he's hooked up with. But while I was down at the Spouter Inn night afore

454

last, I heard talk about a man by the name of Peale. Seems he was askin'—''

"Peale? Damn you, are you sure that's the name you heard?''

"I'm sure," the man answered with growing confidence that he would get out of there with his head intact. "He's a dark, wiry bastard with more guts than brains. He's been hangin' out at the Spouter Inn most days, though he ain't been there much lately.''

Peale, Ryan's mind repeated while his handsome features grew savage once more.

The loose-tongued coward was greatly relieved to find himself thrust aside as Ryan, Josiah, and Ewan bolted from the alleyway and headed for the Spouter Inn.

Hillary was certain it was a woman's voice. She flew to the door and peered outward through the hole. Night had fallen, and the darkened warehouse was lit only by a single whale oil lamp burning atop the same overturned crate that the guard had sat upon for most of the day.

There was no sign of the guard now. He had neither looked in on her nor spoken to her throughout the past several, agonizingly long hours. Plagued by a growing thirst, she had tried asking for water, but he had ignored her. Her stomach was churning with hunger, for she had not had the opportunity to eat anything at the picnic.

Now, as she anxiously strained upward against the door, she saw that there was indeed a woman talking to a man whose back was turned to the storeroom. Hillary recognized the man, however, when he turned a bit so that his face was illuminated by the lamp's soft golden glow.

Peale! Dear God, he had returned, and there was still no sign of Ryan!

She could not see the woman very well, for Peale's dark form obstructed her view. But the voice that drifted through the warehouse toward the back room where she was being held sounded vaguely familiar. She quickly turned her head and pressed her ear to the hole in an effort to hear what was being said.

"You needn't count it!" the woman snapped. "It's all there."

"When do I get the other half?" asked Peale.

"Just as soon as I am sure you have carried out my instructions! Those other idiots nearly ruined the whole thing. I want to make certain it's done right this time! That's why I risked coming down here myself. I want her out of New Bedford and on her way back to Tahiti before morning!"

"I'll have to take her up to Boston first, since there ain't no ships setting a course for the Horn till the end of the week, and none of them are—"

"I don't care! Do whatever you want with her— just get her out of New Bedford!"

"You're a coldhearted little bitch, ain't you?" Peale remarked with a quiet, unpleasant laugh. "Why are you so hot to get rid of her?"

"None of your business! I'm paying you to do a job, not to pry into my reasons for wanting that little slut out of the way!"

There was silence after that. Hillary peered out through the hole once more, only to see that Peale and the woman had moved away to the far end of the deserted warehouse, where there was very little light at all. As the woman turned to leave, however, her proud, distinctive profile was briefly accentuated by the lamp's far-reaching glow. In that moment,

Hillary's suspicions were confirmed.

Alison Bromfield! It was Alison who had paid Peale to abduct her, Alison who was so determined to get rid of her that she would go to any lengths to do so. And it was Alison who would no doubt see to it that Ryan never learned of his wife's true fate until many long months afterward. *Oh Ryan, where are you?*

Her violet eyes filled with increasing alarm as she recalled what she had just heard. Peale was planning to transport her to Boston that very night!

She jumped away from the door when she saw him moving back toward the storeroom. She had to do something! She couldn't allow him to take her away from New Bedford, away from Ryan!

Frantically searching in the darkness for anything she might be able to use as a weapon, her gaze fell upon a sharp, splintered remnant of a barrel stave in the corner. It wasn't much, but perhaps she could use it to stab Peale. She hastily snatched it up, and her fingers curled tightly about it as she concealed it within the gathered folds of her skirts.

"It's time we was goin', *my lady!*" Peale sneered as he unbolted the door and swung it open.

"I'm not going anywhere with you!" Hillary proclaimed with proud defiance, hoping she sounded a good deal braver than she actually felt. She sought to control her erratic breathing, and she battled the dizziness that was brought on by fear, hunger, and the dull, lingering ache at the back of her head.

"It won't do you no good to fight me." His hand clutched two lengths of rope and a dirty kerchief, and Hillary surmised correctly that he meant to bind and gag her. She instinctively backed away, her heart pounding as he merely smiled nastily and began advancing on her. "You and me are gonna get to know each other *real well* before this night's through!''

"No, damn you, no!" she cried hoarsely. Peale smiled again and reached for her. She hesitated only a moment before raising her arm and bringing the sharp piece of stave thrusting down with all her might into the unprotected flesh of his back.

A loud, animal cry broke from his lips as he twisted violently about and sent Hillary crashing against the wall. The splintered piece of wood was buried only half an inch deep in his back, and he ground out a savage curse as he pulled it out.

Hillary, seizing the advantage of his pain, took flight. She raced through the doorway and out into the dimly lit warehouse. Peale was after her in a flash, and he caught her before she had gone far. His fingers closed upon her arm in a brutal grip, and he yanked her roughly back against him, his arm closing like a vise about her slender waist as he cruelly twisted one of her arms behind her back.

"I'll make you pay for that, you stupid little bitch!" he vowed through clenched teeth. His golden eyes were suffused with a feral gleam as he brought his ugly face close to the upturned loveliness of hers, and a tremor of pure, unbridled fear coursed through Hillary.

Ryan! Ryan, help me! her heart cried out.

In the next instant, Peale brought his punishing lips crashing down upon hers. She struggled wildly against him as nausea rose deep within her, and she shuddered in revulsion when she felt his foul, greedy tongue stabbing within her mouth. He twisted her arm higher, sending hot slivers of pain shooting up through her shoulder and tears of helpless frustration stinging against her eyelids.

No! Please God, no! her mind screamed.

Suddenly, the double doors of the warehouse burst open. Peale's head shot up in alarm, and Hillary could feel his entire body tensing when he saw the three tall men who came storming inside.

"Ryan!" she breathed in shocked amazement, her violet eyes sparkling with mingled joy and relief and love. Her relief was short-lived, however, as Peale abruptly drew a gun from his belt and pressed its cold barrel against her temple.

"Hold it right there!" he spat out. "Another step closer and I'll kill her!"

Ryan, Josiah, and Ewan stopped dead in their tracks. Ryan's gaze fastened upon Hillary, and his heart twisted as he read the naked terror in her eyes. He could not know that her fear was for him.

"Let her go, Peale!" Ryan ground out. He, too, held a gun in his hand—as did Ewan and Josiah— and his fingers clenched about the handle while he battled a wave of explosive fury. His desire to kill the man was greater than ever.

"Drop them guns, damn you!" rasped Peale. "Unless you want to see her dead, do as I say!" His arm tightened about Hillary until she could scarcely breathe. She choked back a cry of pain as he jabbed the end of the pistol against her head. "Drop 'em!"

Ewan and Josiah looked to Ryan. He nodded at them in a wordless command, his smoldering turquoise gaze never leaving Peale's face as he slowly allowed the gun to slip to the ground. Ewan and Josiah reluctantly did the same.

"Now I'm gonna take her out of here with me, and you're not gonna do a damned thing to stop me, understand? I swear I'll put a bullet through her head if any of you makes a move!" Peale threatened as he began inching toward the doorway with his captive. Hillary's eyes silently implored Ryan not to do anything rash, for she was certain that Peale would kill them all if they dared to cross him at this point.

"Let her go," Ryan tried once more. His entire body was tensed and ready for action, and his eyes were ablaze with a savagery that Hillary could not recall ever having seen before. "You don't need her, Peale. She'll only slow you down. If it's money—"

"Shut up, *Captain!*" Peale contemptuously growled. "You ain't givin' the orders here—*I* am! And I'm tellin' you to hold fast! It ain't just the money, you high and mighty son of a bitch!" Hillary gasped as he jabbed as her with the gun again. "It's *her!* You let her stay on the *Falcon,* and you'll damn well pay the price for it! She'll be mine now! Mine!"

He had dragged her over to the doorway, where he stood visibly wavering about what to do next. A wiser man would have realized it was useless to try to get away, but Peale was not wise at all. He had been careless, and he had underestimated Ryan's determination.

But Peale now did something completely unexpected and completely at variance with the words he had just spoken. He suddenly thrust Hillary away from him, spun about, and fled.

"Stay with her!" Ryan tersely commanded Ewan and Josiah. Pausing only to snatch up his gun, he took off after Peale. He caught sight of him just as he broke from the warehouse. Apparently headed toward a waiting boat, Peale was running down the wharf amidst the great casks of oil and the clutter of harpoons, lances, boat spades, and other implements of whaling. The wharves themselves were virtually deserted at night, and Ryan had no difficulty spotting his prey beneath the moon's helpful glow.

Peale turned and fired once, but desperation and flight combined to distort his aim. Ryan had soon closed the distance between them, and he lunged for the other man, tackling Peale about the legs and wrestling him down to the hard, oil-soaked planks of the wharf.

The slim, wiry Peale twisted about and jerked up his arm in an attempt to point the gun at Ryan. Seizing the man's wrist in a bone-crushing grip, Ryan forced him to release the pistol, which went clattering across the wharf to land between two seaweed-packed barrels. Ryan brought his fist smashing down across Peale's face, then repeated the hard, punishing blow.

Though blood was pouring freely from his broken nose, Peale refused to surrender. He struggled against Ryan while working a hand down toward his boot. Withdrawing the knife he had concealed therein, he slashed viciously at his opponent with the sharp blade.

Ryan cursed as the gleaming metal tore across the bronzed, hard-muscled flesh of his shoulder. He grabbed Peale's arm and twisted it until his fingers relaxed their grip on the knife. Peale, however, kicked out at Ryan's head with his booted feet, and he broke free long enough to be able to scramble to his feet and retrieve his gun.

He triumphantly spun back around to fire, but he never got the chance. Suddenly, he gasped and staggered backward. His strange golden eyes widened in horrified disbelief as he looked down to see the blade of his own knife buried deep in his chest. A strangled cry broke from his lips before he collapsed, dead, upon the wharf.

"Ryan!" Hillary flew to her husband's side as he climbed to his feet. She cried out softly when she glimpsed the dark stain spreading across the white linen of his shirt. "Oh Ryan, you're hurt!"

"It doesn't matter," he murmured as he caught her up against him and held her as though he would never let her go. "All that matters is that you're back in my arms where you belong." His deep voice was brimming with raw emotion as he told her, "Damn, but I feared I'd lost you!"

Hillary choked back a sob and buried her face against the warm, familiar hardness of his chest. The nightmare was over, and she was indeed back where she belonged.

XVIII

Being the young, spirited, and vibrantly alive person she was, Hillary recovered quickly from the ordeal. She complied with Ryan's orders that she remain abed for the entire day immediately following her rescue, but she adamantly refused to do so for any longer than that. She was determined to put the terrible incident from her mind and get on with her life.

But there was a matter connected with her abduction that still had to be resolved. She had told Ryan of seeing Alison Bromfield at the warehouse, and of Alison's conversation with Peale. Ryan had in turn revealed his own suspicions about the malevolent blonde, and he had vowed to exact a confession from her, no matter what it took. Without a confession, he had reluctantly acknowledged, it was merely Hillary's word against hers, and it was highly improbable that the authorities would lend much credence to Hillary's accusations. The warehouse had, after all, been dark, and there would be few willing to believe the word of a newcomer to New Bedford's shores over that of Alison Bromfield, the cherished daughter of one of the city's wealthiest shipping magnates.

Ryan finally returned to his work at the shipping office two days later. David was able to go with him, though the doctor had decreed that his soon-to-be former patient should remain for only half of the day. Cara, along with Priscilla and Erin, took the children to visit the Ludlows again, while Gillian begged off with a headache.

Hillary, who had also declined Cara's invitation to participate in the outing, was upstairs later that afternoon when a knock sounded at the bedroom door. She smiled to herself, thinking that it was no doubt Agnes returning with her tea, and went to open the door. But it was Gillian, not Agnes, who stood there.

"Why, Gillian!" Hillary breathed in surprise.

"I have a letter for you," the young woman coolly announced. Her gray eyes kindled with a faint, telltale glimmer of scornful amusement when she added, "Actually, it arrived a few days ago, but I forgot about it until now." She withdrew it from the pocket of her skirt and held it out to Hillary. "I'm afraid I opened it by mistake." Her lips curved into a faint smile of malicious satisfaction as Hillary took the letter and hastily scanned its contents.

"Dear God, no! Oh no!" she murmured in sudden anguish. Word had come from Tahiti at last, but it was not what she had expected. Written by Anthony Warren more than three months ago, the letter informed her of her uncle's death.

Uncle Denholm! her heart cried as her eyes filled with tears of dawning sorrow. Oh Uncle, why didn't you tell me? You knew before I left, didn't you? You knew it all along!

Her glistening, pain-clouded gaze abruptly shifted

from the letter in her hands to the other woman's spiteful face.

"Oh Gillian, why? Why did you keep this from me when you knew—"

"You little fool!" Gillian hissed with unexpected vehemence. "Did you really think we would all give in so easily? Yes, I kept the letter from you—I wanted to wait until the time was right, until it would do some good for you to learn of your precious uncle's death! There's no reason for you to delay *your* departure one day longer now! Go back where you belong, damn you!" With that, she whirled about and was gone.

Shocked by the extent of Gillian's hatred and cruelty, Hillary stared after her for a moment, then dazedly moved back inside the room. Her fingers clenched about the letter as the hot tears spilled over from her lashes and coursed, unheeded, down her face.

"Oh, Uncle!" she whispered brokenly. Guilt washed over her when she thought of how he had urged her to go with Ryan. Why, oh why had she allowed herself to be deceived? Why hadn't she been able to see that his 'recovery' was not what it seemed?

Ryan. She had to tell Ryan! She needed to feel his arms about her, needed to hear the comforting words only he could speak. He would understand her grief as no one else could. She had to go to him at once!

Choking back a sob, she hurried from the room and down the stairs. She was unaware of the fact that Gillian stood watching from the parlor as she flew across the entrance foyer to the front door. Desperate to be with Ryan, she could think only of getting down to the waterfront.

Gillian Gallagher's satisfaction would have increased tenfold if she had known of the added bonus to her cruelty in keeping the letter from Hillary . . .

The shipping office was nearly deserted by the time Hillary arrived. Although there was still an hour or so of daylight remaining, most of the workers and all of the young, prospective whalemen had gone to their homes, boardinghouses, or favorite haunts along the waterfront.

Hillary gathered up her skirts and climbed the steps. Tears still slipped quietly down her beautiful face as she opened the door and went inside. Two men stood talking together at the far end of the outer room, and they glanced up in surprise when she swept toward Ryan's office.

The door was slightly ajar. Hillary had done no more than raise a trembling hand toward the brass doorknob when she heard the unmistakable, throaty tones of Alison Bromfield's laughter. Remembering another time when Ryan and Alison had been closeted alone in his office, she wondered, for one fleeting instant, if it was business that had brought Alison there this time as well.

But, how could that be possible? she then asked herself. Surely Ryan had not forgotten that it was none other than Alison Bromfield who had arranged her abduction. Surely he had not changed his mind about making Alison confess to her part in the treacherous deed!

For a few fateful moments, she forgot about her grief over her uncle's death and listened to the two familar voices drifting outward from the office. It was not her custom to eavesdrop, and yet she could not seem to make herself turn away.

"Oh Ryan, my darling, do you truly mean that?"

"Of course I do. What happened the other day made me realize that you and my family have been right all along. Hillary will never fit in here. I never should have brought her to New Bedford. I know that now." He paused and released a long sigh before admitting in a low, resonant tone, "You were right about something else, too. I still love you, Alison."

Outside the door, Hillary drew in her breath upon a soft gasp. The color drained from her face, and misery welled up deep within her.

No! she silently cried out in denial. No, he . . . he couldn't have said that!

"My marriage to Hillary was a mistake," she then heard him declaring. His words tore at her heart.

"But Ryan, why did you marry her if you still loved me?" demanded Alison. "You knew I was waiting for you!"

"An act of impulsiveness, my love—nothing more than that. I'd been away at sea for nearly three years, remember?" There was a discernible touch of humor in his deep voice now. "It's easy for a man to get carried away when far from home, and especially when in the South Seas. Relationships between men and women there are a lot less restricting than here."

"*Our* relationship needn't have been so restricting! You know I gladly would have—"

"I know, Alison. And you can damn well count on my making up for lost time, just as soon as I've decided what to do about Hillary."

"What is there to decide? Simply send her back where she belongs! Send her away now, Ryan, this very night, so you and I can be together as we were meant to be!" Alison urged him. Hillary could hear her silken skirts rustling softly as she apparently moved closer to him. "I love you, my darling. I've always loved you! You must believe that! Whatever

467

I've done, I did because of my love for you!"

"I believe you, Alison. I've been a blasted fool, but no longer. I love you, and I'll never leave you—"

Hillary could bear no more. She dragged herself away from the door and blindly made her way outside once more. Stumbling down the steps, she leaned back weakly against the brick wall of the building.

Oh Ryan, how could you do this to me, to our love for each other? How could you still love Alison after all we've shared?

"You swore to love me forever," she whispered in agonized disbelief. Please God, it . . . it couldn't be true; he couldn't love Alison!

But there was no escaping what she had heard. She had heard him; she had heard them both. Ryan did not love her—he loved Alison Bromfield. The man she loved more than anything in the world had lied to her. He had deceived and betrayed her. And yet the only thing that mattered was that he no longer loved her.

Her uncle's face suddenly swam before her eyes, and she knew what she must do. She had to get away at once! There was no use in torturing herself by remaining any longer; she knew she could not endure seeing Ryan's face when he told her he loved another. No, she could not bear that final cruelty.

She would go home. Home to Tahiti. Home to Starcross.

Meanwhile, unbeknownst to Hillary, the conversation inside the shipping office had taken an unexpected turn.

"You know, Alison, I suppose I never would have realized how much you truly care about me if it hadn't been for Hillary's abduction," Ryan suddenly remarked as he set her away from him and stared down deeply into her green cat's eyes.

"Oh? Why is that, my darling?"

"Come now, my love, there's no need to pretend you don't know what I'm talking about." He forced himself to smile at her as he smoothly lied, "I know you were the one who hired Peale. He mentioned your name just before he died."

Ryan watched as several conflicting emotions played across Alison's pale, aristocratic features. She was obviously tempted to deny the whole thing, but she evidently decided that it was safe to admit her involvement to the man who had just declared his love for her. She knew as well as anyone that Ryan Gallagher was a man of honor, and that he would protect those he loved. In all the years they had known each other, he had never lied to her.

"I only did it because I love you so very much!" she insisted, her shimmering green eyes imploring him to understand. "I was desperate, Ryan, so desperate that I . . . well, I suppose I did go a bit too far with things, but I didn't know what else to do! You were being completely unreasonable, my darling, and I couldn't allow things to go on as they were." Her tone became slightly petulant when she added, "Besides, Peale wasn't going to hurt the little strumpet—he was only going to see that she returned to Tahiti."

"What purpose would that have served? Hillary would no doubt have returned," he pointed out. It took every ounce of self-will for him to control the violent impulses blazing within him.

"Perhaps. But I'm sure Peale would have seen to it that she remained there long enough for me to be able to convince you that—"

"Didn't it ever occur to you that I would go after her?" Ryan quietly challenged. There was something in his low, deep-timbred voice that made Alison's eyes widen in sudden alarm.

"Go after her? But why would you have done that?"

"Because I love my wife, Alison," he now truthfully proclaimed. "I've loved her from the first moment I set eyes on her."

"But that . . . that can't be true!" she sputtered in disbelief. "Why you just told me—"

"Damn you!" he raged at last, his hands closing about her arms with bruising force. His handsome face had become a mask of savage fury, and a dangerous, undeniably menacing light gleamed within the fiery depths of his magnificent blue-green eyes. "I ought to kill you for what you put her through!"

"You bastard!" Alison spat back at him, her own explosive anger making her recklessly defiant. "You lied to me! How dare you! You led me on just so—"

"So I could make you admit to your despicable little scheme!" Ryan finished for her. He suddenly released her arms as though the contact burned him. "Yes, damn it, that's exactly what I did! And now that you *have* confessed, I'm going to make you pay!"

"You'll not make me do anything, Ryan Gallagher! You've no proof of my involvement! It will simply be your word against mine!"

"Not entirely," he dissented with a faint, triumphant smile that boded ill for the haughty blonde. "Hillary saw you talking to Peale that night at the warehouse. My word, combined with hers, will no doubt hold some weight with the authorities. But there is yet another witness, one whom you have

470

apparently—and foolishly—dismissed from your mind."

"Another witness?" Alison echoed sharply, her features suddenly growing wary.

"You and Peale were both careless, Alison. One of the participants in this black-hearted plot of yours has been found, and I'm sure he will be able to identify you as the—"

"But Peale was the only one who ever saw me!" she exclaimed. Ryan shook his head.

"No, Alison. There was someone else there at the warehouse that night, someone who saw you going inside just as he was leaving. It seems Peale hired a man to stand watch over Hillary throughout the day. Two of my men found him last night. It required only a little 'persuasion' to make him talk, for it seems he was afraid he'd be connected with Peale's death."

Alison Bromfield knew then that she had lost. She knew Ryan would never be hers, and she knew it would be useless to try to deny what she had done. Yet, she was far from repentant. Her green eyes continued to flash in defiance as she lifted her aristocratic chin and asserted with disdainful confidence, "My father will not allow you to do anything to me, Ryan Gallagher!"

"The law has been violated," he stated in a cold, clear tone. "I have proof of your misdeeds. Your father won't be able to buy you out of trouble this time, Alison. You *shall* be made to pay!"

Ryan climbed the stairs, anxious to tell Hillary about his enlightening conversation with Alison. When he arrived at their bedroom, however, he found the door standing open and Agnes crying softly within.

"What is it? Where is my wife?" he demanded, sudden fear clutching at his heart.

"Oh, Captain Gallagher, she . . . she's gone!" the little maid disclosed unhappily.

"Gone? What the devil are you talking about?"

"She . . . she came home not an hour ago and stuffed some of her things into that carpetbag of hers and . . . and left! She told me to stay up here until you got home, and to give you this!" she explained as she thrust a piece of paper at him. While he took the note Hillary had left for him and read it, Agnes went on to reveal, "I asked her why she was leaving, but she wouldn't say! I . . . I thought I heard her say something about having been down to the waterfront, but I—"

Ryan's handsome, sun-bronzed features grew savage as he crumpled the paper and threw it aside. He turned away and muttered a blistering oath, then rounded on the pert redhead again and fiercely demanded, "Did she say where she was planning to go *tonight?*"

"No, sir, she . . . she did not!" Agnes breathlessly replied. She opened her mouth to ask him what had happened, but he was already storming from the room.

Sniffing back tears, Agnes reflected once again that it was a heartbreaking thing indeed when the happiness of a man and woman—a man and woman who had seemed to share the romantic kind of love she herself dreamed of finding someday—was so cruelly shattered by . . . well, by whatever had happened. Her curiosity to know got the better of her, and she quickly bent to retrieve the note Ryan had tossed aside. Her eyes grew round as saucers as they

472

scanned the words Hillary had penned in the midst of such pain:

> Ryan—what you told Alison is true. Our marriage was a terrible mistake. I am returning to Starcross, where I am both needed and loved. I leave it to you to make the arrangements regarding the dissolution of a union that should never have been. Farewell—Hillary.

XIX

"You must eat more, Miss Hillary," Tevaite gently
chided as she lifted the scarcely touched plate of food
and placed it on the bamboo tray she steadied against
her hip.

"I haven't had much appetite of late," Hillary
admitted with a disconsolate sigh. She was thinner
than when she had left New Bedford, though her
supple curves were still undeniably alluring and her
beautiful face even more ethereal-looking.

"You do not sleep, you do not eat . . . your uncle
would not be pleased." Though it had been many
months now since Denholm Reynolds had "gone
into the night"—the Tahitian expression for death—
Tevaite still felt his presence strongly.

"I know, Tevaite, but I . . . I cannot help it."

"Your heart is sad for your husband, and for your
uncle. But you must think of the child that grows
within you. It is not good for a baby to know
unhappiness so soon," the Tahitian woman insisted,
her dark liquid eyes full of kindness. She smiled
down softly at her young mistress, then padded back
across the verandah and disappeared inside the
house.

Hillary sighed again and gazed out across the lush, perennially green landscape she loved so well. A always happened whenever she did not keep he mind fully occupied with other matters, her thought were drawn to Ryan. She caught her breath when hi handsome face suddenly swam before her eyes.

"Oh Ryan!" she whispered forlornly, battling ye another wave of the tears that had sprung so readil to her eyes these past several weeks. Her heart twiste painfully, and she cursed herself once more for bein unable to shake the awful melancholy that made i impossible for her to feel anything else.

She had been back at Starcross for a month now and yet it felt more like a year. Ryan's image haunte her day and night, as did the memory of the words o betrayal she had heard him speak to Alison. Ther were other memories to plague her, to invade he dreams and very nearly her every waking moment the day she first encountered Ryan Gallagher . . . hi tempestuous courtship of her . . . their weddin night . . . those happy, adventurous months wit him aboard the *Falcon* . . . the night he rescued he from Peale and then held her safe within the warn circle of his arms for hours and hours afterward—

"No!" she cried out, her very soul in agony. Sh loved Ryan. She would never stop loving him. An God help her, but she wanted nothing more at tha moment than to go back to New Bedford and plea with him to love her in return! There had been mor than one time when she had wondered about th wisdom of her decision to leave, more than one tim when she had wondered if perhaps she should hav stayed and fought Alison for his love. But she ha always realized such contemplation was useless, fo she knew better than anyone that it was impossible t alter the course of love . . .

The sound of hoofbeats startled her out of her miserable reverie. Glancing up to see that it was Anthony Warren riding down the palm-shaded drive, she frowned to herself and rose from the white wicker chair to greet him. She managed a welcoming smile as he came around the corner.

"Hello, Anthony." She extended her hand to him, and he took it and clasped it warmly between both of his.

"Hillary, my dear! You're looking quite lovely this morning," the attractive, fair-haired Englishman gallantly proclaimed. His pale blue eyes were aglow with undeniable affection for her, as well as with a discernible light of purposefulness, and she sensed that his present visit held far more significance than his previous one.

"Please, Anthony, sit down," she quietly directed. Resuming her own seat, she smoothed a graceful hand along her white cotton skirts before smiling briefly again and asking, "To what do I owe the pleasure of this visit, dear friend? Tevaite was inquiring about you only this morning. You have not called in nearly a week, you know. I was beginning to think perhaps you had taken it in mind to have nothing more to do with me. I certainly would not blame you, of course, for I know I have been very poor company indeed!" She also knew she was chattering on in a thoroughly ridiculous manner, but she felt compelled to postpone whatever had brought him there that day.

"Hillary, I came because there is something I wish to discuss with you," Anthony wasted no time in announcing as he took the chair next to hers. He did not appear to notice the way she suddenly tensed, nor the way her violet eyes suddenly clouded with apprehension. "I've spent a lot of time of late

477

thinking about your . . . your predicament, and I firmly believe I have hit upon a solution that should prove favorable to everyone."

"A solution?"

"Yes. You see, I've made certain inquiries, and I think I can obtain a divorce for you under Tahitian law. After all, you *were* married here, and even though the island is a French protectorate—"

"Anthony, what in heaven's name are you talking about?" Hillary demanded in bewilderment. "What is all this talk about a divorce?"

"Why, you'll naturally have to obtain a divorce before we can be married."

"Married?" She stared across incredulously at the man who had proposed marriage to her once before— but not when she was already the wife of another!

"Of course," Anthony calmly responded. "Don't you see? It is indeed the perfect solution. Once your marriage to Gallagher is legally dissolved, you'll be free to marry me. I promise to make you a better husband than he did, Hillary, and I also promise to provide a good home and upbringing for your child. You can rest assured I will—"

"You . . . you know about the baby?" she stammered in further surprise.

The young vice-consul nodded and divulged, "Tevaite told me not long after you returned home. She was so worried about you that she came to see me and . . . well, she told me everything, all about your determination to keep your condition a secret from your husband, and about your stubborn insistence that he be the one to make the arrangements for a divorce. But surely you must realize that all haste is called for in this matter! If you wait for Gallagher to act, it might very well be a year before you are free!"

"I will not do it, Anthony," Hillary declared in a

very low tone. She raised her eyes to his, and he saw that they were sparkling with tears. "While I appreciate your kindness and your willingness to help, I cannot divorce my husband, and I cannot allow you to sacrifice your own happiness on my behalf."

"But it will not be a sacrifice!" he earnestly denied. He leaned forward and took her hand. "I asked you to be my wife before you married Gallagher, remember?"

"Yes, dearest Anthony, and we both know you are no more in love with me now than you were then." Her lips curved into a smile of heartfelt tenderness as she squeezed his hand with hers and said, "I shall never forget what you have offered to do for me. You are a very good and honorable man, and I hope that someday you will find someone to love you as you deserve to be loved, to love you as I love—" She broke off and drew her hand away, and he glimpsed the pain in her eyes before she quickly averted her gaze.

"So you are still in love with him," Anthony reluctantly observed. There was a long moment of silence between them as they both became lost in their mutually troubled thoughts. Finally, he sighed heavily and reached across to grasp her hand once more. "How can you still love him, Hillary? How can you care about him after what he did to you, after he—"

"Oh Anthony, I don't want to love him!" she wretchedly exclaimed as she pulled away and leapt from the chair. She moved to the edge of the verandah, then spun back around to face him. "But there's nothing I can do about it! No matter what he's done, no matter what he is, I love him. I will never love anyone else as long as I live."

"I don't understand," he admitted, rising to his

feet as well and hastening to her side. His blue eyes were brimming with confusion and disappointment. "I don't understand why you are so determined to ruin the rest of your life this way! At least think of the child—"

"I *am* thinking of the child!" she countered sharply, her violet eyes flashing up at him now. "What sort of life would my child have if I were to force myself to marry someone I didn't love? No, Anthony, that would not be fair to anyone!" She released a long, ragged sigh, and when she spoke again, it was with more composure. "My life will never be as I wish, for that . . . that is impossible. But I can strive to the best of my ability to make a good life for my child here at Starcross. I'm well aware of how much the lack of a father's love and guidance will be felt, but Tevaite and I will do everything we can to make up for it."

Anthony Warren was forced to acknowledge defeat once more. He had had no idea she still cared so deeply for her husband. Though her enduring love for the scoundrel was completely beyond his comprehension, he realized he could not fight against it.

He took his leave soon thereafter and rode back to Papeete. His thoughts remained preoccupied with Hillary throughout the rest of the morning and into the early hours of the afternoon, and his anger at Ryan Gallagher increased with each passing minute. He blamed himself in part for Hillary's unhappiness; he should have done more to prevent her marriage to that degenerate Yankee whaler!

When he left the consulate shortly after three o'clock and set off toward the quay, it was with the intention of speaking to one of the French authorities he knew to be conducting an inspection of a vessel docked there. His gaze traveled absently about his surroundings as he walked, and he became aware of a renewed feeling of restlessness within himself. Although he had not yet told anyone, he had asked his superior to try to arrange for his reassignment to the diplomatic corps back in England. He had hoped to return to his homeland with Hillary as his wife . . .

Anthony Warren drew to a sudden halt in the middle of the street. His pale blue eyes widened in profound astonishment as they took in the sight of the tall, handsome seaman who had just disembarked from a ship tying up on the other side of the quay.

Ryan Gallagher! his mind quickly confirmed what his eyes beheld. Why, the last man he had expected to see in Papeete was Gallagher!

Anthony's initial stupefaction was immediately followed by the most intense fury he had ever known. His gaze filled with uncharacteristic violence as he glared across at the man who had so shamefully mistreated a woman of whom he himself was so fond. By damn, he raged inwardly, Gallagher was a fiend and must not be allowed to inflict any more pain or dishonor upon Hillary!

Unaware of the invisible daggers being hurled his way at that very moment, Ryan slung his jacket over his shoulder and moved with long, purposeful strides down the crowded wharf and across the dusty street toward the market, where he planned to bargain with one of the islanders for the use of a horse. There was a forbiddingly set look about his rugged, sun-bronzed features, and his magnificent turquoise eyes gleamed with a dangerously intense light. His turbulent thoughts were so engrossed with his mission that he did not notice the slender, fair-haired man who was bearing down on him with such uncustomary belligerence.

"Gallagher!" Anthony spat out behind him.

Ryan wheeled about, only to find himself the recipient of a surprisingly forceful blow to his chiseled jaw. He staggered backward a few steps before swiftly regaining his balance and shaking his head to clear it from the benumbing effects of the unexpected punch. His eyes first filled with recognition, then smoldered with vengeful ire as they fastened upon the man who had hit him.

"Blast you, Warren! What the devil did you do that for?" Though tempted to retaliate and beat the young Englishman to a bloody pulp, he exhibited admirable restraint and did not. He damned sure didn't want to waste time sparring with Anthony Warren, not when Hillary was less than an hour away!

"Stay away from her, you bastard! She's suffered enough!" Anthony stood poised to hit him again. "You ought to be flogged for what you did to her!"

"What's between *my wife* and me is none of your blasted business!" Ryan ground out.

"I've made it my business! Damn it, man, you've put her through hell! I don't know why you decided to come back here, but I'll not allow you to hurt her anymore!"

"I'm warning you one last time, Warren—keep out of this!"

"Your actions would have been despicable enough as it was," the other man bravely went on, "but to ruin the life of an innocent, unborn child as well, you—"

"*Child?*" He stalked forward and fiercely gripped the lapels of the Englishman's impeccably tailored jacket. "What the hell are you talking about?"

"You know very well what I'm talking about!" Anthony shot back. He brought his arms up to furiously knock Ryan's hands away. "The babe *you* sired, you blackguard, will have no father to—" He broke off when he viewed the unmistakable look of wonderment crossing Ryan's face. "You . . . you didn't know?" Anthony questioned, then suddenly realized that of course the man couldn't have known—why, only that morning during his visit to Hillary, he himself had made mention of her resolve to keep her condition a secret from her husband. Suffering a momentary pang of guilt for the fact that it was a secret no longer, he then decided he was glad he'd told Gallagher. Perhaps now Hillary would listen to reason and allow him to arrange a divorce for her.

Ryan never answered Anthony's question. He left the young British vice-consul standing in the street while he spun about and went to procure a horse—to steal one if necessary—to provide him with immediate transportation. When Anthony last saw him, he was riding like the very devil himself away from Papeete and toward Starcross.

Hillary stepped from the bathing pool and bent to retrieve the towel she had earlier tossed upon the bank. After hastily patting the moisture from her naked curves, she squeezed some of the water from her long hair and smoothed it back away from her face. She expertly wrapped the bright crimson *pareu* about her body, knotted it just above the shadowed valley between her breasts, then sank down upon the cool, mossy earth.

Oh Ryan, Ryan, she sighed inwardly. Anthony's visit had served to make her feel even more sick at heart than before. Her violet eyes darkened when she thought of his offer to help her divorce Ryan.

Though he could not know it, her heart filled with dread each time Tevaite brought her the mail. She feared the day when Ryan's letter would come, as she knew it must. Eventually, he would want his freedom so that he could marry Alison.

She dashed impatiently at the fresh tears glistening upon her lashes and stretched out to trail a hand in the clear, aquamarine waters of the pool. In the next instant, however, she suddenly recalled Anthony's words about the baby. She straightened again, then looked down and gently placed her hands upon the slightly rounded planes of her abdomen.

Her spirits momentarily lifted, for she cherished the new life growing within her more each day. It was her child—hers and Ryan's—and no matter what had happened afterward, it had been conceived in love. She had to believe that; she *had* to!

Hillary released an outward sigh and climbed to her feet. Sternly reminding herself that there were things to be done, she started back toward the path, only to draw up short when she heard a sudden rustling of the foliage just ahead. Her silken brow creased into a slight frown, for she knew that she and Tevaite were alone at Starcross that day.

Suddenly, the very man who came to her in her dreams each night stood there before her. Only it was no dream. Dear God, it was no dream!

"Ryan!" she whispered in shocked amazement. Her violet eyes grew enormous within the delicate oval of her face and her heart leapt within her breast. Her legs weakened and gave way beneath her, and she would have fallen if not for the fact that he rushed forward just in time and caught her up in his strong arms. He crushed her against his warm, lean-muscled hardness, while she clung to him as if she were drowning.

Ryan had come back to her! she rejoiced inwardly. He had come back to her!

Neither of them spoke for the longest time. Then, Ryan startled Hillary by seizing her wrists and forcing them from about his neck. She blinked up at him in astonishment while his handsome features grew savage and his eyes blazed down at her.

"Blast it, Hillary, why did you run away like that?" he ground out. "Don't you realize what you've put me through these past few months? Damn it all to hell, woman, do you have any idea how it felt to go home and find you gone?"

"Oh Ryan, you gave me little choice!" she cried. "When I overheard what you said to Alison that day, I—"

"You obviously didn't hear very well!" His fingers slid up her bare arms to curl tightly about the unprotected smoothness of her shoulders. "I only said those things to Alison to make her admit she was the one who'd had you kidnapped! Apparently, *Mrs. Gallagher,* you didn't stay long enough to hear the conclusion of our discussion, else you'd have known that!"

"You . . . you mean you . . . were *lying* to her?" Hillary stammered in growing realization of the truth. "You *don't* love Alison?"

"Would I have come all this way to be with *you* if I loved *her?*" he thundered. "If you'd only stayed and talked to me about it—"

"But I . . . I thought—"

"You *didn't* think, damn it! You didn't think at all!" He abruptly released her and bit out a curse. His deep, resonant voice was very low and edged with fury when he said, "I was worried sick about you. It took me a full day to find out you had hired that coach to take you to Providence. It took me another

485

day to discover which steamer you'd taken up to New York. And it took me still *another* day to learn you had managed to secure passage on that blasted missionary ship! By the time I was able to make arrangements to come after you, a whole damned week had gone by!"

"A week? But it's been nearly a month since I arrived!" she unwisely pointed out. She drew in her breath upon a gasp as her arms were seized in a near bruising grip.

"Don't you think I know that? Hell, woman, I've counted every day, every minute, almost every blasted second that we've been apart! I would have been here long before now if not for that hurricane we ran into three days out of New Bedford!"

"Hurricane?" echoed Hillary, her heart twisting at the thought of him in such danger. She choked back a sob and raised wide, luminous eyes full of contrition and pain and love to his fury-tightened countenance. "Oh Ryan, I . . . I don't know what to say . . . how to explain . . . I love you so very much, and I could not bear to think you did not love me any longer! How was I to know you did not mean what you told Alison?"

"You would have known if you had only asked me, if you had only trusted me! Damn it, Hillary, you should have known I wouldn't betray you!" Gazing down into the upturned, ethereal loveliness of her face, he felt his anger evaporating. Dear God, how he loved her! These past several weeks without her had been pure hell! He had envisioned all manner of misfortune befalling her, had lain awake nights agonizing over whether or not she was safe. Torn between the desire to wring her beautiful little neck and the desire to crush her damnably beguiling softness against him once more, he muttered another curse and chose the latter.

Her heart sang when she felt his powerful arms encircling her, and her tears of anguish became tears of joy as his lips descended upon hers in a fiercely enchanting kiss that left them both light-headed with passion. But there was still a certain "little" matter left to be settled between them.

"Were you planning to keep the baby a secret from me forever?" he asked in a low, husky tone as he drew away to gaze down intently into her wide, shining eyes.

"Why, how . . . how did you know?"

"Anthony informed me, though I don't think he meant to," Ryan disclosed with a faint, sardonic smile. His handsome features grew solemn again before he demanded. "Why didn't you tell me, Hillary? How could you leave without—"

"I didn't know it myself until I was already on my way back to Tahiti!" she declared honestly. A rosy blush rose to her cheeks when she added, "I think it must have . . . happened while we were still aboard the *Falcon!*" She raised her eyes to his once more, and he saw that they were aglow with all the love in her heart. "I would have told you, Ryan. In the back of my mind, I always knew I would send word to you. I tried to make myself, and others, believe that I could live without you, that I could raise our child and give her the kind of life—"

"Her?" he broke in to challenge, his own eyes gleaming with such love and desire that she felt her pulses racing alarmingly. "What makes you so certain it's a girl, my love?"

"A woman knows these things, my dearest captain!" she retorted, still scarcely able to believe that they were together once more, that he loved her and would always be at her side. She knew that she would never, *never* leave him again.

Ryan gave a low chuckle, then pulled her close to his heart once more as his magnificent blue-green eyes darkened with a raging passion that had been simmering within him for months. Hillary responded with an answering fire, and it was quite some time before Tevaite looked up from her post at the kitchen window to see them strolling hand in hand across the lush, fragrant grounds of Starcross.

The Tahitian woman smiled to herself, and her brown eyes kindled with satisfaction and a certainty that the two lovers would share a lifetime of happiness before they were called to go into the night.

XX

"She *is* a special child, isn't she, Tevaite?" Hillary agreed with a mother's objectivity. She kissed her infant daughter and relinquished her into the Tahitian woman's care, then watched with a tender smile on her face as Tevaite carried the dark-haired cherub off to bed.

Releasing a sigh of total contentment, Hillary wandered back to the upper verandah and gazed out across the sea of gently swaying palms. The brilliant blue of the cloudless sky was turned into a blaze of color as the sun followed its inevitable course and turned day into night. A soft, wonderfully aromatic breeze wafted across the beautifully undulating hills and valleys of the island, and the eternal murmur of the sea breaking upon the barrier reef echoed throughout the tropical splendor that was Tahiti.

In some ways, it was difficult for her to believe that it had been a year since she had come home from New Bedford, and yet the year—or at least the eleven months following Ryan's return—had been one of so many changes.

Starcross was actually prospering again, and Ryan had followed through on his plans to start his own shipping line in Papeete. Although the business was small, it was very successful. Ryan appeared to have made the transition from whaling captain to shipping magnate and plantation owner with relative ease, mused Hillary, her violet eyes sparkling with the undeniable knowledge of his happiness.

The baby had changed their lives more than they ever could have imagined. Frances Loana Gallagher was a joy to them both, as well as being the adored pet of Tevaite and Tehura and everyone else at Starcross. It seemed that little Loana, as she was called by the Tahitians, would grow up having the best of both worlds.

They had received a letter from Ryan's brother only a month ago. David had written that everyone was doing well, and that he and Cara were expecting another child. He also mentioned that Priscilla had been pleased to learn of her granddaughter's birth and had even expressed a desire to see her. And Alison—this David had no doubt written with great satisfaction—had been married off to a much older man reputed to be quite a tyrant.

There had been other letters as well these past few months. Anthony had written from England to say that he had been promoted to an even higher post, and he had strongly hinted that he had finally found someone with whom he wished to share his life. The letter from Connor had arrived soon after Anthony's —it had been something of a shock to hear that Bethany was aboard the *Falcon* with him. Connor wrote that the ship would be calling at Tahiti within the next year, and that he and Bethany were very much looking forward to seeing them again.

Wandering back inside the room that had once been her uncle's, she thought of returning downstairs to see if Ryan was still in the study. Though he tried not to work too far into the evenings, there had been so much to do of late.

"I'm sorry, my love, but I had to finish those account books before morning," his deep voice suddenly sounded from the doorway. Hillary's mouth curved into a warm smile as she turned to face him.

"That's quite all right. I doubt if our daughter is asleep yet, so perhaps you'd care to go bid her good night."

"I've already done so." He closed the door behind him and sauntered across to stand towering above her. "You know, I have this nagging suspicion that she's going to turn out to be every bit as headstrong and temperamental as her mother!" he remarked with a low, mellow chuckle.

"Or as obstinate and domineering as her father?" she saucily parried. She laughed softly as he yanked her against him and imprisoned her with his powerful arms. Her violet eyes lovingly glowed up into the gleaming turquoise depths of his. "It may interest you to know, my dearest captain, that I intend to have at least a dozen children. That is, if you have no objections?"

Ryan grinned wickedly and declared, "No objections at all, my love. As a matter of fact, it will be my pleasure to oblige you!" She gasped in delight when he suddenly scooped her up in his arms and reiterated, "My *utmost* pleasure!"

And it was.